THE
LOCKSMITH

LINDA CALVEY

WELBECK

Published in 2021 by Welbeck Fiction Limited, part of Welbeck
Publishing Group 20 Mortimer Street London W1T 3JW

Copyright © Linda Calvey, 2021

The moral right of the author has been asserted.

A CIP catalogue record for this book is available from the British Library

Hardback ISBN: 978-1-78739-526-8
Tradepaperback ISBN: 978-1-78739-527-5

Printed and bound by CPI Group (UK) Ltd, Croydon, CR0 4YY

10 9 8 7 6 5 4 3 2 1

Dedicated to my beautiful grandchildren,
Samantha, Mia, Emily, Alana, Mano, Lacey and Fletcher.

In memory of Billy Blundell:
A true friend, a true gentleman, a true legend.

FOREWORD BY MARTINA COLE

As I hope some of you will know, I've been writing about dangerous and powerful women for a long, long time and I know how interesting they are.

Linda Calvey is a friend of mine. A strong woman and a woman with a story. Her life reads like it's straight from one of my books, and it's also true. Her voice is real, and like my characters, comes from a world that few can possibly imagine. Linda is also a diamond. She sticks by what she believes and looks after her friends.

The book you are about to read is written by someone who the British authorities considered dangerous enough to lock up for eighteen years. She grew up in the East End, knew – knows – all the faces. She was in deep with the gangsters, robbers, hit-men, gamblers and chancers who controlled the area. It was fast and glamorous and promised money; often violence and definitely power. But things took a wrong turn and she was convicted for murder and went to prison. The papers called her the Black Widow – the men in her life had a habit of turning up dead.

If you've read my books, you'll know that I'm interested in strong women, who take matters into their own hands; women who kill. When a woman writes about crime and violence, they have a different perspective on it than men. Maybe they fundamentally understand it better. They are often on the wrong end of it. Linda Calvey knows a thing or two about that, too.

The Locksmith is a story about a family in east London. At the center of it all is Ruby, who along with her brother Bobby, are a simply a pair of straight, sweet and gobby kids from the tough part of Canning Town – until they are forced to make some hard choices. One step into the criminal underbelly of the East End, soon becomes two, and Ruby quickly discovers a natural talent for negotiating with villians and robbers. So their rise to power begins, with Ruby calling the shots. In this alternative under-world of crime, villains aren't born, they are made.

I loved every page of this story and I think you will too. It's a tale that unfolds as you get to know the characters, their family and the world they inhabit. Some writers write what they know. Linda writes about what she lived, and I believe is the bravest and most authentic new voice in crime fiction.

Martina

PROLOGUE

'Where's the money?' shouted the man wearing a balaclava. He marched up to Ruby and pointed his gun directly in her face. 'Tell us and you live.'

The tall, elegant woman turned to face him, staring down the barrel of his gun. She gave no indication of the lightning jolt of fear now coursing through her veins. Being on this side of the gun was scarier than she'd imagined.

'Give them nuthin'. Open the safe and we're all dead!' yelled her husband Archie from the other side of the room. She caught sight of him, tied up with a gun to his head. Scanning the large lounge, she saw two masked assailants, no security guards or staff in sight. The second man, pointing his gun at Archie, slammed his fist with full force into Archie's face, breaking his nose. The violence was shocking. She wanted to scream but she controlled the impulse. She mustn't show fear. If there was anything she'd learned from the life she'd led, it was that.

Blood ran down Archie's face, splashing onto the white marble floors.

'Give. Us. The. Money.' The first man moved closer, the tip of the gun almost touching her cheek. His voice was a snarl.

Ruby's hackles rose but still she said nothing. She realised immediately that these men were inexperienced crooks, probably a couple of thugs who'd taken their chance and bribed the villa guards. Ruby knew proper crooks and these men weren't it. The staff were away at a festival, something anyone local would've known. *Simple but effective*, she thought to herself. This instinct gave her strength, focus.

'All right,' Ruby said, her voice steady despite the trembling already threatening to take over her body, her heart pounding against her slender chest. 'I'll give you the money.'

'No! Ruby they'll *kill* us, d'ya hear me?' Archie coughed, sinking back into the chair he was tied to. The pain of his injury stopped his plea.

Ruby continued as if her beloved husband was not in the room, as if he wasn't bleeding heavily from his broken nose. A fly buzzed against the huge glass window that overlooked the bay. The hot Spanish sunshine glittered on the turquoise sea as it lapped against the white shore far below.

'I'll do what you tell me, but you don't touch him.' Ruby shot back with authority.

Ignoring her, the second gunman raised his weapon as if to strike the man she loved again.

'You. Don't. Touch. Him.' Her voice was low. Despite her pounding heart, she remained calm, dignified.

For a second, she wondered if the robbers had heard her. She knew they might just shoot them anyway, leave them for dead and escape with the priceless paintings that lined her walls. That would cause them problems, though. They'd have to move the stolen artworks, and looking at the two men, they didn't look the type to have high-class art contacts. They looked downright scruffy. Ruby's instincts told her they were nobodies, and she would bet her life they would keep going all the way, intent on stealing the prize in the form of the rolls of cash in her safe.

'Gentlemen,' she said. 'I'll get you the money but put yer guns down. You're makin' me nervous and I might forget the combination ...' She smiled, knowing the effect it would have on them.

She sensed, like an animal scenting its prey, that they were rattled. Though she could only see their eyes, slits inside their headgear, she noticed their gazes were darting around the room, edgy and wild. She knew they were expecting her – a woman – to panic, to scream and faint, but that wasn't her style. She was the calm negotiator, the steely head that had faced down bigger villains than these two scruffy chancers. They had no idea who they'd come up against. Ruby was no longer the innocent young woman she'd once been. Every second that went past was giving her a creeping advantage.

Reluctantly, both men put down their guns. Ruby, satisfied by their acquiescence, allowed herself a small smile as she slowly began to move to the back of the room, turning her back on the gunmen. Her expensive heels clicked against the marble, the only sound except for the rasp of the men breathing inside their menacing balaclavas. Not exactly beachwear. A balaclava on a scorching hot day was another sign of their need for this money. Why torment themselves unless they had to?

Each step she took brought her closer to the family safe. Now no one breathed. The air was turgid, the heat overpowering. She leaned forward and pushed aside an abstract painting. Behind it was the large metal safe, not the only one in the plush villa, but it was the one they used most and she guessed the burglars didn't know about the others. It wouldn't matter anyway. A plan was form-ing in Ruby's mind. Always sharp, she knew she had a split second to decide the next step.

In that moment, Ruby saw herself as if from a great distance. A woman, still beautiful, still composed, and about to make the most important move of her life. The stakes weren't just high, they were soaring. If she got this wrong, they'd all be dead. Ruby's mind began to clear. She saw herself as a child, sticking up for her friends at school unafraid of the bullies. She saw herself as a young woman, living a good, normal life. And she saw herself making the hard choices, always knowing she wanted more. Well, now she'd got it, all right. She had more of everything: money, glamour, danger . . .

The time had come. Ruby glanced back at the men. She caught the look on their faces, a look of expectation, of riches to come. They looked like they could almost smell their victory – and in that second she knew they'd kill her the moment they laid eyes on the money. She focused her attention back to the dial, taking a deep breath. Click. Click. Click.

PART ONE
THE DECISION

Canning Town,
London, 1990

CHAPTER 1

'Not sausages again, Mum. Can't we 'ave somethin' different for once?' groaned the teenage girl as she nudged her brother, sitting across from her at the small kitchen table.

'Be thankful you've got this, Ruby,' said Cathy Murphy, as she spooned mashed potato onto her truculent daughter's plate. 'You know money is tight, it's the best I can do, love.'

Ruby gave Cathy a sad smile. 'I know, Mum, I'm sorry. I don't mean to rub it in. It's just sometimes I wish we could 'ave steak and chips like they have at Sarah's . . .'

Sarah was Ruby's best friend and neighbour. They'd grown up together.

'You know where her old man gets his cash from, don't ya, Ruby?' Her brother Bobby spoke between mouthfuls of sausage, barely looking up from his plate.

Ruby gave him a withering look. 'Course I do, I wasn't born yesterday. He's a blagger. That's a bank

robber to you, Mum.' Cathy sniffed, showing her dis-
approval but Ruby continued, 'Some say he's big-time
now. All I know is that Sarah wears posh dresses bought
from proper shops while I'm still wearin' dresses from
Rathbone Market . . .'

Ruby looked down at the soft yellow frock she was
wearing. She liked the way it contrasted with her coal-
black hair and brought out her green eyes. It fitted her
slim figure beautifully, though it had been second-hand.
The hems were fraying – again – and she needed to replace
some of the buttons down the back.

'You look gorgeous, Rube, you always do, my darlin','
Cathy looked over at her, trying to reassure her daughter.

The gesture only made Ruby roll her eyes and grin.
'You know what I mean, though . . .'

Their entire world was enclosed within the East End
and the neighbouring roads next to Star Lane. Every
day of Ruby's life had been spent in these streets, surrounded by people she'd known since she was born. It was
a close-knit community, but a place divided sharply into
those who stayed on the honest path – working manual
jobs, eking out their wages until pay day – and those who
walked a very different path. Unlike her family, many of
Ruby's friends, including Sarah and the other girls she
hung out with, had already turned to crime. Most of it
wasn't big stuff: hoisting or cashing fake cheques and
nicking postal orders. Some of her mates' dads did jump-
ups – jumping onto lorries to steal whatever they carried,

or diverting lorries and their contents by dressing up in security garb or fluorescent jackets to lure unwary drivers to offload onto stolen trolleys. From what Ruby heard, it was a trick that worked surprisingly well much of the time, but of course, the drivers might've taken a back-hander to look the other way.

It was how things were done. The attitude was that big firms could afford a loss here and there, so what was the harm? Those were the people who could buy a round in the pub, or go up to the West End to buy proper clothes from real shops like M&S. To Ruby, that seemed like the height of luxury, and something the Murphys would never have.

Everyone, Ruby and her family included, knew what their neighbours were up to, but the code of silence of the East End, one that had existed for generations, still stood. You didn't grass up your own, no matter what they'd done. No police, or Feds as they were known to Ruby, were ever called. What happened in the streets around Star Lane was a world unto itself, and that's the way most people liked it. Most people – except her mum and dad.

Ruby looked around the table in the small kitchen. Everyone she loved was there: her older brother Bobby, her mum Cathy now taking off her faded apron and sitting down to eat, and her dad Louie, who until now had been washing his hands at the sink. Their neat terraced Victorian house might be small, but it was home. And her dress might be second-hand, but they had everything they needed.

'Louie, get yerself sat down and let me dish up yer dinner. You look done in.' Cathy frowned. She worried incessantly about her husband, especially after the death of his father, Jim. It'd been Jim who'd taken in Ruby's parents when Cathy fell pregnant. Cathy's own parents had been quick to see the back of her.

Ruby smiled at her dad, her co-conspirator and ally.

Louie turned to wink at his daughter as he offered his plate up to her mum. 'Don't fuss, love, I'm fine,' Louie said, waving away her concern.

Louie spent his days at the scrapyard on the Isle of Dogs, a few streets behind their house. It was a bustling place filled with stacked-up discarded cars, forklift trucks moving large machinery into piles, and workers and sellers haggling over the price of that day's offerings. It was hard work and long hours for little pay, but Louie grew up around the site, dodging cranes and trucks and following his own dad around after school.

'Darlin' I've been workin' on that scrapyard since I was fourteen, but it's tough work. A man gets tired,' Louie said, picking up his knife and fork and looking at Cathy expectantly.

'I know, love, and your dad always said he'd wanted better for ya. He never wanted ya to leave school and earn a wage in such a place . . .' Cathy started to say, but Louie cut in.

'Look, babe, Dad brought me up on his own. We needed the money. I never regretted it, though sayin' that, I nearly did today; it was a bad day, I'll admit that.'

'Why, Dad?' asked Ruby as she cut up her sausages.

Louie glanced over at his wife, suddenly unsure if he should say what was on his mind. Cathy stopped dishing out Bobby's food. 'Go on,' she said, eyebrows raised. Louie looked like he regretted mentioning it.

'One of the cranes almost took out a pile of scrap. It 'appens. I'm fine and no one got hurt . . . It's times like that I'm bloody sure ya need to make the most of your locksmith apprenticeship, ya won't be followin' in my footsteps, Bobby.'

'Language!' admonished his wife, but her face was worried rather than stern.

'I'm fine,' Louie said. 'Now let's eat, I'm starvin'. And anyway, all I ever wanted was to raise a good family and get a good wife, and I done that.' He smiled at Ruby.

'Somethin else did 'appen today,' Louie swallowed his forkful of heavily salted potato and boiled peas, and leaned forward.

'Not sure I want to hear this,' Cathy said, sitting down and starting to eat. 'Bobby, get yer elbows off the table. We might not 'ave cash to throw about but my kids will grow up with proper manners,' she muttered.

'I am grown up, Mum!' Bobby beamed.

'Go on, Dad,' Ruby interjected, keeping the peace.

'Well, somethin' 'appened today that hasn't 'appened for a long time. I got offered crooked work . . .'

The revelation prompted Ruby to glance over at Bobby, who was looking at their dad in surprise.

'You said no, right, Dad?' Bobby said, putting down his fork.

'Course I did, son, but they were pretty insistent. These blokes I knew at school came in to the yard, drivin' a right old banger of a van. I thought they looked shifty. I went to say hello and shake their 'ands, and they drew me over to the van, opened up the back doors and there it was . . .'

'There what was?' Ruby burst out. She was dying to know the answer.

Louie turned to look at his daughter. He could see the glint of fascination in her eyes. 'It was a safe. They'd nicked it from a warehouse down the docks and wanted me to open it with my welding torch.'

'I could've done that without the mess for a nice fee. Wouldn't take more than a minute to crack a safe open,' Bobby cut in, laughing.

It was clearly a joke, but Cathy frowned again. 'Go on, love,' she said to her husband.

'That's it. They offered me a small fortune to crack it. I told them I don't do that kind of business. I said, "Everyone round 'ere knows I don't do no crooked work, I leave that to the villains around our way."' At this point Louie frowned. 'For a minute, I thought they weren't goin' to take no for an answer,' he said.

Cathy's face registered alarm. She understood what he meant. 'Did they threaten ya?' she asked.

'I think they thought about it,' Louie answered carefully. 'Luckily there were a couple of the lads on site and they saw what was goin' on and came over. But for a minute there . . .'

Ruby saw the briefest glimpse of fear on her dad's face and guessed there was more to the story than Louie was letting on.

'Anyway,' he said with forced brightness, 'everyone knows now, if they didn't already, that I don't work for crooks, so why come to me?'

It was clear to Ruby that this had upset him. Nobody said anything. They all knew that Louie was straight as a die. He'd lost friends growing up because of it; there were pubs he couldn't drink in because he wasn't part of the local crime network. Everyone but everyone knew how strongly he felt.

'I told them to sling their hook, but still, it's a different world these days. Everyone's tryin' to make an easy coin. It ain't right.'

Suddenly Ruby spoke. 'How much were they offerin'?'

'Never you mind how much, you just get on and eat yer dinner,' Cathy chipped in. 'We don't take dodgy money, as Grandad Jim said—'

'A straight pound is worth three crooked pounds,' chimed Ruby and Bobby together, rolling their eyes. They'd heard the phrase a million times. It had been drummed into them by their grandad and dad throughout their childhood.

'Yes, and don't you forget it!' Louie barked. He looked serious. 'If you let in one monkey bastard then they'll all come runnin' and you'll be a crook like all the others, always watchin' yer back.'

Ruby laughed as a memory came back to her, clear as anything. '"Monkey bastards." It's like Grandad is sitting at the table. I must only 'ave been six the first time I heard him say that and I said to him, "Grandad, what's a monkey bastard?" and Mum whacked me one for swearin'.'

Bobby grinned back at her and Louie laughed out loud. Cathy wasn't so amused. She stepped over and smacked her daughter lightly on the arm, just as she'd done when she was a little girl. 'And you're not too old to get another whack now. No swearin' in this house!'

'Ow, don't do that, Mum!' Ruby giggled, rubbing her arm, but she carried on all the same. 'The worst of it was that I was sittin' there thinkin', *When do I get to meet a monkey bastard? They sound so excitin'!*'

Cathy and Louie shook their heads in unison, both now laughing. It was her mum's turn to sigh. 'You're right though, Louie. If you do one job, they'll all be comin' to ya to do the next one and the next one. It ain't worth it . . . I know times are hard right now . . .'

Louie smiled just a little sadly. 'I know, love. The leccy needs toppin' up and I could do with some new work boots . . . but that's not the way we'll do it. Anyway, easy money ain't easy at all, you know that as well as I do. Let's eat our dinner and be thankful for what we've got.'

The moment of jollity evaporated. Underneath the humour was the harsh fact of their life: they didn't have much. But they had each other. Sometimes Ruby wished she could just throw their standards out of the window and enjoy the good life like her friends, but she knew what was important. Ruby was happy with her life, with her small bedroom, her second-hand clothes, with her friends, but sometimes, just sometimes, she wished for more.

CHAPTER 2

'Come on, I've got somethin' to show ya,' Sarah whispered, her face alight with mischief. Ruby was at her best friend's house for the evening while her parents were at the pub.

'What is it, Sar, I want to watch telly,' Ruby answered, barely looking up from her programme.

'Come on, I'll show ya somethin' better than the telly,' Sarah said conspiratorially. Ruby looked up at her friend, whose eyes twinkled in the dim glow cast by the lamplight. She smiled. It was probably just a trick her friend was playing on her but she would humour her. Ruby yawned. It was quite late and really, she should've been getting back home. Her parents knew where she was but she hated staying away from them for too long.

'This way.' Sarah led Ruby out into the thin entrance hall. The evidence of her family's criminal activities showed in the expensive wallpaper, flashy net curtains, the new chandelier that was too big for the small lounge. It was as unlike Ruby's home as it was possible to be, despite being the same size and layout. Ruby liked to run her hand across the wallpaper pattern gently as she walked, thinking one day she'd have posh wallpaper to match.

'Why are we 'ere?' Ruby asked, looking confused. She'd seen the front door and hallway a million times. There was nothing new there except the carpet that had recently been laid, a brand new one with swirling red and brown patterns to match the beige walls. Ruby knew that carpets were expensive. She didn't have any at her house.

Sarah reached down to grab the corner of the expensive flooring.

'What are ya doin'? You'll ruin it!' Ruby gasped.

'Look! Watch me . . .' Sarah lifted the corner and tugged at it until whatever was sticking it down released its hold and the thick polyester carpet curled upwards in Sarah's hand. Beneath it was what looked like a trapdoor, albeit a small one.

Sarah pulled up the hatch to reveal a large black holdall.

'What's in there, Sar?' Ruby asked, though something told her she didn't really want to know.

'You just wait and see,' her mate replied mysteriously, unzipping the bag and plunging her hand inside. Seconds later, Sarah pulled out her discovery.

'It's a bloody gun!' Ruby gaped. She stared disbelievingly at the weapon in Sarah's hand, suddenly frightened. Her heartbeat quickened, her pulse beating inside her brain. She swallowed, digesting this new sight. Every second that passed made her feel more like bolting back home to safety. Sarah, meanwhile, was grinning, transferring the weapon between each hand as if trying on a new accessory. Her friend seemed mesmerised by the black revolver, peering at it from all angles, while Ruby just felt sick.

'Put it back, Sar. We shouldn't 'ave found it.'

'Don't worry, it ain't loaded,' Sarah replied, grinning at Ruby's discomfort. 'And anyway, Dad won't actually use it. He says it's to scare people into givin' him what he wants. So, it's really just for effect.'

'But why would he need it?' Ruby was puzzled. She knew that Sarah's mum was a dipper, a shoplifter, and her dad broke into places to steal things, but this was a whole new level.

'My dad says he's movin' up in the world, he's goin' to be a big-time blagger,' Sarah couldn't hide her pride. She puffed her chest out, then held out her arm, pointing the gun squarely at Ruby.

'Don't bloody point it at me! Put it down. Sar, stop it!' Ruby hissed, making Sarah giggle.

'Don't worry, scaredy-pants, Dad keeps the rounds separate. He says he won't load it, only wave it around when he starts doin' the bigger jobs like robbin' banks for Charlie Beaumont.'

Ruby had heard of blaggers and knew Sarah's dad did some small jobs but had never realised that the people she knew were doing big-time jobs. A blagger, or bank robber, was the top of the criminal hierarchy, everyone knew that.

'Who's Charlie Beaumont?' Ruby said. Her voice sounded strange, as if she had something stuck in her throat.

'Oh,' said Sarah airily, 'he's Dad's boss now. He's a proper crook, a big-time blagger and he knows all the big jobs. My dad's gone up in the world. He says that as soon as the money comes in, we'll move to a bigger house somewhere posh, just like Charlie.'

'Oh, but I don't want ya to move,' Ruby replied, her head spinning. She'd grown up in Star Lane. She knew that petty crime was rampant and people did what they did to survive, but this was something else, something she'd never experienced before.

'You'll come and stay in our mansion, don't worry, we'll still be friends . . . Go on, Rube, try it yerself. It feels heavier than ya think.' Sarah held out the gun but Ruby shook her head. 'I don't like it, Sar. You, your parents and Alan could all be in big trouble.'

Suddenly all Sarah's nice things – the huge television, the Betamax video player – all seemed to belong to a world Ruby didn't understand. She didn't want to admit, even to her closest friend, that the sight of the gun had shocked her, but she couldn't help but shudder.

'Put it back. It ain't right to get it out. Yer dad won't like us playin' with it . . .'

'We ain't playin' with it, Miss Goody-Two-Shoes!' Sarah sneered, sensing her friend's dislike. 'Anyway he's my dad and I can do what I like with it.'

'Go on, just put it back. Please, Sar.' Mollified by Ruby's plea, her friend replaced the handgun in the holdall and zipped it up. Ruby watched as Sarah closed up the hidden hatch and laid the carpet flat again. She felt better once the gun was hidden, but she still had that queasy feeling of walking into new, unchartered territory.

'I've got to go . . .' Ruby said falteringly, trying to smile at the girl standing in front of her. Sarah shrugged her response.

'See ya,' Ruby said. Her friend stared after her as she left through the small kitchen that was filled with boxes of top-of-the-range toasters from a jump-up Sarah's brother Alan had done recently.

When Alan's luck came in, the whole neighbourhood knew about it as him and his dad, Mike, would buy rounds in the pub all night, returning home pissed and singing loudly, waking up the whole street. Sarah would always have a new dress or shoes the next day as well. Ruby had even seen Mike hand a big wad of cash to Sarah's mum, Julie, over the dinner table on the nights she stayed for tea. The family talked about robbing and stealing openly and easily, as if it were the most normal thing in the world. It was the opposite of her own house, but Ruby was used to Sarah's family. Now the gun, the blagging . . . that seemed something else.

Her head was buzzing as she crossed from Sarah's yard to her own via the small alleyway that ran along the back of the Victorian terraced houses.

'Sarah's parents in The Anchor again?' Cathy sniffed disapprovingly as Ruby opened the back door and let herself into the small kitchen. Ruby watched her mum sipping a cup of cocoa, a rare luxury in their house, trying to puzzle out what to say.

'A penny for 'em, darlin',' her mum said softly. She must've spotted something, some expression on Ruby's face. Ruby was different to the rest of the family, but Cathy knew her daughter. Whereas her oldest child Bobby was content with his home and family, Cathy had a feeling that inside Ruby was yearning for something better, a cleverness that wouldn't be content with a small, honest life. The knowledge scared her. She worried for her daughter.

'Did something happen, luv?'

'Of course not. I'm just tired, Mum, I promise. I'm fine. I'm goin' to bed.' Ruby managed a weak smile. There was no way she'd willingly share the news of the gun with her mum. She knew Cathy would hit the roof. Louie, her dad, would go ballistic if he found out what was really going on next door. Ruby'd never be allowed to hang out with Sarah again for sure, so she hurried through the kitchen and up to her room at the back of the house. She needed time to think.

Cathy watched her daughter as she made her way upstairs, a slight thread of concern nagging her, but it was late and she too was tired, so she let it lie.

CHAPTER 3

BANG, BANG, BANG. Ruby startled awake, glancing at the alarm clock by her single bed. It was just past 6 a.m. and the dawn sunlight was only just filtering through her plain curtains.

'POLICE! OPEN UP!'

'Oh my God!' Ruby exclaimed, leaping out of bed and running the few paces to her window. Her small bedroom was at the back of the family home, overlooking their yard and the neighbour's yard too. As she pulled a section of the brown fabric aside she saw heavily armed officers wearing full military-style black gear, guns pointing at Sarah's kitchen door.

'Bloody 'ell, what's goin' on?' Bobby burst into the room rubbing his eyes. His pale blue pyjamas were rumpled and faded from repeated washing, and his sandy-coloured hair was sticking up without the gallons of gel he usually applied to it.

'Shhhh,' Ruby gestured to her older brother to be quiet, putting her finger to her lips and motioning for him to come over to where she stood. There was little furniture in the small room: a bed with a pink bedcover that Ruby had had since she was a young girl, a lamp for reading and a wardrobe. Bobby sidled over next to her and peered out.

'Be careful, you don't want the Feds to see ya!' Ruby admonished her brother.

Bobby shrugged. 'What's it to do with us, anyway?'

'It's bloody Sarah's 'ouse, that's what!' snarled Ruby. Just then there was a loud crash as the door was kicked in and the line of black-clad coppers shoved their way into her friend's home. Ruby's heart was beating wildly, though it wasn't out of fear for herself or her family. Bobby was right, they hadn't done anything to bring the Feds to their door, but Ruby was terrified for her friend. What would happen to the family if they nicked Sarah's dad? What if they nicked Sarah? How would she cope being banged up? Ruby pushed Bobby aside to try to get a closer view.

'Ouch, Bobby!' Ruby elbowed her brother as he trod on her foot clumsily. They peered out of the window, waiting to see what would happen next.

'What'll they do to him when they get him?' Bobby whispered. He seemed shaken by the experience though he'd grown up around criminals and the ever-present threat of them being caught.

The question was answered almost immediately. A young woman's voice escalated to its crescendo, scream-ing for all she was worth. 'Dad! DAD! GET YER 'ANDS

OFF HIM. DAD, DON'T LET THEM DO THIS TO YA!'

It was Sarah's voice. Ruby craned her neck, trying to see her friend, just making out her blonde hair and a flash of her pink pyjamas. Ruby wanted to help and felt desperate knowing there was nothing she could do to stop this. Then came Julie's voice. 'You fuckin' bastards. Get yer 'ands off my 'usband. He ain't done nuthin' wrong. NUTHIN'.'

Just then, they caught sight of Mike being tussled to the ground, almost bringing down a line of washing along with him. Expensive underwear, designer tops and luxury cotton sheets threatened to engulf them all.

Ruby was frantic now. 'Poor Sarah. Oh my God, they're arrestin' her dad. What will they do without him?'

One of the coppers threw off the washing, and was greeted with, 'Oi, you mind my sheets, you FILTH!'

Ruby was unable to tear her eyes away from the scene unfolding beneath her window. She saw Mike kick a bin over, all the while yelling at the top of his lungs.

'Bloody 'ell, they've nicked him, all right,' Bobby exclaimed, forgetting to whisper. One of the officers suddenly looked up, though Mike was making a real racket as he shouted obscenities at the Feds and they couldn't possibly have heard him.

'Shut the bloody curtain!' Ruby never swore in front of her family as she always got a smack for it, but this was something else.

'I can 'ear them takin' him down the alley,' said Bobby. He was right. They heard the sound of metal clanging as more bins were kicked over. The captured man grappled along the back alleyway to where a cop car would surely be waiting.

Both of them peered round the curtain again to see Mike, who was now in handcuffs, disappear, though they could still hear him.

Then several more policemen appeared from the kitchen door, all carrying boxes of the stolen goods that had been piled up in Sarah's house. Seconds later, a copper walked out carrying the large black holdall Ruby knew only too well. At the sight of it, Ruby froze. 'Oh my God, they've got the gun!'

Ruby's voice was low but Bobby heard well enough. He turned sharply to look at his younger sister. 'They've got the what? What the 'ell do you know about a gun, Ruby Murphy?'

'That's exactly what I'd like to know!' Louie's voice thundered behind them. They both turned in shock to see their father standing at the bedroom door, his face wearing an expression of pure anger. 'I 'eard ya, Ruby. What d'ya know about guns?' Louie's hair was still tousled from sleep, but his dark eyes were hard as he scanned his daughter's face. 'Tell me the truth.'

'Dad, I don't know nuthin' really, I promise,' Ruby stuttered. 'Last week Sarah showed me where her dad kept that holdall. The gun was inside it. That's all I know! It was nuthin' to do with me, and I hated seeing it. I know I should've told ya but I didn't want you and Mum to worry . . .' Ruby trailed off miserably, wondering what punishment she would receive for not imparting this information sooner.

At the sight of her distress, Louie changed tack, becoming softer. He ran his hands through his thick black hair and looked back at her, this time with concern. 'Ruby, all we want is for you to be safe. We'll talk about it this evenin', but I want you to swear to me you'll never go round to Sarah's house again.'

Tears started to fall down Ruby's cheeks, but she nodded. She'd heard her friend's distress without being able to help, and she'd witnessed the unthinkable, a parent being arrested and taken away. All she could think of was how upset Sarah must be now – and she couldn't even go to comfort her.

Louie saw the tears, and with a soft voice said, 'Now get back to bed the both of you. I'm just glad neither of you are caught up in all this. We don't 'ave nuthin' to do with crooks from now on, and that includes your friend. Sorry, Rube.'

With that, her dad sloped off back to his bed. Ruby prayed he would say nothing to Cathy about the gun. She couldn't imagine what her mum would do if she knew, but she did know she'd hit the roof good and proper.

Her dad's words stung. Ruby couldn't imagine life without Sarah. They'd been best friends since before primary school, and she knew she couldn't – wouldn't – drop her, even if it meant incurring her father's wrath. She couldn't just leave her to deal with this alone. Somehow she had to try to see her.

Luckily, Louie didn't tell Cathy and so no more was said. The street quietened down, though the neighbours were all buzzing with gossip for days. Ruby was too worried about her friend to care what the local gossips said over the back-yard fences.

It took a couple of days, but eventually Cathy was out working at the local tobacconist and Louie was sorting out something at the scrapyard, leaving Ruby free for the first time since the arrest. She rushed across their yards and knocked softly on Sarah's door. Sarah hadn't been seen since the arrest, which Ruby had expected, but she'd been worried about her friend.

No one came to the door. Ruby pushed it; it was usually open, as were all their doors. Today it was shut. She knocked again, this time harder. Still no reply.

The next day she did the same. Each time her mum and dad were out Ruby tried to see Sarah.

It was over a week later that Ruby saw Sarah coming out of the local supermarket. She ran over, filled with relief at seeing her, but when Sarah turned to her, her expression was hostile. Her friend usually wore pink lip gloss and make-up, but today her face was bare. She looked like she hadn't eaten a decent meal in days and her face looked different, harder. Sarah was the first to speak.

'Dad's goin' away . . . for a long time . . .'

Ruby stepped towards her, desperate to comfort her but not sure what to say all of a sudden. This wasn't the reunion she'd expected.

Sarah took a step back. Before Ruby could say anything, Sarah blurted out, 'Mum says I can't speak to no one about it.'

Tears were now pouring down the girl's face, and she wiped them away roughly. Ruby stepped towards her friend again, wanting to hug her, but Sarah put her arms out to stop her and shouted, 'Don't touch me you *dirty pikey.*'

For a second, Ruby thought she'd misheard. 'Sarah . . . ?'

Her friend's tear-streaked face turned into an ugly scowl. 'Mum says we don't want no more to do with ya. Don't come to my 'ouse again, d'you 'ear me?'

Ruby nodded, unable to speak, so shocked was she by her friend's unkind words. Sarah stalked off leaving Ruby standing alone in the street. Even though it was a sunny spring afternoon, Ruby pulled her second-hand cardigan around her tightly, as if to protect herself from her friend's cruel words.

CHAPTER 4

Ruby was devastated by her friend's rejection of her. For the next few days, she contrived to hide away in her room, trying to think why Sarah had spoken to her so harshly. She wasn't just upset, she was puzzled. Why on earth would her best friend ditch her like that? What had she done wrong? Ruby racked her brains and could think of nothing. Obviously, her Romany roots had upset her friend but why would that suddenly be an issue? The Murphy family was descended from Gypsies, and she had grown up being taught to be proud of her family's past. Louie said people could be judgemental about Travellers, but Ruby had never experienced anyone using it against her – until now.

She was still puzzling over Sarah's words on her way to Rathbone Market a week later.

'Come and get yer apples. Lovely, juicy apples. Oi, darlin', come an' taste one of these beauties,' hollered the fruit and veg man, giving the teenager a wink. It was Saturday morning, the sun was out, and Ruby did what she'd done every weekend for the past couple of years and had taken herself off to the thriving marketplace off Barking Road, only a short walk from Star Lane. She tried not to think about the fact that she usually went with Sarah.

There were stalls of all descriptions running the length of the road, selling second-hand clothes, soft furnishings, fabrics, toys and bric-a-brac, as well as spicy Jamaican food, and fresh fruit and veg. Crammed next to the veg man's stall, filled to bursting with potatoes, carrots, cabbages, oranges, bananas and apples, was a woman selling oversized underwear. Huge pink bras and large lacy knickers wafted in the breeze. Ruby caught herself smiling as she walked past, through the crowds of people, remembering how she and her brother would scream with laughter as children at the sight of ladies rifling through the knickers, looking for a bargain. Cathy would always hurry past, her cheeks red with shame, dragging the two siblings with her as they pointed and giggled loudly. They'd always laughed about it as a family later, even Ruby's mum enjoyed the joke once they were out of earshot of those poor women.

'. . . I've got hairdryers, I've got toasters, I've even got hair curlers. Now come on, ladies, what'll it be today? Yes, you, come and 'ave a go on my curlers . . .'

Ruby moved past the electrical man's stall, wondering where he'd nicked the goods from this time. He was a hoister. Every week he had a different display of nicked goods at knock-down prices. She gave him a smile, which made him doff his cap to her as if she was a proper lady, and Ruby couldn't help but laugh. She loved the sights and sounds of the market – the bustle of the women as they elbowed each other out of the way, haggling over camisoles and bags of peaches, the sound of the stallholders hawking their wares, the passers-by and the smell of Caribbean spices mingling with it all. It was like a hive and the stallholders and customers were like the bees, buzzing around a flower, all looking for the same bit of nectar.

Just then, as Ruby started to feel at peace for the first time since losing her friend, the local troublemaker Freddie Harris stepped out in front of her, blocking her way. Freddie was a mate of Bobby's, though Ruby could never work out why her brother spent any time with him. He was a wide boy, a Jack the Lad who boasted about doing jobs for the blaggers and crime bosses. He thought he was sharp, but Ruby thought he was a loser, doing other peoples' crooked jobs and thinking he was something special as a result. He even looked like a weasel, with greasy brown hair permanently slicked back, a neck-full of gold chains and expensive trainers. Ruby was not impressed.

'What d'ya want?' she said impatiently. 'I've got things to do and I don't want to be bothered by the likes of you.' Ruby could never bring herself to be nice to Freddie. She saw him as a snake, ready to strike. He was always on the take, borrowing money from good-hearted Bobby and 'forgetting' to pay him back.

'That's not very friendly. Ain't no way to say 'ello, eh, Ruby Green Eyes,' he said, his voice oily, his manner reptilian. He always stood too close, and Ruby had to fight the urge to push him away.

'Don't call me that!' Ruby hit out at him, a course of action that only made him grin. She couldn't let him see he'd riled her. He loved the conflict, loved winding people up, especially her, and Ruby didn't want to give him the satisfaction. She sighed to herself. She knew the only way to get rid of him was to listen to whatever he had to say. She could tell by looking at him that he wanted to deliver some news, something unpleasant, most likely. She just had to wait it out then get on with her day.

'Tell me, then,' Ruby said, smiling at him through gritted teeth.

'Tell ya what?' Freddie looked over his shoulder a few times, always wondering who might be coming up behind him.

'Tell me whatever it is you're so desperate to tell me.' Ruby tried to keep the smile on her face but it was hard. Freddie was enough to provoke anyone.

'All right, then, I'll let you into a little secret . . .' He leaned even closer. She could smell the beer on his breath and it revolted her but she stood her ground, waiting for the bombshell to land. Freddie was loving this. He was all smiles as he said, 'People round 'ere are sayin' a few things . . .'

'Oh, and what might those things be, Freddie?' Ruby replied with wide eyes, looking as innocent of the murderous thoughts in her head as she possibly could.

'Oh, it's good, believe me, Ruby Green Eyes, it's really good – though not for you and your pikey family,' he leered. His eyes flicked away, always just avoiding her gaze. Oh yes, Freddie was really enjoying his moment of power.

'What are people sayin'? Spit it out, Freddie, I haven't got all day. And I'd prefer it if you didn't call my family *pikeys*.' Ruby was rapidly becoming weary of this game. She didn't care to spend any more time talking to this weasel than she really needed to, especially if he was going to insult her and her family.

Freddie stepped back as if in shock, though it was clearly part of his twisted performance. 'Don't ya know what everyone's sayin', Ruby Green Eyes?' he said with exaggerated concern.

'No, I don't, Freddie. Why don't you be the one to tell me. I can see you're dyin' to.' This time Ruby stared at him until his eyes were forced to meet her gaze. She knew this always rattled him. She wasn't scared of this loser. Ruby could handle herself where Freddie was concerned.

Now she'd stolen his thunder, Freddie almost reluctantly imparted his information. 'They're sayin' it was either someone who was jealous of them, or it was Gypsies who dobbed in a friend of ours, a friend of ours who is looking at doing ten years for blagging . . .'

Ruby instantly realised Bobby's repellent mate was talking about Sarah's dad. 'What are ya on about? I don't 'ave time for this,' Ruby cut him off. She tried to push past him but he grabbed her arm, stopping her from leaving. Freddie sensed his target had hit home.

'Oh yeah, people are sayin' it was pikeys who done for Mike. Now, d'you know any pikeys who might be jealous of all their pretty things?' Freddie stared straight at her.

Ruby didn't back off though. She squared up to Freddie, anger building up inside her. 'What's that got to do with me?' she said, but she already knew. Even though her family had nothing to do with the arrest, suspicion would fall on anyone with her background. 'My family might not be crooks, but they're not grasses either. Now you know as well as I do, Freddie Harris, that my family don't 'ave a jealous bone in their bodies, and, yes, we are Gypsies, so bloody what? We're proud of our roots, and we don't care what people say around 'ere because we done nuthin' wrong.'

'That's not what people are sayin'. Everyone round 'ere thinks your family are the grasses, so you'd better watch out. I'm doin' ya a favour warnin' ya.'

Freddie was now smiling widely, like the Cheshire cat. He licked his lips as if he could taste her words. With a small shrug of his bony shoulders, Freddie swaggered off, pausing to glance back at her before starting to whistle. Ruby's blood was boiling. Her morning, which had been strange anyway without Sarah, was now completely ruined. It didn't bother her what Freddie thought, but if everyone thought that, then the Murphys were in for a tough time. Her family would be shunned by the community and goodness knows what would happen as a result. The unwritten code of the East End was known by all: no one grassed to the coppers. Breaching the code meant there'd be consequences, and the thought chilled Ruby to the bone.

Suddenly, she lost interest in buying the clothes she'd set out to find today. Her excitement at being able to buy things to wear to her new job in an office up the West End had disappeared. She was due to start in a couple of weeks, but with a sinking heart, she decided to head home. She felt tired and had a desperate urge to get back home to the people she loved.

When she got home Ruby couldn't hide her feelings from her mum. Cathy took one look at her daughter, dragging her feet on the floor, and without a word, pulled her aside. 'Sit with me, love. Now, I know somethin's botherin' ya. Tell me what it is, perhaps I can help.' Ruby looked at her mum's still-pretty face, her fair hair still worn long, her blue eyes full of concern.

'What's wrong, darlin'? You've been so sad about Sarah. Is that what's botherin' you?' Cathy leaned forward, putting her arm around her daughter.

'Mum, I bumped into Bobby's mate Freddie Harris at the market . . .'

'Oh yes,' frowned Cathy. She disliked the weasel even more than Ruby did, if that was possible.

Ruby came straight out with it.

'Everyone's sayin' we grassed up Sarah's dad, and that's why he's gone to prison.' Ruby started to cry. Her mum held her tighter, rocking her gently in her arms. 'What's goin' to happen to us, Mum? What will people do? Are we in danger?'

Cathy took a moment to reply and when she spoke, she was careful with her words. 'That isn't good, Rube. We might 'ave to be a bit careful, but we'll keep tellin' people it weren't us. It weren't us, was it, Ruby?'

'Course it wasn't! I'd never grass on my best friend!' Ruby was stung into defending herself.

'That's all right, then. Listen, I'll speak to your dad. He'll know what to do. If there's any comeback it'll be him and Bobby who'll get it, so they need to be prepared,' Cathy said.

'Comeback?' Ruby asked, wiping away her tears.

'You're not a child any more so I won't lie to you. Perhaps it's best if all of us keep a low profile for a while, for a week or two. I'll tell your dad and Bobby they can't go down the pub on a Friday for a while. People round 'ere don't take kindly to grasses. I'm not sayin' we're not safe, but we need to be careful.'

Ruby shuddered.

Just then, Ruby caught sight of the old black-and-white photo sitting on the kitchen mantelpiece. It showed a beautiful woman, long dead, to whom Ruby bore a striking resemblance. The picture was of her granny, a Traveller who fell in love with her beloved Grandad Jim.

Cathy turned to look at the photograph. 'D'you remember the day that Grandad Jim told you about your Granny Ruby? You never met her, of course, as she died givin' birth to your dad, but by all accounts you're so like her.'

Ruby nodded, tears filling her eyes again. This time she wouldn't cry, though. She was done shedding tears over anything Freddie Harris said.

Ruby spoke in a whisper, smiling sadly at the image. 'She wasn't meant to marry Grandad but her brothers worked with him, so when they fell in love, the Travellers let them get married. Grandad told me about her when he was ill himself. He still spoke so lovingly about her. He told me that my eyes were the exact same shade of emerald green as Granny Ruby's and that's why I was his favourite.' Cathy squeezed her daughter's hand as if to say, 'Go on'.

'When I held Grandad's hand it was so frail and papery. He was dyin' then and I was too young to really understand. He told me that I reminded him of Granny, and that every time he looked into my eyes he saw hers starin' back.'

It was Cathy's turn to look sad. She nodded silently.

'He told me to always be proud of my roots, to be proud of comin' from Gypsy blood.' Ruby managed a smile as she recalled the conversation. Jim had died only a few short weeks afterwards, and it was the last real conversation they'd had together.

'Yes,' Cathy said, after a moment's silence as they both remembered the man who'd given them so much love and happiness, 'he loved Granny Ruby fiercely. He took Louie to Appleby Fair every year to show him what bein' a Traveller meant. He wanted him to know his heritage – your heritage.'

Ruby smiled again as she recalled his obvious pride, his love for the woman who refused to go to hospital and died in childbirth as a result. His love for her had been undimmed by time.

When Cathy finally left, Ruby sat down heavily in front of the small mirror in her bedroom. A beautiful young woman with jet-black hair, creamy skin and those brilliant green eyes that had come down to her through the generations stared back. A thought was forming in her mind, a decision she was in the process of making. Eventually she spoke out loud, not taking her eyes off her face. 'From now on, it's family and only family,' she vowed.

CHAPTER 5

'You ready to go, love?' Cathy smiled at her daughter. She almost couldn't believe Ruby was starting her first job, and as a trainee admin girl in a large, busy office in the West End. No newsagents for Ruby.

'Ready. How do I look?' Ruby said as she descended the stairs. She was dressed in the best she could afford, a pencil skirt from Rathbone Market, a pretty pale pink blouse patterned with tiny flowers, and a pink headband to keep back her shining hair. She had even applied a small amount of make-up, blush for her cheeks and a touch of red lipstick. Cathy felt a sudden urge to cry as she looked at her beautiful daughter; a woman stepping out into the wider world.

Ruby sensed the conflicting emotions her mum was feeling; the strange pull of wanting Ruby to stay a child for ever, and the opposite urge to send her out into the world to find her place in it. She gave her mum a sweet smile and before they could say anything else, she nodded. Cathy nodded back, there was no need for words. They understood each other completely.

'Don't worry, Mum, I'll be back about 6 p.m. for dinner,' Ruby said eventually. 'You OK?' Cathy, who was usually ready with a smile, looked tired. Ruby had noticed dark rings under her eyes lately and she looked a bit paler.

'Course I am, love. Don't worry about me. Off you go and good luck, darlin',' Cathy answered. Satisfied, Ruby picked up the handbag Cathy had treated her to especially for work. It was from the market, and her mum didn't usually approve, knowing they were forgeries or nicked, but she realised Ruby had to look the part so this time she gave way.

Ruby caught the bus, feeling utterly exhilarated, and more than a little nervous. She knew she was lucky to have landed the role. She was given the nod by a friend of a friend whose aunt worked in the administration department. Ruby knew there were many more capable girls, as she hadn't passed her Pitman typing test yet, but she'd somehow impressed her future employers at the interview.

It was Ruby's first big break, and she'd grabbed it with both hands. That day, her future seemed to shine a path in front of her. At the office, the women all looked up as she walked the length of the room, the clicking on the computer keyboards almost universally stopped. Ruby managed a smile, hoping she looked more confident than she felt. An older woman wearing large glasses and with permed hair showed her to her desk.

'You'll be sitting here. Don't worry, it's all quite simple. Once you've mastered the computer you'll be typing out letters to some of the companies we import goods from,' the woman said.

'Thank you, I'm sure I'll be fine,' murmured Ruby, hoping her hands wouldn't shake as she tried her first faltering movements on the great big machine sitting on her desk. It all looked so high-tech, so complicated.

'Yes, we import luxury products from all over the world, and supply places like Harrods and Liberty. I expect you've heard of those.' It was a statement rather than a question.

Ruby nodded, smiling broadly this time. 'Yes, I've definitely heard of those.'

Ruby could hardly believe that she, a girl from Canning Town, was sitting in an office that sent beautiful things like real designer handbags, luxurious clothes and jewellery to the poshest shops in London, and the world. She looked down at the fake Gucci bag her mum had bought her, knowing it would've taken a big chunk out of the weekly budget. *One day, I'll buy real Gucci bags for Mum and designer clobber for everyone*, she thought fervently to herself. *One day . . .*

Work went well and at 5 p.m. Ruby caught the bus back to the East End, walking in just in time for tea.

'It's liver and spuds, sorry, darlin',' Cathy said as she walked in, her face alight at seeing her daughter.

'That's all right, Mum, I'm starvin', I'd eat anythin' right now.'

'Tell us everythin' but wash yer 'ands first and sit at the table, we're waitin' for ya,' her mum bustled, touching her daughter's arm to show her she'd been thinking of her throughout the day.

Louie was already home, eager to hear about his daughter's first day of work, and Bobby had slouched in early too. He was fast becoming a valued member of the locksmith apprentices. He seemed to have a light touch, and almost instinctive way of unlocking even the most complex locks. The firm had already indicated that they would make him an employee when his training was finished.

'Well, go on, sis, spit it out,' Bobby encouraged.

They all looked at her expectantly, making her burst out laughing. 'It was great, really it was. They buy designer clothes and expensive watches from companies abroad and ship them over to London and sell them at Harrods. You wouldn't believe the invoices I've seen today, some of those things cost a fortune, more than we'll all make in a lifetime,' Ruby said swallowing her first mouthful.

'My goodness, that sounds somethin' doesn't it, Louie?' Cathy sighed again, a wistful smile growing on her face. 'Sounds a bit special, that job. Good for you, darlin', for landin' it.'

'Don't forget that they're lucky to 'ave ya,' added her dad, always eager to see the best in her, which she loved him for.

'Don't forget to bring some of that posh clobber home!' Bobby chipped in. 'It's the only way we'll ever see that kind of flash gear! I bet they won't miss a few Chanel handbags. Go on, Rube, nick a few bits for us.'

Cathy instantly snapped, 'You won't "nick" anythin', either of you. I don't want to hear you say that!'

Louie looked stern too. 'It ain't a joke, Bobby. We've got what we've got. If others 'ave the money to throw away on a handbag then that's their business.'

'Sorry, Dad,' Bobby said but he was still grinning at Ruby.

'I won't need to steal a damn thing. One day, I'll be able to buy it for myself. I'll be the head of a business like the one I work for.'

Cathy gave Ruby a small slap on her arm for swearing, but a smile played around her mouth at her daughter's ambitions.

Ruby couldn't help herself. She felt a mixture of elation and pride in stepping out of her small world to go up west each day. It felt like a huge adventure. It would have been grand no matter what, but these days it held an even greater appeal. The family was still under suspicion for grassing on Sarah's dad. Several times, local kids had shouted threats at Ruby in the street, making her put her head down and run to her destination. Louie and Bobby had to stop going to the pub after work on Fridays, and Cathy was worried she might lose her job with some of her regulars, who'd bought their 'baccy' for years from her, now avoiding the shop.

Bringing herself back to the conversation, Ruby continued her tale. 'And the girls were all nice to me. Some of them invited me out on Friday for a drink after work. Can I go, Mum?'

'Course you can, darlin',' Louie cut in after seeing his wife's frown, 'but promise us you won't stay too long. Just be friendly, 'ave one drink, and come 'ome.'

'Thanks, Dad,' Ruby said, loving their protectiveness. It didn't feel stifling. She knew how lucky she was to have their care and concern.

CHAPTER 6

Four weeks in and Ruby was loving work. The computers weren't half as difficult as she'd feared, and though the girls were much posher, they'd all been kind to Ruby. But each evening instead of looking forward to getting home, she dreaded running the gauntlet of locals eager to see the back of any Murphy. The slurs against her and her family weighed heavily on Ruby's young shoulders and she knew she had to do something about the situation. She gathered all her courage and went to knock at Sarah's door again. This time, her friend opened it.

'You're not welcome 'ere,' Sarah said sharply.

'I know I'm not, but you 'ave to believe me when I say it wasn't me, or any of my family. We would never grass. You've known us for ever. You can't believe we'd do this to ya. Look, please meet me tomorrow. I've had my first pay check and I'll treat ya to pie 'n' mash . . .'

This was Sarah's favourite treat. She saw her friend mull it over, hoping against hope that Sarah would give in.

'All right. I'll meet ya at Kelly's tomorrow lunch-time,' was all she said before slamming the door shut. Despite this, Ruby could've shouted with happiness at the prospect of seeing her again.

The next day, Ruby had a quick mooch around Roman Road Market in Bow, before heading to Kelly's, their favourite pie 'n' mash shop. Sarah was inside already, waiting for her, so Ruby ordered the full works for both of them, including hot eels that quivered on their plates. There was an awkward silence as she sat down opposite Sarah. Neither said a word.

It was Ruby who broke the silence. 'Look, it wasn't us. I swear it on my mum's life. Whatever people are sayin', it weren't us. You're my best friend, I'd never grass on ya.'

Sarah nodded. Eventually she replied, 'Oh, Ruby, I know it couldn't be you, but I were just so upset and everyone was sayin' stuff and . . .'

Ruby sighed. The weight pressing down on her lifted. She smiled at her friend, noting she looked thinner these days, a bit unkempt.

'It's OK. I understand. How's things at home?' Ruby said as their food was placed in front of them. She watched as Sarah ploughed into the food ravenously, looking like she hadn't had a square meal for a while.

'Not great,' replied Sarah through a mouthful of food. 'With Dad gone, and my brother bein' a lazy tosser, it's down to me and Mum to bring in the cash. Mum's had to go back to shopliftin' and I'm doin' a bit of this and that. You know, bit of thievin', bit of dippin' . . .'

Ruby tried to smile back at her friend but she couldn't. She was worried Sarah would go the same way as her parents. Her mum Julie had been in and out of prison for years before meeting Sarah's dad, Mike. She'd been nicked flogging stolen designer baby clothes to an under-cover copper and ended up in Holloway. And Sarah's brother Alan, he'd been in trouble since he was knee-high to a grasshopper.

Sarah continued to chew as she spoke, her large gold hoop earrings swaying as she ate. Her hair was pulled up into a scrunchie but it looked unwashed and she wasn't wearing her customary make-up.

'Yeah, so we're skint. Mum'll end up banged up again, and Alan's useless. So, what's new, Rube? I've 'eard you're workin' up the West End now?'

'Yes, and I'm hopin' this is the start of better things, Sar. You should see 'em. All posh, sitting at their computers, orderin' Gucci, Chanel, you name it. And I'm part of it. I want to make a go of it, I want to do well. Maybe I could keep an eye out for ya, let ya know if they have a job goin'. Imagine the two of us workin' in the West End,' Ruby said, her cheeks flushed with excitement.

Sarah looked up from her plate and as their eyes met, she hesitated for a moment, then said, 'That's not likely for me. You've got everythin', Rube, and if anyone can make a go of it straight, then it's you.'

'What d'ya mean, Sar? If I can do it, you can.'

'But I can't. Listen, there's somethin' ya don't know about me, and I ain't told no one about this. I was born in Holloway. I'm a prison baby; I even had a bloody prison number. If that ain't a bad enough start, my dad's banged up for blaggin'. Your posh bint's not goin' to offer a job to the likes of me. I ain't got no chance, Rube. Don't matter what I do, there's no out for the likes of me.'

Ruby cradled her Coke, not sure what to say. She'd known Sarah all her life, but this was new. She watched her friend pick at her food, sucking fish off the bones, and not making eye contact. 'I'm sorry, Sar,' she said quietly. 'I can't imagine what that was like.'

'No, I know you can't,' Sarah replied. 'I was always jealous of ya. Ruby Murphy with her nice family, straight as a die. You had everythin', ya still do.' She finished, looking down at her plate, which was now empty of mashed potato, pie and green liquor. Ruby, in contrast, had hardly eaten a thing.

'What d'you mean, Sar? We don't 'ave nuthin', except each other.'

'That's what I mean, ya silly moo. You've got a family, you're loved. No one's never loved me, no one, Rube . . . What chance did I ever 'ave in life?'

Ruby didn't know what to say to that. Instead she took Sarah's hand, offering the only comfort she could. She'd come hoping to clear the air between them, maybe even ask Sarah to tell people it wasn't them that grassed, but she couldn't add any more weight to her friend's shoulders. She felt powerless to help her and worried that soon Mike wouldn't be the only Riley in prison. Life was so unfair. She could already see that you had to fight for what you wanted, but some people were dealt a hand that meant no amount of fighting would ever be enough. She hoped Sarah wasn't one of those people.

Ruby got to the office early as usual. She was often one of the first in and last to leave. She wanted to make her mark.

About an hour after she'd sat down at her desk, Ruby noticed a bit of commotion at the front of the office. She craned her neck and spotted an elegant woman in her forties strolling along with Mrs Jones, the office manager. The woman had immaculate taste, and was dressed in Chanel. Trailing behind the pair could be none other than her teenage daughter. She was a blonde, picture-perfect replica of her mother, wearing a smart dress and matching kitten heels.

'It's the boss's wife,' whispered the girl sitting next to her. 'Better look sharp.'

Ruby tried not to stare and turned her attention back to her screen, but a few moments later the trio stopped at her desk.

'And this is our newest addition. Ruby has been a godsend. Never had a girl take to the work the way she has. Won't be long till she's managing her own accounts,' Mrs Jones said.

Ruby was struck speechless by the high praise, but before she could muster a response Mrs Jones had moved on.

The girl lingered behind the others and smiled at Ruby.

'Hello, I'm Felicity. I can see you're going to be running this place soon,' she said, conspiratorially winking at Ruby as if they'd known each other for ages.

'Thanks. I just want to do well,' Ruby spluttered. She was feeling rather in awe of Felicity, with her public school vowels and her swish clothes.

'It seems you're well on your way already. We should go for a drink one night—'

'Felicity, do keep up,' called her mother.

'See you.' The girl winked again and sashayed off.

Ruby looked after her. Whatever that girl had, she wanted; that confidence, that natural ease, all of it. Felicity swung her designer bag around, looking a bit bored and grinning over at Ruby as if they were already best friends.

One day I'll be like her, Ruby vowed to herself, feeling like a small chink in that world had opened up to her. It was the beginning of something, she could sense it.

'They think they're the bees knees, lording it over us. And look at those shoes, and that handbag. They're probably worth more than you or I earn in a year.' Mrs Jones had sidled up to Ruby, having seen Felicity and her mother out.

'I think it's lovely they've got nice things. If you don't mind, I'd like to get on.'

There was something in Ruby's voice, some edge of steel, that the office manager picked up on immediately. She gave Ruby an almost curious glance before walking over to a neighbouring desk, immediately spotting a mistake and haranguing the poor girl as she typed. Ruby put her head down, pretending to work, but she knew that she wanted to be like them, to have what they had, to be someone who walked into a room and made people look, just like the boss's wife and daughter did. The realisation crystallised in Ruby's mind, whirring away as she painstakingly copied the work she'd been set. This was a new world for Ruby. She had been more used to avoiding her brother's toe-rag friends, or hanging out with her own friends, who were all mixed up with dodgy men and dodgy business. These new people seemed breathtakingly sophisticated and glamorous. Ruby even went out each Friday evening with the girls from work, staying in the West End and going clubbing, though she refused to drink alcohol, preferring a clear head and slipping off early to get home to her family. The values instilled in her from childhood held strong.

Come that Friday, she looked for Felicity to see if they really would go for a drink, but she hadn't yet reappeared. So Ruby headed to drinks with the girls, imagining what it would be like to slip her feet into Italian heels, or feel the reassuringly expensive weight of a Gucci bag on her arm.

CHAPTER 7

It was Ruby's first Friday night in for ages. She'd decided to give the girls' night out a miss that week. She was flicking through *Cosmopolitan*, which one of the girls from the office had lent her, when there was a loud knock at the door.

'Expectin' someone?' Cathy called from upstairs where she was folding sheets.

Louie shrugged, looking over at his daughter, sitting in the cramped lounge. 'Don't think so?' Ruby said, getting up and opening the front door.

Why was it always her that seemed to end up being face-to-face with Bobby's cocky pal Freddie? Instantly, she sighed and crossed her arms, standing like a sentry in front of the doormat. 'No need to knock, Freddie, no one else does, they just let themselves in.' She delighted in confusing him. He seemed to bring out the devil in her. It was common practice to leave your front and back doors open, especially if you were as poor as the Murphy family – there was nothing of value to steal. She knew that Freddie wouldn't have dared let himself in because he was slightly afraid of decent, upright people like her mum and dad, and possibly even Ruby herself. She watched him regain his composure and flash his gold teeth at her, making her wrinkle her nose in distaste.

Ruby eyed him up. What on earth was a weasel like Freddie Harris doing on her doorstep on a Friday evening? Bobby rarely went to the pub any more, let alone with Freddie, so there was no reason for him to call by. She raised her eyebrows in anticipation. Freddie wilted a little under her scrutiny, then regained his confidence and lent against the door-post.

'What d'you want this time, Freddie?' Ruby sighed.

'Not pleased to see me, Ruby Green Eyes?' he leered, leaning in towards her.

'I wouldn't come any closer if I were you, or you'll 'ave my dad to deal with.'

'Don't get your knickers in a twist, I've come for Bob,' Freddie snapped, his hands now in the pockets of his low-slung jeans, the gold chains rattling as he moved. He kept looking over his shoulder, as if something was there.

'Bobby! You've got a visitor,' Ruby shouted over her shoulder, refusing to move. She wasn't going to let him take one step inside her home. She didn't trust him.

'So, what d'you want my brother for, then?' Ruby asked. She wouldn't normally care what Freddie and Bobby got up to but today was different. The two men hadn't hung out for ages, so why was Freddie sniffing round her doorstep? She wanted to know the answer, and she was damned sure she'd stay right where she was until she got it. It was clear as daylight that something was up.

'Nuthin' to worry your pretty head over,' smirked Freddie as Bobby pushed past her, poking his head out the doorway.

'What's up, Freddie?' Bobby said, grinning.

'Well, er, it's difficult to say, mate. Can we 'ave a little privacy?' Freddie replied, staring overtly at Ruby.

'There's nuthin' you can't say in front of my sister. So, what's it all about, Fred?'

Ruby couldn't resist a victorious smile as she stared back at Freddie, who was now shaking his head, a dangerous grin on his face.

'All right, all right, I see I've got to come out with it,' the dodgy bloke answered.

'And get on with it,' Ruby muttered under her breath. She had just started reading an article about dating and was finding it fascinating. So far she hadn't had much interest in the fellas around their way, but that could change.

'I've got a bit of work for ya, Bob, if ya want it? A couple of the *big boys* need a favour, a safe that needs your kind of . . . *persuasion*.' Bobby looked momentarily confused, but Ruby knew instantly what Freddie was alluding to.

'You want my brother to do crooked work for you?' she clarified, her eyes widened.

'We'd make it worth your while,' Freddie continued, ignoring Ruby completely.

Before Ruby could hit back, Bobby opened his mouth and set his mate straight. 'We're honest people, Freddie. I can't do no crooked jobs, sorry but you'll 'ave to tell your *big boys* no can do.'

With that, Bobby retreated back inside the house, leaving Ruby on the doorstep. Freddie had looked momentarily defeated but as he sloped off towards Star Park across the road, he looked back at her with a wolfish grin.

Ruby shivered. The nights were drawing in and already the leaves were starting to turn brown. She wasn't altogether sure if that was the reason she suddenly felt icy cold.

CHAPTER 8

'We've got something to tell ya both. You'd better sit down to 'ear it,' Louie said as he ushered Ruby and Bobby into the front room. The window, bare of net curtains, looked out onto the road that separated the row of houses from Star Park opposite.

Ruby looked up at her mum and dad as they stood awkwardly by the sofa. She glanced at Bobby; he shook his head in response. What could this mean? Bobby smiled back at her, though he registered something, some confusion evident on Ruby's face. She had noticed her mum looked exhausted these days, and suddenly Ruby wondered if there was something wrong. They sat together, like small children, on the brown fabric sofa, waiting.

'Mum—?' Ruby started to say but Louie interrupted her.

'Don't look so scared, Rube, it's happy news. We're, ahem, we're 'avin' a baby.'

There was silence for a moment as both siblings digested this latest news, news that neither thought they'd ever hear.

'Well, one of you say somethin',' Cathy laughed nervously. 'I know it's a shock but we're not *that* old!'

Ruby looked over at her parents. Louie had his arm around his pregnant wife, and Cathy was leaning into him, looking between the two young people expectantly. At first, Ruby wanted to think it was some kind of joke, but it was clear now it was no such thing. Her parents were having another baby at the age of forty.

'But . . . but . . . you don't look pregnant?' was all Ruby could think to say.

'Well, I'm only three months gone so I won't show for another month or so,' Cathy pointed out, though Ruby saw again how small Mum seemed, how slim and almost frail.

'Bloody hell, Mum!' Bobby interjected making them all laugh. 'How are we goin' to afford to 'ave a baby?'

It was Louie's turn to speak. 'Listen you two, I don't want either of ya worryin' about money. We'll make what we 'ave stretch. Babies don't need much, just your mum and a few nappies.'

Ruby raised her eyebrows. She'd seen friends from school get pregnant and have babies and they were always surrounded by stuff: prams, nappies, toys, bottles, formula and buggies. But those worries could wait.

'We're havin' a baby! That's lovely news. Mum, you need to sit down. 'Ere let me make you a cuppa. Bobby, go and get some biscuits from the corner shop, we're celebratin'.' Ruby smiled as she fussed around her mum. Another baby in the family! In a million years she would never have suspected they'd be welcoming a baby into their lives.

'You don't need to fuss over me, Rube, though I am feeling tired at the moment. The doctor says it's bein' pregnant at my advanced age. He called me a geriatric mother!' Cathy said indignantly, making both Ruby and Bobby smile.

'Shouldn't they do some tests anyway? Just to make sure . . . I'm sure there's nuthin' wrong but it's worth them checkin' ain't it?' Ruby said as she plumped up one of the few cushions they owned.

'I'm fine, Rube, honest. Now where's that cuppa? I'm parched.'

Satisfied her mother was comfortable, Ruby went to the kitchen and put the kettle on the hob. As she waited for it to boil she had time to gather her thoughts. A baby was a wonderful thing, and it made sense that Mum was more tired than normal. She felt a sense of wonder at the thought of having a little one to look after.

Louie came in and shut the door behind him. 'Listen, Rube. I know this is a shock but this is happenin' and, at first, we couldn't believe it either. Your mum needs our support. She's older than when she had you two and she's no spring chicken any more . . .'

Ruby smiled at the dad she adored. 'Course, I'm really 'appy for you both, and all of us. I'll do everything I can to help Mum.' She grinned and turned to give him a cuddle. She breathed in the familiar scent; the cheap soap he used to scrub himself clean after a day lugging metal around the scrapyard, and the lingering smell of other men's tobacco. In his arms she felt safe from everything.

She heard the front door open and Bobby reappeared clutching several packets of biscuits.

'I didn't know which ones to get so I bought them all!' he grinned.

Ruby carried in a tray with the teapot and cups, just in time to see her mum tutting at him for spending recklessly in the shop.

'A packet of digestives would've been enough!' she was saying.

Bobby reached over and planted a kiss on her cheek. 'We're celebratin' so I thought we'd 'ave a treat,' he said, raising his eyes skywards at Ruby, who had to stifle a giggle.

'That means Dolly Crutch was right!' Bobby suddenly said.

'Oh my God, I'd forgotten about her. That old witch always got it right, every time, didn't I tell ya?' Cathy turned to her husband.

Ruby's mum had made an annual pilgrimage to a colourful local character, Dolly Crutch, who lived in a cramped ground-floor flat in Wapping. Everyone knew Dolly. She was the local fortune teller, and most days there was a queue running out of her front door and onto the street; people all desperate to know if good times would ever return. Cathy used to go every year to find out what was in store but after Dolly predicted she'd have another baby, three years ago, she'd stopped.

'I remember comin' home and laughing at how ridiculous it was, vowin' I'd never go back to her, and she was right all along.'

Ruby smiled. She'd been taken to Dolly as a child, hanging on her mother's apron strings. They'd sat in the tiny kitchen with yellow cupboards and a small wooden table, waiting for Cathy's turn to go in. Ruby must've been six or seven at the time, yet she could remember the sight of the old woman even now. They were ushered into an even smaller room, strung with coloured Indian scarves, with a single orange lamp that seemed to throw only a small light in the gloom. Dolly was a sight she'd never forget, with dyed black hair, wisps of grey escaping from the scarf tied around her head. It had small coins stitched to it and it jangled as she pointed to the chair and asked them to sit.

She'd closed her eyes, which were lined crudely in black kohl, and asked for guidance from 'the spirits'. Ruby couldn't take her eyes off her. Dolly had opened her eyes and stared straight at Ruby, yet the little girl had felt no compulsion to look away.

'She has the gift,' was all she'd said, her unblinking gaze staring into Ruby as if she could see right inside her. Ruby hadn't felt scared. She felt she'd been recognised – that was the only way she could describe it as an adult looking back at that strange encounter.

Dolly had eventually turned to Cathy and asked her to hold out her hands and place an item of jewellery into her waiting palm. Cathy'd wriggled off her wedding ring and placed it there, leaning forward just a little, eager to hear of her fate. Ruby couldn't remember anything else from that day except that on the way home, Cathy bought her a chocolate bar, which was a rare treat. As Cathy handed her daughter the chocolate, she'd stopped for a second, as if she'd wanted to say something to Ruby, but at the last minute, changed her mind.

'What was it she said to ya that time I went with ya?' Ruby asked now they were on the subject of Dolly Crutch, so named because she had a peg leg.

Cathy's face clouded over. She hesitated, though it was clear she remembered. 'Go on, Mum, what was it?' Ruby said, her voice quiet now.

'Darlin', you shouldn't go listenin' to everythin' Dolly said. She was a harmless old woman who sometimes hit the nail on the 'ead, and sometimes she was wildly off.' Cathy looked at her daughter but Ruby wanted to know.

Cathy sighed. 'All right then. She said, "Your daughter will be very rich, very wealthy, but she'll always be lookin' over her shoulder . . ."'

Ruby was silent as she digested that, but there wasn't much to make of it.

CHAPTER 9

As time went on, and Cathy's pregnancy advanced, she struggled more and more doing normal things, spending much of the day flaked out on the sofa or resting in bed.

Ruby took on the lion's share of the chores, on top of her work, and fell into bed at midnight each night exhausted, though she wouldn't have dreamt of doing things any other way.

Cathy gave up her job at the tobacconist and so they lost her income, small though it was. Louie worked longer hours at the scrapyard to try to make up the shortfall, which meant he was out for much of the day and evening, leaving Cathy by herself.

She never complained. Even when her labour pains started she waited for Louie to get home that night before telling him her contractions had begun. Neither Ruby nor Bobby were back from work and so she'd been alone.

'Bloody hell, why didn't ya ring the yard?' Louie rarely swore. 'Sorry love, I didn't mean that. Come on, let's get ya to hospital. I'll leave a note for Rube and Bobby, they can follow on later.'

Ruby arrived home just ahead of Bobby and found her father's hastily scrawled note. She didn't hesitate. Both headed straight to Bancroft Hospital in Mile End.

'Where is she? Is she OK?' Ruby had a thousand questions but Louie stopped her at the door to the ward.

'She's absolutely fine. The midwife said she did brilliantly. You can both go in.'

Ruby opened the door and saw her mum, hair tangled with sweat, propped up against her pillows, a gentle smile on her face.

'Come and meet your baby brother.'

'Oh, Mum, he's gorgeous. Can I hold him?' Ruby said in a whisper, holding out her arms. She picked up the warm bundle, inhaling his sweet milky smell, and gazing into his big blue eyes.

'He's gorgeous. Hello, little brother, welcome.'

Bobby looked like he was about to cry. He was a sensitive man, kind to the core, and as soon as the baby was placed in his big arms, the tears started to come.

''Ere, take him back, Rube. I'm too emotional,' Bobby said, handing their brother back to her.

The baby looked up at his big sister, curling his tiny hand around her little finger, his eyes fluttering open.

'He thinks you're his mum, I swear it,' said Bobby.

Just then, Matron bustled in. 'Right, you lot, it's time to leave. Your mother needs her rest.' Ruby handed the bundle back to her mum who barely looked strong enough to hold him. Before she could think any more about this, Louie gestured for them to leave. Cathy gave them all a weak smile as they were shooed out of the ward. The three of them made their way home, yawning now as well. It had been a long evening.

Ruby visited every day after work, catching separate buses to get there and almost missing visiting time on a couple of occasions. A week after George's birth Cathy was allowed to go home, and the whole family turned up in Louie's knackered old van to drive her and the baby. Ruby had placed an extra cushion in the front for Cathy to sit on. As they drove, Louie began to sing an old Romany song, and Ruby, sitting next to him, smiled over at her beloved dad, the first grey hairs only just appearing in his thick black hair. He returned her smile as they travelled to the hospital. He had a good voice, melodious and strong. Louie looked more handsome than ever. He was clean-shaven for once, which showed off his square jaw and high cheekbones. He was a man in his prime, wearing jeans and a blue shirt that seemed to show off his deep brown eyes. They arrived at the maternity unit and before long, Cathy was back home and Ruby had carried her chubby, blonde-haired little brother into the house. His cot was set up next to Cathy's side of the bed, and she lay him down in it. He opened his eyes briefly, staring up at his big sister before shutting them again and drifting off to sleep.

Ruby fussed over her mum, helping her up the stairs and putting her straight into bed too.

'Thanks, darlin'. What would I do without ya?' Cathy said weakly. She seemed exhausted just walking up the stairs.

It's just the lack of sleep, she'll be OK. Ruby tried to reassure herself, but her instincts couldn't be dulled. Something was up, she could feel it in her bones.

A week later, and Cathy didn't seem to be any better. 'I think we should call a doctor,' insisted Ruby.

'Don't fuss, love. She ain't young, and 'avin' a baby this late in life is bound to take it out of 'er,' Louie said, biting into the bacon sandwich Ruby had made for his breakfast.

Ruby stood at the cooker, spatula in hand, and looked over to Bobby for support.

He shook his head. 'You're worryin' too much, Rube.'

'Anyway, the midwife is comin' tomorrow so we can ask her then.' Louie gulped down his tea. 'I'm off up the yard today so I'll see ya both tonight. Don't worry, love, it'll all be fine.'

Just then they heard a wail. George had woken up and needed a bottle. Ruby sighed. She just had enough time to make him one and hand it to her mum before leaving for work.

'I'm comin',' she hollered up the stairs. Quickly, she grabbed a piece of toast and raced up the stairs with the warmed bottle.

'I'll be home at six. Will ya manage until then?' Ruby asked, frowning. Her mum pushed herself up on her pillows with some effort, saying, 'Course I will. Now, off ya go, don't be late.'

That day, Ruby couldn't settle to any of the many tasks she now had. Even walking around the West End at lunchtime didn't distract her. As the hours passed, she had a growing sense of unease. When the call came, she felt she'd been waiting for it.

'You have to go home, Miss Murphy. It's your mother . . .' The boss, a balding self-satisfied man in sharp suits, came straight to her desk. Ruby didn't reply, she'd known something was wrong, very wrong, all day. Instead, she grabbed her coat and handbag and practically ran from the office. The bus couldn't move fast enough for her. As she ran from the bus stop to the house she almost knocked Bobby flying.

'Slow down, Rube,' Bobby said, though his face looked a mirror of the fear she was feeling too. They entered the house together, neither knowing what they would face.

They opened the door. There was, at first, no sound. Ruby's pulse was hammering in her brain. Her sense of unease grew by the second. 'Mum, you there? You all right, Mum? Is little George nappin'?'

Then Ruby stopped. She could just make out a muffled sobbing sound. Without hesitation, she ran up the stairs two at a time, Bobby following on her heels. Was George OK? Was Mum OK?

Ruby burst into her parents' room. The cot was empty. Next to it, Cathy lay on the bed, moaning and crying. Ruby's heart stopped. Her mouth was dry. She almost screamed her question. 'Is it George? Is little George dead? Speak to me, Mum!'

Cathy shook her head and Ruby felt a swooping sense of relief. It was so strong her legs almost buckled and she sat down heavily. 'What's wrong, Mum? Please tell us, what's goin' on?'

Cathy wiped her eyes, which were red raw. She struggled up, saying over and over, 'Oh God, it isn't true.'

Ruby was as still as an animal that knew it was hunted. Bobby sat down next to her. 'Mum, please tell us what's wrong.'

'Oh God, I don't know how to tell ya. I don't know how . . .' Cathy shook her head, her voice a whisper.

'You must,' Ruby said, her voice firm.

'You must, Mum,' echoed Bobby.

Cathy struggled up and wiped her face, though tears still ran down it in torrents. Finally she spoke. 'It's yer dad. Your dad is dead. He's dead . . .'

The air sucked out of the room, or so it seemed. In that instant, Ruby's safe family world shattered, shards of it piercing every part of her body and mind.

'Dad's dead?' was all she could say and her mum nodded, unable to speak.

'What 'appened?' Ruby wanted to know every detail as if to make herself understand the unthinkable. Bobby placed his head in his hands and sobbed.

Cathy burst into fresh weeping, and Ruby fought hard with herself to contain her emotions and the frustration of not knowing.

'He . . . he walked under a crane that was shiftin' a load of machinery parts. Somethin' went wrong, I don't understand it as he knew never to walk under those cranes, but today he did. The crane driver didn't see him and that was that. Louie was buried under six foot of metal.'

The words tore a hole in Ruby's heart that she realised would never be mended. Her dad, always urging them to be honest, to look after each other, to be safe, did something as reckless as walk under the cranes that were notorious for dropping their loads early. It didn't make sense. Nothing made sense. Louie was dead and their lives had changed in a heartbeat.

CHAPTER 10

The next day, Ruby, Cathy and Bobby sat at the kitchen table, still in shock, their faces wretched with grief.

Louie had been dead for less than twenty-four hours but it felt like their world had collapsed. When the telephone rang, Ruby got up to answer it.

'Yes, who is it?' she said woodenly, her mind still blank with shock, her brain half asleep due to the wakeful night she'd spent.

'Hello there. Is that Mrs Murphy?' a voice that sounded rather more posh than she was used to hearing at home said.

'No, but it's her daughter. You can speak to me, I'm Ruby Murphy.'

'This is Mr Anderson from the mortuary. Would you kindly let us know which funeral parlour you need the body of Mr Murphy to be transferred to?' the voice continued.

Ruby hadn't a clue how to respond. She knew funeral parlours cost a lot of money.

'Please hold for a minute,' she said, putting her hand over the receiver to stop her conversation being overheard.

'Mum, I'm so sorry but it's the mortuary. They're askin' where we're sendin' Dad's body . . .'

Even the words 'body' and 'mortuary' sounded so surreal, as if they had no place in their lives. Cathy turned her distraught face up to meet Ruby's apologetic gaze.

'It's all right, darlin'. Tell them I'll be in touch, as we don't know about the arrangement yet.'

Ruby relayed her mother's words, sounding confident but inside feeling suddenly sick. They couldn't afford to send Louie to an undertaker's. They had barely enough to live on. Cathy was in no shape to go back to work, and she and Bobby didn't make much. Where on earth would they find the money for their dad's funeral?

Ruby swivelled round as she heard the worst sound in the world – that of her mum bursting into tears.

'How can we pay for a funeral?' Cathy wailed. Her head was in her hands. 'Your father worked his whole life yet we never 'ad enough to save for one. He'll have a pauper's burial and I can't bear it.'

Bobby was sitting opposite, his face reflecting Ruby's sense of helplessness. A pauper's funeral, was considered a shameful end, especially for a working person. They called it the nine o'clock trot because they'd take the paupers to be cremated at 9 a.m. before the paid-for funerals took place. Everyone would think they didn't care one wit for Louie. People in the East End saved their whole lives to have a 'proper' send-off involving carriages and plumed horses, sleek limousines and a wake to remember for years. Funerals were serious business, and it was a deeply humiliating prospect to say goodbye to a loved one without the trappings.

Ruby knew the pain this would cause her proud mum, and rushed over, pulling Cathy into her arms, trying to impart some comfort. The worst thing was, her mum was right. They had no money. Dad would have to have the basics, and plenty of people round their way would gossip about it for years to come. The Murphy family was already shunned, making up with Sarah hadn't put an end to the rumours. Gossip seemed more powerful than truth.

'There, there,' she said as if she was comforting little George. 'There, there, Mum, it'll be OK. You just get yourself back to bed. You look like you need a sleep. You 'ave to keep your strength up for the baby. Bobby and I'll take care of this.'

Cathy nodded. Ruby gestured to Bobby to make a cuppa, saying she'd help their mum upstairs.

Later, once Cathy had drifted into a restless sleep, Ruby sat with Bobby at the table, both cradling lukewarm cups of tea. They were silent for a long time. What was there to say? How would they afford the cost of their dad's funeral when they ran into hundreds or even thousands of pounds?

'There's no way we can pay for a proper send-off, no way in heaven . . .' His voice was bleak.

'I don't know how we're goin' to put food on the table, how we're goin' to take care of George. It's simple, Bobby, we can't pay for Dad's funeral, and that's that.' Ruby's voice was flat. 'Things 'ave to change, Bobby. Mum was right. Dad worked his whole life at the scrapyard and for what? A pauper's funeral and a family strugglin' to keep the wolf from the door. Somethin' *has* to change.'

Ruby stood at the crematorium, a black veil over her face. There were a few mourners, some of the lads Louie had worked with had done the decent thing and shown up, but few others had come. The only friend of Ruby's that had bothered to show up was Sarah, and even then the rest of Sarah's family had refused to come.

Ruby felt a hard stone in her stomach, a feeling that she didn't belong here any more, even though she was a born and bred East Ender. She was grateful for the solid shape of Bobby standing next to her, awkward in his black suit, sniffing as he shed tears for the father they adored.

None of it seemed real. She was numb with grief. Louie had been so young, barely forty-two years old, and with a new baby that would never know him. Ruby tried to breathe, to stop the oceanic emotions that swelled and rose within her. She saw Cathy almost stumble as she turned to walk away, and was instantly by her side, catching her arm and helping to balance her.

'It's all right, Mum, I've got you,' Ruby murmured. 'It's all right . . .'

Cathy looked through the veil and into her daughter's eyes, which were red from crying, and she just shook her head. Nothing was 'all right'. Everything was wrong. How would they cope without the man who'd loved them and protected them from the harsh realities of life? How could they go on living in a community that wouldn't forgive them for a crime they hadn't committed?

It seemed unfathomable that Louie was gone. Ruby remembered everything that day; how Louie had bounced her on his knee as a child, playing horses, how he had sat patiently with her as she learned her numbers and spellings. She recalled how protective he was when she was a teenager, shooing away the local fellas as if they were a swarm of annoying flies. In her mind's eye she saw him giving one local lad a right earful because he'd whistled at Ruby as she walked past. He'd hated any disrespect shown towards her, and demanded she was treated like a young lady. Ruby always knew how fortunate she'd been, growing up under his loving care. She wasn't ready to say goodbye, none of them were.

'I'm OK now, Rube. I'll be OK, I just lost my balance a bit.' Cathy reassured Ruby as she steadied herself, her face was deathly white and her dress hung off her thin frame, despite the fact she'd had a baby only two weeks ago.

Would she ever recover from her beloved Louie's death? The pair had been like sweethearts up to the day of his death. They'd met in the tobacconist where she'd worked. Louie fell in love with her at first sight, or so the story went. He'd come out of the shop that day and told his dad, Jim, that he'd met the girl he was going to marry. The rest was history – and now, far too soon, the story had ended, and Cathy was left to bring up George without his father.

Ruby remembered how Grandad Jim had insisted she wear an emerald green dress to match her eyes at his funeral all those years ago. Jim had been a careful man. He'd planned his death for years, putting aside a little money each month so there was enough for a modest burial and new black suits for everyone – except his favourite grand-child – who had been resplendent in shimmering green. He and Louie had been working full-time so there'd been enough money to go around and a few pounds each week grew steadily into a reasonably-sized pot. It had been just like him; such a thoughtful, caring man. He didn't want anyone to worry about finding money at such a sad time and he'd spared his son and grandchildren that.

This time it had been different because there'd never been those few coins to spare each week and no one thought they'd need the money so soon.

CHAPTER 11

The funeral over, it was time to make their way to the local pub, The Anchor, for Louie's small wake. Ruby stood with what remained of her family and made small talk with her dad's former co-workers, the kind that won't ever be remembered but was essential nonetheless. They couldn't offer food or a bar tab to their guests, which shamed them even more. Most of the few mourners drifted off after a drink. When the scrapyard boss Terry came over, Ruby thought it was just another set of pleasantries she'd have to endure, smiling and nodding while all she really wanted was to get home, away from people and the strange formalities of death.

'Listen, I don't want to upset ya any more than I 'ave to, but I thought you should know . . .'

'Know what?' Cathy said, frowning, turning to Ruby, who shrugged.

'I was there in the yard that day, and I saw Louie. He didn't look right. He had his head in his 'ands and was visibly shaken or upset about somethin'. I went over to speak to him but he walked off quickly, not lookin' where he was goin' and that's when it 'appened.

'Louie was one of my best men. He'd worked with me since he was sixteen, and he'd never have been so careless, steppin' under that crane . . . He wasn't himself, that's all I'm sayin'. Look, I'm sorry for your loss. I 'ope I haven't upset ya . . .'

Puzzled, Ruby turned to her mum, catching Bobby's eye as she did so. He shrugged. What was Dad's boss on about?

Cathy stood as still as if she'd been carved out of stone. She swallowed, and in a small voice, she said, 'You're right. There was a reason Louie was so upset that day, but . . . it's a private family matter. I'm sorry . . . I can't talk about any of this right now.'

Ruby's eyes narrowed. None of this had made sense from the moment Cathy had told them their dad had been buried alive at work. She'd felt in her bones that something was amiss. Louie had been too experienced to have made such a drastic – and tragic – mistake. No one, except perhaps an inexperienced yard hand, would ever walk under a crane that was loading metal. They knew things could slip out of its grasp, it happened all the time. Louie's mistake had cost him his life, and yet it was a mistake that she would have gambled anything to say could never happen. She looked at her mum, her face pinched and closed.

'Mum?' Ruby said.

Cathy shook her head. Her lips were shut. 'Not now Rube,' she said.

Fear mixed with anger rose in Ruby's heart. She realised there were things her mum hadn't told her, important things.

'When, Mum?' Ruby spat. She couldn't remember the last time she argued with Cathy, but she was as close as she'd ever been right now. Bobby looked back and forth between them, not understanding what was going on.

'I will tell you both later,' their mum said at last, in a way that brooked no argument – at least for now.

Ruby couldn't wait for the last mourner to leave. Eventually, the pub emptied, and the staff waved them off, saying they'd clear up. Back inside the house, Ruby ripped off her hat and veil and turned to face her mother. Bobby stood beside her, looking lost. 'Tell us now. What 'ave you been hidin'?'

Cathy sighed and sank into a chair. 'I wanted to tell ya in my own time, when things had calmed down, when it felt right.'

Ruby instantly felt ashamed for getting cross with her mum. She could see how much strain the last few months, and now this, had placed upon her.

'I'm sorry, Mum,' Ruby whispered.

'It's all right, Rube. I do 'ave somethin' to tell you both, and it's just so difficult. I never wanted to tell you like this.'

As she spoke, a single tear traced its way down Cathy's gaunt cheek. Ruby reached for her hand.

'Go on, Mum. Tell us. I can't bear seeing you so sad.' Ruby's voice broke. She could see the pain her mum was suffering and there was nothing she could do to stop it.

'Well, I know you noticed I wasn't well when I was pregnant with George. I know you saw me losin' weight and bein' tired all the time. You asked me a few times if there was anythin' wrong – and Rube – I kept lyin' to ya both . . .'

Ruby's face was anguished. What was going on? Her head was spinning but somewhere deep down she knew already, she knew the truth. She could see her mum's condition plain as day, and she knew this wasn't good news.

'Will you ever forgive me, you two, for not tellin' you both sooner?'

'There's nuthin' to forgive, but you must tell us now, you must,' Ruby soothed, her heart pounding in her chest. She stared into her mother's eyes intently, trying to give her the courage to say what she had to say.

Bobby stood watching them both, his face pale with shock.

'There's no easy way to say this, but I'm dyin', Ruby, Bobby. I'm dyin' and there's nuthin' any of us can do about it.'

Cathy stopped talking as if her batteries had run out. She flopped back in the chair. They could see her exhaustion, the sheer strength of will that had kept her standing and walking and speaking during the day. That willpower had gone now, and all that was left was a husk of the woman their mum once was.

'I've got ovarian cancer. I knew early on in my pregnancy and I chose to keep it a secret. It was that or get rid of George, and I could never do that. The doctors told me they could do nothing to treat the tumour until after your brother was born, but by then it was too late.

'I knew the cancer had grown and spread but I couldn't face tellin' ya. I was so scared of leavin' you alone to look after Louie and my baby boy. And now this . . . it's so cruel, so cruel.' Cathy burst into fresh sobs.

Ruby's heart had broken with the death of her dad, and now this on top. It was too much for any human heart to bear. Bobby was in tears, sobbing and holding his mum as if he could never let her go.

Suddenly Bobby looked up. 'But what's this got to do with Dad's death?'

'There's more, isn't there?' Ruby said, making Cathy nod.

'The day yer dad died, I'd told him the news only minutes before. He'd come home from work as he wanted to ask me what was really wrong, as he'd guessed too. Gypsy intuition – it's a powerful thing, as you know. So, I 'ad to tell him that I'd be makin' him a widower with three mouths to feed and all the grief that I knew he'd feel.' Cathy looked down at her hands that resembled an eighty-year-old's now and went on. 'He didn't take it well. He got up, for a moment I thought he hadn't 'eard me, and I said, "Where are ya goin'?" but he just sort-of lurched out. I 'eard the door slam and I broke down in tears. I cried and cried, and then, not long after, there was that knock at the door.'

Ruby understood. That knock was the site foreman, his cap in his hand, his face a picture of despair at being the one to share the news of his workmate's death.

'He went to work and he didn't know what he was doin', ' Ruby added, then Bobby spoke. 'So that's why he stepped under the crane. Oh Dad, why did ya go back to work?' Bobby's face was a picture of grief – and understanding now. His soft heart, so obviously broken, was shattering again. Ruby couldn't decide who to comfort, her mum who was now in floods of tears, or Bobby, who was suffering so intensely.

Cathy spoke eventually. 'He was overcome with grief. He was devastated, and I let him go . . . I let him go . . . If I'd 'ave tried to stop him then he'd be alive today, your dad would be 'ere now, makin' this so much easier. It wasn't meant to be him dyin', I blame myself completely. It was meant to be me first, me first . . .'

Both mum and son dissolved into fresh tears and Ruby put her arms around them, wanting so much to protect them from their hurt, even though she was grieving herself.

As she held them she stared at the magnolia paint on the walls, paint that needed redoing, marks from the years of living in the house that was their home. She stared, her feelings freezing as she knew, from this moment onwards, she had to pull her family through this, she had to take up Louie's role and protect them. From now on, it was all down to her. She knew that in the weeks and months ahead, her resolve would be tested, that she'd feel unimaginable grief, yet she had to stay strong for them all; for Cathy, Bobby and little George. Even though her older brother was 'officially' the head of the family, her intuition told her that in reality, it would be her. Only she was tough enough to weather the storms that beset them from every angle.

CHAPTER 12

'With Dad gone, his wages lost and Mum too ill to work, we're sunk, Rube,' said Bobby one evening not long after the funeral.

Ruby sighed. They were both cradling cups of coffee, a precious drink they could no longer afford. Things looked bleak, bleaker than they'd ever known.

'And how are we goin' to care for George while I'm back at work? I'll 'ave to speak to my boss and see if I can cut my hours, though that won't help with bringin' in cash,' Ruby spoke aloud.

'We're barely surviving as it is, and with another mouth to feed . . .' Bobby said. Seeing the downcast look on his sister's face, he added, 'But we'll manage. We'll find a way, Rube.'

Ruby glanced at him and nodded, knowing it was just a platitude. They needed to take action and do *something*, or Bobby was right, they'd be sunk. They could sell the house, but it wasn't worth much and they'd just have to make rent every month somewhere else. So that wasn't an option.

'I'll go in tomorrow and ask to work part-time, then we'll 'ave to find someone to care for George while I'm out. Mum just can't cope with him. She can barely get out of bed. At least we'll still 'ave some money comin' in.'

'I know my job doesn't pay much, but they've taken me on full-time after my apprenticeship, so that's a bit better than it was,' Bobby said, trying to force a smile on his face.

'The main thing is not to worry Mum. She needs to think everythin's OK,' Ruby added. It wasn't unusual for hard-up families to give away children they couldn't afford to keep, but Ruby couldn't bear to do that. *We won't give up George, not on my life. We'll find a way – we have to.*

The next day, Ruby stood in front of her boss's door gathering her courage. She knocked and a voice said, 'Enter!' She stepped into the office. The boss, Mr Armstrong, sat back in his chair, his eyes narrowing as he smiled at Ruby.

'How can I help you, dear?' His grin was wolf-like.

'Thank you for seeing me. I wouldn't be 'ere unless it was really important . . .' She hesitated. 'My dad died recently . . .'

'Yes, I heard. My condolences,' he murmured.

Encouraged, Ruby continued, 'And my mum's very ill and so we need someone to look after my baby brother. Well, that's why I'm 'ere. I want to ask you if I can work less hours, cut my work down . . .'

The smile had left the wolf's face. 'I'd love to help you, darlin', but you see I know a dozen girls who'd kill for your job.' He leaned forward to make his point.

Ruby was stung by his coldness. 'But my brother, who'll look after him? And my mum'll need care too—'

'Sorry dear, it isn't my problem. Either work the hours you're given – or go.'

Ruby got up from her chair and thanked him, though she felt nothing but sheer disbelief. She was deflated, and shocked that her employer, who'd seemed to like her so much, had left her – and by extension, her family – in the lurch.

Standing back outside the door, she tried to compose herself. What would they do? She couldn't work her usual hours and care for George, and they couldn't do without her wage. There was a tightness to her chest and she felt herself struggling to breathe. She wasn't sure how long she stood there, but as her breathing came under control, she realised she'd left the door ajar and she could hear the boss speaking on the telephone.

'Listen! I've told you I'm not prepared to pay that amount of tax. I don't care what you have to do, I won't pay it. All right then, fiddle the books, it's no skin off my nose, but get that bill down. Just change the invoice – say the consignment was teddy bears not Chanel, that'll slice off a fair whack. I'm telling you to just do your job.' And with that, the phone was slammed down. Ruby crept away. She could hardly believe what she'd heard.

The Murphys might be a straight family, but Ruby knew enough crooked folk to know exactly what was going on. The respectable, honest trade she was so proud of was nothing but a sham.

Ruby's mind was whirring. She thought about the wife she'd envied, the daughter she'd hoped to emulate. She'd worked hard, done everything right. Just like her father had, just like Cathy had. And what did she have to show for it? They'd let her go without a care of what it meant for her or her family. They pretended to be straight, they dressed up in their fancy clothes, went to fancy restaurants and pretended to run a legitimate business. But they were all a bunch of crooks. The only difference between them and the folk Ruby grew up with was that in the East End people were honest about who they were.

Ruby gathered her knock-off Gucci, wrapped her coat tightly around her shoulders and headed home. She didn't know what they were going to do, but she and Bobby would figure it out together.

She told Bobby what she'd overheard. But in reality, what she knew didn't really change anything. She didn't have any evidence, and what did she have to gain by saying anything? No one would believe a poor East End girl over a successful businessman. And in the end, she'd still be unemployed, struggling to put food on the table.

The house was quiet and the only sound was the low murmur of the radio in the corner. The doctor had been to administer Mum's medication and give her something to help her sleep, as the pain seemed to be getting stronger every day. Ruby had looked in on her before coming downstairs, opening the door gently, seeing her mother so frail and thin in her bed. It was a relief to see her face relaxed in sleep, but she still got a shock every time she realised Cathy was sleeping in her bed alone now. Too much had changed too quickly.

Little George had gone down for the night. He was such a good baby. He rarely woke up overnight, though he was only a month old, and he took his bottle like a little hungry animal, gulping it down, seemingly oblivious to the fact that Ruby was now his mummy substitute.

'Bobby?' Ruby said softly.

'I don't want to talk about none of it. I don't know what to do, Rube. I don't know how we're goin' to put money in the electric meter this week, let alone with you not workin'.' Bobby didn't look up. He peered down at one of the master keys he was polishing. Ruby decided to go on. She knew he didn't want to talk about it, but they needed to confront reality. There was little cash in the family pot and the gas bill was due, let alone the continual supply of nappies and formula milk she now needed for the baby, and the fact that their mother had terminal cancer. They needed to keep talking because their problems weren't going away by themselves.

'I don't mind lookin' after little George. I understand that's what I must do for our family, but I just don't know how we'll feed our brother, it's as bad as that. Mum only has weeks or even days left. And there's the next problem. It's awful to speak about it, but we're goin' to 'ave to work out how the hell we'll pay for the burial. Please speak to me, Bobby . . .' she pleaded. Ruby had to make her older brother understand that some things, however terrible, had to be faced sooner rather than later.

'I don't want to think of Mum dyin'. Can't we change the subject? I've 'ad a long day.'

Ruby swept her gaze over him, noting the sadness on his face. His features, once full, seemed drawn now. He had visibly lost weight, and worse, he'd lost the spring that had been in his step since childhood. Bobby was the kind of man who got on with life. He wasn't a complicated person. He loved his home comforts, his Friday night beers with his pals and a full roast dinner on Sundays. He'd always been the cheerful one of the two of them, the simple soul with a deep love for his family and little ambition in life. Ruby saw in that moment just how much the death of their dad, and now this new emotional blow, had taken its toll on her beloved brother. She was also discovering that she was a completely different character; strong-willed, able to face reality, someone who was more comfortable in the driving seat than being a mere passenger of life. She knew that she would have to be the one who found a way to get through these days, even though the grief and shock were raw with her still.

'No, Bobby. It's time. We 'ave to talk about it. Mum'll probably 'ave to go into a hospice if the pain gets any worse. We 'ave to think about what we're goin' to do when she's . . . she's gone . . .'

Ruby put her hand upon her brother's, making him stop his cleaning. He raised his eyes to hers. They were pools of anguish.

'Oh, darlin',' she said, tears rushing to her eyes now. 'I'll make us some tea, that'll 'elp, I promise.' She got up quickly and turned her back to make a cup of tea, placing the kettle on the hob and waiting for the first fizz of the water as it started to heat. She didn't want Bobby to see the agony on her face too. He was suffering enough. She had to be brave for the both of them.

The humiliation of her dad's pauper's funeral was still with her and she hated to think her mum might have the nine o'clock trot as well.

Somewhere in Ruby's heart were the dreams she'd barely acknowledged herself. For a brief moment, she'd really thought that if she worked hard she could change her life, leave the East End and find a new way, surrounded by exciting, sophisticated people. But her visions for the future lay in tatters. Now, she had a dying mother and a new baby to bring up. She'd been thrown into motherhood without even the thrill of meeting someone and falling in love. She was chained to her kitchen sink in Canning Town as surely as if she'd married one of the local wide boys and given up her dreams of a better life that way. Ruby could hardly bear to think about what she'd lost. It hadn't been her choice, and beneath it all she felt sore, like there was a fresh bruise on her heart. But if Bobby couldn't face the hard choices, she would.

She waited until the water boiled, making the kettle tremble, and she slowly poured out a drink for them both. She dipped the tea bags into the cups, added the milk, and sugar for Bobby, all the time her mind shooting this way and that. There had to be a way to make this right; to pay for Mum's funeral and to keep them all safe. Please God there had to be a way. Just then there was a knock at the front door.

'Expectin' someone?' Ruby glanced back at her brother who shook his head in response. 'See who it is, won't ya?'

Bobby got up from the table, his movements slow like an old man carrying the weight of the world on his shoulders. Ruby heard muffled voices, then the door to the kitchen opened and in walked Freddie Harris.

'Evenin', Ruby Green Eyes,' he said, all cocky and fidgety as usual.

Ruby sighed. 'Stop callin' me that, Freddie. What d'you want this time?' She felt like disappearing to her room, but something, some instinct, stopped her.

Freddie ignored her question, turning back to Bobby who had reappeared behind him. 'Sorry to hear your news. Terrible tragedy, terrible,' he said, almost convincingly.

'Which news, Freddie? The death of our dad, or our mum bein' terminally ill?' Ruby replied waspishly. Even her mouth tasted sour as she spoke to him, such was her revulsion for the visitor. It wasn't so much that Freddie was harmful; she wasn't scared of him, or any of the local lads, at all. It was more what he stood for. He thought he was the bee's knees because he nicked stuff, or acted as a getaway driver for some of the local blaggers. He really thought he was someone, and he irritated Ruby beyond belief. Freddie always had money to throw about in the pubs, yet when it came to paying anyone back he was suddenly skint. There was nothing to like about him, but more pressingly, what was he doing in their kitchen at 8 p.m. on a Tuesday?

'We don't 'ave no money. I'm sure you 'eard Dad had a pauper's funeral,' Ruby added bleakly.

Freddie had the decency to look embarrassed. 'I did 'ear somethin' like that . . . I'm sorry for your troubles,' he said, finding his trainers fascinating as he looked down and shifted on the spot.

'We don't even know how we're goin' to pay for an undertaker when Mum passes.' Ruby felt a sob rise in her throat, but she was damn sure she wouldn't let Freddie see her moment of weakness. Never Freddie.

'Well, that's where I might be able to 'elp ya.'

Ruby turned away from him, hating the sight of him more with every second he stood in their clean but sparse kitchen. She would've stayed like that, staring at the wall, but his words settled somewhere inside her whirring brain. She'd asked God how they could pay for what they needed right now. She just couldn't believe He'd sent Freddie Harris. She almost shrugged, but instead, she turned back to him, her eyes wide to give Freddie the full force of their dazzling emerald beauty.

'What d'ya mean, Freddie? Why are ya 'ere if ya don't want money?' Her voice was oozing liquid honey now, and she saw the effect on Freddie straightaway, while her brother looked at her like she was having a seizure. Freddie gulped. He couldn't turn his gaze away from her. He seemed to have temporarily lost his tongue, so she took advantage of his indisposition and continued, 'We appreciate your condolences but is there somethin' else you wanted?'

Freddie cleared his throat. Meanwhile Bobby was looking back and forth between his strange new sister and the mate he'd known since primary school, wearing a look of sheer bewilderment.

'All right, Ruby.' It was the first time he'd ever said 'Ruby' rather than 'Ruby Green Eyes'. She seemed to have knocked him off-balance, and that's exactly what she'd wanted. She needed the upper hand when dealing with a weasel like him.

'Go on . . .' She prompted, smiling again, parting her red lips slightly to reveal her small white teeth. She pulled her hand through her thick shining hair, letting it fall down one side of her face.

Freddie looked like a man possessed. He was stuttering now, but finally, business overruled his lust and he managed to tell them precisely why he was there, his eyes darting now between Ruby and Bobby as he explained.

'All right, I'll come clean. There's a job—' At which point Bobby snorted and sat down at the table, clearly uninterested. This was how they all used to react as soon as Freddie, or any of his mates, broached the subject of crooked work, but this time was different. This time it felt like everything was at stake: their mum, their family, their lives. Ruby could feel her pulse quicken. A tiny thread of excitement started to coil inside her. Perhaps there was a way to get themselves out of this mess. They couldn't go on with so little money. They had to find a way to earn it.

'Everyone round 'ere knows you're tight, you ain't got no money and, beggin' yer pardon, Ruby, you can't afford to bury your mother,' Freddie's voice was unusually gentle. Bobby could hold his feelings in no longer. He made a gulping sound then burst into sobs, his large shoulders heaving as he wept loudly, grief overwhelming him.

Ruby looked at Bobby, then back at Freddie who now looked like he wanted to bolt from that room. She wasn't finished with him yet, though.

'Go on,' was all she said as her brother wept openly. Freddie jiggled some coins in his pocket. 'You need the money, you've got no one lookin' after ya and we need Bob . . . We need him to do this one job. He don't 'ave to

94

do nuthin' else, just one job, and it's ready money. It'll 'elp pay for yer mum, at least.'

Freddie looked down at the wooden floor now as if he was in trouble and about to get a bollocking. Ruby stared at Freddie, her mind suddenly clearing. She had never thought the words would come out of her mouth, but they did. 'Suppose we said we'd 'elp you and yer mates by doin' this job, what's in it for us?'

Bobby stopped crying, wiped his eyes on his sleeve and looked up at his sister. 'What are you on about, Rube? We don't do no crooked work. We don't earn crooked money. Don't you remember what Dad said, what Grandad Jim said?'

'A straight pound is worth three crooked,' chorused Ruby. 'Yeah I remember, but where did that get us, eh, Bobby? A life of worry and the nine o'clock trot for our dad, that's where.'

Bobby looked appalled. 'Where are ya goin' with this, Rube, 'ave you lost yer mind?'

Ruby shook her head. She knew Bobby would need an explanation, but this wasn't the time to give it. She looked back at Freddie, who was looking at her now with curiosity. Even though he'd come around, he'd expected to be turned away. That much was clear to her now. He had just been trying his luck. Well, tonight, his luck had finally come in.

Ruby kept her flashing eyes on Freddie, who seemed mesmerised by her. He'd seen a new Ruby Green Eyes, a sharper Ruby, a woman prepared to do anything to help her family. He stepped closer to Ruby, making her stand up straighter, meeting his gaze which was full-on now, designed to intimidate. She brushed back her long hair and smiled slowly. They were almost nose-to-nose.

'You're right, Freddie, we do need the money, so, tell me, what are ya terms?' Ruby could hardly believe she was saying all this, it went against everything she'd ever been taught, everything her parents believed in. Yet, something in this moment, a new sense of power, was just as intoxicating to her as it had been to Freddie, though for very different reasons. Ruby saw instantly that a family facing desperate times had to resort to desperate measures.

A wail from upstairs interrupted the moment. George had woken up for his last bottle of the night. Ruby knew she had to go, but could she trust Bobby to finish this business with Freddie?

'You'd better go and see to the nipper,' sneered Freddie now, stepping back. Ruby realised she'd lost her advantage.

'Bobby will sort out the money while I'm gone, won't ya, brother?' Ruby stared at Bobby and silently he nodded, though he looked mutinous. Ruby grabbed a bottle she'd prepared earlier and which she'd been warming in a bowl of hot water, and stalked upstairs, shooting the weasel a look of pure menace as she went.

As she climbed the stairs, she heard Freddie's low chuckle, knowing that they'd crossed the line that should never be crossed, and she'd done it willingly.

'How much did ya shake on, then?' Ruby asked her brother the next evening when he'd returned from work. He looked tired and she guessed that, like her, he hadn't slept a wink that night. 'I hope ya didn't let Freddie mug you off for a few quid and a couple of beers?'

'Nah, we agreed a thousand nicker. Not bad for a night's work but I still don't like it, Rube. It goes against everythin',' Bobby said, looking anguished.

'I know, I know,' soothed Ruby. She could see the dilemma written on Bobby's face. This move to crooked work was upsetting him, but as she kept saying to him, what else could they do? 'And are ya sure you got a fair price? Perhaps we could've agreed a percentage of the takin's and not just a flat fee?'

Bobby scowled. 'Listen, Rube. You told me to sort the money – and I did. So, leave it. I got us a good deal, don't push it. Freddie let slip that Charlie Beaumont's been eyein' up the same job, so we know it's kosher. I feel bad enough for doin' it, just trust me on this, eh?'

'We're doin' the right thing,' said Ruby hastily. She didn't want Bobby backing out now. 'It's for Mum, it's for George. Just don't forget that. Sometimes you 'ave to do bad to do good.'

Bobby shrugged but his face didn't change. He didn't like it, that much was obvious, but he was a loyal son and brother and he would do it for their mother.

'I need to know, though, Rube: are we plannin' on doin' more jobs or is this a one-off?'

Ruby looked over at him. Her face was in the shadow cast by the overhead light in the kitchen. She didn't reply, not knowing how to.

Bobby wouldn't let it drop. 'Is this just for the thousand pound, to make sure we can pay the bills and give Mum a proper send-off?'

'I think so, Bobby,' she replied, noticing she naturally led their conversations. It was strange for it to be the other way around. She wasn't sure, though, if this was a one-off. Their financial problems wouldn't end with the funeral, she saw that. They would still be there, lying under everything they did, under every conversation, every word or action. Who knew where this would lead? Who knew what would happen?

'Let's just get this done properly, and without you gettin' caught. That's all that's important, Bobby, then we can talk again,' she finished, unsure who she was convincing, her brother or herself.

CHAPTER 13

Ruby pushed the old-fashioned black pram down the grimy street flanking the docks. Huge warehouses loomed over her along with large cranes and chimneys spewing out thick smoke. The dock sludge swayed in oily motion, the water filled with the detritus of industry, a sheen of rainbow-coloured petrol lying over its murky grey depths. Ruby cast a strange figure, walking through the haze. The Isle of Dogs was a place of extreme contrasts, bankers mingling with dock workers, large tower blocks in various stages of development climbing into the sky amid the historic wreckage of London's dockland past.

In the past ten years, the island had become a thriving industrial hub under Margaret Thatcher, with brand new skyscrapers springing up, the gleaming tower blocks of corporate offices and luxury apartments now half empty as recession bit at the redevelopment of this ancient tongue of land jutting into the mighty Thames river.

Ruby glided through a mix of office workers and men clad in fluorescent jackets and hard hats, pushing baby

George. She was all but invisible to everyone except a handful of young male bankers who whistled as she walked past.

Ruby wore sunglasses and had pulled back her hair into a tight bun, looking for all the world like a young mum out for a stroll in the weak spring sunshine. Taking her little brother out with her had felt like the perfect disguise. After all, who really noticed a young mum? Who really cared what she was up to? Ruby felt as invisible as if she'd worn a wig and glasses, blending into the background, looking as innocent as it was possible to be.

Thankfully, George had been sleeping peacefully as she bumped the pram down from the DLR, getting off at Island Gardens and walking north along Westferry Road. She was heading for Millwall Docks and the offices inside an old warehouse, which was the target of the heist agreed with Freddie. Ruby insisted to Bobby that she'd case the joint beforehand. She didn't trust a hair on Freddie Harris's head, and so she'd set out that day, at around the time that workers took their lunch, hoping to be less visible among the crowds, even if she was stalking through the less salubrious parts of the docklands.

She walked for a while then slowed as she realised the building was coming up on her right. As luck would have it, there was a bench overlooking the water almost directly in front of the offices she was scouting out.

'Our luck's in, little George,' she murmured as she manoeuvred the pram to the seat and sat down at an angle, pretending to fuss with the sleeping baby's blankets. As she did so, she was afforded a full view of the site where the robbery was due to take place that evening. She hooked her sunglasses onto her head and turned to inspect the site.

Unfortunately the building was flanked by large security gates, which meant she couldn't get access inside to scout it properly. It worried her that she was limited to walking round the building, looking for possible exits, checking the number of people coming and going, and getting a feel for the building and its surroundings. She was starting to realise that she would have to take Freddie's word for it that this job was kosher, but he was the last person she wanted to trust.

Luckily, the alarm system was clearly visible, the main entrance below it. Ruby didn't know anything about locks or alarms but she could see the brand was a security company she recognised, and she could give Bobby that much information.

She looked around for security guards or cameras tracking her movements but could see no one or nothing that would cause problems.

'We'll wait 'ere for a minute, George, and see if anyone comes,' Ruby said, stretching her shoulders back and gazing out at the river. Her eyes rested on a large tanker that was negotiating the stretch of water, but her senses were on full alert. Nothing much happened over the course of almost an hour. Someone who looked like a foreman came out and stood smoking a cigarette. He even said 'hello' to Ruby, who smiled back at him. She got up and walked around the building as best she could, but there was no getting to the back. There was a main front entrance, and tucked away at the side of the building was a small doorway. She didn't dare get too close in case anyone spotted her, but she saw that was probably the way they'd force their entry.

But what about getting away again? She looked up and down the road. There were only two main escape routes, alongside the dock going in either direction, but then again she hadn't seen the back, so there could be routes there too. She bit her lip, deep in thought. It was a risk. It was a huge risk, but what other choice did they have? If they wanted to earn the thousand pound that Bobby had shaken on to open the safe, then she had to trust Freddie.

More time passed and there was still no sign of any further external security. Ruby sighed. She set off again as George started to stir, back in the direction of the train station. She walked quickly now, her stomach churning, knowing she would give the go-ahead despite the risk.

Ruby returned to Star Lane and dropped George round to a neighbour who would look after him while she spent a few hours with Mum. Cathy had been moved to a hospice as her condition worsened. She needed round-the-clock care and pain relief, and Ruby sadly saw that her mother needed more than her help now. Their mum's days were numbered.

Sitting at her mother's bedside, Ruby smiled though her nerves were getting to her. The heist was tonight, and her mum mustn't know a thing.

'All right, darlin'? Why the frown?' Cathy gasped, trying to sit up but failing.

Ruby rushed round her bedside to help her, glad her mum couldn't see the expression on her face. She realised her feelings were transparent – to her mum, at least.

'Nothin', nothin' at all.' Out of Ruby's lips came the first real lie she'd ever told her mum. She felt sick as she plumped up the pillows, avoiding Cathy's honest gaze. 'Just tired . . . and worried about you. Now, shouldn't you be gettin' some rest?'

'Now, I've been thinkin' about things, especially my funeral—'

'Don't even mention it, Mum,' Ruby interjected.

'Rube, it's important, you mustn't worry. I'm not bothered about all the fuss. I want ya to know that, no matter what happens, I'll always love you, Bobby and George. I don't want ya to go short with money. You've got enough on your plate lookin' after George. I'm worried about how you'll survive without me.'

Ruby knew that her mum was telling her, in her own way, that she would be happy with a pauper's funeral, but

Ruby didn't want to hear it, didn't want to acknowledge her mum's death, let alone what she and Bobby were doing to see that didn't happen.

'Don't be silly, Mum,' Ruby said through cold lips, 'we'll manage. Bobby's got work and so 'ave I. We'll be fine . . .'

At that moment a nurse popped her head round the door. 'Sorry, Mrs Murphy, visitin' hours are over. Time to go.'

Ruby smiled again, kissing her mother on the forehead, praying that nothing in her expression would give her away.

'I'll be in tomorrow, Mum. Love you.'

Ruby left, pondering how life could be so cruel. How could they lose two parents within months of each other, neither of them old enough to justify dying? The anger simmered inside her, and she knew she couldn't let it out, not now, perhaps not ever, because she had to stay in control, for all their sakes. It was her the nurses spoke to, her they checked her mum's medication with, her they came to with questions about what would happen when she died. Ruby couldn't break down. She had George and Bobby to care for. She had her mum to do right by, and she was happy that she could, in private at least, tell the end-of-life team that they would be able to afford a proper East End funeral with the same undertaker as Grandad Jim had, a fleet of limousines and flowers, though those arrangements would come later.

Ruby felt exhausted when she arrived home, but she fed George and tucked him up for a nap before reaching into the fridge to work out what to cook for dinner. She didn't feel hungry, and she could tell with one look at her brother's face as he walked in from work that he didn't either.

'Too nervous to eat, Rube. Don't bother with a dinner. I'll 'ave somethin' later. You look tired, though. Go and 'ave a lie-down while George is asleep.'

Ruby shook her head. 'I'll wait up for ya, I won't be able to sleep anyway.'

There was a strange atmosphere, both felt equally guilty at taking this unfamiliar path, but Ruby realised she felt something Bobby clearly didn't, a twinge of excitement.

She hadn't been lying when she said she wouldn't be able to sleep but it was because her nerves and fears were mixed with a rush of adrenaline she hadn't expected to experience. What they were about to do was against everything their parents had taught them. Growing up, Ruby had wanted to please them. She'd turned away from her friend Sarah's choices, watching as she, and others like her, ended up with a bad lot in life: parents in prison, homes full of dodgy goods and always having to look over their shoulders. Ruby could hardly believe she'd finally taken a step down the same dark path, though she knew she wouldn't stop Bobby going tonight. They needed that money to survive, and it should buy their mum a good burial too. There was no choice that Ruby could see. Do this robbery or fail their mum completely.

Bobby got changed out of his work clothes. He walked back into the kitchen dressed head-to-toe in black. He was clutching a small bag of tools containing his skeleton keys, which he called twirls. Ruby almost gasped. The sight of her flesh and blood dressed up like some common criminal was almost too much. Ruby thought again of baby George, and knew they must do this for him as well as Mum.

'You ready?' she asked softly. Bobby nodded. He shoved his balaclava and black gloves into the bag. He gave her a last look before leaving, a look halfway between regret and fear.

'Just a one-off,' she whispered to herself. 'Once this is done we'll 'ave some money in our pockets and things will work out.' Even as she said the words, she wondered if she was trying to convince herself.

Ruby saw him in her mind's eye, walking to the pub for a pint and to meet Freddie and his accomplice. She saw them walk down to the warehouse she had already cased out on the Isle of Dogs. She imagined him finding the safe in the back office, kneeling down next to it and working his magic until click, click, click, the door swung open and its contents were quickly stuffed into Freddie's bag. She saw the accomplice keeping watch at the side door, a sawn-off shotgun in his hand. She saw Bobby lock the safe again before him and Freddie left the building. Bobby would turn the outside alarm system back on to make it look like an inside job, which had been Ruby's idea. She had no notion of where it came from.

CHAPTER 14

ROBBERY! POLICE SAY IT'S AN INSIDE JOB!

The headline screamed out from the front page of the local newspaper. Ruby, who was on her way to the supermarket with George in his pram, snatched up a copy, her eyes scanning the front page. It *had* to be the job Bobby had done only a few days earlier.

'Oi, you goin' to buy that or what?' the newsagent shouted over at her from inside the shop.

'Oh, yes I am . . .' she said, fumbling in her handbag to find her purse. 'There you go, no need to get stroppy with me!' Ruby's hands were trembling as she stepped inside and handed over the coins.

'Sorry, love, didn't mean to frighten you. You OK?' the shopkeeper, a young Asian guy added. He obviously thought he'd been the one to unsettle her.

'What? Oh, don't worry, it ain't you,' Ruby muttered. She dashed out to the pram and stood in the street, reading every word of the news story.

It was the same job.

Then she gasped. One line of the text stood out. She read it again to make sure she'd understood, then as comprehension dawned, fury rose within her like a striking snake.

'Oh my God, he's mugged us off. Freddie Harris, you don't know what's comin' to you, but I won't let ya get away with this.' Ruby could hardly believe her eyes and yet she'd known not to trust him. She'd known Freddie was a weasel, but this? This was something else.

Quickly, Ruby headed back to Star Lane, all thoughts of getting supplies of milk, bread and nappies forgotten. Once she'd settled George, she whacked the paper down onto the table as if the table itself was to blame, then paced around the house for the next two hours, waiting for Bobby to come home. She couldn't settle on anything. She showed George his picture books, but her mind raced and she couldn't concentrate. She cleaned the kitchen and lounge, but that bought no respite. In fact, her agitation increased as time wore on until, eventually, she heard the key turning in the lock.

The minute his footsteps sounded through the front door, Ruby grabbed the paper and ran to greet him.

'Whoa there Rube, what ya doin? Pleased to see me at last?' Bobby grinned. He'd clearly had a good day at work and was mellow from a drink in the pub. Bobby had been welcomed back into the pub and the community as soon as he'd agreed to the safe break. No longer were Ruby's family seen as outsiders. Now they were complicit.

They'd crossed the line, become as crooked as everyone else. Well, Ruby was about to ruin his good mood.

'Look,' she hissed. 'Look how much money was in that safe!' She thrust the paper under her brother's nose. Bobby's mouth turned into a perfect 'o' shape as he understood why Ruby was so angry.

'Ah . . .' was all he said. He'd clearly seen the same paper, or heard the gossip in the pub and was hoping Ruby hadn't.

'Ah? AH? What 'appened when I had to leave you and Freddie together to agree the deal that night, eh, Bobby? Did ya lose yer brain?'

Bobby sighed a long, drawn-out sigh. 'Listen, Rube, Freddie offered me a grand to do that job. It was more than enough to put food on the table, pay the leccy and have money left over for the . . .' Even as their mum's health worsened, Bobby still couldn't say the word 'funeral'.

'He mugged you off, and he mugged me off. That's what 'appened when I left you two 'ere in our kitchen to go and see to George. He took you for a fool, and me with ya.'

Bobby walked slowly into the kitchen, slumping down onto a chair.

'Rube, I shook 'ands on the deal. It was what we agreed. A one-off job to get money.'

Ruby stood next to him. She was too angry to sit. Her pulse was hammering in her head. Her blood was up. She started to read the article out loud, as if somehow that made it clearer.

'". . . the company chief executive said that the robbers had taken staff wages amounting to £10,000." Ten. Thousand. Pounds. And how much did you shake on with Freddie? A mere thousand. It ain't right. They would never 'ave got into that buildin' without ya. You were the most crucial part of the operation. Freddie knew this, and he let ya shake on a thousand.' Ruby was shouting now.

Bobby glanced round, guessing that George was napping. 'Shh, you'll wake the baby. So what if I got less? It doesn't matter, Rube. We got our share, so drop it.'

Ruby stared at him as if she'd never seen him before.

'Drop it?' Her voice was cold, measured, now. Her fury mounted. 'I won't drop it, Bobby. No, I won't do that. D'ya know what I'm goin' to do?' Ruby's eyes bored into her brother's.

He looked away. Her anger frightened him. 'No, Rube, what are ya goin' to do?' he said, cautiously.

'I'm goin' round there and I'm goin' to 'ave this out with Freddie. That's what I'm goin' to do.'

Bobby seemed alarmed.

'You mustn't Rube. We shook on it. It's as good as a contract.'

Ruby looked at him again. She saw her soft-hearted brother, always thinking the best of people, always ready to share what he had and take little for himself, and she knew in her bones that she was made of different stuff. She had no fear of Freddie Harris and his mates. Let them see.

Without a word, Ruby turned and stalked out of the kitchen.

'Ruby?' Bobby shouted after her, but her only reply was, 'Stay where you are. Look after George.'

Ruby blazed through the streets until she got to the council flat where Freddie lived with his parents and younger sister. She knocked and seconds later, Freddie came to the door.

'What an honour! Ruby Green Eyes comin' to my door. Perhaps you want that date now? 'ave you decided to play with the big boys like meself?'

'Big boys!' spat Ruby, laughing mockingly. 'You're hardly a *big boy*, Freddie. Whatever you are, there's one thing I know about you and that's the fact that you mugged off me and Bobby.'

Freddie's oily charm immediately dissipated. He seemed to know instantly what all this was about. Now, he got down to business.

'Bobby agreed a grand. We shook 'ands on it so don't come round 'ere accusin' me of anythin'.' Freddie was acting flash, smiling at her cockily, as if she was just some silly local girl who'd fall for a bit of flattery and a few notes in her hand. What he didn't seem to understand was that Ruby wasn't silly, she wasn't stupid at all. In fact, she was pure class, and if Freddie didn't know that by now she was going to remind him.

Ruby took a step closer. She turned her piercing green eyes on him. 'I've spoken to Bobby since ya did that job. He told me you knew about the safe because your girlfriend works in the office. I'll bet any money ya knew how much was in there that night. I'll bet any money you set the fee with Bobby knowin' full well there was ten grand in there.'

Freddie sized her up and down. 'All right, Rube, maybe I did know, maybe I didn't. What's it to you? Me and Bobby made a deal.'

'Oh, did ya? Well, I'm tellin' you that the deal was a bad one and ya mugged us off. I know you stole this job off Charlie Beaumont. You wouldn't want him to know ya nicked his job on purpose, would ya? Charlie might forgive someone accidentally takin' his job, but doin' it on purpose? My Bobby wouldn't 'ave a problem, but you would.'

Freddie's face hardened. He shuffled his feet again. His eyes narrowed as he opened his mouth. She'd hit the target.

'Well, Bob shook 'ands on the deal for a thousand,' he replied weakly.

'Well the term's 'ave changed. We want half the money, and if we don't get it you won't 'ave a hand to shake if Charlie Beaumont finds out.'

'So, now you're a "proper" gangster are ya, Ruby Green Eyes, turnin' up 'ere and givin' me grief?' Freddie sneered. 'Wasn't so long ago you'd turn yer nose up at workin' with the likes of me, and now you're round 'ere playin' with the crooks.'

'Oh dear, Freddie, you could be in a lot of trouble . . .' Ruby almost burst out laughing at seeing the discomfort on his face. Then she went in for the kill. 'I want our half of the ten grand at mine tonight. You bring it round or I go to Charlie and let him know he's been mugged off too. Would you like that, Freddie Harris?'

The shifty man's face was pale now. His eyes still refused to meet Ruby's but instinctively she knew she'd won.

'You might think we're mugs but know this: my brother will never work for you and your "big boys" again unless ya give us our half.' Ruby said defiantly, staring hard at the weasel. 'So, let me tell ya what I want. I want five thousand pounds, in cash, brought round to me tonight. Is that clear? If ya don't bring it, I'll 'ave a word with Mr Big.' Ruby smiled a slow smile of satisfaction. Freddie looked as uncomfortable as a man could possibly be.

'Look, Ruby, darlin', I'll 'ave a word with Bobby. We'll sort this out man-to-man.' Freddie tried to charm her but Ruby cut in, her voice low and dangerous, 'You deal with me from now on. You take my terms or nuthin'.'

Ruby stood, her head high, her back straight. Her hair fell down her back, almost to her waist and she held Freddie's gaze until he pulled away. She'd won. It was a feeling she would never forget. If she could face a villain, what else could she do? A sense of possibility grew inside her.

Freddie nodded reluctantly, looking over her shoulder. He plastered a sly grin on his face. 'I'll be round later. Got some business to do first but I'll be there.'

'You'd better be,' Ruby said grimly.

She stalked off, her heart pounding, but it wasn't fear, it was pure exhilaration. Yes, she wanted a fair share of the takings, but suddenly she realised *this* was what she was born to do. *This* was power, pure and simple, and, in that moment, she realised she liked the feeling of it. She realised she could use her brains, and her brother's skills, and they'd never want for money ever again.

Ruby arrived back at the house to find George being given his night-time bottle by Bobby in the lounge. Her brother's face was still pale. He looked up as she entered the room. Ruby knew her face was flushed, her heart still raced, yet she felt calmer now, back in control.

'I got the money. Freddie's bringin' it tonight.'

'You what? Are ya mad? Freddie knows some big-time villains. You don't know what you're messin' with, Rube.' It was Bobby's turn to hiss at her.

Ruby didn't look away. She knew Freddie Harris was rotten to the core, but she also guessed that he had no real friends in the criminal underworld. He was too dodgy, too stupid, to be a player. She was betting everything on him being the loser that she'd always thought he was.

'Believe me. Bobby, he's comin' 'ere tonight with the cash. Five thousand nicker.' Even though her confidence had begun to drain away, Ruby tried to appear certain. Now she was back home, she couldn't believe she'd done what she'd done.

Bobby looked stunned. George stopped gulping, eyed up Ruby and smiled, emptying the contents of his gummy mouth onto Bobby's hoodie.

Bobby sighed, not for the first time that day. ''Ere, take George, will ya? I'm goin' to get changed, and get me head round all this. You've done somethin' there, Ruby. You don't know how this is goin' to pan out,' he said as he departed.

Ruby was left in the sitting room, holding her baby brother, his warm milky scent made her smile, bringing her back to her reality and family life. She kissed his forehead and he smiled back, kicking his little feet in happiness at seeing her. 'I wouldn't let anything or anybody harm ya. I'll sort out those nasty men, oh yes I will, even if Bobby don't believe I can do it,' she said softly. Little George's fingers curled around hers as he gurgled with the sheer joy of seeing his big sister and hearing her voice.

Ruby smiled back at him. She searched her heart, yet she couldn't find any regret at challenging Freddie the way she had. They had to stand up for themselves or every villain round there would think they were a soft touch and try it on. That's if they did any more jobs.

'Everythin' I do is for you, little one,' she crooned, bringing the bottle back to his lips and watching as he sucked contentedly. Once she'd burped him and read a storybook about baby ducks to him, he yawned and she realised it was time to put him down for the night. Her heart swelled as she lay him down in his soft, clean cot and sang him an old Romany song, which her Grandad Jim had taught her as a child.

She drew the curtains, smiling to herself as she sang, remembering how Grandad Jim had always replaced the words so he sang 'green-eyed baby' to her as a child. She murmured the words quietly now until George's eyelids drooped and he fell fast asleep.

Downstairs, Bobby was in the lounge reading the paper again. His face was still pale. He looked shocked as he read. 'Makes it real . . .' he said haltingly.

Ruby nodded. She'd felt that too upon seeing the headline, but her feelings had soon been overtaken by the rage that followed.

Just then, there was a knock on the front door.

Bobby stood up. 'I'll get it,' he said, taking charge this time. Ruby stayed silent. What would happen now? Would Freddie hand over the cash, or were they about to find out what happens to people who defy the local crooks? Anyone could be out there. Freddie could've called in a few favours. He might not have been lying about his big-time contacts. The next few seconds would reveal what they were up against. Ruby braced herself, suddenly feeling small and vulnerable. 'Don't harm George, just leave the baby alone,' she whispered to nobody but herself.

She heard Bobby open the door. She stared at the clock ticking on the mantelpiece, constant, slow. She swallowed. Her hands went cold, her throat dry. There were murmurs from the doorway then the sound of the door shutting and being bolted from the inside, something they rarely ever did.

Ruby stood up, her head swimming. Bobby walked back in. Without saying a word, he handed her an envelope; a thick brown envelope. She opened it, half expecting it to go off in her face.

Inside was a stash of notes. She pulled the wad from its container, gingerly. What did she expect? Would Freddie poison them or give them fake money? She checked a couple of the notes against the overhead light. She saw they were real. Hands trembling for the second time that day, she started to count. Ruby looked up at Bobby. A shadow seemed to fall across his face but perhaps it was a trick of the light. They shared a look of disbelief, which changed rapidly to wonder.

'It's all there . . .' she said. A smile began to form on her face. They'd done it. *She'd* done it.

Bobby looked down at the notes, then back up to Ruby. 'What 'ave ya started?'

Ruby looked at him, her love for Bobby, George and her mum filling her up, making her feel like weeping where she stood. 'We 'ave to hide this. Mum can't know,' she said, handing the money to Bobby.

'It would kill her,' he replied.

'I know, Bobby, but we 'ave to think of little George now. It's all down to us.'

'But what about everythin' Mum and Dad taught us? What about goin' straight, livin' an honest life?' Bobby sounded like a young boy, not the strapping man he had become.

Ruby sighed. Why didn't her brother see it? 'That life is gone, Bobby, it's gone. From now on, we work together. I make the deals and you do the jobs. If we play this right, if we're choosy and pick our targets carefully, then we'll never 'ave to worry about money ever again. We're foolin' ourselves if we think we 'ave any other way to survive. Without Mum, without Dad, and me havin' to take care of George . . . there's just no other way.'

Bobby looked mutinous, then great fat tears came into his eyes.

Ruby turned away from him. She knew their mum mustn't know. She knew it would destroy her to think her beautiful children had grown into crooks, like everyone else they knew in Canning Town, but she was already realising the opportunities, the ways they could earn enough, or maybe more than they needed, and the idea was intoxicating.

'Listen, Bobby, I won't say nuthin' to Mum, but this is our life now,' Ruby reiterated, looking down at the little tower of bricks still left on the floor from earlier that day. Bobby and her had played building bricks with their little brother. He'd been squealing with delight as they put one block on top of the other, creating a tower that wobbled and swayed, staying up long enough for George to whack it and bring it all tumbling down. For a couple of hours life had been simple and filled with joy.

Bobby noticed the direction of his sister's gaze. 'Just make sure, we ain't like that tower, with no foundations, pushed down by anyone strong enough,' Bobby whispered to her, and though it upset her, Ruby managed to keep a smile on her face.

We'll 'ave foundations, don't you worry about that, she thought to herself.

Bobby handed Ruby the wad of cash. It felt weighty in her hands, and again she felt a thrill she'd never experienced before.

'Oh Bobby, just think of the good we can do with this. We can look after little George, we can buy everythin' Mum needs from now on. We could even get her extra care at the hospice, get a private nurse to go in every day and check she's OK.'

They both stared again at the money she held.

'This 'ere is our chance,' Ruby added, 'this 'ere is freedom.'

CHAPTER 15

'What's this, Mum?' Ruby took the folded envelope that Cathy offered, hands shaking with the effort. She'd taken it out of the side table next to her hospice bed. The dying woman's breath was rasping, her pallor grey. She lay back on her pillows, exhausted, her eyes searching Ruby's face.

'Open it later . . . when I'm gone . . .' Cathy said with difficulty as she dissolved into a coughing fit.

'All right, Mum, just settle back,' she replied, her heart aching at the sight of her mother.

Ruby had kept a vigil at her mum's bedside for the last two days, knowing the end was near. Their neighbour Mrs Brown, from two doors down, a stout and motherly woman with five kids of her own, was looking after little George as Ruby ate and slept by her mum's side.

Ruby inspected the crumpled envelope in her hands. Her mum had written her name, and hers alone, on the front. She could sense Cathy watching her, and she looked over and her mum nodded as if to say, 'It's for your eyes only'. Ruby looked back again. It had clearly been written a while ago as it was stained with handling, but it obviously meant a lot to her mum so she placed it into her handbag, the knock-off Gucci that Cathy had bought her at Rathbone Market when she started her first job.

'How's yer job goin', love?' Cathy asked, as if reading part of Ruby's mind. Without missing a beat, Ruby looked up to her and smiled. 'It's great, Mum, really great. Mrs Brown is lookin' after George and we're managin' fine. There's nuthin' for ya to worry about. But you must rest, Mum, you're tired.'

Ruby was adept at lying to her Mum now. She'd lied about still working. She'd lied about Mrs Brown looking after her brother all the time. She'd lied that there was nothing to worry about. *Just little white lies*, she thought to herself. Cathy closed her eyes and suddenly her breathing became more laboured.

'Nurse!' Ruby rushed to the door, almost bumping into Bobby as he arrived. He looked around in alarm as a nurse sped into the room.

'Now then, dear, let's adjust the oxygen levels. That's better. Is that better, Mrs Murphy?' the nurse said.

Cathy made a small nod and her breathing began to slow, though it seemed like hard work.

Once the nurse had written on Cathy's chart and left the room, Ruby and Bobby sat either side of her, each holding one of her hands. Ruby looked down at the gnarled hands of her mother, a working woman who'd slogged all her life, working in the tobacconist, who'd cooked, cleaned and ironed for others. She remembered the cool touch of her mum's hand as a child on a hot day, checking her forehead for sunburn, smiling down into her eyes. Ruby felt a wail rise up inside her. She wanted to shout, 'Stop!' She wanted her mother's death to stop, her life to return to the happiness she'd felt as a child, secure and safe in her family. Time wouldn't stop though.

It only took a second for Ruby to realise that the oxygen pump was working but her mum wasn't breathing. It was a second of complete stillness, before she saw their beloved mother had passed. Ruby picked up her mother's hand, now floppy and still, and kissed it, feeling the warmth already draining from her body. She placed it down, bent her head onto the bed and wept. She wept for them all, for Bobby, for George who would never know his mum, for her dad who was now reunited with the woman he adored. Lastly, she tried to weep for herself but that was where the crying stopped. Her tears had run dry. She would never shed a tear for herself ever again. It was as if her emotions had frozen, and she'd changed into a woman whose heart ran cold.

There was a blur of activity in the room. Nurses came. They checked their mum over. She heard the words, 'I'm sorry, Miss Murphy, Mr Murphy, but your mother has passed away.' She didn't know who had spoken them. She didn't care. Her world had shattered into a million pieces. Nothing would ever, ever be the same again, and their future, the one where they protected themselves, looked out for themselves, had already begun.

Later that night after all the rush of nurses and officials, after her brother's tears had stopped flowing, Ruby was finally alone. She didn't dare open Cathy's letter until she was in bed, George sleeping peacefully in the cot beside her.

She sat in what had been Cathy's room and tonight, it gave her comfort. The house was silent, the only noise coming from the street with the occasional cat yowling, a drunkard singing tunelessly, a group of young men laughing then shouting, their voices like pinpricks in her mind.

When she was ready, Ruby opened the letter. She almost couldn't read it, so powerful was the sense of her departed mum as she saw her handwriting scrawled across the lines, the writing of a woman old before her time, a woman knowing she was dying and would never see her baby grow up.

Ruby took a long breath and began.

Dear Ruby,

My darling, I know I don't have long, my doctors in the hospice are kind but I know my time is short. I can't believe I'm writing this to you as a widow, facing the end of my days without your father with me, while my youngest child is still a baby.

I want more for you three, my gorgeous children, which is why I'm writing this down rather than telling you. You all look so frightened, though you try to hide it, every time you come in and see me, which is every day. You look so fragile but so grown up at the same time, and it breaks my heart knowing I won't be there to comfort you, protect you and advise you as you go through life.

This letter is all I can give you. I don't have money to leave you. I don't have wealth to give you. All I ever wanted for you and your brothers was a quiet life, an honest life filled with as much love as me and your father could give you. I won't be around to protect you any more. I'm breaking my promise to all of you, the promise I made every time the nurse handed me my newborn babies: 'I'll keep you safe. I'll do anything to keep you from harm. You're loved and safe, and I'll always be here to make sure that's true'.

And yet, I won't be here, and by a cruel twist of fate, neither will your father. You will all be left as orphans. As I write this, the tears are starting to come and I can't see the page too well through their blur, but I must finish this as time is so short.

I have weeks left to live, and that's the truth. Ruby, by the time you read this, I'll be gone, but one thing I can promise you is that my love for you and your brothers will never die. I believe I will watch over you all from heaven.

No mother should ever die with a baby to love and bring up, but that's what will happen to us. Ruby, I'm writing this specifically to you because you will have to take over my role. It's you who will bring up little George. It's you who will hold our family together. Your brother Bobby is a sweetheart but he isn't resilient in the way that you are. I've seen your father's direct nature in you but I don't know where you get your courage, your strength. You shine a light so strong that sometimes I have to shade my eyes, just like on a summer's day. I've always been so proud of you, my darling. So proud of your courage, of the way you have never cared what other people think. You've always gone your own way, made your own decisions without being swayed by anyone else and I've always admired you for that.

Now, I need to ask you to step into my shoes. I need to know that when I'm gone, there will be someone to care for George, to comfort Bobby as he grieves for both me and your dad, and someone to stay strong for the family.

I know I'm asking a lot, and I wouldn't ask it of you if I didn't know you could rise to it. Look after your brothers, see that they don't fall into bad ways with bad people. Keep them out of trouble, and please, please remember your father's advice. An honest life is the best life. Stay away from bad men and dodgy fellas who promise the earth. My love for your dad was for ever. He was my first sweetheart and the man of my life. I hope you know the same joy, Ruby, the same love as I did. Lead an honest life, and remember you were brought up with love. Your grandpa Jim, your father and I might be gone, but somewhere up there, in the heavens, we'll always be loving the three of you.

Keep my baby safe, Ruby. Keep Bobby safe too, and keep yourself safe. Remember your father's words and know that I love you.

I love you all.
Mum x

Ruby folded up her mother's letter carefully. The words touched her deeply, but she knew even now that she couldn't follow her mother's wishes. She'd keep them all safe, but the only way she could do that was in a way her mother would never approve. She'd made her choice. She was the head of the family now. Her sweet brother Bobby and little baby George needed her to be strong, just as her mum said, and that meant not looking back. How else would they survive? Ruby stared into the distance. They were three orphans in a harsh world, and she would protect them all come what may, in any way she could, and by any means possible.

In that moment, as she mourned her adored mum and her wonderful father, her heart hardened. It had to. Everything had changed. Where once she was appalled by crooked work and making easy money, now she was focused only on providing for her family. She thought about Bobby, about his skills at lock-breaking, the skills that were a rarity in the underworld, and she knew which path she'd chosen.

PART TWO

NEW LIFE, BAD HABITS

Canning Town,
London, 1993

CHAPTER 16

A runner for a big-time blagger Charlie Beaumont came to their door. He already knew to ask for Ruby. The brother and sister team had a reputation for getting jobs done.

They were still small-time though, doing carefully chosen break-ins, but they could feed themselves and take care of their small family. They'd even managed to give Cathy the kind of send-off their mother deserved – horses in black plumes, a Victorian carriage to carry the coffin and a limousine to carry Ruby, Bobby and George. But most of all Ruby was grateful they had enough money that she could spend time with George, and give him the care he needed instead of trying to hold down a job while being a full-time mother to a small baby. Over the last two years George had grown into a boisterous, happy toddler and while they still missed Cathy and Louie, they were happy.

Coming to the attention of someone like Charlie, though, wasn't something that Ruby had planned for. But gossip in the pubs and shops spread to Charlie's ears, and now she had a shady-looking geezer slouching in their doorway. This could mean trouble or opportunity, but either way Charlie Beaumont wasn't someone you said no to.

When Bobby got home she handed over George, who screamed in delight at seeing his big brother. Some people said taking care of children was woman's work, but they hadn't seen the way Bobby was with little George.

'All right, little man. It's good to see you, too,' Bobby laughed as he juggled the squirming bundle of little boy. As soon as he got George settled he turned his head to speak to Ruby, but was left with his mouth hanging open as he took in his sister.

Ruby was dressed in her best, hair done, heels on.

'Goin' somewhere special, sis?'

'It would seem so,' Ruby answered. She knew Bobby wasn't going to be happy when she told him about Charlie, but they were a team. 'We had a visitor earlier, a runner from Charlie Beaumont.'

'Charlie Beaumont! What would the likes of him want with us?'

'About what you'd expect,' Ruby answered. 'Seems he's interested in your skills . . .'

'Rube. I don't know. Pullin' some small jobs, getting by . . . That's one thing. But workin' for the likes of Charlie? That's another thing altogether.'

'I'm not sure we 'ave a choice, Bobby. He's asked to meet me, and that's what I'm goin' to do. Besides, this could be our big break! Just think, we could soon be rakin' in cash hand over fist.' Ruby laughed and smiled at her brother, but inside she was a mix of terrified and excited.

She was going out, alone, to meet an armed robber who inspired an equal mix of fear and celebrity in the East End. The idea of working for a blagger had been unthinkable even a year or two ago. Now, it could be the next step on the path Ruby had chosen.

'I don't like it, Rube,' Bobby said, his face stern in the low light of evening. He held little George close to him as if his bulk could protect him from what they were getting into.

'It's fine, Bobby, it'll be fine,' Ruby murmured. 'Working for Charlie could be a different world. We'd be looked after, 'ave bigger jobs, more respect, more money. It could be a good thing.'

Bobby nodded. They both knew what working for a big-time villain meant. It meant you were accepted. It meant nicer things, bigger cars, nicer clothes, but, most importantly, it meant you had a protector, someone bigger to lean on, if you did things right.

'But what if we do somethin' wrong? What if we don't like playin' these games? What do we do then?' Bobby insisted.

Ruby smiled but, inside, she shuddered. 'We 'ave to play. We 'ave no choice.'

Ruby left Bobby with little George and headed out. She'd taken care dressing herself, selecting a new silk blouse and a smart red skirt. She'd dusted on face powder gently, and pulled a mascara wand through her long lashes. She was as ready as she could be.

As the door of the Beckton Arms shut behind her, a hush formed over the smoky bar that smelled of cheap aftershave and expensive beer. For a moment, Ruby felt like she'd walked into a saloon, as all heads swivelled to stare at her, and conversations stopped mid-sentence, every man in that place wondering what on earth a woman was doing there unaccompanied, especially one who exuded glamour like she did.

Ruby stared back boldly. She looked a million dollars, and the sight of their amazement served only to bolster her confidence. Slowly, she navigated the crumpled, sticky carpet, walking up to the bar, her head held high, as if she owned the place. She flicked her long hair and stood in front of the barman, who was looking at her like a cartoon dog might look at a bone, his eyes almost popping out of their sockets.

Two men standing at the bar moved aside, putting down their pints. There was a feeling of expectation in the room. What would happen next?

'Gin and tonic, please,' Ruby said without hesitation, watching her words land in the silence with wry amusement. She had never been in a pub on a Saturday night, and she had certainly never been to one alone. It wasn't the done thing. In many ways, life in the East End was like being in a time warp. Decent women didn't go to bars alone, only prostitutes ever did that.

Somehow, everyone in that pub knew she wasn't a whore. So, what then was she doing there? Ruby smoothed down her pencil skirt, relishing the feel of the expensive silk lining against her skin. She was tall in her heels, and she made sure she looked the barman straight in the eyes.

'Right, love, well, why don't ya sit 'ere at the bar with me? I'll keep ya company. Don't want a pretty girl like you to get lonely.' The barman grinned sleazily as he poured a generous shot of gin.

Ruby reached into the bag that she always carried, the knock-off her mum had bought her. She preferred to keep this handbag, it was like keeping a piece of Cathy with her. She was about to bring out her purse when a familiar voice sounded.

'I'll get that, mate. Well, well, if it ain't Ruby Green Eyes.' It was clear that Freddie Harris had put away a few pints already that evening as he swayed slightly on the spot. His mate Smithy was standing next to him, a pale lad with dark hair and eyes that glinted, sizing up Ruby and clearly liking what he saw. Both men grinned like foxes eyeing a chicken coop.

'Freddie, I can't seem to get away from you,' Ruby smiled, making a couple of the men within earshot smirk. 'No matter how hard I try.'

Freddie, cocky as ever, swaggered up to her. Ruby turned to him, her eyes meeting his, flashing under her thick, dark lashes. Freddie smiled widely but stepped back all the same. 'And what brings you out, *Ruby*?' Freddie said, emphasising her proper name.

Ruby considered ignoring his question, but assuming her contact wasn't running late, he'd know what she was up to soon enough. 'As it happens, Freddie, I'm meetin' someone,' she said.

Freddie looked about to launch another of his smarmy come-ons, but before he could move, the door of the pub opened for a second time. Glancing over, Freddie caught sight of the area's number-one crime boss, big-time blagger Charlie Beaumont, dressed in a sharp Savile Row suit with flash gold jewellery and trailing expensive cologne. Freddie stopped in his tracks. It wasn't every day he got to smarm up to a proper villain.

'All right, Mr Beaumont,' Freddie said. 'Nice to see ya.'

Charlie ignored the weasel, his gaze turning instantly to Ruby. For the second time that evening, the tables went silent. Even the thick fug of cigarette smoke seemed to still.

Ruby looked at the man who was both feared and respected in the underworld, a man who was a big player, someone everyone knew not to mess with.

'You must be Ruby,' Charlie said to the young woman. He looked her up and down, seeing the effort she'd made, the style she carried herself with, and he nodded his approval. Out of the corner of her eye, Ruby could see Freddie looking between her face and Charlie's, at a complete loss, until realisation began dawning on his face. *This* was the man Ruby had arranged to meet. This man, this crime boss, was Ruby's reason for being in the notorious crook hangout at 8 p.m. on a Saturday night. Ruby almost laughed out loud as the look of comprehension spread over Freddie's thin face, his beady eyes flitting between them both. Well, this'd give him something to stare at.

'Yes, I'm Ruby. You must be Charlie Beaumont. I'm pleased to meet ya,' she said, extending her slender hand for him to shake.

'Not botherin' you, is he?' Charlie said, his eyes not moving from Ruby's face. It was clear he meant Freddie, though.

'Oh no, he's nuthin' to worry about,' Ruby smiled, enjoying every moment of Freddie's discomfort.

'Let me know if he's annoyin' ya and I'll sort it. Now, you're lookin' too good for in 'ere, and there's too many ears. Let me take you to a place I know where we can talk.' It wasn't a question, it was a command.

Despite Charlie's fearsome reputation, the violence he perpetrated, the robberies he'd pulled off and the adversaries he'd beaten, Ruby didn't feel unsafe. She knew he wasn't a ladies' man. He'd been married for years and, unlike the other big-time crooks, wasn't seen sporting girlfriends on his arm with a wife tucked away somewhere out of the limelight. By all accounts he'd stayed faithful to the woman he'd married. He'd robbed banks, had underworld contacts all over the city, and was known for dealing swiftly, and decisively, with any betrayal, but above all he was a businessman. Ruby understood business. Her choice was made. She nodded her agreement.

Charlie nodded back to her. 'I'll take you for somethin' to eat and we can talk, but let's get out of 'ere.'

Ruby let the gangster steer her out of the bar with the lightest touch on her back. As he opened the door for her and stepped aside to let her through, she couldn't resist throwing a look of pure victory at Freddie Harris and Smithy, who were standing at the bar still, their mouths open, gawping at this new, unexpected turn of events.

Once outside, Charlie opened the door of his shiny black Merc and Ruby slid into the front seat, feeling the intense thrill of sitting on white leather seats. Charlie drove them north to Epping. They eventually stopped outside a small family-run Italian restaurant. Leaving his car on the double yellow lines as if he was above the law in all things, Charlie opened the car door and helped Ruby out and in through the inviting doorway. It was clear Charlie was a regular, as the staff greeted him like a visiting dignitary.

The owner of the restaurant appeared, a balding Italian man in a grey suit, and personally ushered them both through the restaurant, past the diners at their tables, to a back room. Inside this room was a single table, already set up with white tablecloth, white roses and a bottle of wine set to chill. Ruby stared round, taking it all in.

Charlie pulled out her chair for her and she sat, hoping the flush of fear mingled with excitement wasn't evident on her cheeks, betraying the fact that every sense in her body was on high alert. Her heart was pounding and her palms were sweating, but she felt strangely at home with this feared man, in this room far away from everyone she loved.

The waiter simpered, then poured wine into her glass. After he'd presented the day's specials to them, Ruby took the chance to assess the man who now sat in front of her. He was an attractive man in his fifties, she guessed, with a dark grey suit cut perfectly to fit his strong frame. He had piercing blue eyes, matched only by the winking gold of his cufflinks and designer watch, worn so effort-lessly. The scent of rich aftershave, warmed by his tanned skin, was a light undertone in the room. For a moment, a brief second, Ruby wondered if this was a seduction, and everything she'd heard about how he was faithful to his wife had been wrong. Then Charlie leaned in, his elbows planted on the immaculate tablecloth, and spoke in his low, authoritative voice.

'We've got a job we want doin'.' His manner was firm yet friendly, his smile seemingly genuine.

'We?' Ruby said, her throat dry. She took a small sip of the wine. She knew power when she saw it, and Charlie oozed it.

'Some associates. You don't need the details, Ruby,' he said, waving away her question. 'Just know that we need a job doin' and your brother's name has cropped up in some circles of mine.'

Ruby nodded, taking another sip. The white wine was dry and cold.

The candlelight flickered as Charlie leaned in still further. 'It ain't the biggest job, I'll admit it, but your brother—'

'Bobby,' Ruby interjected.

'Bobby, I'm sorry I forgot my manners,' Charlie continued, 'well it seems like it'll be right up his street, and I need to test him, to see if he's loyal.'

'Oh, he's loyal all right, but I need to know what the job is before I agree,' Ruby said, staring back at the gangster.

Charlie laughed at that. 'I 'eard it was you who done the deals. That's fine by me. I like to see a woman with brains takin' charge – and you look like a smart bird. Listen, Ruby, this job would be a way in. If it went well, then there might be other "work" I'd put his way, if you get my drift?'

Ruby nodded. She understood completely. 'Go on,' she replied.

'If you like, it'll be a test of his skills and loyalty under pressure. You sure Bobby is up to it?' Charlie said, leaning back now and taking a long slug of the expensive wine. Out of nowhere, a waiter scurried over and refilled his glass.

'Depends what he'll be doin'. What did you 'ave in mind, Charlie?' Ruby enjoyed the thrill of using the boss's first name. She'd seen how others virtually bowed to him, and called him 'Mr Beaumont', and she'd decided in that instant that she would be different. She'd call him Charlie and consider herself his equal.

If he thought she was being too familiar, Charlie didn't show it. 'There's a bookie up the West End who – how do I put it? – who is out of favour . . . We did some business but he screwed us for part of the money, 'scuse my language. We know there's at least sixty grand in the safe, and we want to teach him a lesson not to fuck with us.'

Ruby sat back, a little startled at his turn of phrase, but not threatened by it. 'And you want my Bobby to unlock that safe.'

'Exactly. But I need to know if he's up to it. Is he up to it, Ruby?'

Charlie met her eyes. He'd ended up ordering for both of them; a plate of spaghetti with veal and a dressed salad, which was now being placed carefully on the table in front of them both.

'*Buon appetito*,' the waiter said softly as he left the room, closing the door quietly behind him.

Charlie picked up his fork, which caught the light, before sinking it into the pasta and swirling spaghetti expertly around the prongs. Ruby watched him, momentarily fascinated by the deftness of his movements. Charlie looked up and caught her intense interest. He laughed at the sight of her, all thoughts of the dodgy deal they were making lost for a brief second as he decided to teach her how to eat Italian food properly.

'You pick up the fork like this . . . then you turn it so the spaghetti catches on the fork and as ya turn, it gathers more and more, then . . .' Charlie opened his mouth and neatly popped the pasta into his mouth, dabbing the tomato sauce off afterwards with a pristine white napkin.

'You 'ave a go,' he said, smiling.

Ruby couldn't help herself, she giggled.

'I'll give anythin' a go, within reason,' she countered, scooping up a forkful of the dish and delicately nibbling at the pasta.

Charlie laughed. 'I 'ope you're better at makin' deals than you are at eatin' dinner!'

Ruby blushed. She looked over at him and, placing her fork down, she said, in all seriousness, 'Look, Charlie. My brother's a good man. He's the best at what he does, no one is more gifted – or more loyal – than him. In fact, he's too good a bloke, which is why I step in and do this bit. He'll do the work if the money's right, and I'm the one who makes sure the money's right. I'd like to check out the place beforehand, go down there with Bobby and make sure he's happy and we know what we're gettin' into. If you're happy with that, and we can agree the fee, then it's a deal.' She had started to tremble inwardly as she spoke. He might be friendly enough, but she had the feeling that what she was doing was more akin to baiting a lion. He looked happy but at any minute he could pounce, and then there would be his giant jaws, his large teeth biting down on her.

Ruby kept her hands folded on the table in front of her now, all attempts to eat the meal abandoned. She couldn't show him how scared she was, how out of her depth she felt right now.

'Tell me what you've got in mind and I'll tell ya if we'll do it.'

Charlie stopped eating. He dabbed his mouth rather theatrically. The air went still, even the candles seemed to stop flickering. Charlie looked up at her, and she thought, *This is it, now is when he attacks.*

Suddenly, the big man's face creased into an amused smile. 'So, this is how it's goin' to be, is it? All right, Ruby Murphy, I think we could make a good team. If Bobby turns off the alarms and gets into the bookies, he can keep half of what's in there, which is thirty grand for you. I'm reliably informed there's sixty in there.'

Ruby almost gasped. Thirty thousand pounds was a small fortune to them. They'd never had that much money in all their lives. If Bobby did this one job, they could move away, somewhere nice in the country, somewhere where little George could run and play outside.

Steady yourself . . . steady, Ruby, she admonished herself. *Hold it together.* The young woman smiled. 'I think we 'ave a deal, Charlie.'

Charlie nodded. 'We do, conditional on me meetin' Bobby.'

Ruby understood. He didn't take anything on trust. 'Of course,' she demurred.

With that the kingpin lifted up his glass. 'A toast to us and a new workin' relationship.'

'To us,' Ruby murmured, holding in her sigh of relief. She felt instinctively that this crook was taking her seriously.

'To new business, and to a beautiful woman,' Charlie smiled, taking a drink, at the same time as shooing away the waiter who had appeared to fill the glass again. 'I'm drivin' and I want a clear 'ead as I've got more business after this. It's been a pleasure meetin' ya, Ruby. From now on, you're under my protection, until we see how Bobby does.'

Charlie stood up. The meeting was clearly over. Ruby had barely touched a morsel of the delicious dinner. She'd been too nervous to eat, but she was now filled with a new feeling, a buzzing sensation that seemed to stem from her brain down the length of her body. She'd done it. She'd met a man who could've destroyed her and her family in seconds, yet she'd warmed to him, even felt that she was now under his wing. She knew that this was the beginning of a new way of life, a new path that had appeared under her feet. She didn't know where it would lead, but she knew that Charlie Beaumont was going to take her there.

CHAPTER 17

By Thursday afternoon, Ruby had scrubbed the house from top to bottom, ashamed at their humble home. She imagined that Charlie lived in a mansion somewhere flash, with servants and Rolls-Royces, and the sight of her basic home, with its utilitarian furniture and few comforts, made her feel strangely vulnerable. Bobby came in from work, his face like thunder. Ruby arched her eyebrows at him. She didn't need to speak a word. He got the message and said, 'All right, Rube, I'll put a smile on my face. I won't let ya down, I promise.'

Ruby sighed. 'I know ya don't like it, but think of the rewards, think of the money we'll make with Charlie behind us. And it ain't just about the cash. With Charlie on our side we'll be safer. No one will try to mug us off knowin' we're in with him.'

'Listen, Rube, it's one thing crackin' a safe, it's another thing working for the likes of Beaumont. We don't know nuthin' about him except he's a blagger and he runs things round 'ere. We don't know what we're gettin' into.'

Ruby knew her brother was nervous. If she admitted it, she was more than a little anxious herself. Even though they'd met just once, she had the feeling she could work *with* him, and not just as a minion.

'He's kosher, and we'll be fine, I promise ya. Your talents are wasted on break-ins at offices, Bobby. They should be used to do the really big jobs, the big banks, big warehouses. We could clean up.'

Bobby grimaced. 'Yeah but the big jobs come with long jail stretches, Rube. It's riskier.'

'Maybe, but Charlie's been at it for years. It could be safer workin' with a big-time crook who knows what's what,' Ruby butted in. 'I know this is 'ard for you but it's the only choice we 'ave. Charlie will do right by us.'

'If we do right by him, you mean,' Bobby said, but he nodded in agreement anyway.

'Right, you can take George, while I get changed,' Ruby said, handing the warm bundle to her brother. Bobby's face changed instantly. He smiled beatifically down at his little brother's sweet face and began whispering endearments to him while George chuckled and wriggled in his arms.

Ruby smiled, this time, genuinely. Things were really OK between her and Bobby. He just needed a bit more time to get used to it all. She stood in the doorway for a second watching her soft-hearted brother's face light up as he talked to the toddler. He was a born father, a family man to the core. She had to tread carefully to keep him happy.

An hour later, Ruby was dressed in a new outfit, a black dress and heels, with a matching jacket. For the first time in her life, she could afford to buy new clothes. It was a nice feeling, and one she didn't take for granted. Bobby had put George down for the night, crooning over him as he gave him his milk, and had only had time to have a swift wash and change out of his work clothes when the door knocker sounded.

'That'll be him,' Bobby said unnecessarily. Ruby glanced nervously at him, then walked slowly to the door. She stopped, took a breath, then opened it to see Charlie on her front step looking like a king would.

'Please come inside,' she said graciously, as if entertaining crime bosses was something they did as a matter of course. She could feel his masculine presence as he followed her down the dark narrow hallway to the front room.

She gestured for him to enter but he said, unexpectedly, 'I'd prefer to meet in the kitchen. I find a kitchen table is the best place for business, if ya don't mind, Ruby?'

'As you wish,' Ruby murmured and seconds later all three of them were standing around her table.

'Please take a seat,' she said as if hosting a banquet. 'Do you want tea?'

Charlie shook his head. He sat himself down, his impeccable suit and tie, that expensive waft of cologne and his Italian shoes as out of place in their home as it was possible to be.

'I'm not 'ere to drink tea. Nice place you got 'ere, though,' he said politely, giving Ruby a nod, which made her blush.

'It's home and it's clean,' she stated a little defensively.

Charlie turned to look at her and nodded. It was a small gesture to himself, as if to say he understood everything. 'I was born in a council flat in Poplar near the market. My wife Maureen came from the Isle of Dogs when it was real rough. We know what 'ard times are. D'you know where we live now?' It was more of a rhetorical question. Bobby just stared at Charlie, hardly able to believe that a kingpin, a man so feared, would be sitting inside his house about to talk business. 'We live in Chigwell, the posh bit, in a mansion. I've got seven bedrooms, three bathrooms, and my wife spends half the year out at our villa in Spain. I'm guessin' you might like a life like that too.'

Bobby shrugged but his gaze never left Charlie's face.

As if understanding the locksmith's reticence, the crime boss nodded.

'So, you're the one with the talent,' he said to Bobby. 'I'm told you've got a way with locks. I'm told you're the best in the business.'

Bobby shrugged again but this time he smiled at Charlie. 'All I know is I find it easy, Mr Beaumont—'

'Call me Charlie. Now, what I need is someone loyal, someone who won't talk, someone who won't squeal. Are you that person, Bobby?'

Ruby looked at her brother, willing him to agree. She knew he was reluctant. Would he let her down?

He didn't. Bobby nodded, 'I am Mr . . . Charlie. I won't let ya down. I'm the best there is and I'm loyal.'

With that, Bobby excused himself and left the room, leaving Ruby if not triumphant, then pleased at least.

'I take it you're the brains behind the operation.' It wasn't a question.

Ruby grinned. 'I am – but my brother isn't stupid. He's smart as they come when it comes to gettin' into anythin' or anywhere you might wish.'

She knew that Charlie would be able to spot honest men – or liars – a mile off. You didn't get to be an under-world boss without instinct. It was hard to believe, but Ruby could tell by looking at Charlie that Bobby had passed the test with just a couple of words and steady demeanour. He knew already from Bobby's reputation that he was capable, now he knew he'd keep his mouth shut. That's all Charlie needed to know.

'Listen, Charlie, we want to go big-time. We want bigger jobs – for bigger rewards.' Ruby's eyes glittered in the dim light.

Charlie nodded. 'I can see you're ambitious. I like that, especially in a woman. You've got a lot to learn, though, Ruby. I'll take you both on, see if you're up to it, and if you are . . .'

'. . . if we are?' Ruby tried to keep the excitement from her voice.

Charlie chuckled. She didn't fool him. He could feel her desire to be better, have better than this. If he was being cruel he'd describe their home as a hovel. *Well, good.* He liked people with nothing to lose, and something about Ruby made him want to help her up the ladder.

'We'll talk more when this job's done.'

Perhaps it was his fatherly instincts kicking in? He'd lost his only son Michael in a motorcycle accident at the age of nineteen. Neither him nor Maureen had ever got over the loss fully, and here were three orphans, needing direction if they were going to navigate the shark-infested waters of the crime network of East London.

He nodded his head as if he'd communicated all this to her. Charlie had given his consent to the job. He'd sussed out her brother. The interview was over.

Without a word, Ruby stood up. Charlie smiled. There was a connection between them, nothing sexual, but he saw something in this woman. He saw her beauty and her elegant ways, and more than that, he understood the raw anger and ambition that lay beneath her calm exterior. *I can use these two. I can take them far,* he thought to himself. He brushed off imaginary crumbs, stood up and held out a hand to Bobby, who had reappeared in the doorway.

'It's 'appenin' tomorrow night. Be ready at 11 p.m. Meet my associate at The Anchor and he'll go with ya. Get in, get the money and get out. If ya can do this then there's thirty grand in it for ya, half the takin's. Not bad for a night's work.' Charlie's instructions were for Bobby.

Ruby showed him out. As he left, he handed her a piece of paper with the address. 'So you can case the joint,' he smiled.

When she'd shut the door behind him, she moved into the lounge, sinking into their old brown sofa. She looked around, trying to see everything through Charlie's fierce gaze. She wasn't impressed. The TV was an old one, too small for even this tiny room. The curtains were old and had a brown floral pattern chosen by Cathy many years ago. She'd always hated them, so dark, so cheap. The sofa itself was in surprisingly good nick considering it'd been around for as long as she could remember but she knew in that glance that none of it was enough for her any more. She wanted nice things, expensive clothes, a beautiful home, but more than that, she wanted a future for them all. They'd been scraping by for too long. Even with the small crooked jobs they'd been doing, they were only covering the basics. Ruby had some new clothes, they had food, and a roof over their heads, but she knew she wanted more. She wanted comfort and ease, and there was only one way people like her could get it.

If there was any doubt still remaining, it went in that moment. *I want everythin' Charlie has – and more*, she thought to herself and smiled, imagining the fine leather seats she'd have, the diamond rings on her fingers, the designer clothes for George. She could almost taste the luxury, the refinement. They were only just beginning.

Bobby was pacing the kitchen, his balaclava and black gloves in his bag, his jewellery all removed and hidden away so if he got caught or seen he couldn't be identified that way. He looked over at the clock. It was almost 11 p.m. and it was time to head down the road, his small holdall containing his twirls. Ruby had insisted on waiting up for him. She nodded as Bobby said, 'It's time.' She watched him head out through the back door, creeping along the alleyway and circling around the houses to get to the end of the street. Bobby usually got a bit nervous before jobs, but as this was the first for Charlie Beaumont, he seemed to be more anxious than usual.

He walked quickly, head down, black holdall gripped in his hand. He walked straight into The Anchor, the meeting place, and saw the landlord had been 'briefed'. There was only one other customer in the pub.

'Ready?' the man said.

Bobby replied, 'Yes, mate.'

The pair of them headed off.

Bobby and Ruby had already been to the betting shop and sussed it out. Bobby knew the alarm system was one he could handle. They'd gone inside and placed a bet at the time, checking where the locked doors to the back rooms were and getting a feel for the place.

Once inside, Bobby gingerly opened the safe. The other man, whose name Bobby didn't know, looked inside and whistled softly.

'What is it?' Bobby hissed.

'You don't want to know,' the man said, reaching in and bringing out armfuls of notes, which he started to stuff into the black holdall. The man appeared to be doing some mental arithmetic as they worked, but Bobby was too keen to get the hell out of there to take much notice.

'Done?' Bobby whispered.

'Done,' the man said.

CHAPTER 18

After Bobby left, Ruby made herself a coffee and sat down, flicking absent-mindedly through a magazine. She didn't read a single word. She was thinking of Bobby, wondering where he was and when he'd be back. It was just past midnight, and she was dozing in her chair when the back door creaked open. She awoke instantly. Bobby walked in, yawned then threw his holdall onto the table.

'How was it? Did you get the money?' Ruby searched Bobby's face as he sat down heavily, placing a large black holdall, stuffed to the gills, on the table.

'There weren't sixty grand in there. The safe was massive but it was 'alf empty. I don't know who gave Charlie the information but they was lyin'.' Bobby looked anguished.

Their first job for Charlie Beaumont and this had happened. Ruby swallowed hard. Her brain began whirring though she was exhausted, adrenaline kicking in as fear stole through her body.

'Tell me everythin',' she commanded.

'We got there. I sorted the alarm system no trouble, while the other geezer did the lookout. He knew where the safe was, which is why Charlie had put him on the job. We went inside, found the safe, again, no trouble. Then, I opened it. There was money, but I knew it weren't as much as he'd said there'd be. We didn't 'ave time to count it. We stuffed it into the bag then did the usual: he went and checked the exit was clear while I locked the safe up, re-set the alarm and crept out. Charlie told him to give the money to me and so 'ere it is. It was a nifty job, no security, no problems except the bloke I was workin' with seemed surprised when I opened the safe. I'm thinkin' there wasn't as much in there as they thought, which isn't good news for us.'

'Oh Christ,' Ruby swore. She knew if Charlie had set them on the job, it was because it was a big haul, not their usual small robberies of office safes or pub takings.

'So what do we do, sis?' Bobby said in a small voice, perhaps already imagining the punishment Charlie Beaumont would mete out on him.

'We count it,' said Ruby, firmly. Ruby tipped the contents of the black bag onto the Formica tabletop. Notes scattered and fell on the floor, though most of the money was in wads of one thousand pounds. They spent the next hour counting and re-counting.

'You were right, Bobby, there's forty grand. We're twenty short and my guess is that Charlie will think we've pocketed the difference,' Ruby said slowly.

Bobby stared at her. 'We're dead then. No one cheats Charlie Beaumont.'

Ruby sat for a moment, thinking. 'There's only one way to handle this, Bobby. We've got to tell him straight, and not just that, we've got to insist on our fee, the full thirty grand,' she said at last.

Bobby almost choked.

'What are you on about? 'Ave ya lost ya marbles?'

'No, but you're goin' to 'ave to trust me.'

Did she have the courage to do what was in her mind? She sat still for a long time after Bobby went up to bed, even though the urge to sleep was almost irresistible. She wanted to be absolutely sure of the next step. Their lives might depend upon it. Did she have the guts to face Charlie, to take the risk? Somewhere, deep down, she knew she did.

The next morning, Ruby picked up a wad of money, and, leaving Bobby to gape after her, little George in his arms, she walked out of her home. 'If I'm not back by dinner time then take George and get the hell out of London,' were Ruby's last words as she closed the door behind her, leaving Bobby, pale and shaken. She wasn't feeling too good herself. In truth, she had never felt so scared, so unsure of herself, yet she knew what she was going to do – and she knew that whatever happened next would be their making, or their downfall.

Ruby met Charlie at the agreed place, a greasy spoon café in Old Street. He drew out a chair for her as if they were dining in The Ritz rather than about to sip from mugs with chips in the rim.

Ruby swallowed. 'I've come with the money, but there's a problem . . .' Ruby's throat was bone dry. Every nerve in her body was straining. She felt nauseous, and wondered for a second if she shouldn't just throw the money at him and run.

'It's good to see ya, Ruby,' Charlie said, stirring a heaped teaspoon of sugar into his cup. His eyes were ice blue as they locked her gaze.

Ruby's hands shook in her lap. *Calm down, it's just business, just business* . . . she tried to soothe herself. Carefully, she placed the bag on the table. 'There's ten grand in there,' she said, looking him full in the eyes.

He leaned forward as if to hear her better, his muscular frame towering over her.

'Whoever told ya there was more in that safe was lyin',' she continued, her voice shaking just a little, though she kept her gaze steady. If he was going to threaten her or hurt her, now was the moment, though perhaps it would be worse than that. Perhaps she would end up buried in concrete, or her body dumped on local wasteland. She swallowed again.

Charlie looked down at the bag then up at her. Her gaze was defiant, strong now.

'There was only forty grand in that safe, and we agreed thirty for doin' the job, so if my maths is correct, then that leaves you with this. A deal's a deal.' Ruby felt her skin prickle with sweat. She could hardly believe she was saying this to a man who could kill her as easily as look at her.

Charlie stared down at the bag. His face was harsh, lined and scarred, but he was still a handsome man. If he chose not to believe her then he'd demand all the money, leaving them thirty grand down and with a formidable enemy. Had she played this right? The next few seconds would tell. Ruby knew with one word in the right person's ear, she'd be dead before tonight.

Eventually, Charlie looked up at her, his face expressionless. She stared back, refusing to drop her eyes, refusing to submit to this dangerous man. She knew they'd done nothing wrong. She only prayed he'd realise it.

Suddenly, he barked with laughter. 'You're as ruthless as you're beautiful,' he said with genuine amusement. 'I don't think 'alf the men I employ would 'ave the balls to say to my face what you just did.'

Ruby started to speak again but Charlie stopped her with one wave of his hand.

'You've got some nerve, comin' in 'ere and tellin' me I'm twenty grand short and wantin' me to believe that it weren't you and Bobby who nicked it.'

'It's true,' she said simply. In that moment, she sensed that this would be OK.

Charlie sat back in his seat. 'You're in luck. The associate of mine I sent with Bobby wasn't just there to show him the safe. I needed to know you were kosher. He told me the cash was short.'

Ruby gasped. 'So, it was a test? You made me sweat to see what we'd do?'

Charlie nodded. 'And I'm impressed, girl, I really am. You've got balls, Ruby Murphy, I'll give ya that.'

Ruby felt enraged, then elated. It was her first big test of courage – and she'd passed with flying colours.

'I can teach ya stuff, Ruby, show you how it's done, shape you into somethin',' he continued, wiping his mouth with a paper napkin, which he placed carefully under the now empty mug. 'I've got plans for you – and your brother – but first I've got a present for ya, though I can't decide whether to give it to ya now you've cost me a fair few nicker. It's from my wife, she chose it.'

Ruby looked at him quizzically.

'Just open it,' was all he said, handing over a large Louis Vuitton shopping bag. Ruby almost whistled as she pulled out a black snakeskin bag worth thousands. She knew its worth because she'd seen one just like it in her magazine, never thinking she'd ever actually own one.

'You need to look the part. Can't 'ave ya meetin' contacts with scruffy gear.' Charlie said, looking pointedly at her worn handbag.

Ruby placed her arm over it almost protectively, want-ing to refuse the immaculate gift, but she knew he was right. She had to look the part. It was no good walking into the kind of dodgy big-money deals that she sensed she would be doing from now on with a knock-off from the market, even if it had been the last gift her mother had given her. Almost sadly, she stuffed her old bag into the shopping bag and placed the designer bag on her arm.

Back home, she packed away the drooping market bag, placing it like a precious relic inside tissue paper and storing it at the back of her wardrobe. She felt an ache in her heart as she closed the wardrobe door, shutting her past away for ever.

CHAPTER 19

'So, what's the job, Charlie?' Ruby said, twirling the spaghetti around her fork expertly. She was comfortable now in the presence of the gangster, this time back in the Italian restaurant, sensing she was under his protection. He'd told her he'd make sure Bobby did the best jobs, but he needed him full-time. For the past few weeks she'd been meeting Charlie regularly, and he'd told her which jobs her brother would do – if she agreed to them.

'It's an easy one this time, Ruby,' Charlie said, dabbing the corner of his mouth with the starched white napkin. He leaned forwards, his muscular arms clad in his expensive suit resting on the table. 'All Bobby has to do is open the warehouse and make sure the alarms don't go off.'

'What's inside this warehouse, Charlie?' Ruby asked, taking a small sip of her wine. She never drank much. She hated the feeling of being tipsy and so she only ever had a few small sips to be sociable.

The crime boss looked over at her. 'I 'ave it on good authority that a lorry will be inside that warehouse on the night with a full load of cigarettes which 'ave cleared customs. All we 'ave to do is get inside and it's rich pickings.'

'And when you say "rich pickings", what does that mean for my Bobby?' Ruby smiled, sitting back in her seat and looking over at the man who had become so important in her life. A few weeks ago she barely knew him, only having heard of him through Sarah's dad who had done some work for him years ago. She'd known he was the local hard man, and remembered wishing she'd never meet him. In a million years, she'd never have thought she'd be sitting across from the same dangerous man enjoying a perfect Italian meal and being treated as an equal. Times had changed but so had Ruby. She knew Bobby's worth. She knew that good key-men were rare, and those who could work quickly and expertly were worth their weight in gold. Ruby had grown up in the crime-ravaged back streets of London. Her family might've been honest but she heard the gossip, she saw the winners – and losers – and she had ears to listen.

It was Ruby's mission now to convert that expertise to gold, and Charlie was her champion, if the price was right.

'I wondered when we'd get to that. Always sharp, ain't ya, Ruby,' Charlie chuckled. He eased himself back. In many ways he was a man in his prime. He had streaks of grey in his thick brown hair, which was cut expensively, yet he retained his good looks despite the life he'd led and the battles he'd won.

Ruby shrugged but the smile didn't leave her face.

'We'll split it fifty-fifty. I can't say fairer than that. So, Ruby Murphy, is it a deal?' It was Charlie's turn to grin.

'It is, Charlie, but on one condition . . .' Ruby replied, her eyes twinkling with mischief in the low light.

Charlie raised his eyebrows. He was always surprised by this woman. He never knew quite what she'd say or do, and that's what intrigued him. In many ways, she reminded him of himself as a young man, keen to prove himself, to know his value and take a risk for high stakes.

'My condition is that you let me buy dinner,' Ruby laughed, which made Charlie roar. He shook his head. 'Well, it's been a while since a woman paid for me, but go on then, I'll give ya that. Now, do we 'ave a deal?'

Ruby nodded. She put down her fork and placed her napkin on the table. It was her turn to end the meeting, she'd decided.

With a small gesture to the attentive waiter, she placed a wad of cash on the table. 'And that's a tip for you,' she finished, smiling at the young man who seemed lost for words.

Charlie looked on. He liked a woman who took charge, and who looked after those around her who weren't considered to be so important. He nodded his approval and stood up. Driving her back home, he got down to business. 'Bobby will be picked up for this one. They'll drive there. I won't say where it is but believe me, it's all good, all sorted.'

Ruby liked to stake out targets herself, but for once, she decided to trust Charlie on this. It sounded like the warehouse was a journey away so she nodded her agreement. One of them had to be at home to take care of George. The time and date was set, and all Ruby had to do was wait.

Back at home, she went over the details with her brother, who listened placidly as she outlined the plan. 'All you 'ave to do is open up the place, then a couple of other lads will drive the lorry out to a different warehouse where they'll unload it. You'll need to lock up the original storage place so when the mobile security does their checks, there'll be no suspicion of the robbery.

'It's an inside job and it's bona fide.'

Bobby nodded and shrugged. 'Sounds simple enough to me, Rube. What's our cut?'

Ruby looked over at him and allowed a small smile of triumph to creep onto her face. 'It's fifty-fifty. Charlie knows how to keep a good key-man onside.'

That made Bobby laugh even though he was shaking his head. 'You were born for this, Rube.'

'Maybe I was, Bobby. Maybe I was . . .'

Ruby yawned. She picked up her Louis Vuitton bag and headed upstairs, checking in on George, who was now sleeping in his cot in her old bedroom at the back of the house. She'd taken the main room at the front that used to be their parents' room, which meant that Bobby often heard George overnight more than she did. She was dog-tired, though, and her head spun with the mixture of good food, good company and the good deal she'd struck.

Happy to see George was sleeping peacefully, she crept into her room, closed the door and breathed out a long sigh. Every time she came back to her house it felt smaller and shabbier, although it had been her whole world growing up.

The raid went perfectly. Bobby did his part swiftly and with the minimum of fuss, gaining everyone's respect. Charlie dropped round with their share of the money, a large holdall filled with rolls of notes. It was becoming somewhat of a routine for them. 'There's ten grand in there,' the kingpin robber said. 'Ain't it time you got yerselves a better place?' he added, looking round the small kitchen.

Ruby could see Bobby was riled by this sentence. She put a hand on his shoulder to steady him, and said, 'I've been thinkin' for a while that we need to move up in the world. Little George needs a garden and I want a kitchen I can be proud of.'

Bobby stared at her, hurt written across his face.

'I know, Bobby, I know. It's our childhood home. It's where Mum and Dad brought us up, and loved us, but they're gone now, darlin'. We've got money now, enough to buy a bigger house. It's time to move on,' she said softly.

Charlie looked at Ruby's brother. 'I didn't mean no offence, Bob. I'm sorry, really I am.'

Bobby was looking down at his hands but he nodded.

'There was no offence taken, Charlie. But how do we buy a new place with crooked money?' Ruby got straight to the point. She had no idea how to bypass the rules and regulations when it came to buying property. It was fine to splash their cash buying designer clothes and bags, and a new car for Bobby, but how on earth would they secure a home?

'Leave all that to me,' Charlie murmured. 'Is this place rented?'

'No,' said Ruby, unable to keep the pride out of her voice, 'Grandad Jim bought it lock, stock and barrel. It's ours.'

'Good,' replied Charlie, 'get it on the market and we'll get a crooked accountant to sort the money . . . problem.' With that, the gangster made his excuses and left, leaving Ruby and Bobby in the kitchen.

'I'm sorry, Bobby, but what Charlie said is true. It's time to move up in the world. Don't ya want a garden for George? Don't ya want more space, perhaps a garage for your BMW?' Ruby's voice was wheedling now, persuasive.

Bobby smiled reluctantly. 'I do, Rube, it's just that all my memories of Mum and Dad are 'ere. I'm worried if we leave, we'll be leavin' them behind too.'

Ruby nodded. She understood, but she also knew that memories lived in her heart and not in the stuff of life. They didn't live in things – sofas, tables or curtains; they

166

lived inside themselves, and a change in residence would never alter that.

'They'll always be with us,' she added gently. 'Mum and Dad are always with us. Don't you feel them? I do. I know they're 'ere with us, and they'll come with us wherever we go.' Ruby instantly knew this to be true. She wanted Bobby to feel the same way. He was simpler than her. He didn't go in for big ideas or big thinking, he left all that to his younger sister. She looked over at him and saw the tears gather. Wrapping him in her arms, she held him, feeling his pain, but also knowing Charlie was right. It was time to go.

CHAPTER 20

Ruby took little George with her in his buggy to the local estate agent, who put their home on the market, and within days a reasonable offer was made. Bobby was coming round to the idea that it was time to go, though he still felt the pain of it.

'Where are we goin' to go?' he said the day they rang the estate agent to accept the offer on their home. The pair were just leaving the house to visit Charlie and his wife Maureen.

'Chigwell,' Ruby said, smiling.

'Chigwell? To be nearer to Charlie Beaumont?' Bobby replied, starting the ignition. George was strapped into his child seat in the back.

'Why not?' Ruby said. 'I can think of worse places, and it gets us out of 'ere.' She looked out of the window as the car moved off, seeing the overflowing rubbish bins, the litter drifting down the pavements which needed a good weeding.

'Listen, Rube, you might turn ya nose up, but Star Lane is where we was born and bred, never forget that,' Bobby said harshly.

'Sorry, Bobby, I didn't mean to upset ya. Of course it'll always be our home, but it's OK to want to move on. It's how Charlie got where he is today.'

Bobby grunted a reply.

Ruby smiled to herself. Bobby was unfailingly loyal, and she loved him dearly for it, though she didn't share his nostalgia for the bleak-looking roads and houses. As the car left the urban highways travelling through larger streets with trees and gated houses, Ruby exhaled. She loved the feeling of space, of possibility.

Charlie's wife Maureen had invited them over to the exclusive part of Essex for lunch at their palatial home. Ruby, Bobby and George, wearing their best gear, pulled up on the long driveway, Ruby relishing the crunching sound of the tyres on gravel. Bobby whistled.

In front of them was a large white mansion with a water feature in front of the doorway. There were ornate bushes planted in huge pots outside the front door, which opened as they stepped out of the car.

'Welcome. Charlie's told me so much about you all,' said a petite blonde woman with immaculately groomed hair, wearing a chic Chanel two-piece suit.

'Meet my wife, Maureen, she'll show ya round, get a feel for the place. A drink, Bob?' Charlie gestured for

Bobby to follow him into the drawing room, while Ruby and George followed Maureen in a tour of the home, which was filled with vases of fresh white lilies.

'It's like a palace,' said Ruby dreamily, which made Maureen laugh.

Her accent was as strong a cockney voice as her visitors, made rough from years puffing on her Cartier Pearl Tipped cigarettes.

'You should've seen where I grew up, darlin'. It weren't like this. We had a shared lavvy and two rooms between six of us in the Isle of Dogs. My mum used to 'ave to carry the pram up four flights of stairs to get to our rooms, which were damp all year round and had buckets to catch the leaks when it rained.'

Ruby nodded. She gazed around the immaculate bedrooms, walking on thick pile carpets before heading down to the designer kitchen that backed onto a landscaped garden.

'It's a different world,' Ruby said at last.

Maureen turned to look at her. There was something motherly in her gaze. 'Just imagine, you could 'ave a similar place one day.'

Ruby smiled. *She would have a place like this.*

Maureen nodded as if she knew what the young woman in front of her was thinking. Patting her gently on the arm, she said, 'Why don't I come lookin' at properties with ya?'

'I'd like that, thank you,' Ruby replied.

'It won't be as big as this yet, darlin',' but we'll find you somethin' gorgeous,' Maureen added, smiling.

The two women had taken to each other at once. The only time Maureen's smile had faltered during the tour was when she showed them Michael's room. 'This was my son's. He died very young in an accident . . .'

Ruby didn't know what to say, except, 'I'm so sorry for your loss, Mrs Beaumont,' her heart breaking for this composed and elegant women.

'Call me Maureen, and thank you. It was a long time ago, but somehow you never forget, never.' She smiled sadly back at her.

Feeling a little shaken, Ruby followed Maureen downstairs, wondering how a mother ever got over the death of a child. It didn't seem possible, and yet, at first glance, she'd never have guessed the tragedy that had befallen them.

By the time they got to the dining room, Charlie and Bobby were chatting like old friends, Maureen had recovered herself and was back to being the charming hostess.

The four adults settled down to a lunch of roast chicken, potatoes and an exotic salad made with fruit neither Bobby nor Ruby recognised.

'It's mango!' Maureen laughed. 'Don't tell me you've never tasted mango before?'

Ruby and Bobby shook their heads. George clapped his hands, smearing the sweet, sticky fruit Maureen had given him all over his face as he sat on his big sister's lap, making everyone laugh.

'Well it's time I taught you both a few things, brought you up to speed.' Maureen added, 'Now, eat up, there's tiramisu for dessert.'

She sounds so posh, Ruby thought. At the sight of Ruby and Bobby looking blank again, both Charlie and his wife laughed even harder. Their bemusement was clearly comical, and Ruby realised she had so much to learn, and she couldn't wait to try out all these wonderful new things.

A couple of weeks, and about a hundred house visits later, Maureen found the perfect property for the small family. It was a three-bedroom house with its own large garden, a summerhouse and a garage. Best of all, it was only five minutes away from the Beaumonts.

The first time Ruby walked into the large entrance hall, she noticed the sense of space, the light, so different from their narrow, dark home in Star Lane. She knew straightaway that this was the right place. She looked over at Maureen who started to giggle.

'You've found your home, Ruby,' was all she said.

Ruby walked around each room as if in a daze. She could picture little George, chocolate smeared all over his mouth, toddling around the garden. He was nearly three years old and already trying to chase anything that moved, including birds that tweeted from the trees. Her adorable scamp would have room to run and play. He could have a play house, a swing and a climbing frame for when he was older, and there'd still be plenty of room left over to grow flowers.

Within weeks, the home was theirs. Ruby bought new furniture, ordered new curtains and blinds for each room, and decked the house out like a palace, though her taste was naturally refined, and she had each room painted white with the luxurious furnishings in muted shades. Before she had time to really settle in, Charlie appeared one day with a stranger beside him.

Ruby, a little flustered, ushered them both into her dining room, a white space with a long cherry-wood table and a set of elegantly carved seats.

'I wanted you to meet Marcus Lawrence, an art dealer associate of mine. Marcus only deals with the wealthiest and most exclusive clients.'

He had trendy red glasses, swept-back hair and a tweed jacket over designer jeans and slip-on leather shoes. He looked every inch the London art buyer. She could see him sizing her up the same way, but with a slight air of puzzlement. Ruby was not your average crook. She dressed expensively now that Maureen had taken her up west for a shopping spree in Bond Street. Today she was wearing a coral-coloured dress that fitted her slim figure to perfection, with white slingback heels and beautiful jewellery. She wore her hair long, shining down her back, thick and lustrous, and used only the barest touches of make-up.

'To what do I owe the pleasure?' Ruby waited for Charlie to lead the conversation, sussing out every inch of this wealthy man as she did so.

'Marcus arranges for paintings to be—'

'Requisitioned,' interjected the man.

'Stolen,' finished Charlie. 'He's a high-class dealer who only deals with the super-rich. His clients are some of the richest men – and women – on the planet. He gets them the paintings they want, no matter how.'

Ruby looked over at Charlie. 'So, how can I 'elp?' she said.

'I hope I can rely on your discretion. There is a certain painting a wealthy private collector is interested in,' the dealer said, simply.

'And you want my brother to get it for ya,' Ruby finished, smiling over at Marcus.

'Exactly,' he replied.

'Whatever you do, make your terms specific because Ruby 'ere don't mess about. She'll take whatever you offer and not a penny less,' Charlie smiled, winking at Ruby.

Ruby didn't disagree. She was pleased her reputation as a tough talker carried before her. She wanted them to know that if she didn't approve, then it was a no to the job, and nothing or no one could talk her round.

'If the money's right and the job's sound then I'm happy,' Ruby smiled. 'Would you like a coffee, or somethin' stronger?'

Both men shook their heads. Charlie checked his flash watch. 'Can't stay long, Ruby, I've got things to do. So, what d'ya think?'

The sun streamed into the bright room at that exact moment, making the white lilies in a large vase on the table seem to shimmer.

Ruby took this as a good sign. She nodded and sat down, waiting to hear what the plan was, and, more importantly, what the money was.

'Let's get down to business, shall we?' Ruby said, looking down at her manicured nails, the perfect matching shade of coral.

'I'll cut to the chase. We're all busy people,' Marcus said. 'Twenty K flat fee for the job, assuming nothing goes wrong and you get the painting in question. It's a straightforward break-in. Very nice place in Kensington. The owner just bought a Matisse but he's going to be away in France for the next few months. There's no family, and no staff to complicate matters.'

'And you've got a buyer lined up who can make it worth your while . . . ?' Ruby finished his sentence.

'Yes. All your brother has to do is disable the alarms. We've got others who will go in and do the actual robbery. The picture needs specialist care. Then, of course, he'll have to set the alarms again and get away without being caught. It's a standard system, nothing to trouble your brother too much, I don't think.' Marcus glanced at Charlie. 'Can you do it?'

Ruby looked at Charlie, who gave her a slight nod of his head. She looked back at Marcus. 'Twenty grand to disable the alarms. Yes, Marcus, I think we can do that,' Ruby agreed, shaking both their hands to seal the bond.

'I'll send word, Ruby. Meanwhile, enjoy ya new home. You've got it lookin' nice. My Maureen would approve of the lilies,' Charlie said. The two men left as quickly as they'd arrived.

Ruby watched them go from the lounge window, the sleek cars gliding away down the tree-lined street. Bobby appeared with George in his arms. George held out his chubby little arms to his big sister, and her expression changed instantly to a beaming smile.

'Come 'ere, my darlin'. Come to your big sister Ruby.'

'So, who was that?' Bobby asked as they walked out into the garden. It was a warm summer day. They settled down on the grass under an apple tree, George happily playing with his toy cars on the grass.

'Just an art dealer friend of Charlie's. He's got a job for ya. It's a no-brainer, Bobby. It's no pressure, and we'll make good money,' Ruby said eventually, shading her eyes from the bright sun.

Bobby couldn't hide his expression from her. 'I know this is all great, and we've gone up in the world but was it the right thing to do, Rube?'

It was a question she knew how to answer. Firmly, decisively, Ruby said, 'Yes it was, Bobby. It was the right thing to do, for us and most of all, for little George. He'll go to the best school, 'ave more toys than Hamleys, and he'll 'ave the best life we can give him.'

They both watched as their baby brother collapsed into giggles clutching a stray dandelion, his sweet face looking over at them.

'It's all for him,' Ruby said, love shining out of her emerald green eyes.

CHAPTER 21

'To us,' said Marcus holding up his champagne flute, one that Ruby had purchased from Harrods with the spoils of the painting heist. She'd also paid out a large sum to land-scape the garden, and she, Charlie, Bobby and Marcus were sitting in the summer sunshine, admiring the lush planting on her newly built decking.

Everything had gone to plan, the painting had been stolen and sent abroad to Marcus's contact, and over the months since, Bobby had done several more jobs for Charlie's dodgy dealer. He'd cracked open a jewellery store in the West End and helped with several other robberies. The money had been good, and it was clear Charlie trusted the brother-and-sister team.

Charlie had called another meeting, telling Ruby that this one was a big job. This one could change their lives for ever.

'To Ruby,' said Charlie, winking over at his protégée. It had become clear that this was a winning partnership.

'To all of us, and to my Bobby,' smiled Ruby behind her expensive Lagerfeld shades. She was dressed simply in a chic linen shift, gold sandals and a smattering of jewellery; subtle diamonds in her ears in contrast to an armful of bangles.

Looking round the garden, seeing how far they'd come in such a short time, made Ruby's head spin, though she concentrated hard on appearing serene. 'So, shall we talk, gentlemen?' she said, giving each of them her dazzling smile in turn.

They all looked at the art dealer, who lifted up his Ray-Bans and placed them on top of his chestnut hair, revealing his tanned face. 'I'm delighted with how everything has gone so far, and my clients are also very pleased. I think we all agree that this . . . partnership . . . is one that benefits us all.'

Ruby nodded, though she was alert to every word this man said. Charlie had advised her never to shout, never to get agitated or cross, and instead to listen, to be slow to speak, to threaten using a soft voice and never to show weakness. None of this had been new to Ruby, and her natural manner used all those ways of dealing with people, but she felt shored up, protected by the crime boss's advice.

'Go on,' she murmured, staring directly at Marcus, who smiled a wolf-like grin back at her. She knew he liked her, and she also knew that she wasn't interested. He was too upper class, too privileged to ever understand the path she and Bobby had taken in life. No, she'd shut down any thoughts of attraction to him a long time ago, though Marcus clearly hadn't.

He looked back at her and only her, his deep brown eyes staring into hers, but Ruby was only interested in the job he was proposing. She returned his gaze coolly, with just the right amount of interest, making it clear she was in the mood for business – and only business.

Charlie had noticed Marcus's attraction and he looked amused at how Ruby was handling it, his respect for her growing by the day.

'Go on, I want to enjoy this champagne before the bubbles die,' Bobby said, winking at Ruby. Even though her brother had been reluctant to take the crooked path, he looked better than he ever had. His skills were in demand, and it was a good feeling for him. He was a respected key-man now, the go-to man for safe-breaking, and Ruby could see he walked taller these days.

Their bond, if anything, had grown stronger now that they were in this venture together. Ruby never made a decision without discussing it with him. He might be the kind of bloke who preferred a pint in the pub to a glass of bubbly, but he was her right-hand man, the only person she really trusted, because family was everything to them both.

Just then the baby monitor announced that George was waking up from his afternoon nap. Bobby stood up. 'You carry on, I'll see to him.'

'Thanks, Bobby,' Ruby said gratefully. 'So, gentlemen, let's get down to business.'

Marcus adjusted his glasses and leaned towards her. 'I've got a very wealthy Arab client. He has a vast collection of pieces, many of which the Louvre or the Met would bite his hand off for. He wants two paintings, both Impressionist, both worth a lot of money, and both currently sold to a new private collector who has come late into his cash and doesn't have – how should I say it – the required security . . .'

'And you want us to steal them,' Ruby finished for him, arching her eyebrows. 'We can consider that when we know who this private collector is, where they live and why they don't have the right set-up, oh, and the money, of course. The money has to be right or my Bobby won't do it.'

Marcus smiled but his eyes didn't twinkle. Ruby had ruffled him. His suave charm disappeared instantly, replaced by a serious tone as he leaned in to the circle and, with a low voice, explained the details.

'The private collector I hope we will steal the paintings from inherited a great deal of money from an obscure relative. He lives in South Africa, but one of the first things he did with this new wealth was to buy a huge apartment in Marylebone, and start buying artworks.'

'I see, and so what 'appens to the pictures once they're stolen from him?' Ruby was curious about all aspects of this type of business. Her hunger for knowledge meant she asked questions perhaps others wouldn't. The art world meant nothing to her parents or grandparents. It was an exclusive club that only the most privileged or educated could enjoy. It fascinated Ruby, but only as a means to an end. They could make big money here, or so she hoped.

'Well, in this case, my Arab associate will probably keep them hidden in his underground vaults, far away from the public eye,' Marcus replied.

'Seems a shame though don't it?' Ruby said almost sadly. 'Why would you want to steal somethin' so beautiful in order to hide it?'

Marcus paused for a second. 'Because my clients desire beauty above all things, and they are greedy for it. They're prepared to pay large amounts of money to acquire something that only their eyes will see. That's the worth to them – the knowledge that they, and they alone, have access to these paintings.'

'If we can continue?' Charlie coughed, breaking the spell of Marcus's words. Ruby understood the desire to own beauty, to hide it away, even. It was an interesting insight, and one she stored away in her mind.

She smiled. 'Do carry on.'

'It'll be harder to access the flat without being seen, but once inside there won't be anything to cause you any trouble.' Marcus sounded incredibly relaxed about what he was suggesting; an audacious heist that would make international headlines. These paintings were world-class objects, pictures that were known, and loved. Stealing them would be like robbing the Queen of her crown, almost an act against God.

'How much are these pictures worth?' Ruby said, straight to the point.

'If I'm honest, I negotiated the sale of them myself and it ran into several million pounds. They'll be taken to the London apartment for one night only before they're shipped off to Africa. That's our chance. I'm offering to pay you a vast sum of money to disable the alarm system. Again, I'll get my own contacts to do the actual robbery. I just need a key-man to let them in then lock up again. I'm willing to pay Bobby a cool two hundred K to do just that. Don't forget I have large expenses. Doing this type of job incurs a great deal of cost – and risk.'

Ruby glanced over at Charlie. She knew just what he was thinking. If those paintings cost a few million then she would bet anything that Marcus would be paid that at least to rob them from his own client. He had to offer them more. But was it worth the risk? There was big money at stake – but big repercussions too. There would be a lot of attention on this theft, more than any job they'd done before. If they got caught then they'd be in for a long stretch. Who would look after George if they went to prison?

Ruby sat back. She stared over at the summerhouse, which she'd had repainted and surrounded by beautiful urns spilling over with flowers. She saw what crooked money had bought her so far. She knew there was always a risk, but was this too dangerous?

Charlie sensed her fears. 'Listen, Ruby, I wouldn't put you or your family in unnecessary danger. This job is one hundred per cent, and I'll guarantee that.'

Marcus nodded. 'Ruby, it's easy pickings, just very lucrative pickings. Yes, sure, you don't want to get caught, but none of us do.'

Ruby looked between the two men. She took her time, weighing up the situation. There was more risk for Bobby and, by extension, for her and George. Their fee had to reflect that.

'All right, if we do this job, and I ain't sayin' we will, but if we do it, we want a bigger cut,' she said.

'How much bigger?' Marcus asked.

'Name your price, Ruby,' encouraged Charlie. 'This job will change your life, and your little brother's. You won't ever want for money again.'

It was certainly a persuasive argument.

'Bobby will do it if you pay him half a million pounds. We won't take any less,' Ruby said, feeling her cheeks flush with excitement and terror. She was glad of the sun's glare, as no one would be able to tell.

Charlie nodded discreetly, a gesture she caught out of the corner of her eye. She felt giddy at the sums being discussed, but she knew she had to let Marcus know she wasn't some mug who was glad of the work. Her entire family was at stake – they couldn't mess this up. It was a far cry from her wage at the import office, almost an inconceivable amount of money. Charlie was right. It would change their life for ever.

At that moment, Bobby reappeared, holding George, who was reaching his arms out for her. She stood to take him from Bobby, planting a big kiss on his chubby cheek, and turned to Marcus. 'Do we 'ave a deal?'

Bobby looked over, taking in the tense silence, the look of expectation on Charlie's face, the frown on Marcus's.

'We have a deal, Miss Murphy,' the art dealer said eventually, planting a smile on his face, and coming over to kiss Ruby's cheek. *In another world, perhaps another time, I would fall for your charms, but not now,* thought Ruby to herself as she raised her cheek. She brushed her lips against his fashionable stubble and almost laughed out loud. Five hundred thousand pounds! An absolute fortune.

She raised her glass. 'Cheers. To another successful business arrangement.' She flicked her eyes over to Bobby, who raised his eyebrows, wondering what they were celebrating. He knew enough by now though to judge Ruby's expression and so he stayed silent, picking up his glass and bringing the bubbles to his lips.

'Cheers, 'ere's to business,' Charlie said, 'and I'd better not forget to say, but you're all invited to our villa in Spain. Maureen is most insistent. You won't disappoint her, will ya?'

'To business,' Marcus echoed.

'. . . and pleasure.' Ruby smiled. 'Of course we'd love to join you in Spain.'

She moved off with George, leaving the men to their conversation as the sun shone. She knew that every job they did meant their future was more and more secure.

CHAPTER 22

'Come on, girl, 'ave another glass,' Charlie grinned as he held the bottle of champagne. 'We've got to celebrate another successful job, and the biggest one yet!'

Ruby giggled. The bubbles had already gone to her head. The heist had gone as planned. Bobby had worked his magic, disabling the alarm system and opening the door to the apartment where the paintings were being stored. Within five minutes the two paintings had been cut out of their frames, rolled up and stashed in the bag carried by Bobby's accomplice, one of Marcus's best men.

'And now we can go shoppin' for a villa for you,' Maureen beamed, raising her glass. 'What a shame Bobby couldn't 'ave been 'ere too, but I bet he's enjoyin' doin' the house up while you're away.'

Ruby shook her head. She could hardly believe her luck. They were sitting on one of the balconies of Charlie and Maureen's villa in Spain, the remains of a seafood dinner cooked by their resident chef on the table, as the sun went down. They'd arrived only a few hours earlier but already she felt like she might never want to go home.

The fee had already been siphoned through a crooked accountant contact of Charlie's, who'd run it through various offshore accounts. By 12 p.m. the next day, the money would be clean and polished, and sitting in Ruby's new, legitimate account in the UK, minus the twenty per cent accountancy fee, of course.

'Look, you need somewhere to put that money,' Charlie said, 'and we've come up with the perfect place. This is a very exclusive development, very expensive and no questions asked. I've already 'ad a word with the bloke who owns it, another crook originally from Poplar too, and he's 'appy to take your money. So, tomorrow, that's settled, you and Maureen can chose a holiday home.'

'How can I refuse?' Ruby laughed.

She'd swum in the sea for the first time in her life that afternoon as Maureen built a sandcastle for George on the beach. The next morning, Ruby insisted on heading out to the local village to buy fresh bread for them all to eat for breakfast. She ambled down the hill, enjoying the feeling of the morning sunshine on her skin. She was wearing a white Prada bikini covered by a coral-coloured kaftan. She carried a raffia bag with just her purse and keys. The insects were already buzzing in the palm trees and exotic flowers, and she felt a giddy sense of freedom, one she'd rarely, if ever, felt before. Ruby queued at the small bakery, buying enough bread for the day. She pottered around some of the stalls being set up for market day as it was still early, before heading back to the villa.

'You look so happy, darlin',' Maureen remarked as she walked in to the villa.

Ruby felt it. Seeing George's wonderment at the sight of the sand and the sea had woken something of that feeling in herself too. They spent the morning building new sandcastles while George giggled and shouted, 'My bucket!' They helped him to fill it up, the gentle waves lapping against the shoreline.

Later, Maureen, Ruby and George met with the developer who showed them a smaller but no less luxurious villa only a few moments' walk away.

'It's the last one left,' he said.

Ruby stared at the white walls, the big open windows and the view of the sea below them. She turned to Maureen and said, 'We'll take it. Bobby won't be able to believe his eyes when he sees it.'

The developer nodded and the deal was done. Charlie would handle the purchase.

'Thank you, Maureen, thank you, Charlie, it's beautiful,' Ruby said that evening as they opened a bottle of wine to toast the villa.

'It's what ya deserve,' Charlie said, waving away her thanks.

The phone rang and Maureen rose to answer it.

'Hello, who's that?' she said, then went silent as she listened.

Suddenly, Ruby felt a prickling sensation on the back of her neck. She knew something was wrong.

'Everythin' all right?' Ruby called, but Maureen didn't reply.

Seconds later, Charlie's wife reappeared, looking flustered.

'I'm so sorry, darlin', but I've got to fly back to England. My mum's had a heart attack and I 'ave to be there for her. That was the nurse at the hospital. I hate to be rude, but we've got to go now.'

Ruby jumped up from the table and took Maureen's hands. 'I'll help ya pack, we'll get the first flight out of 'ere—'

'No, darlin', stay 'ere with George. Finish your holiday,' Charlie interjected, taking charge. 'There's no sense in us all goin' back. I'll go make the arrangements.'

Maureen's face was pale.

'Come on, we'll get you packed in no time. I'm sure she'll be fine, she's in the best hands.' Ruby tried to comfort her friend.

An hour later, and the flight had been booked. Goodness knows how Charlie managed to get seats, but he did.

Ruby waved off the Beaumonts, praying they'd get there in time. Maureen had said it didn't look good. She couldn't settle for the rest of the day; Ruby could think of little else apart from Maureen's mother.

The next morning, the phone rang again.

'It's all OK, Ruby. Mum's shaken but it wasn't a big heart attack. Everythin's goin' to be fine. Now, you just enjoy yourself. Charlie's sortin' the villa purchase from 'ere so there's nuthin' for ya to do except relax.'

'I'm so glad, Maureen, I was so worried,' Ruby said, thrilled at the news.

'There's a lovely restaurant right on the seafront we hadn't been to if you're lookin' for a nice place to eat. They do lunches for children too so George will be happy. Listen, enjoy yourself, that's an order from Charlie!' Maureen rang off.

Her friend's words echoing in her ears, Ruby made a decision to go and see this place. It sounded lovely and she knew Maureen would like to think of them eating out there.

She took George down to the beach and they spent a happy morning together. At midday, she went in search of the small restaurant, finding it easily further along the bay. It had curling vines as a canopy and palm trees in ornate pots between the charming tables.

'This looks lovely, George. Hold there, I'll get you out of your buggy,' she said, lifting up her brother and settling him on her lap. It was still early for lunch and Ruby was the only customer. She ordered a *café con leche* and *bocadillo* alongside an ice cream for her brother from the waiter.

Ruby looked particularly elegant that day in a white Chloé dress with matching heeled sandals and a little make-up. Her pale skin seemed to shimmer and her green eyes shone as this luxurious new future rolled out in front of her. Although she worried on the nights Bobby was out doing the jobs, she never felt afraid that there would be consequences. She trusted Charlie, and her own intuition, implicitly, and so far she hadn't lost a night's sleep over the robberies they'd done. The moral side of it was less easy to shake off. Ruby told herself that the businesses they robbed were very wealthy and could afford a few losses here and there. She reasoned to herself that insurance would cover most of them, except the paintings, of course, but, again, they were seriously wealthy people, and theft must go with the territory. No one ever got harmed, no one was ever hurt as they were all done at night when the staff were asleep in their own homes.

Lost in her thoughts as she chatted to little George, she didn't see the two handsome men who had spotted her and made a beeline for the restaurant.

'Isn't he a handsome boy,' said the deep, masculine voice above her.

Ruby jumped.

'I'm so sorry, I didn't mean to scare ya.' The man sounded genuinely sorry. Ruby looked up. Her gaze met the most startling pair of blue eyes she'd ever seen. They belonged to a man about the same age as her, dressed expensively in a crisp white loose shirt and designer jeans. He had a muscular physique, tanned skin, dark blonde hair that he pushed off his face, and a smile that sent a shiver down her spine.

'I was sayin' that I've just told my brother, Alfie 'ere, that I've met the girl I'm goin' to marry but I can see I've been beaten to it,' he grinned again.

Ruby smiled warily but shook her head. He might be attractive but he was a bit too sure of himself. *Too cocky*, she thought. A thought that must've shown on her face.

'Too much?' the man said, and she nodded.

The stranger looked down at her brother. 'I bet your mummy adores you, little man,' he cooed.

Ruby watched him intently. He seemed genuinely interested in George, though she knew that wouldn't last if he was a player like most of the men she'd grown up around.

'Like children, do ya?' she said rather caustically.

The man, whom she noticed was wearing a very expensive Rolex, cocked an eyebrow. 'I do, as it 'appens. I practically brought up my twin brother.'

The remark made the other man laugh. 'My bruvver 'ere thinks he's Mother-bloody-Teresa but I gave him hell, that I will admit.' He looked identical to his brother except his face was somehow harder, more angular.

'I'm Archie, and this is my brother, Alfie. Please excuse my manners, I've been hangin' around with my twin for too long. Can I ask your name?' the handsome stranger said in a softer voice. 'Do you mind if we join you?'

Ruby hesitated. Her first reaction was to say no and carry on with her lunch but something stopped her. He might be a bit cocky but he seemed nice as well, and he was, admittedly, very attractive.

'I'm Ruby,' she said.

'I'm George,' her brother chipped in, making them all smile.

'All right, I suppose we can make room for ya both.'

'Thank you,' Archie said, and his manner seemed to change completely. The cockiness had vanished, and he seemed rather serious, sincere, even.

'So, this is your little one? He's a gorgeous boy.'

Ruby smiled. 'I think so, but no, he's not my child, he's my little brother. My parents died leaving me and my older brother to bring him up. I'm as good as his mum. I love him like one, anyway.'

Archie nodded as if he understood. He leaned in as Alfie ordered drinks. 'I know how that feels. Our mum died when we was young. Our dad brought us up, but I always say it was me that done it.'

Alfie grinned, 'Bruv, you're probably right. Didn't do such a good job though, did ya,' he laughed.

There was an awkward silence as Ruby digested this news. 'I'm sorry to 'ear that, I really am. Life can't 'ave been easy,' she said.

'We didn't go short for nuthin'. We had all the love in the world from Dad,' Archie said. 'Doesn't matter who the kid has love from, as long as it's there.'

Ruby smiled, relaxing into their conversation a little, though she was still wary.

She watched as Archie began to entertain George, pulling faces which delighted him, and pulling coins from his ears.

'My dad used to do that with me,' Ruby said, stirring her coffee and taking a sip.

'I bet you weren't so easily fooled,' smiled Archie, which made Ruby giggle and shake her head.

'You're right, I always knew it was a trick.'

The three of them carried on chatting as the waiters busied about with plates of paella and spaghetti bolognese for George. The little boy smeared the sauce all over his chubby face as he ate greedily, which made them all laugh.

After they'd finished eating and the plates had been cleared, Archie smiled and said, 'Well, we'd best get goin'. It was really nice to meet ya and sorry for disturbin' your lunch. I hope we see each other again soon.' He grinned.

There was something very appealing about him, and it wasn't just his looks. Ruby had noticed during their lunch that he had actually listened to her. He didn't talk over her or interrupt her like the boys around Star Lane did, all puffed up with their own egos. He seemed different.

As he stood up to go, Ruby had the sudden feeling she didn't want him to leave. She looked up and they exchanged a glance, his blue eyes meeting her green ones, and she felt a strange sense of warmth flood her body. She had the strangest feeling, as if she was safe at last.

It would've been natural to feel suspicious, threatened even, by the sudden appearance of this man ingratiating himself into her company, but Ruby just wasn't. The longer she looked back at him, the more potent the spell he was weaving. She couldn't explain why.

Eventually, she cleared her throat. 'It was nice to meet ya . . . both. Thank you for the food and for entertaining my brother,' she said as Archie picked up the cheque and waved off her attempts to pay.

Alfie had already left the table leaving the pair of them to it, and was smoking a cigarette on the beach.

'Listen, let me take ya for lunch again. I've got a few other tricks I haven't shown George and I know he'll like them. What d'ya say, Ruby?'

She shivered. He said her name in a way that was almost tender.

She blushed, hoping he couldn't read her thoughts, and for a moment couldn't think what to say.

'All right, but just lunch. I'm not lookin' for a boyfriend.' Her voice sounded weak even to her.

'Understood, all above board, I promise ya.'

Ruby found that she still couldn't look away from Archie as they exchanged numbers. His blue eyes seemed to strip her bare, leaving her torn between the desire to run away from him, and the opposite – the desire to get very much closer indeed.

The sound of the telephone echoing through the large villa woke Ruby up from her reverie. She was stretched out on a sun lounger while George played happily beside her, when she leapt up and made a run to catch the call. 'Ruby speakin'. Oh, Maureen, it's you. How are ya? How's your mum?'

The voice at the other end of the phone broke down.

'Oh my God, I'm so sorry, Maureen that's tragic. What can I do to help ya?' Ruby said, holding the receiver to her ear. Her friend's mother had died suddenly after a second, fatal, heart attack. 'Do you want me to come back? I can help with arrangements. You'll need a friend there . . .' Tears had sprung to Ruby's eyes. It reminded her of her mum's last hours and how it all happened so quickly in the end.

'No, darlin'. That's very kind of ya but you stay there,' Maureen sniffed. 'I'll be all right, I promise. I don't want ya to spoil your holiday.'

Reluctantly, Ruby agreed to stay, but the day was soured and she struggled with the echo of her own tragic losses, and worry for her friend.

'Come on, George, let's go and get ice cream. We 'ave to find a way to cheer ourselves up.'

Her tear-stained face hidden by designer sunglasses, Ruby headed out with George. It was late morning and the shops were already starting to shut for the long afternoon siesta when suddenly, a familiar, handsome face appeared.

'Ruby?' Archie said, a slow smile spreading across his face as he recognised her.

She wasn't sure why but she gasped, then felt utterly foolish.

'Everythin' OK?' He seemed to sense her distress.

She tried to reply but suddenly felt tears welling up. She was going to blub and make even more of a fool of herself.

'You're not OK, are ya? What's happened?' His voice was gentle. He was a virtual stranger yet he seemed to care. He took her elbow and steered her towards the café where Alfie was sitting.

'Hello, darlin', good to see ya . . .' Alfie's voice trailed off as he caught Archie's expression.

'Can we 'elp ya?' Alfie added.

Ruby calmed her breathing and felt the tears pass. The strange thing was that she didn't feel stupid. She could see both men were actually concerned.

Just then George started to wiggle in his buggy, making it clear he wanted to get out. Without a word, Archie leaned over, unstrapped him and put him on his knee, as naturally as if he was the little boy's own father.

Alfie laughed his throaty, tobacco laugh. 'Don't get too comfortable, bruv, or you'll be next.'

Archie looked scornfully at his twin. 'And I'd count myself lucky. Family is everythin', you know that. Now, sit down, Ruby, and tell us what's happened.'

Ruby did as she was told. She sat down and started to speak. Somehow she found herself telling them about Cathy's death, how Maureen's mum had brought back painful memories, and how sad she was not to be able to help her friend.

Neither Archie nor Alfie said a word until she stopped talking. They weren't like other men, butting in, taking over the conversation. They both just listened.

When she'd finished Archie nodded. 'D'ya want me to get you a flight home? I can do that, no problem.'

Ruby caught sight of that watch again, the one which cost tens of thousands of pounds and wondered, not for the first time, who this man really was.

She shook her head. 'We fly back in a week, honestly it's fine. Maureen said to stay and I know she'd be heart-broken if she thought she'd ended our holiday.'

'All right. Let me buy ya lunch, then I'll run ya home. If you want I can make a call and get that flight, if ya change your mind.'

'Oi, waiter, menus, *por favor*.' Alfie's terrible grasp of the Spanish language made Ruby giggle, and they all burst out laughing. George grinned, happy to see his sister's good cheer.

'How would you like another ice cream, eh?' Archie grinned down at the little boy who commanded Ruby's heart. She sat back in her chair, watching the two men. She saw straightaway that Archie was the more refined of the brothers. Alfie was harder, rougher, even. He had a tattoo poking out from his shirt sleeve and he chain-smoked fags. Archie was better groomed. He looked calmer, more in control than Alfie, who had a wildness about him that she sensed.

They ate lunch, Ruby learning more about their dad Lloyd, who brought them up.

'Mum died when we was six, we never really knew her. I only know her face from photos,' Archie said sipping from his cold bottle of beer.

'Dad did everythin' for us, everythin',' Alfie added, making Archie nod in agreement.

'He must be a very special person. It must take some-thin' to bring up two young boys like he did. My Grandad Jim brought up my dad Louie by himself. His wife, who I'm named after, died givin' birth to him. Times were hard but he refused to give up my dad,' Ruby said.

'He sounds pretty special too,' Archie smiled.

Was it her or did her heart race as he looked at her?

'I really must go,' she stammered, getting up too fast and almost knocking their beers over.

''Ave we offended ya?' Alfie said gruffly.

'No, not at all, I just 'ave to go now,' Ruby said.

Archie stood up. 'Wait 'ere. I'll get the car. I'll be two minutes.'

'No, really, it's no trouble to walk . . .' Ruby's voice trailed off as she saw Archie's determination. He strode off, leaving her alone with Alfie who coughed nervously and lit another fag.

'I 'ope ya feel better,' he said awkwardly as a brand new Porsche stopped at the roadside. ''Ere's your ride,' he said, and Ruby was left with no choice but to get into the car. Archie was already packing in the buggy while George opened his arms to be lifted up to sit with Ruby in the front seat.

'It'll only take a minute, we're close by. George'll be fine,' she said.

They arrived at the villa gates. 'Drop me 'ere, thanks Archie,' Ruby said, and she meant it.

'It's no trouble. Look, if ya need anythin', ya call me. If I don't hear from ya then I'll be 'ere in a week to take you and George to the airport.'

Ruby tried to tell him they could call a cab but he waved away her words. 'I want to 'elp ya. I don't expect nuthin' in return, just your company for the journey,' he said sweetly.

She stood and watched as the Porsche drove away wondering how on earth she'd managed to meet a man who, for all the world, appeared to be a gentleman.

You can't go out with him though, Ruby, she thought to herself, *because you're a crook and you can't be with someone straight, however lovely.* The realisation made her sad, but it was a fact. She couldn't bring a 'normal' into her life, it was too much of a risk, there was too much at stake and he'd never understand her lifestyle. She tried to put him from her mind, hard as it was, yet those blue eyes that seemed to have *seen* her, seen who she really was under the designer clothes and flash sunglasses, just kept creeping back.

CHAPTER 23

She heard him before she saw him. The purr of the car's engine signalled his arrival, exactly when he said he'd be there. As the week had progressed, and she'd heard nothing more from Archie, she'd decided that despite his sincerity, it was probably the last she'd see of him. Men always made promises, but did they keep them?

She'd managed to put his good looks out of her mind, concentrating on spending time with George and enjoying what was left of their holiday, though she was glad to be returning so she could support Maureen and attend her mother's funeral.

She'd been on the point of calling a cab to get to the airport when the Porsche arrived. As Archie stepped out, he smiled and the sight of him, so gentle, so like her own dad in many ways, made her heart leap inside her. *Perhaps some men do mean what they say?* she thought as she watched him.

'Hello Ruby, I made it,' Archie said, opening his car door for her. He smiled as if he knew she'd suspected he wouldn't show up. 'I put a car seat in the back for George. Hope that's OK?' he said, making Ruby blush as she nodded her head. His thoughtfulness had caught her off-guard.

'Thank you,' was all Ruby could say. This man seemed to know what she was thinking even as she thought it.

They arrived at the airport early and it was then that Archie turned to Ruby as they sat in the car.

'Listen, I know I come across as a bit of a ladies' man at times, I overdo it, but I mean it when I say that I like ya, Ruby, and I want to call on ya when we get back to England.'

Ruby sighed even as a small thrill of pleasure sounded through her. 'Archie, look, I can't be with ya. Our lives are . . . well, it's hard to explain, but they're too different . . .'

She was surprised to see Archie smile.

'Are they? I don't think so, Ruby Murphy . . .'

'How did ya know my name?' she felt startled. Was he some kind of stalker?

Her expression made Archie laugh out loud. 'I'm not a stalker, if that's what you're thinkin'. Listen, I know Charlie Beaumont. I know that's his villa I took ya to the other day. I was even hopin' to put some work your bruvver's way when we get back. In fact, I'd already had a word with Charlie before meetin' ya. It didn't take much to work out who you were.'

Ruby was taken aback, but only momentarily. 'So who are you?' she said simply.

'My dad is Lloyd Willson. He's a blagger. You know what one of those is, don't ya?'

Ruby nodded. They looked at each other, both revealed who they were, both part of a dangerous criminal underworld.

'Go on,' added Ruby.

Archie shrugged. 'It ain't an unusual story. Dad was a blagger in London. He pulled off some big jobs, high profile ones, if ya know what I mean and he did time for it. That's where he met Charlie, in prison. We were grown up by then but it was hard with Dad bein' put away.'

'And there I was thinkin' you was straight!' Ruby said, and they both started to laugh.

Archie took Ruby's hand and held it to his lips. He kissed it so lightly she barely felt it but it sent a shiver down her back. He didn't treat her like all the other blokes she'd known. He talked to her as an equal. He didn't look at her as some dolly bird to shag and then boast about. He treated her like a human being, and it was a heady feeling.

'I'll call on ya when you get home. Until then, Ruby Murphy . . .'

'All right. Until then, Archie Willson . . .'

As Ruby boarded the flight, carrying little George, she couldn't stop a smile spreading across her face.

The flight landed on time at Stansted Airport. Even though she'd enjoyed being away, she was relieved to be back on home soil. Maureen's Merc drew up silently in the VIP parking bay. Both women were dressed entirely in black.

'I'm so sorry. How are ya?' Ruby said, hugging the older woman, breathing in her expensive perfume.

'Don't you worry about me. Look, Ruby, I'm sorry but we went ahead with the funeral. I didn't want any fuss, just me and Charlie and a few friends. I didn't want ya to come back from your trip and 'ave to go to a funeral. You've been to far too many.'

'As 'ave you,' Ruby replied, tears in her eyes.

'I took the liberty of ordering flowers in your, Bobby's and George's names from the same place as your mum had for her funeral. She died quickly, and she didn't feel any pain, so I'm grateful for that at least.'

'That was thoughtful of ya. I'm so sorry I wasn't there though.' Ruby sat in the front passenger seat as Maureen drove them home, little George already snoozing in the back.

'Don't worry, darlin', I told ya to stay. Is the villa sorted?' Maureen asked.

'It is,' Ruby replied. Charlie had phoned her the day before to say he'd put her cash deposit down and it should be hers within weeks.

There was a slight pause in the conversation, then Maureen spoke. 'A little bird tells me you met a certain Archie Willson?' Maureen glanced quickly over at Ruby, who found herself blushing.

'How did you know that?' she burst out indignantly, making Maureen laugh.

'You crack me up, Ruby. One of our friends saw you and Archie havin' lunch. I'm told Alfie was there too, but it wasn't him who was leanin' in to talk to ya . . . He's a very attractive boy . . .'

'You know him? Of course you do. He said his dad Lloyd had done time with Charlie,' Ruby said. 'But I'm not goin' out with him. I ain't seein' anyone while I've got baby George to bring up.'

'Oh well, that's a shame . . . It won't be long before he's snapped up, girl. I say go for it.' Maureen added pointedly, 'His father Lloyd is a big-time villain. Did he tell you that?'

'He did,' said Ruby. 'He also told me about his dad bringing up him and Alfie after their mum died.'

Maureen nodded. 'It was tragic, she was so young. Breast cancer. It takes the best of 'em. Charlie will tell you more about him. He'll fill you in. Archie's a catch so mind ya don't lose him before some other woman bats her eyelashes in his direction.'

Ruby changed the subject but thought about the conversation all the way home. Charlie was waiting for them, announcing he'd booked a table at their favourite restaurant. Over a meal of tapas and Spanish wine, the conversation turned to the Willson twins.

'Oh yeah, I know their father, Lloyd, all right. He was doin' time for a big job, robbed a well-known bank and stole hundreds of thousands,' Charlie started to say.

'That's not exactly the best recommendation for a boyfriend!' Ruby laughed but she looked worried.

'Listen, girl, it's better he comes from our world. A straight goer ain't goin' to fit in. His dad is one hundred per cent. He's the real deal. He's a gent, and he's got ambition, if you know what I mean. I'm sure his sons are the same. He did right by them when their mother died and he's earned our respect for bringin' them up.

'Listen, Ruby, Archie's got money and he's goin' places – in the underworld.' Charlie took hold of Ruby's hand and looked into her eyes. 'But what do you think of him?'

Ruby blushed – it felt like she was always blushing these days.

'I liked him,' she said simply.

'Well then, darlin', it's about time you got yourself a boyfriend and had a little fun. Life ain't just deals and George, though they're important. You've got to live a little too.'

Maureen nodded over at her husband. She'd clearly briefed him to say the right things. 'It's true, Ruby. We all want ya to be 'appy. You deserve some love. You've been through so much. Why don't ya just meet him and enjoy his company? It can't do any harm, can it?'

Ruby blinked. Why did she suddenly feel tearful? The thought of being looked after, being treated and taken out seemed overwhelmingly appealing. She considered herself an independent woman. She didn't need a man to complete her – yet she couldn't deny there was something about Archie, something that made her feel safe and excited at the same time.

CHAPTER 24

Perhaps it was that conversation, over good food with beloved friends, that made her agree to Archie coming to dinner. She'd regretted letting him have her number because he'd rung her every evening, making her laugh, drawing her ever closer to him. She'd also regretted saying he could come over because thinking of him made her feel so flustered and jittery. She wanted control in her life after so much had gone wrong, but these feelings for Archie were the total opposite of that. He made her feel like abandoning everything she'd worked for and sinking into his arms instead. It was a feeling she didn't trust at all.

He arrived straight from the airport, carrying a huge bunch of white lilies and a smile as wide as the open sea. Stepping out of his shiny red Porsche, his face lit up as soon as he saw Ruby in the doorway. She'd dressed carefully for the meal in a black silk shift, a single diamond necklace and low heels. She wore her hair down as always, but had dressed up her make-up, wearing startling scarlet red lipstick.

As Archie walked up her driveway, her heart swooped down to her belly, and every nerve ending in her body felt alive. She knew herself as a woman who regularly faced up to some of the underworld's most devious, hardened crooks yet she felt at a loss in front of this man.

She had spent hours cooking a roast dinner with all the trimmings, knowing she wanted to impress him but at the same time warning herself to keep her cool. It was all very confusing, but it was too late now. He was here – and she had to get on with it.

'Delicious, Ruby, thank you,' Archie said as they ate.

Bobby smiled between the two of them. George made happy noises as he chewed on a Yorkshire pudding. As soon as he'd finished eating, Bobby got up and, picking up George, announced he was going out for a walk.

'I think that's a subtle hint,' Archie laughed, making Ruby giggle.

'Very subtle,' she agreed, raising an eyebrow.

They heard the door shut and there was suddenly silence in the house. It wasn't an uncomfortable silence, more an expectant one.

Archie got up off his chair and moved round to Ruby's side of the table. He picked up her hand and held it as if it were a crystal glass, precious and fragile.

He raised it to his lips and planted the softest kiss on her skin. Ruby shivered, feeling flustered and out of her depth.

Archie seemed to sense Ruby's discomfort. He slowly lowered her hand and returned to his chair, giving her the space she needed.

His voice was huskier when he spoke. 'When your bruvver gets back, I want to speak to him about puttin' work his way.'

'Oh we're back to business, are we?' Ruby's eyebrow was arched this time. She started to collect up the plates but Archie stopped her.

'I'll do this, you sit and relax. Sorry, I'll talk business with Bobby later,' he called now from the kitchen where he began stacking the dishwasher.

'Actually, it's me ya need to speak to when it comes to makin' a deal,' Ruby said in the doorway. 'Bobby does the work, I make the deals, that's the arrangement.'

Archie stopped what he was doing and looked back at her. She could tell he was impressed.

'You are most definitely not just a pretty face,' he murmured, stepping towards her. The air seemed to still as Ruby looked into his eyes, and he got closer and closer. Archie put up his hand to stroke her face.

The door opened and Bobby walked in with George toddling beside him.

'Oh, sorry. Didn't mean to interrupt,' he said sheepishly.

Quick as a flame igniting, Archie dropped his hand and stepped back.

Ruby exhaled. Bobby looked between the pair of them as if there was electricity in the room.

'You weren't interruptin',' Ruby stammered, making Archie smile.

'I was just tellin' Ruby I want to put some work your way but she tells me I make the deals with her,' he said.

Bobby grinned. 'Yes, it's Ruby who does the deals. That's who the mastermind is.'

'There's a safe in a pub not far from 'ere. I want it emptied, and I've been told your brother Bobby is the man for the job.'

Ruby nodded.

'Can ya do it?'

'That all depends . . . if the price is right, and I check it out first,' Ruby murmured. 'Isn't that right, Bobby?'

'My Ruby likes to make sure everythin' is kosher first. She won't agree to a deal unless she can check it out first,' he agreed.

Archie nodded.

'All right. I'll give ya the address. So what are your terms?' He directed this to Ruby.

'Half of whatever's in that safe,' she said, crossing her arms and staring straight back at him.

Archie rubbed his chin. He looked over at her. 'It's a deal, Ruby Murphy. How could I refuse ya?'

He held his hand out, this time to shake. She took it, feeling his skin against hers and she couldn't help herself, she shivered. If Archie noticed he didn't say anything. Instead, almost as an afterthought, he put his hands in his jacket pocket and drew out a distinctive blue Tiffany box.

'For you,' he winked, giving it to her and walking off to his car before Ruby could answer. Once the low throaty hum of the car had vanished, she opened it slowly. Inside was a bracelet strung with a neat row of diamonds. She held it, mesmerised, as the rocks glittered in the sunlight. Was this a promise of things to come?

CHAPTER 25

'You know Archie wants you, don't ya?' Bobby said as they sipped their drinks in the Bermondsey pub they were casing.

Before Ruby could answer, the landlord, a man in his forties who was propping up the bar, laughed loudly. Heads turned to track the sound.

Ruby fidgeted. 'What do you think of him? Would it be terrible if I did go out with him?'

Bobby took a swig of his pint.

'Listen, Rube, I want ya to be happy. He seems a diamond geezer, and he's respected by Charlie. At the end of the day, it's your choice, sis.'

It was Ruby's turn to sip her white wine.

She looked around. 'We've got a job to do, and right now that's more important than whether I fall for Archie Willson,' she said, batting his words away.

Bobby arched his brow. 'Not avoiding the subject, are we? All right, Rube. Let's 'ave a proper look at this place.'

'You know this job is so that Archie can see if he can trust us. We've not done a pub break-in for ages, but soon we'll be doin' bigger jobs than ever before. Charlie wants us to go big-time now he knows we do what we say we'll do,' Ruby said, her manner now businesslike.

Bobby nodded.

'As your reputation grows, we're going to have to stop casing joints ourselves. It won't be good to be seen somewhere that gets done over a few days later. People will put two and two together—'

'And make four,' finished Bobby.

Ruby had ordered the drinks at the bar, and the landlord had openly eyed her up. They were becoming too visible, their reputation growing too steadily in the underworld, to risk casing joints for much longer.

'Let's do this and get home. George is only in nursery for the afternoon so we don't 'ave loads of time. I'll pop to the ladies' and see if I can get an idea of the layout,' Ruby said.

'Be careful, Rube,' said Bobby amiably, keeping one eye on her as she walked off to the toilets.

Ruby was in luck. The ladies' was directly opposite a door that, when opened, led upstairs to the private flat above the pub.

Looking over her shoulder to reassure herself she couldn't be seen, she slipped through the door and walked as slowly and quietly as she could up each step. Pausing at the top, she waited for a moment. There was no sound from any of the rooms. Ruby peered round the doorway into the first room, which seemed to be the landlord's bedroom. It was messy with men's clothes hung over the end of the bed, and a stale smell of sweat. *Needs an airing*, she thought, wrinkling her nose.

On she crept, to the next room, which was an even messier bathroom. It was obvious the landlord lived alone. Towels were strewn over the side of the bath and there was a line of scum around its rim; tooth-paste was splattered over the sink. She moved on again. This time, she found her target. The door creaked as it opened. *Better warn Bobby*, she thought. The door led to a small office with a desk piled high with papers, shelves which had folders and files placed in a higgledy-piggledy mess on top, and a large safe in the corner. *Bingo!* Ruby smiled to herself. The noise from a door flying open downstairs made Ruby freeze. She could hear someone on the stairs. She edged behind the door and waited.

There was another creak and the sound of distant foot-steps, but they were now walking away. Ruby breathed out. *Time to get out of here.* She tiptoed to the staircase. She couldn't see if anyone was at the bottom as it wound round to reach the upper floor. She listened again, strain-ing to hear but there was nothing to alert her and so she started to descend. Just as she pushed open the door at the bottom that led out to the pub, she was stopped by the landlord.

'And where are you goin', young lady?' he drawled, grinning at her like a hunter who'd found a rabbit in his trap.

Ruby had to think fast.

'Oh, silly me,' she giggled. 'I was lookin' for the ladies'. I'm so sorry, I must've taken the wrong door.' Was it convincing enough? If the landlord guessed she'd been upstairs then the whole operation might be blown. He'd be suspicious and could even move the cash out to somewhere more secure. She had to pull this off. Their first job for Archie had to go off without a hitch.

He looked her up and down as if she was something delicious to eat. Ruby pouted. 'Do you know where I need to go?' She made her eyes as wide as possible, her face as blank as a Barbie doll.

'Course I do, darlin', you're in my pub,' he smarmed. Ruby knew instantly she'd fooled him. He leaned against the door-frame almost trapping her where she stood. She moved quickly, turning her body sideways and extracting herself from his presence. 'Oh, there it is. I am daft. I'm so sorry to bother ya,' she twittered, moving away and throwing him a smile as she went. 'Thank you.'

Once inside the ladies', Ruby leaned against the sink, staring into the mirror and exhaled slowly. 'That was close, Ruby Murphy,' she muttered to the young woman who stared back at her.

'You waitin', love?' a woman barely out of her teens said as the door banged open.

'No, sorry, just leavin',' Ruby replied, and pulling her gaze away from the mirror, she walked out and over to Bobby, who by now was looking worried.

'Rube, where the hell 'ave ya been?' he hissed.

'Sorry, Bobby. I didn't mean to worry you. I did manage to get upstairs, though,' she smiled, enjoying Bobby's reaction.

His face changed from worry to amusement. 'Trust you, Rube. Always up for takin' a risk.'

'Bloody hell, I almost didn't get out of that one!' Bobby panted when he marched in through the front door, heading straight to where he knew Ruby would be waiting.

It was the early hours of the morning, the sky still black as coal, when Bobby arrived back from raiding the safe for Archie.

'What is it? Are you all right?' Ruby stood up abruptly, almost spilling her cold coffee. Minutes earlier she had been yawning with exhaustion but now she was wide awake, senses on high alert.

Her brother threw his black holdall onto the elegant dining table, ripping off his black jacket and gloves.

'I'm fine, Rube. Didn't mean to startle ya, but there was a . . . hitch . . .'

'Was it Archie? Did he do us over? Oh my God, 'ave I been stupid and let him charm his way in?' She was wild-eyed now, the tiredness suddenly dropping on her like a great weight.

'Nah, nuthin' like that, at least I don't think so. Look, if Charlie says Archie is kosher then he's kosher,' Bobby answered, dragging his hands through his dishevelled hair.

'So, what went wrong, then?' Ruby asked, sitting down again.

'The bloke was still in there!'

'You what? But Archie said he'd be out all night.' Ruby frowned.

Bobby, seeing the expression on her face, shook his head. 'It ain't what you're thinkin'. I don't think Archie mugged us off. I think the bloke who owns the pub probably went out but pulled a bird and came home early.'

'Oh Christ,' Ruby whispered, feeling the sudden urge to laugh.

Bobby saw the amusement she tried to hide, and continued, 'As I crept up the stairs, keepin' my feet right on the edge of each step to stop them creakin', I could 'ear him. He was screwin' her'

Ruby looked down at her manicured nails, currently painted bright red.

'So they were . . . screwin' . . . in his bed. Go on,' Ruby said with distaste. She hated the casual way men talked about sex, as something funny or dirty. She might still be a virgin but she had an inkling from the love that her parents always showed each other, and the love Grandad Jim felt for Granny Ruby all those years after her death, that it could be something much more special, more meaningful, than mere 'screwing'.

'I carried on goin' up the stairs, what else could I do? You'd told me which door was the one for the office. The only tricky part was gettin' past the bedroom door, which was open! I had to watch them at it till there was a moment I could get past and into the office.' Bobby snorted now with hilarity. 'God, I don't think I'll ever forget the sight of his arse goin' up and down!'

'But did you get the money?' Ruby interrupted him.

Bobby wiped his eyes and nodded. 'All of it. The landlord won't realise until he checks it for the wages, and then all hell will break loose!'

'Good. So our side of the bargain was kept. Now we wait and see what Archie has to say for himself.' Her eyes narrowed. Bobby hadn't come that close to being caught in a long time. If there was any whiff of Archie lying to them, she'd know.

When Archie arrived, Ruby gave him a frosty greeting, making the gangster arch his eyebrows in response.

''Ave I upset ya, Ruby?' he said as they walked into her sun-filled kitchen. Even though it was early autumn, the light flooded the pleasant space. Bobby sat at the table with little George, watching as Ruby dealt with Archie.

'Bobby was almost caught last night. Your information was wrong. Bobby got inside the pub to find the landlord still in there. He tells me we can trust you but if you were muggin' us off . . .'

Archie looked stunned. 'What d'ya mean? I had it on good authority he was out with the boys last night.'

Ruby stood facing the man she had been in danger of falling for, her long red nails on her hips, eyes flashing with anger.

She studied his face. His puzzlement looked genuine.

'My Bobby had to creep into the office while the landlord was . . . *busy* . . . with a girl he'd pulled.'

'Bloody hell,' exclaimed Archie, whistling through his teeth. 'Jesus Christ, what 'appened Bob?'

'Mind your language, please, in front of my George,' Ruby said, her voice thawing just a little.

'Sorry, Ruby. Bobby, I 'ave to know what 'appened. Did you get out OK? Were ya seen? I'll make this right, I promise ya.'

'It's fine, Archie, me and your mate disabled the alarm. He stayed outside to keep watch while I went in. It was all goin' swimmingly when I 'eard a noise.' Bobby grinned. 'The geezer was gruntin'. I thought, "Oi, oi, what's this?" and then I heard a woman goin', "Oh, oh, oh" . . .'

Archie looked at Bobby's face, which was alight with humour, and over at Ruby's stony expression, her arms now folded, and burst into laughter.

'Sorry, Ruby, I can't 'elp it. Bobby, mate, you're a diamond.'

Ruby sighed. She was still angry at Archie so she refused to smile at him, but she had to admit, they'd still pulled off the robbery. Bobby's holdall was stuffed with cash, which she'd counted and halved, as per their agreement.

'The cash is all there,' she said spikily. 'Fifty-fifty split as we agreed.'

Archie smiled over at her. 'Nah, don't worry, you keep it all. It sounds like Bobby needed danger money for that job!' At which point both men doubled up with laughter.

'I never did it for the money, Ruby,' Archie said. 'All I wanted was to hear that geezer screamin', and he will be when he realises. I wanted revenge, not cash. He did my dad over years ago, before he knew what was what, and I've waited a long time to mug him off.'

Ruby stared at him. She didn't judge him. She knew how she'd felt when Freddie Harris mugged them off, and knew that she was just as capable of wreaking revenge, though she wished then and there she'd never have to.

The next morning Bobby whistled a jaunty tune as George spooned his Weetabix into his mouth, making happy hungry noises as he ate. Ruby smiled over at them. Today, the world felt good. They'd had a lucrative night, and her brother had got back safe and sound. There was plenty to be grateful for.

The sound of the letterbox being opened heralded the arrival of the postman. There was a thud as the post hit the carpet.

'I'll get that,' Ruby said, carrying her cup of coffee to the front door. There was an array of bills, but one letter stood out. It was scrawled with her name, the handwriting like that of a child's.

She frowned. *Who could this be?*

She opened it, scanning the single page and saw her friend's name at the end. 'Oh Sarah, what's 'appened now?' she muttered to herself, knowing this couldn't be good news.

Ruby read the lines as best she could, though the words were barely legible. Sarah was banged up in Holloway Prison – just like her mother had been so often over the years. She'd got six months for shoplifting and needed a tracksuit and essential supplies. Seemed her mum and friends couldn't be relied on, so could Ruby help?

Inside the envelope was a VO, a Visiting Order, and so, without hesitation, Ruby rang the number and booked her visit.

Within a week, she was standing in the queue, grateful for her decision to leave George with Maureen for the day as she watched the line of families waiting to see loved ones. The woman in front of her was a downtrodden looking lady with scruffy clothes that could do with a clean, and two young children who were asking how much longer they had to wait before seeing their mum. Ruby felt desperately sorry for them. She was dressed modestly, though in stark contrast to the other visitors, in beautiful clothes, all black and without flashy labels showing, but worth more than these people might ever spend on themselves in a lifetime. Never had she seen so starkly how far she'd come – and how high the stakes were. Her life was a risky one. Her deals were getting larger and larger, with more and more money changing hands. She shivered, hating the austere gloom of the place.

'Takes ages to get in, babe, and the way they search us, you'd think we was all criminals,' the woman turned and said to her.

Ruby laughed but it felt hollow. This was the distinctly unglamorous side to their business – the risk of ending up in here. The thought made her sweat under her expensive clothing.

'You look a bit posh to be in 'ere,' the woman said, her grandchildren both hanging off her worn cardigan.

Ruby didn't reply. She felt rattled and, in truth, was dreading seeing her friend brought so low.

Once she'd been searched, Ruby was directed to a table. She sat down and waited. Within minutes, Sarah was led into the room. Her face lit up at the sight of her childhood friend. Ruby, in turn, had to hide her shock at the sight of her. Her hair was greasy, her skin grey and she looked skinnier than Ruby remembered.

'I'll get us some drinks,' Ruby offered, returning with two polystyrene cups with coffee for herself and hot chocolate for Sarah. Ruby sat silently sipping the vile liquid as her friend talked.

'I really thought he was a good 'un. Typical me to meet the dodgiest guy around then believe all his lies. He screwed me right over, Rube. He told me I could make some easy cash for us both, and like the silly cow I am, I believed him.

'He got me nickin' clothes to order, nice stuff from the big sports store up town. He wouldn't give me no brown until I did the work.'

'Don't tell me you've got into that mucky drug stuff. What's goin' on? You never did anythin' worse than 'ave a drink, and now this bloke has got you into heroin!' hissed Ruby. She was furious at her mate for sinking so low.

'Oh don't worry, I can't get hold of the stuff in 'ere, so I been cluckin' badly. I can get benzos but they don't really do the trick.'

'Oh Sarah . . .' Ruby now felt just sadness for her friend. She'd never really had a break in life.

'It ain't my fault. I just get in with the wrong people,' Sarah ended, sniffing and looking around the room. 'It's not too bad in 'ere. They let me 'ave my fags, and a few of the girls are OK . . .' Her voice trailed off. 'Don't forget me Ruby, will ya?' she pleaded, fidgeting with her sleeve.

Ruby smiled tenderly at the girl she'd known. *There but for the grace of God*, thought Ruby, knowing her life could so easily have gone the same way.

'I'll never forget my roots. I'm 'ere for you. I know your family ain't good to you, but you've got me, at least. When you get out we'll go and 'ave pie 'n' mash again. D'ya remember how we enjoyed that?'

Sarah nodded, her eyes filled with tears now.

By the end of the visiting time, Ruby waved her friend off, impatient to be out of that forbidding place. Stepping outside at last, she felt the sun on her face, the air on her skin, relief flooding her, but there was something else she realised now, a dark shadow that had slipped in beside her, warning her. Ruby shivered as she walked to her car despite the sun's warmth.

CHAPTER 26

'Say that again, Bobby. You did what?' Ruby glared at her brother, who was refusing to meet her fierce gaze.

'Rube, I'm sure no harm will come from doin' a job for Freddie . . .' he said weakly, still unable to look her in the eye.

'Bobby, how could you even say to him I'd consider it? I swore we'd never work for that weasel Freddie Harris ever again,' Ruby spat. She was furious with Bobby for giving Freddie the time of day, let alone asking her to speak to him about doing a job.

'Look, Rube, you know how it is. We had a few beers and Freddie came over and said he'd offer us one hundred grand to do a job. He told me it's a hundred per cent. He goes out with the girl in the office and she says there'll be three hundred grand kept in the safe for one night only. The company specialises in rare diamonds, have done a big deal, and it's our opportunity—'

'The only opportunity that Freddie would offer us is doin' his dirty work for him,' Ruby cut in. 'I don't trust him, Bobby, you know that. I don't like him either. He's only out for himself, and I thought we'd left him and his dodgy deals behind. You're askin' me to deal with the least trustworthy crook in London, one who's mugged us off before.'

'Just hear him out, Rube. It's big money if we can pull it off.'

Ruby gritted her teeth and nodded.

She could just picture Freddie swaggering over to Bobby in the pub after watching his beloved Hammers at their home ground. Her brother, who had been named after Bobby Moore, the captain of the England World Cup winning squad and a West Ham player, would've been celebrating their win when the weasel sidled up to him. In her mind's eye, she could see Freddie buying Bobby a pint, getting chummy with him, waiting until his guard was down to strike. Her musings were interrupted by a knock on the door. 'I'm guessin' that'll be Freddie,' Ruby said archly as Bobby went to answer the door.

She was right.

'Ruby Green Eyes, it's been too long.' Freddie was as oily as ever as he stood in her hallway. He wore a designer tracksuit with gold chains around his skinny neck.

'Spit it out, Freddie,' Ruby replied, her eyes narrowing.

'Listen, Ruby, I know there's bad blood between us but this is my way of makin' things up to ya, my way of sayin' sorry, if you like. There's a job, a big job, and I need Bob to do it.'

'Go on,' Ruby replied.

'He's probably filled you in but I've been shaggin' the girl in the office for months now, 'scuse my French, and she tells me she's seen the contracts. The money's comin' in next week, and all we need is someone to charm the safe open so we can relieve them of it.'

Ruby didn't take her eyes off Freddie's face.

'Look, it's the best offer you'll 'ave all year. There's three hundred thousand in there, split three ways with you, Smithy and me. It's a winner.'

She paused as she thought. The money was appealing, very appealing. With a hundred grand in their pockets they'd have even more financial security.

She was still reluctant, and her first instinct was to call Archie. He was going to and fro from Spain, but they spoke most evenings, and they were becoming closer each day that passed. He'd taken her out for meals at some of the best restaurants in London, The Ivy, Nobu and The Savoy. Ruby had started to confide in him about work, to ask for his opinion, even though it was always her judgement that she relied on most. Archie was meeting an important contact that day so she knew she couldn't speak to him.

Freddie coughed. 'Sorry to rush ya but I need a decision. Bob's the best but there are other key-men I can ask. I wanted to put the deal to you first, as a sign of goodwill, to make up for things. So, what d'ya say?'

'All right, we'll do it. Shake hands on a hundred grand today and Bobby will be there,' Ruby said at last.

'You made the right choice, Ruby Green Eyes. There's one thing, though: you can't risk them being suspicious if you turn up at a diamond warehouse. Sorry, Ruby, but you'll 'ave to trust I know what I'm doin'. I'm sendin' Smithy, my best man, in with Bob. He knows the ropes and he's been in there with me when I've picked up Lisa.'

'Lisa?' Ruby asked.

'The girl I mentioned. She's not important. Anyway, wait for my message. It's next Wednesday.'

Freddie turned and left just as Charlie was getting out of his BMW. 'Freddie Harris, you're the last person I'd expect to be 'ere – and to get out alive. Seen Ruby, 'ave ya?' Charlie smirked. He walked inside and immediately turned to Ruby.

'What the hell was that weasel doin' 'ere?'

Ruby frowned. 'I've just agreed to do a job for him, and I'm startin' to regret it, however much he wants to pay us . . . I'll just call him and cancel.'

It was Charlie's turn to frown.

'You can't do that, Ruby. As you once said to me: a deal's a deal. You've shaken 'ands on it?'

Bobby nodded.

'Well then, it's a cert. You can't go back on your word. I just hope, for your sake, he's talkin' sense.'

With a sinking feeling in her stomach, she knew Charlie was right. They would look like right mugs if Freddie spread the word they'd reneged on a deal. These things got round.

'I promise you this, Ruby, if he does try and 'ave you both over, then I'll deal with him myself. You and Bobby, and little George of course, are family to us now. And we look after our own.'

Ruby smiled at the man who'd come to mean so much to her. He'd taken her under his wing, introduced her to people who wanted to pay good money for Bobby's skills without fear of being mugged off because they were under his protection. She had no choice – she had to trust him.

Finally, she nodded. It was her turn to refuse to meet Bobby's eye. 'I need to go and wake George, he's been sleepin' too long,' she said, feeling suddenly tearful. She didn't want to admit it, but she'd come to see Charlie and Maureen as surrogate parents, and their protection meant a great deal to her, though she wished they didn't need it.

'A hundred thousand nicker, Ruby. Just think, you could buy yourself a bigger home with that,' Bobby added, glancing at Charlie, hoping he'd back him up, try to soothe her.

Charlie whistled. 'That's a nice fee, Ruby. I wouldn't turn down money like that.'

The night of the heist arrived. Ruby had become increasingly nervous and restless as the days passed, so that she was almost relieved by the time it came to watch Bobby go through the same ritual he did before every break-in. He'd come to the kitchen, peeling off his gold chain and the signet ring of Dad's that he always wore. He'd hand them to Ruby and ask her to keep them safe. She nodded her reply, as he stuffed a black wig, black leather gloves and the skeleton keys into his holdall. He was already dressed head-to-toe in black clothing.

The plan was that Freddie would pick Bobby up in his van just past 11 p.m. and they'd drive into central London together to a large jeweller in the West End. Inside was the safe containing the fortune that Freddie had promised to share.

It was just gone 11 p.m. when Bobby looked over at the clock and announced he was off.

Ruby said nothing, hoping that the feeling of unease might finally disappear.

It didn't.

He walked out of the front door, pulling it gently to behind him. They weren't overlooked but they did have neighbours, and she didn't want anyone to spot Bobby going out dressed as he was.

'Don't worry, Rube, I'll be fine,' Bobby whispered as he shut the door, giving her a last look. His face was in shadow as he spoke, then he disappeared off into the night. Ruby was left standing in the hallway of her immaculate home, the scent of lilies in the air, the silence closing in around her.

'Come back safe, Bobby,' she replied softly before turning round and walking back into the kitchen. Her vigil was just beginning.

The hours passed slowly. Ruby was too fidgety to sit still, too restless to watch TV or read a book. She paced backwards and forwards, never settling to anything, her nerves preventing her from dozing while she waited – and waited.

Several hours later, she heard the soft click of the front door opening. Seconds later, Bobby appeared. He was grinning.

'It was all fine. No trouble. No bother from Freddie. Everythin' went smoothly. He'd paid off the security guards and everythin' was as Freddie said it would be. Are ya happy now?' he said, yawning. The initial adrenaline rush after a successful raid had clearly started to wear off and Bobby looked pale in the low light.

Ruby stared at him, then her shoulders relaxed. Perhaps she'd misjudged Freddie after all. Perhaps he really had let the past lie.

Just as Ruby stood up, Bobby threw a small package onto the table, almost as an after-thought.

'For you from Freddie,' he winked. 'He said he could either give it to his bird, or to you, so he chose you. Told ya he was kosher. Now let's get some shut-eye. George'll be up in a few hours and I need my beauty sleep.'

Ruby glanced at the slim, black velvet box.

'I'll look at it in the morning,' she said. 'I'm beat. Thank God it all went well. I was worried, I'll admit it, and you were right, Bobby.'

Her brother nodded to register her apology.

He yawned again. 'Freddie'll be 'ere in the mornin' with the cash. Let's get some rest, eh Rube.'

Ruby followed Bobby up the stairs leaving the long, thin jewellery box untouched on the table.

CHAPTER 27

BANG! BANG! BANG!

Ruby woke up abruptly. It sounded again. Her alarm clock showed it was 5 a.m.

Christ, what's goin' on? They'll wake George. Stupidly, her first thought was for her little brother rather than the immediate problem that someone was trying to break in – loudly.

'POLICE! OPEN UP!' Ruby sprang out of bed. She raced into George's nursery, and pulled him, still sleeping, out of his cot. She ran to the top of the stairs in time to see Bobby lurch to open the door.

'GET DOWN! NOW!' A black-clad officer screamed as the door was pushed open. Three coppers carrying guns were pointing their weapons at her brother.

'Oh God, oh God,' Ruby choked, not knowing what to do or whether to run for it. Bobby seemed just as thunderstruck.

He dropped to his knees, holding his hands in the air.

'Are you Bobby Murphy?' the officer shouted as he stood over Bobby, while the other two Old Bill started to search the house. One ran straight upstairs on seeing Ruby, who was holding George, quickly checked the rooms, then gestured for her to go down to kneel next to her brother in the hallway.

'Shit, shit, shit.' Bobby rarely swore but he had his head down and was shaking his head as he cursed.

'Shhh. Don't show them you're rattled. Be calm, Bobby.' Ruby had the sense to mutter to him under her breath, eyeing up the nearest copper who stared hard at them both. She managed to pull herself together quickly, but she wondered if Bobby would do the same. He seemed terrified.

'I'm Bobby Murphy. What d'ya want?'

'Where's the money?' One of the policemen circled the prostrate man, pointing his gun directly at him as he moved.

Keep calm, Bobby, keep a cool head, Ruby intonated, hoping he'd say little and perhaps this wouldn't be as bad as it looked.

'I don't know what you're on about, mate,' Bobby replied.

At this point, George suddenly started to wail. He'd been too sleepy to react when Ruby had grabbed him but now he was awake – and making his presence felt. He struggled in Ruby's arms, so she held him tighter to her, taking her attention away from her big brother.

'Look what you're doin'. You're upsettin' the little 'un,' Ruby hissed, more as a tactic to attract the coppers' sympathy. It failed as they proceeded to ignore her completely.

'Where's the fuckin' money?' The copper, who'd stopped circling them now, said quietly, 'Don't bother lyin'. We know it was you who pulled off the jewellery robbery last night. We 'ave it on good authority, so tell us or we'll tear this house apart . . . Look, Bobby we know you did it. You've been grassed, mate.'

Ruby looked at Bobby and back at the Fed. This was serious. It didn't get more serious – and she knew exactly who'd done the grassing.

Suddenly there was a shout from the kitchen. One of the officers appeared, and threw the unopened velvet box over to the copper who was glaring down at Bobby.

'Just what we've been lookin' for.'

The copper holding the expensive-looking box threw it to Bobby. 'Open it.'

Bobby, hands shaking visibly, opened the box. Inside was a diamond bracelet.

'So, tell me, why do you 'ave the director's birthday present for his wife on your dining-room table?' The officer was smiling now. They had all the proof they needed to link Bobby to the robbery.

Why didn't I think to hide it? How could I have been so stupid? thought Ruby. *Freddie Harris, you bastard, you've stitched us up good and proper. You planned this all along. This is your revenge on me for threatenin' to go to Charlie, maybe even for being the ones Charlie took under his wing. You took a risk, shaftin' us, and so it seems you do 'ave a pair of balls, but we'll get you back. We'll make you wish you'd never been born.*

George was crying harder now. Ruby tried to placate him, shushing him and trying to tickle his tummy but he knew something was up and he wouldn't be soothed.

'Just tell them, Bobby,' Ruby said in a small voice.

He looked up at her briefly, then nodded his head.

'All right. You got me bang to rights.'

'You're bloody right we 'ave,' the copper snarled.

'It's all right, darlin', it's just a game. Bobby's playin' a game with the policeman,' Ruby said as George sobbed. Even to Ruby's ears she sounded unconvincing.

It was Bobby who spoke next.

'All right, all right, but it was just me, no one else. I won't give ya any names or nuthin' but I will take the rap.'

The officers nodded to each other. Holding their guns aloft now, they surrounded him. 'Get up, and open the safe.'

They all stood up.

Bobby led them all into the lounge, where the safe was hidden behind a cupboard. 'There's £25,000 in there. That's all we've got in the house. I know I've been set up, and I know who set me up,' Ruby's brother said.

One of the officers stared now at Ruby, who refused to meet his gaze. 'We could nick your sister as an accomplice,' he said, leering at her. Ruby ignored him. Her heart was hammering in her chest. How would this end? Would they throw her in the nick as well? If they did, who would look after George?

Nobody spoke. The seconds ticked past.

Again, it was Bobby who broke the silence. He'd got the hint. The coppers were crooked. They wanted paying off and he was more than happy to oblige to keep Ruby out of it.

Why had she listened to Freddie Harris? She should've known he'd wanted revenge for her turning the tables and making a mug out of him last time. It'd been years, but Freddie must have got tired of how the blokes had laughed at him because a woman had made him pay up. She'd been too soft-hearted. She saw in that instance how different she was to her brother. She had a nose for trouble, was always anticipating a sting, yet she'd fallen for Freddie's lies, too – and it had led to this.

'So, we're playin' dirty are we?' Bobby smiled. That at least he could understand. 'I can't let you take Ruby to prison. I won't let that happen. She needs to be 'ere for our brother.'

'How are ya goin' to make it worth our while, Bob?' the copper who'd led the raid into their home asked. He stepped closer to Bobby. For a moment they locked gazes, then Bobby spoke. 'Why don't you gentlemen take five grand as "evidence" then split the remaining twenty between ya? No one need ever know we had this conversation, and no one need do anythin' hasty with Ruby.'

The Old Bill looked at each other and nodded. It was agreed.

They counted out the money, stuffing rolls of cash inside their protective gear. The plan had worked. Bobby walked out of the house in handcuffs, without another word to Ruby. He didn't look back, dipping his head into the back of the police car, driven away from her to an unknown future.

As soon as the cop car disappeared down the road, Ruby picked up the receiver and dialled Charlie's number. It was coming up to 6 a.m. and she knew he was an early riser. He was away at the moment, at a hotel in Devon with Maureen, but she knew he'd want her to call him.

'Who is it?' Charlie's voice was gruff. Perhaps they'd slept in after all.

'Charlie it's me, Ruby. I need your help. I got Bobby nicked because of that Freddie Harris job. I knew I shouldn't 'ave agreed, but I did, and now he's been taken off by the Feds and—'

'Slow down, girl. Tell me. Where's Bobby now?' Charlie was instantly alert.

'I think they'll 'ave gone to Barkingside Police Station. Freddie mugged us off. He gave me a bracelet and stupidly I left it on the table, then Freddie grassed us up. It could only be him, Charlie. The coppers came and saw the bracelet. Bobby's shafted, and it was me who done it,' Ruby was beside herself. The realisation of what she'd done to her beloved brother was almost too much to bear.

'Do nuthin'. Carry on as normal. I'll call my best lawyer and get him down there. We're comin' back.'

'No, Charlie, you can't,' Ruby interrupted.

'We're comin' and that's final. We'll be back by lunch-time. Don't worry, Ruby, we'll sort this.' Charlie hung up, leaving her holding the receiver.

Ruby spent the morning pacing, and trying to keep George calm. She sat on the floor with him, reading books to him and creating a tea party for all his stuffed toys. Times like this, even amid all the stress and drama of their lives, were golden moments for her. Later, she made him an early lunch, sticking him in front of the telly while she tried to take a moment to think.

Why didn't I realise when Bobby threw that bracelet onto the table that instead of a gift from Freddie, it was meant as evidence? Her mind was going round and round in circles.

Why did I even think I could do a deal with Freddie? I ignored my instincts and the result is that Bobby's been nicked and we don't 'ave the money, it's all in that slime-bag's hands. How could I have been so wrong? Ruby went over and over the conversation she'd had with Freddie. She'd known even as he stood there in her kitchen that he couldn't, *shouldn't*, be trusted, yet she'd gone ahead anyway. She'd fallen for the lure of easy money that her mum and dad warned her of.

Ruby became increasingly guilt-stricken as the hours wore on. Her confidence in her own decision-making had taken its first real hit. Up until then, she'd thought this game was easy. Well, she'd found out the truth – it was only for the hardened, only those prepared to pay the ultimate price of their freedom, or life. Well, Bobby would be paying the price of her misjudgement in his police cell tonight.

We 'ave to get him out. I 'ave to put this right, Ruby vowed to herself. For all her cunning, her intelligence, her charm, she'd been the one to mess up – and it was her brother taking the rap.

'If I could swap with him in that cell, I'd do it in a heartbeat,' she murmured to George, who hadn't a clue what she was talking about. He chuckled, thinking it was a great joke, and Ruby smiled sadly.

Why do I always 'ave to learn the hard way? she thought to herself even as she smiled back at her little brother.

Time and time again, she'd learned her gut feelings were spot-on, were to be trusted, and, from now on, she would never forget it.

Lunchtime was approaching, and Ruby realised she'd heard nothing from Bobby or Charlie. Impatient for news, and feeling still more unsettled, she dialled Maureen's mobile number. It rang for a few moments before a strange male voice answered.

'Who's this?' said Ruby.

'Are you a relative?' the voice asked.

243

'Look, what is this? I just want to speak to Maureen. It's very important. You 'aven't stolen her phone, 'ave ya?' Ruby was puzzled. 'I'm the nearest thing Charlie and Maureen 'ave to a relative, why are you askin'?'

'This is Avon and Somerset Police. I'm sorry to have to tell you but there was a road traffic accident, a pile-up on the M4 motorway earlier today. I'm sorry but I can't tell you any more as you're not a family member. I have a number for the hospital if you'd like to ring there. You might have more luck that way?'

Ruby froze. None of the words made sense to her.

'Did you hear me? I can give you a number to call . . .'

'Sorry,' Ruby managed to say. 'I'll just find a piece of paper and a pen.' Her mind was whirling.

She swore as she scrambled for what she needed, scribbling down the number and putting the phone straight down. Shock was ricocheting through her body. Seconds later, before she had a chance to collect herself and call the hospital, the phone rang again. She almost dropped the receiver picking it up in haste.

'Is that Ruby Murphy, sister of Bobby?' It was a different voice, a well-bred privately educated male voice at the end of the line.

'Yes it is, who's this?' Ruby felt bewildered.

'I'm representing your brother. I'm here at Barkingside Police Station. Bobby has been formally charged with robbery. He'll be here overnight so if you want to bring him some clean clothes and any medication he might need . . .'

'All right, I'll sort it,' Ruby managed to say before putting the phone down.

She instantly dialled the number of the hospital.

'I'm looking for news of Charlie, Charles and Maureen Beaumont. They were in a car crash this morning. Yes, I'm a relative,' she lied.

'I'll put you through to ITU,' said the voice at the other end.

'Hello, yes, I'm their daughter, Ruby. Ruby Beaumont.'

Then she heard the worst news possible.

'I'm so sorry to tell you that both Mr and Mrs Beaumont were declared dead at the scene. You'll need to speak to . . .'

Ruby dropped the receiver, the voice echoing into the space.

She heard the sound of a woman screaming, and realised it was her. She crumpled into a heap on the floor, her heart breaking all over again, screaming and screaming. George ran into her arms, terrified by the sound but she couldn't stop. Perhaps she would never stop. Charlie and Maureen were dead, and her life was smashed to smithereens. Bobby would be banged up, unable to help, unable to do anything. It was just her left now, her and her thirst for revenge.

This is all your fault, Freddie Harris. If you hadn't stitched up my Bobby, I'd never 'ave had to call Charlie and Maureen. Their blood is on your hands and I promise this, I will make you pay, by God I will. You won't know what's hit you. Until now I've tolerated you but that's all over. Freddie, you will die for this, I give you my word.

Ruby lay in a heap on the floor. Little George wailed as she wept. She rocked him in her arms and the only thing that soothed her was the thought of what she would do next.

CHAPTER 28

Ruby sat in front of the lawyer. He was a well-bred, well-spoken corpulent man whose name she now discovered was Rupert Smithers. His office, a large plush room spanning the top floor of the law firm, was filled with legal books all bound with leather covers.

Mr Smithers leaned back in his chair, smiling over his glasses at the young woman who faced him with her direct gaze. She looked pale, but it only seemed to intensify her beauty. Her eyes might have shadows beneath them but they were clear and direct, emerald jewels that looked at him unblinkingly.

He cleared his throat. 'I imagine, Miss Murphy, you're wondering why you are here.' It was a statement rather than a question.

Ruby looked down at her white hands clasped in her lap. 'I am, because you told me this wasn't about my Bobby?' she said.

'Indeed. This is about your great friends, and mine, Mr and Mrs Beaumont. Firstly, I want to offer my sincere condolences. Charles and Maureen were clients of mine for many years. Their deaths were a tragic waste of life.'

Again, Ruby said little, murmuring her thanks for his kind words, waiting to hear why she had been summoned. It was only two days since Charlie and Maureen had been killed, and she was still in shock, unable to sleep except for a couple of restless hours each night. Part of her couldn't believe that they were gone; her protectors taken from her in her hour of need. Charlie had said he'd be there to back her up if the robbery went wrong with Freddie, and now he was gone, his promises mere ashes now.

'Look, Mr Smithers, I don't mean to be rude, but my brother has been charged with a serious offence and he's all I 'ave left now, so if we could make this brief.' Ruby attempted a smile but failed.

'Of course, Miss Murphy, but first there are pressing matters we must attend to,' the lawyer replied.

'I've had to leave George with my old neighbour in Star Lane to come 'ere, now please, can we get down to business?' Ruby almost got up and walked out. They were wasting time, precious time she could be spending working out how on earth to get Bobby off the charge.

'Well, I have some good news for you.' Rupert Smithers smiled as he opened a leather-bound file filled with papers. 'I have the will of Mr and Mrs Beaumont here.'

Ruby shrugged. What was any of this to do with her? She had no interest in Charlie and Maureen's will. Yet,

Mr Smithers kept smiling at her, almost as if he was keeping her in suspense.

"Excuse me, but what is goin' on? I don't know any-thin' about Charlie and Maureen's will. I think you've got the wrong person.' Ruby started to get up to leave. She'd had enough. She was exhausted and grieving, and didn't want to be here a moment longer than she needed to.

'Oh, but Miss Murphy, it has everything to do with you,' Mr Smithers said. 'You are the main beneficiary of the Beaumonts' estate. Didn't you know? As of now, you are a very rich young woman indeed.'

The words hung in the air between them. Ruby frowned. 'Say that again,' she asked, weakly.

'When you walk out of this room you will be a mil-lionairess. There's a small sum of £10,000 which has been set aside for a lady who used to clean the Beaumont residence, and some personal effects, some watches and a ring for your brother Bobby Murphy, but apart from that, everything is yours.'

Ruby didn't recall leaving the office, or making her way home. She'd phoned George's babysitter and said she'd been held up and would be a couple more hours. She needed time to think, to make sense of it all. She dropped her keys and bag upon entering her front door, kicked off her high heels and padded upstairs to lie on her bed. Her best friends were dead, her brother was weeks away from his trial, and now she was a millionaire.

This means we can fight for Bobby. We can get a barrister like Rupert Smithers, and we can fight like dogs to get ya out of a jail sentence. There was at least this one glimmer of hope.

The money was a bizarre twist. She had enough money now to never work again. She could afford the most expensive lawyers for Bobby. She could buy any-thing she wanted – yet the only thing she desired, beyond Bobby walking free, was to see her beloved friends again, and that was never going to happen. She lay there, in complete shock at this latest news. Suddenly, the phone rang. It was Archie. She'd tried calling him after she'd discovered the news and left a message, brief and to the point. 'Charlie and Maureen are dead. Bobby's goin' to prison. Please come.'

'I've landed at Gatwick. I'm on my way to ya.' Archie's voice was low, his tone gentle. How she'd missed him while he'd been in Spain on business.

'Thank you, that means a lot to me, Archie,' she said as the tears came. His tenderness had opened the dam, and he waited until she'd finished crying before he spoke again.

'Listen, Ruby. I'm on my way. I'll always be there for ya and there's a reason for that . . . I've fallen in love with ya.' She stopped crying and let those words sink in. She searched her own feelings and saw how drawn she was to him, yet how scared she was of being with someone, of being let down, of being vulnerable.

'I know you 'ave, Archie,' she sniffed, 'I know . . .'

He put the phone down and Ruby sat, thinking. She saw how, at heart, she was still just a little girl inside. All the people she'd loved had left her; Grandad Jim, Mum and Dad, and now Charlie and Maureen. She'd experienced loss after loss. Perhaps that was what made loving another so hard? Too scared to lose Archie, she'd kept him at arm's length. But no more. Something had changed. She realised she was falling for him too, yet even then, she couldn't bring herself to say the right words back to him.

An hour later and Archie was standing on her doorstep. He pulled her into his arms and kissed the tears from her face.

'You'll never be alone again, I promise ya Ruby,' he said, his face buried in her hair. She wept again, and he held her. He stroked the tangles away from her face when she'd finished crying and bent his head to kiss her full on the lips. Her heart hammered and she could do nothing but respond to his embrace. It felt so natural, like they'd always been lovers.

'Where's George?' he asked eventually, pulling away from her.

'Star Lane. Our old neighbours. Couldn't think where else to take him at short notice,' Ruby replied.

'Right, I'll go and pick him up. You 'ave a bath, make yourself feel a bit better. I'll order in food. We'll get through this,' he added, and she noticed he'd said 'we' not 'you'. She watched him go. He was a dangerous man to love. He was a gangster. People in his trade, along with hers, were notorious for ending up banged up or dead. Could she bear to trust him, to love him? Deep down, she already knew the answer.

Cradling cups of hot sweet tea, Ruby and Archie talked after they'd eaten and George was fast asleep. Her thoughts had crystallised during her bath. Her manner was now completely changed; firm and decisive. The softness, the fragility had vanished, for now. She knew what she had to do. If she let Freddie off with this, her and George might never be safe. She had to ensure no one would ever think to mess with the Murphys again. This was business, and she'd sworn revenge of the worst kind against the weasel who'd set the tragic events in motion.

'I want him dead.' Her voice was soft, and so low Archie barely heard her.

He looked at her. He saw a woman disturbed by grief. 'I know you're grievin' but d'you know what you're sayin'? You really want me to kill Freddie for stitchin' up Bobby?'

Ruby met his enquiring gaze. Her eyes were cold now, brilliant as gemstones. 'Yes. I know exactly what I'm askin'. The deaths of Charlie and Maureen are on Freddie's hands.

'He grassed up my Bobby but, in doin' so he took the people I loved. More than that, Archie,' her voice was now almost a whisper, 'I want you to make him suffer.

I want him to know it was me who planned his murder, me who ordered it, me who showed no mercy. I want the whole of the underworld to know I'm a force to be reckoned with and I don't take betrayal lightly.'

Archie looked away. If he was disconcerted by the difference in the woman he loved, he didn't show it. He thought about it all for a few seconds then nodded his head.

'All right, Ruby. It can be done. It will be done, if you're certain.'

'Do you ask the men in your circles if they're certain? Do you question them like this?' Ruby's temper flared up.

'Course I don't, but then, I don't love 'em,' Archie replied simply.

Ruby's anger disappeared as quickly as it came, 'I should hope not,' she smiled. 'Archie, I mean it. Freddie Harris has had it comin' all his life. If I let him get away with this, I won't 'ave a reputation, I won't 'ave the respect I deserve in our world, and neither will Bobby.' Her eyes narrowed. 'He's taken the people I love from me. He's destroyed three lives, including my brother's. I've vowed to take my revenge, and I'm askin' for your help. Do this for me, kill Freddie Harris, and I'll be yours.'

'You're not serious?' Archie said.

'Deadly.' Ruby replied.

'You drive a hard bargain, Ruby, but yes, I'll do it. I'd do anythin' for you, you must know that by now.'

In the silence that followed, Ruby realised that, yet again, her life had flipped upside down.

'Rumour has it that Freddie has gone to Spain with the money,' Archie said. 'I called a few associates on my way to collect George, and they say he's already been heard boastin' about screwin' you over and takin' the cash. Freddie Harris has always had a big mouth. He'll be boastin' so loudly he'll be easy to find.'

Ruby nodded.

Archie stood up. He planted a kiss on Ruby's fore-head. 'Seems like I'm goin' back to Spain. I won't call. I won't do anythin' to link you to me. Don't ring my number, don't do anythin' that might link his death to you. Freddie will 'ave a tragic accident. He'll 'ave been so drunk on his spoils that he missed his step and fell off a cliff into the ocean . . .'

'Don't tell me any more, just do it,' Ruby said quietly, turning away from her lover. 'Just help me take my revenge.'

A tense week later, Ruby and George were playing in the garden when there was a knock at the door. George was clambering on the climbing frame Ruby had installed in the garden for him. She lifted him down and went to the door, her heart beating faster. Standing outside were Archie and Alfie, identical twins with their sun-tanned faces, expensively cut blonde hair and Archie's red Porsche on her driveway.

They walked in without saying a word.

'Hello, Alfie.' Ruby smiled at him though she felt the tension. Neither answered as they headed straight to the back of the house.

Archie shut the patio doors that led to the garden.

He and Alfie exchanged a glance before he spoke.

'Go on,' Ruby said, then she came to her senses. 'Come on, George, let's put a cartoon on for you in the lounge,' she called in a sing-song voice and ushered him out of the room. A few minutes later she returned. She shut the door to the hallway, and looked between the brothers.

'It's done,' Archie said simply.

Ruby was surprised at the force of emotion that hit her. The anger, the grief, the sheer despair of the past few days seemed to rise up and then vanish. She had wondered how she'd react. Would she feel sick? Would she break down with regret? Would she be overcome with the fear of being found out? She noticed, with a small thrill of surprise, that she felt none of these things. In fact, she felt the opposite, as if a great good had been done to right the wrongs done by the weasel. She searched her conscience. Again, nothing but a growing sense of elation.

No one moved. No one spoke. She almost laughed out loud when she realised the twins were waiting anxiously for her response.

'He's dead?' she said, nodding.

'He is,' Archie replied.

'Good,' was all she said, holding Archie's gaze. His brow wrinkled as if he was checking her reaction, but when he saw her certainty, her serenity about it, he nodded back.

'He weren't in Spain though,' chipped in Alfie, 'he were back in London, tellin' some fine tales about how he'd done you and Bobby over.' Archie threw him a look to try to stop his twin from continuing but Alfie carried on blithely. 'He had himself an accident, and so the pigs at the pig farm won't go hungry today!'

There was a moment's silence.

'You fed him to the pigs,' Ruby said quietly.

'Sorry, Ruby, you weren't meant to know that.' Archie glared at his brother.

'Sorry, bruv, sorry, Ruby, I didn't mean no harm. I thought you wanted him dead. He was a waste of space by all accounts, and if we hadn't done him in, it was only a matter of time before someone else did.'

'That doesn't help. Why don't ya go and wait in the car?' Archie commanded.

'It's OK, Archie. It's best I know. I'm glad. He deserved it. I'm glad Freddie Harris has gone. He was nuthin' but trouble. I couldn't let him live and hold my head high. And, more than that, I want everyone in the underworld to know that the man who screwed us over ended up being eaten by pigs. I want them all to know that no one, but no one, mugs us off.'

Just then, the door banged open. Ruby's heart almost jumped out from her chest. Both she and Archie swirled round to see Alfie, grinning, holding two large black bags.

'We almost forgot – the money,' Alfie laughed, dumping them on the table. 'There's your hundred grand share, and there's Freddie's. We didn't let him get away with the cash.'

Ruby stared at the bags, bulging with stolen cash and before she could stop herself, she laughed out loud. She realised in that moment that she regretted nothing. Freddie was dead at her word, and she felt nothing. She had sanctioned the killing of someone she had known all her life, and yet she knew she'd done the right thing. She couldn't have Freddie boasting about doing her over. Bobby might still be going to prison, but she doubted anyone else would try it on with them for a very long time indeed.

She turned to Archie. 'Thank you,' she said.

CHAPTER 29

Charlie and Maureen's funeral took place at Hermit Road cemetery, organised with Archie's help, and attended by all the underworld crooks and blaggers. Ruby was dignified in black, greeting mourners, but she was glad when the day was over.

Ruby was a rich woman in her own right now, with the Beaumonts' mansion in Chigwell to move into as soon as the legal procedures were complete, and the large villa in Spain she would also inherit, meaning she had four properties, while Bobby had been left Charlie's collection of expensive watches and his diamond signet ring.

However, Bobby was still on remand, waiting for his case to come to Crown court. The date had been set for two months hence, and Ruby had spent more hours than she cared to in Rupert Smithers' office, seeking legal counsel, with Archie constantly beside her.

'Can't we say that Freddie framed Bobby and has now disappeared? That's the truth, after all. All the coppers 'ave got is a bracelet as proof, but we can say that Freddie planted it,' Archie said.

Rupert looked at him over his glasses. 'Yet Bobby has confessed. That puts us in a difficult position.'

'He can say he was tryin' to protect Freddie as they'd been friends since they were at school together? Surely my Bobby can plead not guilty and if there's any doubt, they'll 'ave to let him go free?' Ruby was almost pleading herself.

Now they knew Freddie was disposed of, and couldn't give evidence, they could put the blame squarely on his shoulders, say the whole thing was a set-up from the start.

'You can try, but if the jury thinks he's trying to manipulate the system, or lie, then it'll be worse for him. He'll get a bigger sentence if he pleads not guilty but is found guilty after all.'

Ruby nodded. She'd guessed that much, yet they had to try.

'Let me speak to him. I'll try and convince him to take back his statement. He was flustered at the time, he didn't know what he was signin',' she said, squeezing Archie's hand, knowing she was avoiding the real truth.

Ruby found herself back in a queue to enter a prison waiting room. Bobby was being held on remand at Brixton Prison. She smiled at him as she took her seat at the table.

'How've ya been?' she said.

'I'm fine, Rube. How's little George?' Bobby replied.

'He's a cracker, but he's missin' ya.'

'Tell the little so-and-so his big brother misses him too – and to behave.'

Ruby sighed. 'Look, Bobby, I wanted to ask ya somethin'. Me and Archie 'ave been speakin' to a top barrister, Charlie's man,' even his name brought tears to her eyes, 'and we could try goin' not guilty. Say that Freddie set you up. Tell them ya didn't mean what you said, tell them you was tryin' to protect Freddie . . .'

Bobby shook his head. 'No, Rube, I can't do that. I won't see the barrister, I'll go guilty.'

'But why, Bobby? Why've ya done this?' Ruby couldn't understand. They had the money. They could afford the best lawyer so why not give it a try?

'I'm doin' it to protect you and little George. Those coppers were bastards. They'll come after you if they don't get me. No, I've made up my mind. I'll go guilty. I'll take it on the chin. Let it go, sis.'

'But, Bobby. You've done loads of jobs they suspect ya of and never caught ya. They'll throw the book at ya!' Ruby's voice had risen and Bobby shushed her.

'Let it go, Rube. That's my final word. You've got to be there for George. We promised Mum we'd never let him down, we'd look after him for ever, and this is my way of doin' that.'

Ruby couldn't argue with that.

Only a couple of weeks later, she watched from the docks of Southwark Crown Court as the sentence was read out.

Bobby had pleaded guilty and the only question was how long he'd spend in jail. Archie was with her. He'd moved into her home now, and they'd become inseparable.

She was grateful for his solid bulk beside her.

There was a wait as papers were shuffled, then the judge spoke. 'It is clear, Bobby Murphy, you are a menace to society. Your counsel tells us of the hardships you have endured through your life, the loss of your parents, the bad crowd you fell in with, but in a case such as this, you have pleaded guilty to a serious crime, that of robbery, and the law says you must be imprisoned. Although you are only in front of me for this one crime, the police believe you to be behind many unsolved crimes, so I give you the full penalty, and therefore, sentence you to fifteen years in prison.'

There were gasps from legal counsel on both sides. No one had expected such a tough sentence. Ruby felt her head swim, as if she would faint, but she gripped the wooden bench and stood up so that Bobby could see her.

He stood in the dock, no reaction on his face. He held her gaze as the officers on each side of him gestured for him to be led back down into the bowels of the building. Before he disappeared, he looked back and nodded as if to say 'I'll be fine, don't worry about me', then he vanished, a long stretch ahead of him.

Ruby stared at the space where her brother had just been. She looked around the courtroom, at the judge, the barristers and lawyers, the people who had good starts in life, who were given privilege and the ability to earn money legally. They were the people who had the real power.

She realised as never before that people like her and Bobby, from poverty, from rough backgrounds, had no other choice but to find other ways to survive. She saw the gulf between her people and these, the unbridgeable gap, and she felt a new sensation sweep her body. She had money. She had plenty of money, more than most of the people in that room, yet she realised it wasn't enough. For her to carry on and protect those she loved, she had to have power to wield, the power to make choices, the power to stop these bastards and the system crushing her. She felt a focusing of her desires to one single concept like the sharp point of a knife; she would never be weak again. She couldn't help Bobby. The system had swallowed him up – for now. But she could learn to think differently.

As she held Archie's arm and walked out into the winter sunlight, Ruby knew she was a changed woman; ruthless where once she was merely hardened, determined to be a major player in the underworld, where once she hovered on the edge of it. Now she would make her presence felt, she would learn everything she could from Archie and his family, and one day, one beautiful day, she would be so powerful even the law couldn't touch her.

Nothing and no one would stand in her way ever again. The past was gone. The future was for seeking power, whatever price she had to pay.

PART THREE
POWERFUL FRIENDS

Marbella, Spain, 2006

CHAPTER 30

'Bobby! Belle!' shouted the young girl as she ran to Archie's Porsche. Ruby stood at the doorway of the palatial villa she'd inherited from her beloved friends Charlie and Maureen, watching her daughter Cathy run to meet her uncle and his wife.

The years had been both kind and cruel to them. Bobby had done ten long years. He'd missed the birth of his only niece, and most of little George's life. They'd visited him in prison as much as they could, but it wasn't the same. It had taken months for George to stop asking for Bobby, and the bond that had once been so strong between them was but a thin thread now. It still pained Ruby to know she'd played a part in Bobby going to prison, but she took a small amount of comfort from the fact that Bobby had met the love of his life there. Belle had been his art teacher, and Bobby had courted her ceaselessly, then married her as soon as he got out of prison. The two were blissfully happy now.

In the intervening years Ruby and Archie had built their business into a small empire. Archie's father Lloyd still headed the family, but it was clear where Archie had gotten his respect for women. From the moment she'd married Archie, she'd been one of the family. Lloyd valued Ruby's opinion and negotiation skills, and wasn't one to waste such assets. He'd taken Ruby under his wing, teaching her the ins and outs of running a drug empire. One day he hoped to retire and pass the business on to Ruby and Archie. Meanwhile, Alfie spent much of his time in South America building their connections there.

As Ruby watched Cathy hugging and practically dancing around Belle and Bobby, she felt a huge sense of contentment. Though Bobby had been out of prison for three years, he'd been on parole and unable to leave England. Instead of joining the family in Spain, Bobby and Belle had taken up their old house in Chigwell. Now, with their arrival, she felt her family was finally coming back together. And she had the type of power that the Freddie Harrises of the world would never dare mess with.

She turned her attention to her daughter, enjoying the happiness that emanated from her. Cathy was a slim girl of twelve. She had her father's dark blonde hair, but her eyes were as green as her mother's.

Bobby managed to extricate himself from the tangle of limbs that was his niece and walked straight up to Ruby. 'Sis, it's good to see ya,' he said, wrapping Ruby's petite frame in his big arms.

'Bobby, ya know if I could turn back that clock and do things differently, I would've done—'

'What's done is done. We're 'ere now and the past is gone. New start?'

'New start,' Ruby nodded before breaking into a smile. 'Come inside, I've got so much to show ya.'

Cathy skipped ahead of them, filled with excitement and childish glee. Ruby had done everything she could to shelter their daughter from the realities of their world; the deals, the danger, but sometimes she wondered if she'd done too good a job. Cathy was one of life's innocents. She was without guile, a generous soul who loved her family and wanted nothing more than to spend time with them. Ruby's musings were broken by Archie who, looking round, suddenly said, 'Where's George?'

Ruby sighed. It wasn't the first time she'd sighed over her little brother. 'I don't know, darlin'. I called him, told him everyone had arrived, but he just grunted and carried on with playin' his video game.'

Archie frowned. 'I'll drag him down 'ere myself if I 'ave to,' he said as he marched inside to look for him.

The contrast between Cathy and George was never more stark than at moments like this. Cathy was excited to see her family. She adored Belle and Bobby, and wanted everyone to be happy together. George, on the other hand, had turned from a delightful little boy into a troubled teenager. He sneered. He swore. He wouldn't do anything

Ruby or Archie asked of him. He'd been expelled from two schools already and there seemed to be no way to get through to him. Ruby worried about him constantly.

'Look who I found sulkin' in his room,' Archie announced as he marched a scowling George, who was fifteen years old, onto the vast patio area beside the infinity pool where everyone had wandered.

George grunted, 'Hi,' before trying to turn away, but Archie stopped him.

'George, it's good to see ya,' Bobby said, coming over to them, his face a picture of concern.

George, who was wearing a black hoodie over low-slung baggy jeans, shuffled on the spot. 'All right, Bobby?' he said gruffly, as if it was an effort.

'Yeah, mate, I'm all right. It's good to be 'ere. Must be lovely bein' able to come 'ere durin' the school holidays?' Bobby attempted to start a conversation.

George shrugged and said nothing.

Archie raised an eyebrow and exchanged a glance with the teenager's older brother. His look said, 'We'll talk about this one later.'

'He's fine, Ruby, Archie, don't worry. He's a teenager, he's got other stuff goin' on,' Bobby tried to reassure his sister, but he could see the pained expression on her face. 'George, let's 'ave a chat later. I ain't been around for ages so it's difficult. I'd like to hang out with ya while I'm 'ere, get to know ya again.'

George nodded, though he still didn't speak.

When the teenager had slunk off up to his bedroom seconds later, Ruby turned to her brother and Belle.

'I blame myself. I gave him everythin' and I created a spoilt brat. It's my fault he's the way he is. I should 'ave kept him 'ere with Cathy in Spain, put him in the international school with her and kept us together,' she said dolefully.

'Don't blame yourself, Ruby. You did everything you could for the right reasons. He might've had the same troubles there too, and you thought you were doing what was best for him by putting him into good schools back home,' Belle soothed.

Ruby looked over at her sister-in-law. Belle had curly, almost frizzy hair, which was hennaed a red colour. She wore a red shift with coloured scarves and silver Indian bracelets which tinkled as she moved her hands. She was a kind soul.

'Belle's right, it ain't your fault George is the way he is. He's had every chance in life. You're not to blame if he don't take those chances. He's in the best boarding school in England right now, and why? Because they can straighten him out,' Bobby added, putting his arm around his wife.

Archie moved over and sat beside Ruby. She turned to look at him and felt that familiar thrill that this man was her husband. He had aged well, with a few streaks of grey in his blonde hair but, if anything, he looked more rugged, more attractive. He wore an immaculately cut shirt with chinos and brown leather slip-on shoes.

'It ain't nuthin' to do with you, Ruby. You've been like a mother to him. George is almost a man and it's time he realised he's got to grow up. He's back for the holidays and perhaps he needs time to adjust.'

As the adults spoke, the maid, Maria, handed round cool glasses of sangria with thick slices of orange and lemon in them. Cathy had been listening to every word. She got up from the floor where she'd been sitting cross-legged and smiled at her mum.

'I'll go and speak to him. He'll be all right, I promise you,' she said, making Ruby smile back at her.

'Go on then, darlin'. If anyone can work their magic with him, it's you.'

Cathy brushed back her long fair hair and skipped off up the huge marble staircase to George's room. Ruby watched her go, her heart swelling with pride and love for her daughter. Her and her uncle George were only three years apart in age, but the difference between them was as vast as a galaxy. Even so, there was a bond between the two that neither Ruby nor Archie fully understood. Virtually siblings, protected from the criminal world and the circle they mixed in, each child had been brought up the same way, with lots of love and attention, yet George was against the world. He seemed to hate Ruby and Archie and everyone around them. He lied and stole, cheated and ran riot, but what could they do? He was their flesh and blood and Ruby had vowed to her dead parents that she would bring up their child as her own. Ruby sighed again.

She'd never expected that vow to be as troublesome as it was. 'Well, if there's one person who can charm George, it's Cathy. Let's 'ope she can magic him into joinin' us for lunch. Is everythin' prepared, Maria?'

Ruby smiled over at the maid, a young woman from the local village, who nodded back.

'Yes, Mrs Willson, the food is ready when you are.'

The adults gathered around the table. Food was served and wine poured. For Ruby it was a moment of celebration that she'd waited years for.

As the dessert was served, Archie caught Ruby's eye and she gave him a nod.

'So, Bobby, 'ave ya given any thought to rejoinin' the family business?' Archie grinned, his eyes twinkling.

'It's been a while, Archie. My key-man days might be over. There're new alarm systems now, more sophisticated. I wouldn't want to risk my freedom.'

Belle squeezed his hand and nodded. They'd obviously given this question some thought. Ruby looked over at them. She was happy Bobby had found a soulmate but she was still surprised that he'd managed to find a straight one. Belle wasn't stupid; she knew he'd been crooked – she'd met him in prison, after all – but Ruby couldn't see how she'd approve of any law-breaking now, which is why she'd come up with a plan for him, one that didn't explicitly involve crime.

'I've been thinkin' how you can come back to work. I know you've played it straight, workin' in a bar for the past three years while you've had to check in with the parole officer—'

'And he still wants to play it straight, Ruby,' Belle said firmly.

Ruby nodded. 'I understand, Belle, I really do, which is why I wanted to ask Bobby if he'll manage a pub we've just bought in Chigwell. It's just down the road from ya, and we'd pay you well. I've got plans for it. It'll be an upmarket wine bar eventually and it needs a good manager with experience of workin' in pubs. I can't think of a better person.'

Ruby sipped her wine. They'd eaten slowly, talking and laughing round the table, enjoying the freshly cooked Spanish food. A couple of hours had passed but already the cicadas were vibrating softly in the palm trees outside, the gentle breeze drifting through the white floors and walls of the villa. Ruby kept the vases full of white lilies, in tribute to Maureen, who'd loved them. She could smell their sweet scent on the warmth of the late afternoon air. How she missed her friends, even now.

Bobby glanced at Belle, who looked pleased at the idea.

'All right, I'll do it. Runnin' me own pub, that'll be somethin'. Thanks, Ruby, thanks, Archie.'

Ruby waved away their gratitude. They toasted their success. A new venture. A new life for Bobby. A new start for them all as a family.

The day passed and evening drew in.

'I've got plans to show ya both the local markets tomorrow so I need my beauty sleep,' Ruby murmured.

Archie followed her up to their room. She sat on their luxurious bed, covered with starched white Egyptian cotton sheets, and watched as he took off his watch, slipped off his shoes and started to unbutton his linen shirt.

'So, ya didn't tell him everythin' then . . .' He raised an eyebrow at his wife.

'No, no I didn't Archie. The less Bobby knows about the pub, the better,' she demurred.

'And is that wise?' Archie leaned over to kiss her neck. She moaned softly and lay back, pulling at his belt.

'It's . . . necessary. Belle won't be happy with him doing any crooked work, but Bobby's still a proud man. He won't want a handout, and with his prison record what kind of job would he get? He did ten years for us and I want him to have a good life. We need someone we trust to manage the bar. He doesn't have to know we're laundering money through it. The less he knows, the safer he is, and the happier Belle is. No, this way he's taken care of and protected.

'Now, let's not talk business any more . . .' Ruby began to kiss Archie back, their desire for each other igniting like a flame.

CHAPTER 31

A fly buzzed as it tapped against the huge expanse of glass that looked out onto the glittering ocean. The sky was a blue haze as the heat of the morning melted into midday. Palm trees sat in elegant urns outside the window, and if she craned her neck, Ruby could see her luxurious infinity pool, its blue water stretching out to the heavens from their hilltop position.

Bobby and Belle had returned to England, excited to be running the pub Ruby had acquired. Having them all with her in Spain had been a dream come true, and though they'd had to head back, she knew it would be the first trip of many.

Despite the dangers of this chosen path, sometimes it all still felt like a fairy tale to Ruby – this life with her beautiful things, her plush homes and her husband, who was talking alongside his father with the dangerous stranger sitting across from her in their office.

Archie looked tanned and relaxed, though she could tell he was listening to the man intently as he talked about shipments across the Adriatic Sea. She watched her husband, marvelling at her good fortune in finding a man she desired and respected in equal measure. On his wrist he sported a watch that cost more than her parents would've earned in a year.

He was a kind, considerate husband, and a ruthless, dangerous businessman. She'd seen him smile winningly at an associate then weeks or months later, order them to be despatched when it turned out they'd betrayed him or the company. Yet he was always loving to her.

Ruby had taken a couple of years out of the business, bringing up Cathy and George. But once they'd gotten older she'd begun to sit in on meetings, and when she did, all the while she was thinking, *I could do a better deal than that*, as the men chatted around her.

Lloyd and Archie had always been keen to use Ruby's talents, but it was a meeting with a particularly charming Spanish mafia tycoon that had cemented her position in the Willson business. She'd listened in, watching the man, knowing he was skirting the important issue of the delivery point for a shipment of coke from Colombia. Afterwards, she told Lloyd and Archie straight, 'You should've asked them to deliver the goods to England, as now you've got the problem of shipping it from Spain.'

Both men had looked at her. It had been Lloyd who'd spoken first, 'Archie, I think it's time we let your wife in on the negotiations. She's a sharp thinker.'

Archie had winked at Ruby. 'Dad, you've never met anyone more devious . . .' which made them all smile.

'It's settled, then,' Lloyd had said, glancing at his Rolex. 'I'm expected somewhere so I'm off out. Sort Ruby out with an office. She's officially on board.'

Ruby had missed the adrenaline rush when a deal came off. She'd missed the buzz of staying one step ahead of the criminals they dealt with, always watching for the catch, sussing out their opponents and watching their backs.

The Albanian stranger shifted slightly in his seat, drawing Ruby back to the present.

'My associates tell me you are looking for a large shipment of goods for the European market. Why should we supply to you when we have others who are interested?' he said.

Archie smiled. 'Because, unlike the others, we'll pay you on time and in full.'

Ruby looked at Saban, the drug baron. He was smiling but it didn't reach his eyes, which were cold and calculating.

Archie added, 'And we want decent gear.'

There was a slight pause, and Ruby, who was sitting away from the men in a soft velvet chair, looked up, her instincts alerted.

'Of course, our cocaine is the very best on the market. I'm sure we can do business with you and your charming family.'

Saban fiddled with something on his sleeve, and in that small gesture, Ruby knew he was lying. She couldn't put her finger on it, but something told her not to trust this charming, eloquent man.

She also knew she could do a better deal than the one being struck.

Ruby looked over at Lloyd. He was checking his watch, seemingly with only half an eye on the deal being discussed, but he didn't fool Ruby. She knew Lloyd was as sharp as it got, and he'd be listening to every word.

Lloyd had been running the drug cartel since he'd left the UK, running coke via a complex web of contacts, but it was Archie and Ruby who were now handling the deals. Lloyd was looking to the future, to a time he might hand over the reins. Ruby saw her husband's strengths – and weaknesses – just as she seemed to do with others around her. She saw that he was more of a blunt instrument, made to be a blagger or a crime boss, not a drug baron. Archie was tough, there was no doubt about that, he was ruthless, yet he wasn't a subtle negotiator. He lacked Ruby's mercurial mind, her way of seeing things from every angle.

'We require the goods immediately. We have contacts who tell us the market is ready,' Archie said, at which point Saban gave an exaggerated sigh.

'Unfortunately, our associates in Guatemala can only get your shipment over here to Spain in a month. We can do no more than that. I am so sorry.'

The stranger smiled, and Archie nodded in response.

'We appreciate you putting your suppliers forward. I think we can agree this is to our mutual benefit . . .' Archie said eventually.

Both men stopped talking and stood up, ready to shake hands.

Lloyd looked over at Ruby. It was her turn to speak. The three of them had a natural dynamic, a way of dealing with negotiations. Lloyd would look bored to the point of uninterested, though he heard and saw everything, while Archie did the majority of the chat. It was only at the end that Ruby, as swift and as sharp as an arrow in flight, would enter the conversation, hitting the bull's eye as she spoke.

Ruby returned Lloyd's gaze, acknowledging his trust in her, and just as Saban reached out his hand for Archie to shake, she stood up and walked the few paces to the men's sides.

'Saban. Am I to understand that your cartel is only willing to supply to Spain, and your only guarantee is in a month?' Ruby said, holding her head high and meeting the man's gaze directly.

The Albanian looked to her, and then back at Lloyd and Archie. 'You did not tell me this woman was part of the negotiations,' he said coldly, all his previous charm vanishing instantly.

'You'll find she's very much part of it,' Lloyd replied, looking pointedly at his watch again. Ruby could almost imagine him yawning with boredom right now and she had to smother the urge to laugh out loud. She loved the dance, the game of it. The power battles, the cunning and speed both sides had to employ to get what they wanted – it all enthralled and excited her. She was grateful to her father-in-law for keeping back, for giving her the chance to step up into the role he had retired from.

She spoke again. 'You need to know that we'll only do this deal if you can guarantee the shipment reaches our contact in Glasgow. If you deliver to Spain then it's our problem to smuggle it into Britain and we won't do that.' Ruby smiled and pushed her sleek hair back, revealing her delicate neck decorated with a single string of perfect emeralds. She took strength from their brilliance, their toughness, and knew herself to be made of the same stuff.

Ruby continued, 'I know for a fact that you've got a shipment ready to go as I've spoken to someone in your warehouse. They left your ... *employ* ... shortly afterwards, a few thousand dollars richer, but the goods are there, so why are you sayin' they'll take a month to cross the Atlantic?' She held his gaze, her eyes now as cold as his. Saban flicked his gaze around the room. He fidgeted, staring back at Lloyd, then Archie and finally Ruby as if trying to work out the new power balance in the room.

Archie smiled over at Ruby, who was dressed in a Prada sundress with Louboutin heels, her huge diamond rock flashing on her ring finger.

'I don't believe you've met my wife,' he said, grinning. Archie was clearly enjoying her input, knowing she was going in for the kill, her teeth bared and ready to rip this man to bits.

Ruby smiled. 'We know you 'ave the capability to deliver to our contacts in Glasgow, in two weeks' time. We've seen it for ourselves. So, I ask you again, will you deliver the shipment to the location we've selected for the money we've agreed and to the timescale we want?'

The air in the room seemed thicker as she waited for Saban's answer.

Briefly, he looked like an animal cornered, but the slick smile soon covered his momentary discomfort.

'We 'ave other suppliers who would be more than happy to deliver what we need, when we need it,' she added. Her voice was low and soft, just as Charlie had taught her. There was no need to shout, no need to raise her voice even to normal volume. Her manner said it all.

Saban narrowed his eyes. He'd underestimated her quiet presence. He pulled on his Armani sunglasses, and laughed reluctantly, stepping towards Ruby and taking her right hand in his. She saw Archie flinch but there was no need to worry. She knew she had this man hook, line and sinker.

Strangely, even though he was a good-looking wealthy man, she felt her flesh crawl as he touched her and wondered what this meant. She couldn't look into his eyes as the shades concealed them. That small seed of doubt implanted itself further into her mind.

This one needs watchin', she thought.

Saban said, finally, 'OK, OK. Two weeks, you say? You are very well informed. Perhaps you should come and work for me . . .'

All four of them laughed politely, the tension still rising in the room.

'I will do as you ask. The goods will be at Glasgow Dock when you require them, though I will need to charge you more, dear lady, for transporting. There are dangers . . .'

'Naturally,' Ruby murmured, 'but we've set the terms. We will pay what we've agreed and you will transport the cocaine to Glasgow.'

Ruby could sense Saban's anger building, though he gave no outward indication.

'How can I refuse such beauty?' he said at last, through teeth that to Ruby looked like they wished to devour her.

Archie stepped closer. He was smiling but she knew he was wary, feeling protective of her.

'It's been a pleasure,' Ruby replied, giving him a wide smile and, at the same time, taking back her hand, feeling the skin burn where he'd held her.

Archie's instincts were always to protect her, but Ruby knew she could look after herself. With a dazzling smile, she turned to the wine chiller and poured glasses of champagne for them all.

'To success,' she said.

'Success,' they all chorused back. Without taking a single sip, Saban looked at his watch and made his excuses.

He looked back at Ruby as if to question her.

'Two weeks,' was all she said, then turned away.

Lloyd showed Saban out, leaving Archie and Ruby alone in the office.

'You did it, Ruby.' He bent his head and kissed her neck softly.

Ruby moved towards him, returning his kiss, the thrill of the adrenaline rush still surging through her veins. Making deals was in her blood.

CHAPTER 32

'You what? He's been expelled, again?' Ruby said, holding the receiver to her ear.

The posh voice at the other end hesitated. 'We don't say that he's expelled, Mrs Willson, but we won't be accepting your fee for this term – or any other in future.'

'Same bloody thing!' Ruby swore. Using bad language was testament to how cross she really was.

'I am sorry, but the school governors have given this a lot of thought. George won't be welcomed back to Darlington Grange next term.'

Ruby hung up, her heart pounding.

'George! Where are ya? We need to talk!' Ruby burst into his bedroom in their mansion in Chigwell. The family was back in the UK briefly to settle George back into school – and now that wouldn't be happening.

'What?' George said sullenly, his ears covered by headphones, a gaming device in his lap.

'You can stop playin' that bloody machine and look at me,' Ruby shouted. She was at breaking point with him. Being expelled once was unfortunate, she could make believe he'd made a mistake, and could learn from it. Being thrown out a third time, from a very exclusive school that had promised to help him, well, that was another matter.

'I need ya to listen to me. What the hell were ya playin' at, dealing weed to your classmates? Why did ya do it?' she said, starting to calm down. She plonked herself down on his bed feeling grateful that Archie wasn't there right now, as he'd go mental at this latest trouble from her little brother.

'For fuck's sake, Ruby, you're not my mum, now leave me alone!' George snarled, looking back to the screen.

'Please don't swear at me like that, George. I've spent my life tryin' to help ya. Now tell me what happened. The school says you can't go back.'

'Good,' George said. 'I hated it there. They thought I was dirt cos they're all so snooty and up themselves.'

Ruby sighed. She sighed a lot when it came to George. 'They were tryin' to help ya. Now, I know I'm not your mum, God knows that's true, but we're family and I've raised you as my own . . .'

At that point Cathy walked in.

'I heard shouting . . .' she said, looking between the pair of them. 'George, what's happened?' She came and sat on the floor next to her uncle, and gently lifted off his headphones. He submitted to her, and Ruby wished, not for the first time, that she had her daughter's way with him, her gentleness.

'Look, Cathy, I hated that school, and they hated me. All I did was sell a bit of weed to my mates. They overreacted. Everyone was doin' it, they just picked on me cos I don't 'ave a judge for a dad like some of them there.'

There was something in what he was saying.

For a moment, Ruby saw the courtroom when Bobby went down for the robbery she agreed to. Along with the familiar flush of guilt, she remembered the smell of privilege in there, how she could never join that world, never be considered an equal no matter how much money they had.

She looked at her little brother and understood what he was saying but also despaired of him ever fitting in anywhere. 'Look, so what you do is ya don't give 'em anythin' to throw at ya. If they're lookin' down on ya, you work to be the best, you don't give them the rope to hang ya. You've got a lot to learn, George. Now you'd better pray my husband takes the news better.'

Ruby glanced down at him, now playing the video game with Cathy who was giggling as they raced cars across impossible terrain. She could see how far he'd shut down his emotions, and she despaired for him.

As predicted, when she broke the news to Archie, he lost the plot. Storming into George's room, his voice could be heard through the house. 'Don't ya know how much that place cost us? We want the best for ya, so why ruin it every single time?'

'Archie, don't yell at him,' Ruby ran to the doorway.

'Don't tell me what to do! You're not my dad!' George shouted back. Same old argument. George was right. They weren't his parents, but who else did he have? George barged past Ruby, almost knocking her over. Archie turned and tried to follow him but Ruby barred his way.

'Cool down. Go for a run or 'ave a shower. We'll speak to him later, together.'

Archie nodded without saying a word. He ran his fingers through his tousled hair.

'What are we goin' to do about him?' was all he said, and Ruby didn't really have an answer.

'George'll come round. He's just findin' his feet. He'll calm down and we'll find him a better school. Maybe that place weren't right for him . . .' Her voice was soothing though her heart was beating fast. She wasn't even sure she believed what she was saying, but she had to calm the situation down. She felt agitated and confused. The same old thoughts went round her mind. Was she to blame? Had she done enough for her little brother? Again, there were no easy answers.

Archie looked down at his wife's face and must've read her thoughts because he pulled her towards him. 'We'll speak tonight,' he said, 'and Ruby . . .'

'Yes, Archie?'

'You've done nuthin' wrong. Nuthin'.'

Ruby gave her husband a rueful smile. *If only I believed that was true*, she thought. *If only.*

Something was wrong, deeply wrong, with her little brother, and she had no idea how to make it right.

CHAPTER 33

The Albanian deal had come off, and the shipment had long-since arrived in Glasgow, netting Ruby and Archie a cool million. A new deal had been struck on the back of the success of the first one, an even larger shipment, but this time the cocaine would come to Spain to pass on to a Middle Eastern connection.

Ruby and the family had returned to Spain after finding George yet another school. She sincerely hoped that this one was a better place for him. She'd considered bringing him home with them, finding him a local school, but George had been adamant he wanted to stay in England. He didn't particularly want to go to the new place, but he'd finally relented when he realised the only way he would get to stay was if he went to the school.

With George in England, Cathy at school and Archie out for the day, Ruby had the house to herself for a change. Not one to let a moment go to waste, she figured she would check in with Maria about the family dinner they were planning for next week. Lloyd would be back and she wanted to do something special for him.

Maria was her favourite amongst the staff. Ruby liked to keep an eye on everyone. She wanted her staff to be happy working for her. Perhaps it was her upbringing, the old-fashioned values instilled in her to look after others, or perhaps it was the fact that she didn't grow up with staff or privilege and so saw her maid as a person rather than just as her worker. After walking through the villa, Ruby tracked Maria to the bedroom where she was hanging some of Ruby's clothes.

'Maria, about the menu we discussed, I was thinking instead of mango we could use raspberries. What do you think?'

At the lack of response from Maria, Ruby looked closer at her maid. Maria's face was tight, her usual joyful expression absent. Whatever was going on, Ruby knew that something wasn't right.

'Maria, are you OK?' Ruby said, fiddling with an earring as she sat in front of her dressing table.

The maid started as if she'd been lost in thought.

'Yes, I'm . . . I'm fine,' the woman said but she was avoiding Ruby's gaze and staring at the floor now.

'Maria, what's troublin' ya? Perhaps I can help. Look, give me a hand with this earring will ya? I can't seem to untangle it.

The earring was a delicate gold design strung with tiny diamonds.

Maria walked over but she seemed reluctant, not at all her usual friendly, helpful self. 'Ah yes, I see. It's got caught on one of the strings. I can fix this for you,' she said, but as she worked to untangle it, Ruby noticed her hands were shaking.

'There's somethin' wrong, I know there is,' Ruby said gently. 'Please let me help ya. Is it your mum?'

Maria had confided in Ruby that her mother was very ill.

'Mrs Willson,' she stammered.

'Call me Ruby,' she replied, looking back at the woman who had shrunk back from her, the earring still clasped in her hand.

'What is it, Maria?' Ruby asked softly. 'What's wrong?'

The girl looked terrified now. Still refusing to meet Ruby's eyes, Maria whispered, 'I can't tell you. I can't. I don't know what they'll do to me, or my mother . . .'

Ruby felt the air shift in the room. Every sense was on high alert. 'Who are ya talkin' about? You know you can tell me anythin'.'

Maria started to cry. She wiped away the tears almost fiercely.

'I can't help ya unless I know what's goin' on. Are you in trouble?'

'I— I— I know something,' the maid stammered at last.

Ruby blinked. 'What, Maria? What do you know?'

The Spanish woman ran a hand across her lips, then started to pace up and down the room. 'I overheard them . . .'

'Who, Maria? What's the matter? It's OK, I promise it'll all be OK.' Ruby was really concerned now. Maria was acting very strangely.

'My boyfriend and his friends, I heard them speaking about you and your family . . . I was cooking supper for them last week in my flat, and they talked. They thought I couldn't understand because they were talking in their own language but I know much more than they realise.'

'Which language were they speakin' in?' Ruby asked quietly, the thud of intuition now sounding in her mind.

'Albanian . . .' Maria replied and burst into fresh sobs.

Ruby felt her skin prickle.

'We met in a bar a few months ago. He treats me nicely, buys me things, takes me out . . .' The maid's voice trailed off, as if she too could suddenly see the light.

Questions were already forming in Ruby's mind, as she pieced together the information she'd been given.

Had her maid been groomed for information about Ruby and Archie? Had the Albanian only gone for her because he knew she worked for the Willsons? It seemed obvious he had. But what would Maria be able to tell them that was of any value? Ruby treated her staff well, but she didn't talk openly in front of them.

'It's OK, Maria. I'm not angry with ya, and we'll protect you from any trouble you might be afraid of, but I need to know what you might 'ave told them.'

'I didn't tell them anything. He asked me about you and Mr Willson a few times. Asking about people that came to visit, any fancy parties you might have thrown. I thought he was just curious what it was like to live such a glamorous life . . . but I don't know anything, and I'd never share details about you and your family.'

'That's OK, Maria. I understand. I'd never 'ave suspected anythin' either and I know you wouldn't go tellin' tales about us.'

Ruby put her hand on Maria's shoulder, looking to comfort her when she lifted her downcast eyes off the floor to look Ruby in the eye. Her voice was low as she spoke. 'I know something, something that is bad for you . . .'

'Go on,' Ruby murmured.

'My boyfriend says that you and your husband are being set up. The cocaine they're promising to supply is dodgy and . . . and . . .'

'Go on,' Ruby urged, her blood suddenly running cold.

'And they're going to take your money and shoot your husband.'

CHAPTER 34

Ruby knew in her gut that Maria was telling the truth.

She recovered herself far quicker than the girl, who was still crying, her whole body shaking now.

'What will you do?' she asked.

'Don't worry, we'll protect ya. You're safe with us, but we need you to stay loyal, to tell us if anythin' changes over the coming days.'

Maria nodded.

'Do you know when they're plannin' on strikin'?' Ruby asked, getting straight to the heart of the matter.

'Soon. They'll do it at the handover. When you give them the money, they'll give you bad coke, fake stuff, and when Archie realises . . .'

'They'll shoot him,' Ruby finished for her.

There was a slight pause as they both digested this information.

'Right, Maria, the most important thing now is to do nothin'. Carry on as normal. As long as he don't suspect you've been talking to us, you'll be in no danger from him.

I'll sort this, I promise. I'll keep you safe, but only if you trust me. Do you trust me?' Ruby stared hard into the girl's eyes.

Her face was pale under her olive skin but she nodded, and Ruby saw a steely determination there, not unlike her own. It must've taken great courage to tell her. This girl had risked her life.

Our lives hang in the balance, always, thought Ruby. Life was merely a turn of the cards, a roll of the dice, a kind gesture that unravelled months of plotting.

A plan was already forming in Ruby's mind but she needed this girl to stay silent, to carry on as before. Was she up to it? Could she be trusted even now? *If she can't, we're all dead*, thought Ruby grimly.

'Just do nothing. Understand?'

Maria nodded again.

'If they 'ave any idea you've told me, the first person they'll kill is you.'

The two women stood staring at each other for a moment.

'I won't say anything,' whispered Maria.

Reassured that the young woman would play her part, Ruby nodded for her to leave the room. She needed time to think, alone. She didn't want the Albanians to know she'd discovered their plot yet. She had to keep her family safe.

She walked to the front of the villa and signalled to the security guards to close the gates guarding the property. Her instinct was to increase the number of security, to get more men with guns around the estate, but she knew this might alert the Albanians, so she could do nothing but smile and carry on as normally as possible.

'Archie, Lloyd, we need to talk,' Ruby said as she went back into the cool, air-conditioned villa. She was smiling but her face belied her concerns and the men followed her into the office she shared with her husband. It was a vast room with a wall made entirely of bullet-proof glass. Behind it the sun shone over the sea, making the view hazy with the heat.

She got straight to it. 'We're bein' set up.'

'The Albanians?' Archie said immediately.

Ruby nodded. 'But I 'ave a plan.'

'Course you do. But who told ya, and can they be trusted?' Lloyd spoke this time.

Ruby turned to him. 'It was Maria, my maid, who told me. I'm sure it's the truth. The Albanians plan on supplyin' bad coke, takin' the money and then they'll strike.'

She looked between the two men. Both wore serious expressions as they took in the situation.

'You'd better tell us what you're plannin', then,' Archie said.

Ruby made sure she was at the final meeting with the cartel the day before the shipment was due to arrive. This time the coke was being bought to a disused warehouse several hours' drive away. The agreement was made. Archie and Lloyd would go alone to meet Saban and his bodyguard.

No one else was to be there. The men shook hands on it, and Ruby smiled winningly at Saban as he took her hand again and kissed it lightly.

'Business with you is such a pleasure, dear lady,' he'd murmured.

'And with you, Saban. I think we understand each other,' she'd replied, batting her eyelashes at him, and inwardly laughing as she saw the effect on him.

He might be a drug baron but he was still a man, and she could turn on her charm just as easily as he could if it meant business went well. She wanted to flatter him, to make him think his plan was bullet-proof. They'd all played their parts well. Saban couldn't possibly be suspicious.

Archie came up to his wife and grabbed her hand. 'If I was a jealous man, I'd 'ave somethin' to say about the way you flirted with him.'

Ruby laughed. 'It's lucky you ain't then,' she said, slipping her hand into her husband's. 'Seriously, Archie, this is still a risk. I'm worried for us all . . .' She turned to face this man, the only one she'd ever given her heart to. Life without him would be unbearable. She shuddered, and Archie caught her momentary fright.

'So am I, darlin', but there's nuthin' we can do. We 'ave to tackle this now, Ruby, or they'll come for us another time. Don't lose your courage now, babe.'

She knew this was true. They had to deal with these bastards now, or they'd forever be looking over their shoulders.

There was no guarantee they'd come out alive, though.

Ruby gestured to Maria to follow her into her bedroom.

Ruby spoke first. 'There's a bag there for you inside the closet. Go and open it.'

Maria hesitated but walked to the built-in wardrobe that spanned the side wall, reaching down for an unremarkable-looking travel bag. She unzipped it. It was stuffed full of hundred-euro notes.

'A car will pick you up from your flat at midnight. Take your mum and leave. I've made all the arrangements. You'll be taken to a different part of Spain. There's a flat rented for you there. It's all sorted. You'll be safe, I promise.'

Maria took in the information. She held a couple of the bundles of euros, her face incredulous.

'I'm so sorry, Ruby. I didn't know he wanted information when we met – I thought he wanted me . . .'

Ruby's heart could've broken at the sight of Maria's pitiful expression. 'You 'ave to stay strong and carry on as normal, then go,' Ruby said firmly. This wasn't the time to break down. 'You cannot stay. They'll kill ya both. This time tomorrow, if your boyfriend survives, he'll know it was you who grassed them up, and they'll come for ya. You'll never know a night's peace again – unless you do what I'm askin' ya.'

She felt wretched, knowing the pain this was causing the young woman.

Tears were sliding down Maria's face.

'I know, I've been so stupid thinking Besim liked me . . .'

'Is that his name?' Ruby replied. 'I never thought to ask, sorry.' She put her hand on Maria's arm and felt her body tremble. 'They've left us no choice, but you will be safe as long as you get in that car. You've got enough money to last ya a few years. I'm sorry Besim was using you . . .' Ruby added awkwardly.

Maria managed a small smile. 'Thank you, I will do what you ask,' she said, wiping away more tears.

'Compose yourself, then carry on with your duties. If anyone asks why you're cryin', tell them your mum's ill. Say nuthin', do nuthin' – and we might survive this.'

Ruby got up and left the room, rushing to answer the phone.

She picked up the receiver. 'Hello, Ruby Willson speakin'.'

'Hello, this is the head of pastoral care. Do you have a moment to speak about George Murphy?'

Ruby's heart sank. She knew instantly her brother had got into trouble again.

'I have a minute, but that's all,' she said, more sharply than she'd intended. Her hackles were up already. This call couldn't have come at a worse time.

'It won't take long,' said the teacher with a cut-glass accent, one that had never known what it was to struggle, Ruby could be sure of that.

'I'm sorry to inform you that we have had to exclude George pending a meeting with the school governors because he was found selling cannabis to his classmates. This is simply unacceptable behaviour, and disappointing as George hasn't been with us for long. This school has the strictest policy concerning illegal substances.'

'Where is he now?' Ruby interrupted the posh voice. She didn't want to know the details and give the snooty bastards at this latest school a chance to belittle her family. This was the fourth time her brother had been chucked out of school. Enough was enough.

'He's with the contact you gave us, your brother Bobby Murphy. Mr Murphy and his wife came to collect him yesterday evening.'

Ruby put the receiver down on the table without another word, then bent her head towards it, gripping the marble top. George in trouble again! When would this end?

'Mrs Willson? Are you there, Mrs Willson?'

Ruby heard the voice at the other end piping out from the telephone but she didn't want to speak to it. She knew they'd expel him – it was obvious. And she had enough trouble on her hands without her little brother upping the stakes.

'I've had enough of you toffs – and of my brother's behaviour,' she said to herself.

Without answering, Ruby put the receiver back onto the cradle. She couldn't bear the sound of that posh woman's voice, a voice of privilege and confidence, the likes of which her family had never known, and probably never would. The school had looked down on them from the start. Ruby insisted to Archie, who wasn't in favour of private education, that their money was as good as anyone's but now she wasn't so sure. They didn't have police chiefs or judges in their family who could help them. She knew how crooked straight people could be, she'd seen it at her first job, and it was those people who could wave a magic wand, speak to a few contacts, and – hey presto – get the charges dropped, an expulsion turned into a detention. No, they had to live with the consequences of their actions because they were working class, jumping way above their station, and being reminded of the fact at every available opportunity.

She picked up the phone again and dialled Bobby's number.

'Bobby?'

It was obvious her brother had been expecting her call. There was no small talk, no 'hello', just straight down to the business in hand.

'He's 'ere. He says he didn't do nuthin' wrong. He didn't want me to ring ya yesterday, he thought they might take him back. I take it they haven't?'

'No, they haven't,' Ruby said stiffly. 'Hand me to him,' she insisted. 'George? What happened?'

'Rube, they stitched me up I swear it,' George's voice was angry, and a little self-pitying.

Ruby knew by the sound of it that her own flesh and blood was lying to her. 'Did they now. So, why would they do that, George?' she said, keeping her tone light, her manner calm.

There was a pause. George stayed silent on the other end of the phone and it gave her a chance to collect her thoughts. She knew Archie would despair when he found out, which is why she didn't plan on telling him until the handover was done – and the Albanians sorted.

Ruby spoke first. 'What do I keep tellin ya? Don't give them anythin' to take you down with! Let others do the dirty work. And anyway, why would you deal drugs? Surely you 'ave enough money, so why bother?'

George was silent still.

'I didn't do nuthin',' he replied eventually, a barely adequate answer, making his older sister sigh.

'All right, George, I believe ya,' she answered, though she didn't at all. She just didn't want an argument when there was so much at stake in Spain right now. 'Stay with Bobby and we'll fly back as soon as we can. All right?'

There was no answer from George, then her older brother's voice reappeared.

'It's Bobby. He's gone off to the kitchen. He doesn't seem fussed, Rube. Doesn't care about school at all. Listen, we'll look after him. Perhaps he needs a break from all those lessons. He's fine with us – don't worry, sis.'

Ruby hung up, her mind not put at rest by her brother's words but wanting to believe them, nevertheless.

'George, I ain't forgotten you. I just need to sort this first, then I'll be home,' she whispered to herself.

At that moment, Archie walked into the hallway.

'Anythin' wrong?' he said.

Ruby straightened up. 'Nuthin', nuthin' at all,' she lied. She'd wait to find her moment to tell him. One storm in a day was more than enough for her to handle.

CHAPTER 35

The night of the handover arrived.

Ruby, Archie, and Lloyd packed the holdall filled with money into the back of their armoured Range-Rover.

Ruby climbed into the back, while Lloyd sat in the front passenger seat and Archie drove the car, waving to the security guards to let them out of the main gates.

'We want them to see us leavin', let them know we're on our way,' Lloyd said in a low voice. 'They'll 'ave people watchin' the villa, and the guards might be paid off by them anyway.'

Ruby nodded. She'd suspected that many of her staff were on Saban's payroll. Well that would all change once they'd sorted this.

The drive was a long one. They didn't stop, though. Archie wanted to get there before Saban and his henchmen. There was no doubt in their minds he'd be bringing more than just one bodyguard.

Pulling off the road, Archie peered at what looked like an old, dusty farmhouse.

'I think it's down 'ere. Yes, look, there's the warehouse.'

The car tyres made the gravel crunch as they drove towards the neglected building. There was nobody about.

'We're early. That's good,' said Lloyd, craning his neck to look round the site.

'Let's do this,' Archie said, waiting for Ruby and his father to nod their assent. Archie opened the door and got out, going straight to the back of the car to open the boot.

Ruby stepped down onto the dirt road, her heels making stiletto marks in the dust.

'Ready?' Lloyd said, beside her.

'Ready.' Archie replied, lifting out a large suitcase. The mood was fraught with tension. The three of them walked up to the warehouse.

'We'll stop here,' Ruby said, looking around.

Archie put the suitcase down on the ground carefully.

'Stand behind me, Ruby,' he commanded, as he spotted a puff of sand being thrown up on the road.

'They're here,' Lloyd stated.

Ruby felt her heart freeze. She watched the vehicle draw closer, her palms sweating. If she got this wrong they'd all die today. She glanced around. She didn't want to disappear here, in this bleak place in the middle of nowhere.

Hold your nerve, hold yourself, Ruby. She centred herself.

The car pulled over to one side and Saban got out. He stood for a moment, grinning, a cigar held in his teeth, his gold Rolex winking in the sunshine, as the back doors all opened. Out of the back of the car came three burly men, and out of the front came the driver, all carrying guns, which were now pointed at them.

'Such a shame you came today. I can't bear to see such beauty do such dirty business,' Saban sighed exaggeratedly.

Ruby took a deep breath and smiled back at him. 'Nice of you all to drop by. I can see you've brought your . . . *friends*. That wasn't the agreement, Saban,' she said, ignoring his rather clumsy attempt at seduction.

'Ah, what can I say? I never travel so lightly. You cannot expect me to agree to such terms. Only one bodyguard? Why, I'd have been outnumbered.' Saban held out his arms as if to make his point.

'Enough. Show us the goods,' ordered Archie.

Stay calm . . . . keep it together . . . Ruby thought. *Don't rile them yet.* She could see the strain building on her husband's face.

'Yes, of course, we have it all here,' Saban clicked his fingers and one of the men ran round to the back and brought out a large sports bag. Whatever was inside it was clearly heavy. The gunman dumped it on the ground halfway between the two parties then ran back, picking up his weapon and pointing it directly at her husband.

'It's all there. Please, help yourself. Test the product. You'll find it's of the highest quality.'

'I will, thank you,' Archie said, striding over to the bag, ignoring the gun-wielding Albanians as he did so.

He drew a knife from his pocket and, pulling out a bag of white powder, cut through the plastic and dipped his finger inside it.

Sucking the powder, Archie glanced back at Lloyd. That glance told Ruby everything she needed to know. The gear was bad. It had been stamped all over, perhaps cut with glucose or baby teething powder. She kept her eyes on Saban, but the hairs on the back of her neck had risen.

Time seemed to slow down.

Her heartbeat slowed, seemed to deafen her as she reached down to open the suitcase. Lloyd was beside her.

'Let me, darlin',' he said as if he was playing the gent. Ruby demurred, holding back but feeling for the handgun she had hidden in her jacket lining.

The suitcase lock clicked open.

'Come and see your money. It's been good doin' business with ya,' said Lloyd. Before the Albanians could see what was inside the suitcase, Lloyd pulled out a machine gun and opened fire.

Two of the bodyguards were killed instantly, but Saban was quick. He'd pulled out a gun and with one single blast shot Archie in the chest. Archie fell backwards as Ruby fired her gun, pointing at Saban's head.

BANG. Blood sprayed from Saban's forehead, and for a moment he stayed there, swaying, looking at Ruby with something like disbelief.

Then he staggered back, blood running down his face, soaking his expensive jacket, his shirt, even his chinos.

BANG, BANG, BANG!

Ruby stared at the cartel boss as he fell to the floor. Gunshots rang out behind her and within seconds the henchmen she'd sent to the warehouse the day before walked out of the shadows, each holding an automatic firearm. One of them was instantly recognisable. It was Alfie, Archie's twin. Ruby had recalled him from South America. She'd realised they'd need all the loyal back-up they could get.

'Take that, you lyin' fuckers!' grinned Alfie, his eyes wild. He released another round of bullets, pumping them into the air, crowing with delight. 'DIE, YOU FUCKERS!'

Blood, thick and red, soaked into the earth. All five Albanians lay dead in the dirt.

Ruby turned round, still holding her gun aloft in case there were more but the place was silent. Then she dropped her weapon and ran to her husband's side. He'd hit the floor hard but as she cradled his head in her arms, his eyes fluttered open.

'Bloody lucky I wore a bullet-proof vest,' he said, smiling up at his wife. She kissed him gently on the lips.

'Bloody lucky,' Ruby said, as she tried to blink back the tears threatening to spill. She could have lost him. If he hadn't worn his vest, if she had been a second slower with her gun. She'd shot her first man, but all she could think was how grateful she was that she'd been quick enough. Trembling with adrenaline, she tried to direct Archie's attention away from her shaking frame. 'Look who's 'ere. It's Alfie. He's come home to help us out.'

Archie smiled up at his brother, the spitting image of him, yet so unlike in other ways, and took the arm offered to help him up.

'Bruv, good to see ya,' Archie said, hugging his twin.

'It's been too long. Look what 'appens when I leave ya, you get into all sorts of bother!' Alfie laughed. He slapped Lloyd on the back as his dad greeted him.

'Alfie, son, it's good to see ya. Still got spirit, eh?' which made the twins laugh.

'You don't know the 'alf of it, Dad.'

'Sorry to break this up, but we need to go before the Old Bill arrive,' Ruby reminded them all with some urgency.

The twins nodded.

'I thought you was a goner there, son,' Lloyd laughed to Archie, throwing the suitcase into the boot while the twins and the other bodyguard got into the back seat.

'Leave the dud coke, and the bodies,' Ruby commanded, 'when the police come they'll write it off as a deal gone wrong.' She was amazed at how steady her voice was. She'd killed a man and it hadn't bothered her one bit.

Lloyd glanced over at his daughter-in-law as he drove the car away at speed. She was sitting in the front passenger seat, staring out of the window.

'You did well there, girl. You did well.'

Ruby smiled over at him, then turned back to her thoughts. The Albanians might be fixed but she had more trouble to deal with – her brother George.

CHAPTER 36

'Look, Archie, I can handle it. Give me a box of weed and I'll double your money by Monday,' George wheedled.

Archie looked to Ruby, whose face was like thunder. They were standing in the lounge of their Chigwell home after flying back to sort out George. His stay at Bobby and Belle's had been, on her older brother's account, fraught, as their little brother had refused to talk about school or what he would do next.

'I'm not havin' ya dealin', got it? I won't allow it,' she said, knowing how this would rile her younger brother, who appeared to do nothing all day except play video games or go out with his mates.

'For fuck's sake, Rube, you ain't my mother. You don't tell me what to do,' shouted George, turning to her.

Quick as a flash, Archie went to Ruby's side. 'Don't speak to your sister like that. She's as good as your mum, and you'll treat her with respect,' he warned.

'Or what?' George sneered.

The sixteen-year-old was wearing his usual gear; a black hoodie pulled up over his dark hair, and slouchy jeans worn low at the back. A single, thick gold chain hung around his neck and he was wearing an expensive pair of new trainers. The effect was menacing, and Ruby almost recoiled.

'I know I'm not your mum, but you are my responsibility. I promised our mum I'd look after ya, and that doesn't mean sendin' you out to deal drugs!'

'Ruby's worried about ya, we all are,' Archie added, which made George even more furious.

'You ain't my father either. I don't 'ave a fuckin' dad, or a mum, so you can drop that shit right now.'

'I do understand. I lost them too . . .' Ruby said, her snappy mood disappearing in an instant at the familiar recognition of their orphan status. It still caused her pain to know how much she, George and Bobby missed them.

But Archie wasn't fooled. He almost exploded with rage. 'Never talk to Ruby – or me – like that again. I don't ever want to hear it. Don't give us that shit about bein' an orphan, playing that old card again. Ruby's done everythin' for ya, and more, so it's time you grew up.'

The air was tense. Both men squared up to each other. Ruby wasn't sure who'd win if it came to a real fight. Archie was tough and muscular but George was fiery and once his temper was up, there was no telling what he'd do.

'Go fuck yourself. Just give me the fuckin' drugs,' George swore. He seemed jittery on top of the temper.

He paced up and down the room, only stopping to face her husband. They looked like two fighting dogs, ready for the whistle.

'I won't give ya any *fuckin'* drugs. You're not a dealer, whatever you like to tell the mugs you hang out with,' Ruby snapped.

Archie was quiet now. He'd mastered his anger, which only seemed to rile George more.

'What 'appened to you, George? Ruby and Bobby are good people, but you, you're rotten to the core—'

'That's enough,' Ruby interrupted them. She stood up out of the silver velvet sofa in her immaculately designed lounge, a tasteful setting with vases of fresh-cut flowers, a marble table and matching armchairs.

Ruby's husband looked almost pale in the light from the table lamps. The family had been back in England for a few months since Ruby insisted they come home and take George back to their Chigwell house to try to work out what to do next. The situation was so serious they brought Cathy with them, taking her out of the international school temporarily and employing a private tutor in England instead.

Now, George was actually asking Archie if he could supply him drugs.

Before she could speak again, George lost his temper completely. He yelled, 'Don't fuckin' lecture me. I know what you do for a livin'! I know you're drug dealers so don't come all innocent with me. You run coke from

Colombia to Spain! You supply half the fuckin' dealers I know! So, why shouldn't I get in on it? I'm as much a part of this family as Archie is and yet you never let me into the deals and the money.'

For a moment, Ruby was stunned.

She wasn't naive enough to think that George had no idea of *what* they did, but she hadn't realised he knew as *much* as he did. She and Archie had made a pact early on never to talk about business in front of George, and certainly never to let him do anything dangerous or take on any role within the cartel. It was simply too risky, and Ruby's instincts were always to protect him, just as if she really was his mother.

'Didn't ya think I'd realise why we always 'ave security guards with us? Didn't ya think that some of the guys at school would talk? They're not stupid. They can see you don't run a legit business, that's fuckin' obvious. The only thing is, you never told me! You think I'm an idiot, well I'm goin' to prove you wrong. I fuckin' hate you both!'

There was silence for a moment. Archie looked like he might pounce on George. The vein in his neck was prominent, showing he was stressed. He was gripping his fists tightly. Ruby knew she had to calm this down.

'We never meant to lie to you, George,' she said, imploring him to listen to reason.

'Bullshit! You lie all the time. You've always lied. Nuthin' you tell me is ever the truth,' he spat back at her.

'I've told ya, don't speak to Ruby like that, you little fucker,' Archie shouted now. 'She and Bobby are good people.'

'Good people? *Good people?* Don't make me laugh,' George spat. 'My big brother's been banged up and my sister and you are drug dealers. You're as much scum as I am. The only decent person in this family is Cathy.'

It was then that Ruby saw how drawn he looked. Where he'd once been a well-built boy, he had lost weight on his face and he had dark shadows under his eyes. He was sweating now, and he seemed agitated. Again, he was fidgeting on the spot, almost dancing from foot to foot and he kept running his fingers through his short hair, peeling off the hoodie then placing it back over his head, covering his eyes,

Suddenly, she knew what was going on. 'George, you're on drugs right now, ain't you?' Her voice was quiet, her manner calm. She could see that George was on a knife-edge. 'Tell me, what have you taken?' Ruby stepped towards him, her hand held out to him. Her heart ached at the realisation that, under their eyes, George had gone deeper than she'd ever realised into the underbelly of their profession.

The human cost of their work was something she knew about, but had rarely seen first-hand. The lure for her was always the power – and the excitement.

Suddenly, the real cost of running drugs was revealed to her, in her own house, with her own little brother.

Some part of Ruby crumbled inside, yet she felt inexplicably angry with him. They were meant to be on the winning side! They were meant to be the ones supplying the drugs, selling them, moving them, profiting from them. They weren't meant to be the ones falling foul of them, being broken by them. What had gone so wrong?

'I knew I should never 'ave sent you to boarding school. In my heart I knew it was wrong to abandon you in England while we returned to Spain,' Ruby murmured. 'And this is what it's led to. Oh George, I'm sorry, we let you down, I can see that now.'

Her words fell on deaf ears. If anything they made George nastier, more spiteful, more keen to hurt her in any way he could.

'I. Don't. Give. A. Shit. I want your husband to sort me out with some puff, and I want it tonight,' George snarled.

Ruby stepped back as if she'd been slapped.

'We can't do that, George,' she replied.

Archie stepped towards her, protectively.

George looked at them, then shouted, 'Hypocrites!' before pushing past them and slamming the lounge door loudly behind him.

Seconds later they heard the front door slam. It was then that Alfie appeared.

'Didn't want to interfere ... he's bang out of order. D'ya want me to 'ave a word?' Archie's twin grimaced and stared straight at Ruby, who suddenly felt deflated.

'No, leave him,' she said, giving her brother-in-law a small smile.

'That boy needs a taste of reality. Let me sort him,' Alfie said menacingly. He looked livid. George had riled the whole house up – except for one person.

Cathy sidled in.

'Did you hear the argument, darlin'?' asked Ruby, and Cathy shook her head. 'I just heard voices. Is George OK?'

Archie looked over at her and his face reflected her relief. Cathy hadn't heard the nitty-gritty; that her parents were big-time dealers.

'We've just had a stupid argument, and George walked off. Nuthin' to worry about,' Ruby lied.

'Don't worry Mum, he'll come round. I'll speak to him, make him see he can't behave like that. Honestly, it'll all be fine.' Cathy was always the peacemaker, always determined to see the best in people.

'Look, love, why don't we go out for dinner, somewhere nice like The Ivy. You need a treat, and it'll give George time to cool off?' Archie said. 'I think we all need a bit of space . . .'

Ruby thought about it for a moment and then nodded. 'All right, that might be for the best. Cathy, why don't you wear that lovely new dress I bought for you last weekend?'

'Oh, Mum, I won't come. Honestly, I'd rather wait in for George. You go.' Cathy pretended to shoo them all away.

Ruby smiled at her daughter, her worries receding. 'You'll be all right?' she said to her daughter.

'Course, Mum!' Cathy laughed.

Ruby wasn't completely sure. The mood in the house had been ugly, until Cathy appeared.

Her attention was distracted by Archie, who was now speaking to his twin.

'Alfie, fancy a bite at The Ivy? It's your last night, we need to do somethin' special with ya after all that!'

'Sounds good, bruv.'

Ruby made her way up the stairs to her bedroom. She sat on the bed heavily, her mind racing. She wondered when it was that she'd failed her little brother so badly, and whether she could ever make it right again.

CHAPTER 37

Ruby, Archie and Alfie went up to the West End in a cab. Archie was well known by the staff at The Ivy and always got a table.

'We'll find an answer, I promise ya,' Archie said as they were seated, picking up on his wife's sombre mood. Ruby smiled at him, trying to hide her sense that all was not well. She barely ate anything though, so instead she sat and listened as Archie and Alfie talked business. Alfie had a fresh contact in Colombia, someone high up in the police force who could prove very useful to them.

'We'd 'ave more chance of safe passage of the goods, no questions asked, if we put Matias on the payroll,' Alfie said, winking at Ruby.

Ruby smiled back at him, watching the men as they talked. Where Archie was always well groomed, his hair tousled expertly, his face freshly shaven and smelling of expensive cologne, Alfie looked wilder. His hair was cut much shorter now and it made him look older. Alfie had stubble and wore more gold jewellery than his brother.

Archie only ever wore discreet embellishment, his Rolex and his wedding ring, whereas Alfie loved a bit of bling. He wore gold chains and gold rings, making him appear harder, more threatening, than his brother. Perhaps that was what he intended. He had to keep up certain appearances while doing the dirty, dangerous work of drug-running in South America. He would be used to casual violence on a scale Ruby was glad she had avoided so far for the most part. Alfie looked the part of a dealer and businessman in one of the most dangerous regions of planet Earth.

Much later, when the twins had knocked back a good bottle of expensive wine and eaten their fill, it was time to leave.

As Archie called a cab, Ruby took her mobile out of her bag and called home. She rang and rang but no one picked up. She tried George's mobile – no answer, but that wasn't unexpected. She dialled Cathy's mobile – and when her daughter didn't pick up, her instincts sharpened. Something was wrong, badly wrong, she knew it.

'Get me home, Archie,' she said.

Instead of waiting for the ordered cab, Alfie jumped out into the road and waved down a passing black cab. They piled in. 'Chigwell – as fast as you can,' Archie said. 'There'll be a fifty quid tip in it if ya can do it faster than I would in my Merc.'

A hair-raising journey later, the three arrived back at the house, the cab driver having secured his tip.

Ruby ran up to the front door, then stood stock still. She took in the lack of lighting. It was pitch black inside the enormous house. No light from the kitchen or the lounge. No sound from the televisions or music. No sound of the kids squabbling or laughing. It was all wrong.

'Cathy, love, where are you?' Ruby shouted, though her throat was suddenly dry. Her heart hammered as she headed straight for the stairs. Something told her she would find what she was looking for up there.

'Cathy? CATHY?' She stopped again. The sound of weeping filtered through Cathy's closed bedroom door.

Ruby's heart almost stopped. It wasn't childish upset, it was raw, choking sobs.

'Oh, darlin', what's the matter?' Ruby said, pushing open the door.

At first she couldn't make out her daughter's shape, but as her eyes adjusted to the gloom, she saw her, curled up on the bed. Ruby felt a rush of icy shivers go through her. She felt cold to her bones.

'Darlin',' she said again, softly, approaching the bed. 'What is it? What's happened? Oh, Cathy!'

At once Ruby saw the state of her daughter. There was blood smeared across her face and an ugly red mark forming across her cheek. Her T-shirt was ripped and her jeans open at the top but pulled up haphazardly.

'Who did this to you?' Ruby cried, reaching her arms around her sobbing child. Eventually, Cathy's sobs subsided enough for her to speak. She wiped her hand across her face, moving the blood up into her hair.

'Where's George? Is he OK?' Ruby was breathing fast now. 'Tell me, Cathy. What happened? Who did this?'

She stared into her daughter's swollen red eyes, her blood pounding in her ears. It was as if her heart *knew* the answer, knew with every beat.

'It was . . . it was . . . Please don't be angry with him, Mum. He didn't know what he was doin'. He was actin' all weird and drugged. He was off his head. I was tryin' to comfort him but he got it all wrong and then he just grabbed me, wouldn't let me go, and then he . . . he . . . raped me.'

The words were sharp in Ruby's ears as if made of steel blades that slashed into her mind. *It couldn't be . . .*

'Tell me, Cathy.' Her voice was low. She felt like a tiger in the long grasses, waiting to pounce.

'It was . . .'

'Go on, love.'

'George,' Cathy whispered.

But Ruby had known already.

And now Archie and Alfie did too.

Both men were standing in the doorway, their eyes wild, their faces twisted with rage and grief.

'I'll tear him to pieces. I'll rip his dick off. I'll feed him to the pigs while there's still breath in him!' Archie looked half demented. His fists were bunched tight. The shock of Cathy's revelation filled the room. Waves of disbelief and horror lapped at the walls.

'Stop, Archie.' Ruby turned to look at her husband and brother-in-law. Archie stared at her from the doorway, holding back while she tended to their daughter, his eyes dark in the evening light. She felt his need for revenge, the need for blood to be spilled, as a visceral force.

She nodded, acknowledging his savagery, accepting it completely.

Something had to be done – and fast. This unthinkable crime against their beautiful girl could not go unpunished. There would be no police called, no trust placed in the authorities. They'd handle this themselves.

Ruby's gaze was steady, her decision made.

'Find him,' she said.

CHAPTER 38

'Come on, darlin', I'm takin' you to Uncle Bobby's. You'll be safe there.' Ruby held her daughter tightly, knowing she had to protect her from whatever was coming next.

There was a slight pause. 'From what, Mum?' Cathy had stopped crying, and instead she turned to face her mother, looking directly into her eyes.

Ruby stopped and stared back. She couldn't tell Cathy what she instinctively knew inside. She couldn't tell her that George, when he was found, was a dead man walking, yet Cathy sensed enough to even ask the question.

'I don't want you around when they find him. You've had enough trauma for one night,' Ruby said eventually.

It was enough to satisfy her daughter.

Cathy nodded. 'OK, Mum, I don't really want to see him anyway. I'll go to Bobby and Belle's, just promise me one thing . . .'

'What's that, darlin'?'

'Don't let him suffer,' Cathy said, tears welling up in her eyes again. Ruby's heart broke again at the sight of her, looking so young and forlorn, her innocence ripped from her so brutally.

She pulled Cathy into her arms again. 'I promise, darlin', I won't let that happen.' Ruby felt a thud of guilt, which she quickly dismissed. She knew that George would not survive the night. Her brother would be hunted down like prey. His life was worthless now. Archie would not let him live after raping their daughter. It was the way of the underworld, the law of survival. George had transgressed the line that separated man from beast, and he would pay the ultimate price. Ruby couldn't begin to understand her own shock, her own desperation.

There was nothing Ruby could do to protect him, no matter how torn she was. On the one hand George was the baby brother she loved with all her heart, on the other hand he'd brutalised her daughter, the other innocent who Ruby had sworn to protect.

She went to her daughter's wardrobe and pulled out a thick fluffy dressing gown and soft underwear for her to change into. She watched as her daughter winced with pain as she gently pulled off her jeans and knickers, revealing scratched skin and yet more blood from George's violent attack.

The sight was almost enough to make Ruby break down. *Stay strong for Cathy, stay strong, you can fall apart later*, she chanted in her mind, gritting her teeth to stop the tears and shock coming.

'We'll put you in a nice, warm bath and Belle will stay with you day and night. You're safe now, Cathy,' Ruby murmured as she worked, dressing her daughter with the tenderest care, all the while trying to hold in the emotions that seized her.

Maternal love is as fierce as it is caring, and Ruby felt a swirling torrent of grief, rage and sadness inside her, yet no one would've guessed. The years of keeping a poker-straight face in business deals were so ingrained in her now that she was able to care for her daughter without exposing her horror. Ruby knew if she broke down, she wouldn't be able to do what she knew she had to.

Ruby helped Cathy into their new Bentley, and drove off into the night, her headlights dipped to try to avoid attention. Ruby rang ahead as she drove.

'I can't say nuthin' but we're comin' over. Cathy's been attacked. I need you two to look after her,' Ruby said. Her voice was low, her tone serious.

'What's 'appened, Rube?' Bobby said, his voice sounded instantly alert.

'I'll explain later. Cathy needs to be kept safe. We're almost at yours.' Ruby hung up.

A couple of minutes later, she pulled into the drive of the house they'd once lived in, now Bobby and Belle's home. They were already standing outside the house, Belle in a dressing gown, Bobby in his day clothes. They had clearly been preparing to go to bed when she rang.

'Let's just get inside,' Ruby ordered. She helped Cathy out of the car. Her daughter had been silent through the drive, and in a strange way, this frightened Ruby more. It didn't seem natural to be so calm after the attack she'd suffered.

'Belle, please run Cathy a bath. Bobby, I need to speak to you urgently,' Ruby said sharply. Belle looked to her husband and he nodded. She smiled at Cathy, putting her arms around her as she led Ruby's daughter upstairs and into the bathroom.

Ruby marched into the kitchen. She started to pace up and down, holding her head in her hands. Bobby looked alarmed.

'What is it, Rube? Tell me,' Bobby said, grabbing her by the elbows and forcing her to stop walking.

Ruby's face, when she brought it up to hold Bobby's gaze, was grief-stricken. 'It was George. George raped Cathy. Archie won't let him live. He has to go, Bobby, and I can't bear any of it.' Ruby felt herself starting to fall down a deep, black well of emotion. She *had* to be strong. She *had* to get back. The night wasn't over yet.

'Fuckin' hell. Fuck!' Bobby let go of her arms like she was made of hot coals. It was his turn to pace.

He shook his head, disbelief fighting with anger.

'Our little brother was high on drugs, Bobby. We had a terrible argument earlier in the day and he stormed out. We went out for a meal to try and calm it all down . . .' At this point, Ruby felt a pang of shame and guilt so strong it almost knocked her sideways. 'I can't believe I left her.

I can't believe I left Cathy in the house alone. I let this happen, Bobby.' Tears streamed down Ruby's face now. They were unstoppable. The dam had burst. 'Cathy was in the house. She said she'd 'ave a quiet word with George when he got back but I knew he was high, I could see it and I left her . . .'

'It wasn't your fault. You're not to blame for our brother's actions,' Bobby burst out.

'Maybe. Maybe not. The truth was that George went and took more drugs, God knows what he scored, and he came back . . . and that's when he raped my little girl . . .' Ruby keened, doubling up with terrible pain at the violence, the worst crime that can be inflicted upon a woman.

Bobby was now sitting at the kitchen island, his head in his hands, crying softly. Eventually, Ruby stood up and wiped her eyes.

'I promised myself I wouldn't let Cathy see my pain. This has to be about helpin' her, and her alone. Listen, Bobby, I need you and Belle to stay up with Cathy, all night if you 'ave to, as I 'ave to go back. There's more to be done. Justice needs to be done.' Ruby's face was dark in the shadows thrown by the overhead light.

Bobby looked over at her pleadingly, 'Don't go back, Rube. Stay 'ere with Cathy. She needs her mum tonight . . .'

Ruby shook her head. 'I'll be back later but there's somethin' I need to do first . . .'

Bobby knew not to ask.

Ruby obviously looked as desperate as she felt, because Bobby nodded and said, 'All right, go, do what you 'ave to do.'

A look of understanding that went beyond words passed between the two siblings. Evil had to be put right, it had to be avenged, and they both knew that Archie and Alfie would stop at nothing.

CHAPTER 39

Back at the mansion, Ruby walked in. The house was silent. Suddenly her mobile buzzed. She opened it and saw it was her husband calling.

'Archie?' she said, putting her Gucci handbag down on the marble worktop.

'We've got him. We're on our way.'

Ruby hung up. She put her phone back in her bag and looked around the room, waiting. Everything appeared the same, yet everything was different.

The minutes felt like hours as she waited. Then she heard the sound of the car wheels on the gravel. Glancing up at the clock, she saw it was now almost 2 a.m. The darkest hour of the night.

But there was no sound of footsteps. Suddenly, she saw the lights go on in the plush garden office outside. Picking up her handbag, Ruby prepared to walk out to meet her adored little brother, who had become a monster.

Fear wrestled with fury as she walked across the immaculate lawn. She could hear Alfie shouting, and she willed him to quieten down. They didn't want to alert the neighbours.

Her hand trembled as she opened the office door. Alfie was screaming in George's face. Her little brother had a black eye and was cowering on the sofa. He had clearly taken a beating.

'Careful, Alfie, or you'll 'ave the Old Bill breathin' down our necks,' said Ruby quietly. There was something in her tone that had authority, that men like Alfie – violent, reckless men – seemed to obey instantly.

He backed off, glaring into George's face, which was red from crying. Her gaze travelled over him. His clothes were dishevelled, as you'd expect if he'd taken a kicking, and he was clutching at an injury on his arm.

'Where was he?' she said eventually, looking over at Archie, who was standing by the window, his back to the three of them. It was as if he could not bear to even look at her brother.

It was Alfie who replied.

'He was at his mate's house. Big-time dealer boy 'ere was crouching low at his friend's house gettin' fucked up on crack.'

Ruby nodded. She looked over at her brother and, in that moment, felt a surge of pity. He was a pathetic sight, sobbing and shaking, as the effects of the drugs wore off, and the knowledge of his attack sunk in.

Ruby saw she needed to take control. It was only a matter of time before Archie's pent-up anger would be released, and she could see Alfie snarling next to her. He'd always reminded her of a dog bred to fight, an animal straining at the leash. Well, soon he'd be freed to set upon her brother, the shivering, swaying mess that had brutalised her girl.

'Leave us,' she said.

Archie looked round. He spoke at last. 'I'm not leavin' you alone in 'ere with him. No way, babe.'

'Leave us, please,' Ruby said, 'both of you. I want to speak to my brother.' She looked into her husband's eyes, seeing pure revenge there, and she nodded. 'I understand. I still want to speak to him . . . whatever he's done, he is my brother, and more like a son to me . . .'

Archie saw his wife's determination and relented.

He signalled to Alfie to follow him out.

'We'll be right outside if he tries anythin', fuckin' ponce,' Alfie sneered.

Ruby waited until the door was shut behind them.

She came over to the sofa where her brother was sitting. She put her arm around him, feeling the sweat soaking through his clothes, the smell of fear leaching from him.

'Why did you do it?' she asked.

George shook his head. 'It's the drugs. They make me mental. I don't know why I did that to Cathy. I love Cathy, she's the best one of all of us . . .' George snivelled, snot and tears running down his face. 'I'm sorry, I'm so, so sorry. Promise me somethin', Ruby?' he sobbed.

'What's that, darlin'?' Ruby replied, rubbing his back to calm him as if he was a child again. How many times had she rubbed his tummy when it was sore, or soothed his night terrors as a child? Far too many to count. How many times had she wiped away childish tears, calmed his frustrations and fussed over imagined injuries? It seemed like their whole life together was suddenly in front of them and Ruby was left to pick out the memories: George smiling with an ice cream on a hot summer's day, holding him as he giggled in a bubble bath as a baby, walking him to school on his first day. It had all led to this, this degradation, this disgrace, an unforgiveable crime.

'Promise me you won't let them hurt me.' George turned his face up to hers and the pain and regret was there to see.

He burst into fresh tears and Ruby found herself comforting him again, saying, 'There, there, it's goin' to be OK.'

'It isn't Ruby, I know . . .'

Ruby felt her heart lurch with the love she bore this young man, her baby brother, now a rapist. He was her flesh and blood, whatever he'd done. She looked back into his eyes. They were filled with desperation, and he clung to her, shaking and crying. She could feel his tears soaking into her blouse.

Her decision had been made hours ago yet she almost balked, almost turned away from the path she needed to follow. Her love for him had to stay strong or she wouldn't be able to do it. She held him closer. Behind her was the Gucci bag, now open, and she placed her hand inside it.

The seconds stretched out yet George didn't appear to notice.

She mustn't wobble. She mustn't hesitate.

'I promise I won't let them hurt you,' she said. 'I love you, darlin'.'

As she said the words her hand grasped the cold metal of the handgun she carried with her always.

She brought the weapon gently to the side of George's head.

She had to do this. She had to show mercy because she knew her husband would not.

Ruby took a deep breath – and pulled the trigger.

BANG!

Blood, gristle and bone shot around the room. George's skull exploded into a million fragments. Drops of red were sprayed across the room, covering the sofa, the floor in front of them and Ruby herself.

His body, now a dead weight, slumped onto the sofa cushion, and she dropped the gun on the wooden floor, a sound which would stay with her for ever.

The door burst open.

Ruby didn't look up. She was leaning over him, cradling the lump of bone and blood that was her brother.

'It's done,' she said.

No one spoke. Nobody moved. It was as if they'd been frozen in a terrible spell, a nightmare with no beginning or end.

Then the spell was broken.

'Fuck!' yelled Alfie.

'What did you do, Ruby? What did you go and do?' Archie said as he ran over to his wife.

Slowly, Ruby stood up. It was as if everything went numb. The world slipped away and all she could hear was the rush of blood and grief in her head.

'Get her out of 'ere. Now!' Alfie shouted to his twin, who seemed as stunned as Ruby was. 'Take her inside. Get her to take all her clothes off. Put Ruby in the bath, quickly. Grab the clothes and bring them back 'ere,' Alfie commanded. He was a practised killer and knew the drill.

'Why did ya do this, Ruby? Why?' Archie said, staring up at his wife with new eyes.

Ruby didn't notice the blood trickling down her face, covering her hands, soaking through her silk dress. She felt like she was in a trance as she looked back at the man she married so long ago.

'For love . . .' was all she said, taking his arm and letting herself be led away to the house.

'When you've undressed her, put everythin' in a black bin liner. Her shoes, her handbag, everything',' Alfie added. He was already dragging the body onto the floor.

'Go!'

Archie led Ruby up to the main bathroom where there was a wet area and a roll-top bath. She was shaking violently now, but let herself be taken.

Slowly, carefully, as if undressing a small child, Archie peeled off her clothes. Ruby barely noticed. In her mind's eye she was still at the scene of the crime, witnessing what would inevitably be coming next.

As Ruby stepped into the shower, as the rivulets of blood ran from her body, swirled in the plug hole and disappeared, she knew what her husband's twin would be doing.

In her mind's eye, she saw him strip George's body, putting his clothes and shoes into a bin bag. She saw him take another, smaller bag, and fill it with his rings and his gold chains, all covered in his blood. She saw him shave his head, pull out his fingernails and toenails with pliers before pulling out her brother's teeth and placing them in the same small bag. She could almost hear the crack of splintering bone, the grunts of the effort required to rip apart a human being, one she still loved dearly despite his terrible crime against Cathy.

Ruby stepped out of the shower and let her husband pat her down, before stepping into a bubble bath for the final part of her cleansing.

'Thank you,' Ruby murmured at last as she sank down into the sweet-smelling water.

They heard a sound. An electric chainsaw. It was a strange sound for the depths of the night but she knew exactly what it was being used for.

Alfie would've laid down thick plastic sheeting on the floor, then dragged George's remains onto it. The final part of the macabre theatre of her brother's death was playing out. He would have to saw off his limbs, cut the trunk into several parts, and cut everything; his arms, legs, body, neck, spine, into bits small enough for the pigs to digest.

In Ruby's mind there was no other way they could hide the body. George's body would be taken in large sacks to the pig farm that lay just outside London, in Essex. Pigs couldn't digest fingernails and toenails, something to do with the protein in them, so they would pass straight through them. That's why the nails, hair and jewellery would have to be disposed of another way. She knew that Alfie would then take a car on the Woolwich Ferry and throw those remains over the side, letting the water carry away the evidence.

Archie asked, softly this time, 'Why did ya do it, Ruby?' His face looked ghastly in the light thrown down by the ceiling spotlights.

Ruby turned to the man she loved. She wouldn't lie, she didn't need to. She said bleakly, 'I had to. I killed my brother because if I didn't then you and yer brother would've tortured him first, you would've made him suffer for what he did and I couldn't bear that. Truly, it was the kindest way. It was an act of mercy.'

CHAPTER 40

Come 'ere, darlin', yes that's it, one foot in front of the other! What a good boy you are, you've taken your first steps. Oh, George, you beautiful boy, come to me, come to your big sister. The little boy gurgled with delight at his prowess, walking alone, wobbling from side to side in a shaft of sunlight. Ruby realised she was back in her old family home in Star Lane. The kitchen was the same, clean but basic with the yellow Formica table and the small yard out back. For a moment, just a mere moment, Ruby could sense her parents there too, though that wouldn't have been right. Surely they were dead by then? Perhaps she could feel their ghosts looking over their third child, the one left to Ruby and Bobby to bring up. Ruby felt puzzled, but she knew they were there, watching over her, asking her to look after little George, to protect him, to shelter him . . .

Ruby awoke out of her dream, the smell of burning leaves seeping into her bedroom. She yawned, trying to shake off the unsettling memory of her little brother taking his first steps unaided, the dream she'd plunged into upon falling into a dead sleep. Even though she was now awake, she could almost feel George with her, how warm he'd been in her arms as a baby, how much he giggled when he realised he could walk by himself. She wanted to stay there, in that strange dream state, far away from what awaited her.

Ruby got out of bed slowly and walked to the window. Archie wasn't beside her and his half of the bed felt cold. Perhaps he hadn't been to bed at all.

In the garden she could see her husband was tending to a bonfire, heaping the piles of autumn leaves left by the gardener a few days previously onto a smouldering fire. From where she was standing, she could just see the cuff of the silk dress she'd worn last night peeking out at the bottom.

Ruby shuddered and turned away. She felt panic rising inside her and a sudden urge to throw up. Instead, she started to cry for the loss of the brother she loved so dearly, whose life she had taken so effortlessly.

Would she ever move on from this? Would her love for him, her guilt at being the one who killed him, ever be fully erased? She doubted it. She knew this guilt would become part of her. All she could feel then was the emptiness of life without the boy she'd brought up. She'd failed him, she knew that. She'd tried so hard to be like a mum to him but she knew it had never been enough. She could never replace his mum, Cathy, and dad, Louie. She saw that now, and she saw how confused and damaged he'd been by the loss he'd suffered so young. Yet, none of it seemed equal to the crime he'd committed against her daughter.

It was time to think about Cathy. Her daughter would be traumatised. She'd been raped – her virginity taken from her by the uncle she loved dearly. Ruby had to move past the events of last night and focus everything on her now. Would Cathy ever get over it? Ruby didn't know, but she would be with her every step of the way.

Must get up and go to her, Ruby thought. She could only have had a few hours' sleep, and she felt it. *This is nothin' compared to how my Cathy must be feelin'* . . .

Somehow they all had to move past the horror.

Ruby pulled on her silk dressing gown and headed downstairs, straight to the coffee machine. Archie walked into the kitchen and she turned to look at the man who was as much a part of her soul as her own spirit.

'Is it sorted?' she asked, seeing the exhaustion, the dark rings under Archie's eyes and the night's stubble still on his chin.

'It's done. Now, we move on,' he replied.

She nodded. She didn't ask him how he'd disposed of George's body. She knew without saying that all it would've taken was a large back-hander to the pig farmer who would've fed them his limbs, brain and muscle for breakfast. Just like Freddie Harris. Just like so many who ran up against the strict codes of the underworld.

You don't hurt your own. You don't mug off your own. Simple, brutal, and effective.

At that moment, Alfie walked in. He looked like he hadn't slept either.

There was an awkward silence as the three studied each other.

Ruby broke it by offering coffee.

Alfie shook his head. 'Get Cathy,' was all he said. Alfie might not be a sensitive type, but today he saw the heart of the matter. Nothing else mattered but taking care of Cathy.

Ruby nodded.

'Alfie, my wife's traumatised . . .' Archie started to say, but this time it was her who butted in. 'It's OK, darlin'. Alfie's right. I need to see Cathy.'

'All right, babe. We'll go together. Alfie can finish the cleanin' up.' He leaned in to kiss Ruby, and for a brief second she yearned to cling to him, to sob and beg for forgiveness, for redemption, but she knew she couldn't break down.

She walked upstairs like a zombie, pulling on the first outfit she saw and tying her hair back with a hairband. She caught sight of herself in the mirror. She looked older, weary and very afraid. Not for herself, but for her daughter. The hardest part was facing Cathy now, the lies she would have to tell to protect her daughter.

Just around the corner from Bobby and Belle's home, Ruby pulled over and turned off the engine of the Bentley.

'What's the matter, babe? Why 'ave we stopped?' Archie, whose face was grey, turned to her in the car.

Ruby composed her thoughts. Archie had to understand her way of thinking or they could face losing Cathy for ever.

'I don't want either of us to tell Cathy what happened,' she said.

Archie nodded. 'So what do we tell her?'

'We both know if we tell Cathy I murdered George, she'll never forgive me, so we've got no choice. We 'ave to lie to her, tell her that we've sent George away somewhere . . . I need to know you can do that, Archie.'

Archie thought for a moment. 'It's the only way, I see that.'

Ruby nodded, turning on the ignition, and continuing the journey. Their pact was sealed. The truth would stay hidden, to protect Cathy, to protect them all.

CHAPTER 41

Belle and Cathy appeared to be fast asleep, though the young girl was beginning to stir. She was lying on the bed, while Belle was in a nearby chair.

Cathy opened her eyes as Ruby walked in softly. For a moment she looked just like the sweet, happy girl she was, then as she woke up, her mind cleared and her eyes clouded over as the memories of the night before came rushing back.

'Darlin', it's Mum and Dad. How are you? Oh my lovely girl, come 'ere.' Ruby embraced her daughter as Cathy began to cry, holding her close and rocking as she sat on the edge of the bed. Archie hovered close by, agony written on his face. It was every father's worst fear, a daughter being raped and powerless to have prevented it.

Belle's eyes flickered open. She yawned deeply, and her face looked puffy with tiredness. Bobby was standing in the doorway holding a tray with four mugs of sweet tea.

'Drink this, it'll make you feel better,' Bobby said, looking at Ruby.

'What happened, Ruby?' Belle said softly, but her eyes were sharp. Until now, Ruby had thought Belle a pleasant-enough woman, but now she realised there was a keen intelligence underneath the hippy exterior.

'Let's talk later,' Ruby said, this time looking at her brother Bobby.

'Belle, love, why don't ya take Cathy and get her some breakfast. She needs to eat.'

Ruby helped Cathy up off the bed, crooning, 'Put your dressin' gown on, that's it. Now, what would you like? Eggs on toast?'

'Bobby?' Belle cut across them, looking straight at her husband.

'We'll speak later, I promise. Take Cathy down, love, please?' he replied.

'It's fine, darlin', I just need to speak to Bobby. You go and eat. Aunt Belle will look after ya,' Ruby said to Cathy as she passed her over to Belle.

Belle's face was mutinous but she took the girl anyway, and Ruby was thankful to hear her speak softly to her daughter as they went.

'Did ya find him?' Bobby asked, but Ruby's face told him everything he needed to know.

Archie stood at the doorway, saying nothing.

'Jeez Rube, did they kill him?' Bobby said, his voice a whisper.

Ruby shook her head, and before Bobby could reply she said, 'No, I did.'

There was silence.

Bobby looked over at her. 'Tell me it ain't true. You killed George?'

Ruby sat down heavily onto the bed. 'Yes,' she said flatly. 'I killed our brother. I did it to stop my husband and his twin rippin' him to bits.' A single tear ran down Ruby's face.

Then she heard Bobby break down. With his head in his hands, he sobbed. 'Our bruvver, our little bruvver . . .'

'I know . . . I'm so sorry. If there'd been any other way . . .' Ruby said.

Archie said nothing.

She waited for Bobby to finish crying. His face when he turned to her was red raw. 'I can't believe George's dead.'

'I can't believe it neither,' Ruby replied, 'but it's dealt with. He was a dead man the minute he touched her.'

Archie coughed. 'We couldn't do it no other way. He sealed his fate and paid the price for attackin' our daughter,' he said.

'Listen, we can't tell Cathy ever. She must never know what I've done,' Ruby added.

'So, what do we tell her?' Bobby replied. He knew the truth would kill her, and in his own way, he accepted the simple fact: George's murder must be hidden from her.

'We tell her we found him and gave him money to leave. We say he's not welcome back, and won't be returnin'.' Archie took charge.

'We'd better go to her. If we stay up 'ere too long, she might suspect—'

'That we're lyin' to her?' Bobby said bleakly.

'Yes,' Ruby said simply. 'From now on, we 'ave to stick to the story, and we 'ave to make her believe it. We'll tell her that George has gone to America. He won't ever be back.'

Downstairs Cathy was nibbling at a piece of toast while Belle sat next to her looking anguished.

'She doesn't want to eat. It's the shock. Everything OK?' Belle said, looking straight to her husband for an explanation.

Bobby shook his head.

'Baby girl,' Archie said tenderly. 'We found George . . .'

'You found him?' Cathy looked up. Her face was white as death, her eyes red from crying and lack of sleep.

'Yes, love, and we dealt with it. He won't ever be back. We gave him money to leave,' Ruby said, not able to meet her daughter's eyes.

'Leave?' Cathy looked like she couldn't take in her mum's words.

Ruby glanced at Archie, sharing each other's concern.

'I'm sorry, darlin', but George has gone for good. He knows he's not welcome in our family any more.

He's gone for ever.' Ruby searched her daughter's face. She was unusually quiet. Where were the tears? The shock? Where was the need for revenge, the agony at his departure?

'Mum?'

'Yes, darlin'?'

'Is that the truth?' Cathy's question almost floored Ruby. She steeled herself for the lie that had to be told.

'It is, love, now eat up. You need your strength.' Ruby felt a chill as she spoke.

God, forgive me, she thought, *I'm doin' this for you, darlin', to keep you safe, so that your innocence isn't totally destroyed by it all.*

Deep inside the pit of her stomach, she could feel the doubt seeding like an acorn deep underground.

'We gave him money – a lot of money – and he's gone to America.' Ruby listened to her words like they were flies buzzing around a carcass. Regret, shame and guilt hummed inside her heart but she carried on anyway. This was all to protect Cathy, wasn't it? 'It's best he's gone, for all our sakes. He won't see any of us ever again. He knows never to return. If he does, your dad and Alfie will kill him.'

Tears slid down Cathy's face now, and it took all Ruby's willpower not to break down and confess the truth, to beg forgiveness of the daughter she adored. *I have no choice, I have to protect her from any more grief.*

The thought steadied her. Cathy's gentle tears would be nothing compared to the wild grief she'd feel if she knew that George was already dead.

Cathy turned her tear-stained face up to her mum's. 'I would've forgiven him, you know.'

CHAPTER 42

Ruby watched from the kitchen as the last wall of the office was pulled down. She stayed there as the base was covered with decking, destroying and covering the evidence piece by piece. She thought of the unwritten rules, the codes of conduct that were followed by the criminal world, and how deeply they were enmeshed in lies and secrets. She thought of Bobby's natural grief, grief that was as raw and unfiltered as hers was buried and hidden.

Ruby had watched him, seeing the pain she had caused him, knowing there had been no other choice for her. She told Bobby she did it for love of their brother, not for revenge. He'd understood that Alfie would've maimed him, abused him and revelled in the killing, so it had to be her. Yet, despite this, she sensed a distance open up between them.

Somehow she knew that, in that one act, everything had changed. For Cathy's sake, she also knew that they'd try to be the family they once were, but it wasn't the same. Their family would never be the same again.

This knowledge made Ruby's next decision seem obvious. She would relocate to Spain with Cathy and Archie, and leave England behind for ever. Alfie had flown back to South America on the first available flight after George's death, and there was now a sense that she was rewriting history, remaking their future far away from the terrible truth.

Too many questions were already being asked in the week since Ruby killed George. Several of his mates had rung asking for him. People were commenting they hadn't seen him. Archie put the news out on the grapevine that George had gone to America after being kicked out of yet another school, but the murmurs didn't stop. Why hadn't George said goodbye? Why was his mobile turned off? *Because it's at the bottom of the Thames*, Ruby thought as she answered yet another phone call, this time from his pal in Chigwell who'd bought tickets for a gig for them both and wondered why he hadn't heard from her brother, and demanding to be paid.

'He's not takin' my calls. Tell him he owes me for the tickets and two bags of weed. He's bang out of order,' the voice said before hanging up.

Ruby sighed. She turned to Archie. 'Make sure that kid gets his money, and understands that we're movin' on. We won't ever live back 'ere again.'

All she wanted was to start a new life away from this place, especially for Cathy. She wanted her daughter to live far from this house where she'd been raped. She sensed that the only way her daughter would heal from her uncle's violation, if indeed she ever did, was away from here, away from the memories. At least, Cathy could grieve the loss of her innocence somewhere where the sun shone and she had friends.

Ruby chartered a private jet to take them and their belongings over, while Archie managed the Chigwell mansion, shutting it up and installing state-of-the-art security cameras.

Stepping out of the aircraft, feeling the winter sun on her skin, Ruby felt the first spark of hope since the tragic events. She looked at her daughter, hiding behind big, dark sunglasses, pulling a hoodie around her though it was a mild afternoon. Her once-sunny, sweet daughter was a shadow of her former self. Where she used to prattle away, chatting and giggling with her parents, she was now quiet and withdrawn. Ruby knew that only time, and possibly a good therapist, could help her, but the sight of Cathy grieved her beyond measure.

'You all right, darlin'?' Ruby asked.

Cathy nodded, but didn't say a word, and yet she understood. Ruby saw that her daughter's sense of security had been stolen from her in the attack. She hadn't just lost her virginity – and her uncle – she'd lost her safety.

Sometimes Ruby wondered if Cathy knew in her heart that George had been killed. And sometimes she wondered if Cathy would feel safer knowing George could never hurt her again. But she knew, deep down, it would destroy her gentle daughter to know her mother had killed her uncle.

She would never tell her the truth.

Ruby worried constantly about her daughter as the months passed and she stayed as quiet as a mouse, keeping to the rooms of the villa or the pool, but rarely venturing any further unless it was to go to school. Ruby organised a top-class therapist to speak to Cathy, and every week, drove her to the woman's office. Gradually, Cathy started to come out of her shell, even to eat dinner with the family at the dining table or outside on one of the verandas.

Ruby's worry for her daughter's well-being began to ease with each step she took toward healing. She had taken the last few months off from the business, leaving Archie to run it alongside his father, so she could always be on hand if Cathy needed her. Lloyd knew the truth about George, Archie told him as soon as they'd arrived, and he'd accepted it as just another underworld killing; effective and necessary to resolve a bad situation. Ruby trusted Lloyd with her life, and she knew he would never betray her secret.

Meanwhile, all the staff had been replaced – and security doubled – after the Albanian set-up that almost cost Archie his life. There were now twenty-four-hour guards with dogs and machine guns patrolling the boundaries of their estate. She hoped it helped Cathy feel safer, though the real threat had come from inside their home.

Winter bled into spring and spring into summer. Cathy had become increasingly active, and confident. Ruby saw she didn't need to fuss around her all the time now, and with that knowledge, Ruby was back in business.

'I want to be in on the next negotiations,' she said to Archie and Lloyd one evening as the three of them sat round the large antique dining table eating the supper their new chef had prepared. 'I need life to get back to normal,' she added.

Lloyd nodded and looked at Archie.

'Course, darlin', whatever you want. We've missed your sharp mind, and timing couldn't be better. We have the Russian coming tomorrow.'

The three of them smiled at each other and then swiftly moved the conversation on as Cathy entered the room and took her spot at the table. Both Archie and Lloyd fell straight to eating, but Ruby noticed that Cathy only seemed to be moving her salad around her plate.

'Not hungry, love?' Ruby said, her attention instantly drawn to her daughter.

Cathy raised her gaze from her plate and looked directly at her mum. 'I want to know where George is.'

Ruby stopped chewing. She looked at Archie.

'Darlin', I thought we said it's not up for discussion. I don't even want that boy's name mentioned in this 'ouse again. He's gone, that's all ya need to know,' Archie said, more forcefully than he'd intended.

There was a moment's silence.

'Mum?' the young girl said, this time pleadingly.

Ruby gulped. 'Your dad's right. It's in the past now. We don't even know where George is ourselves, so we couldn't tell ya anyway.' She put down her knife and fork, her hunger gone.

Cathy did the same, then slowly pushed back her chair, got up and walked away from the table.

'Let her go. She'll come round,' Archie soothed, but Ruby wasn't sure.

She smiled at her husband. 'Course she will, love.' Ruby stared after Cathy for a moment, but Lloyd interrupted her thoughts.

'Ruby, we need your attention.'

'Sorry, Lloyd. Yes, tell me everythin' you know about this man, Vladimir Ivanov,' she replied, looking between her husband and father-in-law.

'Our contacts in the East have been tailin' him for a while. He's a big player, most likely ex-KGB.'

Lloyd nodded as Archie spoke.

'If we can get him onside, it would make us the single biggest player in Spain, and potentially Europe. If we could gain a partnership with him, we'd be set.'

Ruby dipped her head in acknowledgement.

She could sense Archie's excitement.

Here were new possibilities, new challenges, new dangers. Almost reluctantly, she had to acknowledge that the thought thrilled her.

CHAPTER 43

The day of the meeting, Ruby pulled on a Chanel suit and matching pearl necklace. She wore her hair back in an artfully messy chignon, finishing her look with a spray of Chanel No. 5.

Stepping into a sky-high pair of Manolo stilettos, Ruby stood and looked at the finished result. She'd researched Russian protocols in doing business, and formal dress was expected. So, did she look business-like? Yes. Did she look focused? For sure. Did she look dangerous? Definitely. The glint in her eye told her what she already knew. She looked like a woman to be reckoned with.

Vladimir was escorted through the villa by two guards. He walked with an air of royalty, stopping to admire a drawing by Picasso, which Archie had recently acquired through Ruby's dodgy art dealer, Marcus.

Ruby took her chance and sidled up to him.

'Beautiful, isn't it?' she said, close behind him.

He turned swiftly, and she saw a brief look of desire before he shut down his reactions.

'Exquisite, dear lady, much like yourself,' the wealthy drug baron replied.

He took her hand and placed a kiss gently on top of her fingers. It was strangely intimate, and Ruby shivered, despite herself. He appeared to know exactly who she was. He'd done his research, which both impressed and alarmed Ruby.

This was someone to watch.

Vladimir Ivanov was handsome. His high Slavic cheekbones, dark hair streaked with silver and tanned skin complemented a natural charm that seemed to ooze from him.

He stepped in beside her as she walked him to the office where the meeting would take place, slightly too close for such casual acquaintance, yet Ruby found she didn't mind. His conversation was mild, he chatted as they walked, his arms in hers as if they were the greatest of friends – or lovers.

Ruby was relieved to see Archie and Lloyd already inside the room. Archie was wearing a white linen shirt, unbuttoned at the neck showing his tanned skin, with slacks and slip-on whiskey-coloured Italian leather shoes. Lloyd favoured suits and was wearing his signature cut, a bespoke mid-blue Westwood. Vladimir's eyes swept around the room, taking in every detail.

The men shook each other's hands then it was down to business.

'Tell me, Mr Ivanov, what exactly are you proposing?' Ruby opened the conversation, straight to the point.

They'd agreed the night before that Ruby would make the opening salvo with the Russian. They thought it might knock him off balance.

The Russian looked momentarily confused. He turned to Lloyd and said baldly, 'I don't usually deal with women . . .'

Archie smiled as Lloyd looked to him. 'You do now. You deal with my wife or there's no deal.'

There was a pause as this information was digested.

'Perhaps it is my confusion with the English language,' Vladimir murmured. 'Naturally I'd be delighted to listen to your wife.' His smile was almost convincing.

He looked over at Ruby and said, 'My apologies. How can I have been so ungracious. It will be my pleasure to negotiate with such beauty.'

Ruby didn't dignify that with a response. She carried on, 'It seems to me, and forgive me if I'm wrong, Mr Ivanov, but we can help each other. I understand supply has been a bit of an issue.

'We know there's been a big bust. And a couple of shipments have been light.'

The Russian smiled. 'You are very well informed, and yes you are right. There have been problems. Supply not being what it should be.'

'We've had similar problems. At the moment, I believe they play us against each other. If we can strike a deal, work together, we would leave this other party with no room to manoeuver. Together we would be the single biggest player in Europe. No one would dare deal with anyone else. It looks to us like a partnership would be mutually beneficial,' Ruby said smoothly.

Vladimir looked at her frankly, sizing her up and evidently liking what he saw. He smiled and shifted in his seat, adjusting his designer suit and leaning towards her.

'This is true. It would be "beneficial", as you say, if we could secure our supply chains.'

'So, let's talk numbers, Mr Ivanov.' Ruby smiled.

'Call me Vladimir, please. Let us not devolve into numbers just yet. We must get to know each other first. To help our negotiations, I have brought a small gift for you, a sample of the product here to prove to you that it is the best on the market.'

Vladimir handed Archie a small decorative box. Archie inspected it. He looked up at Ruby and nodded.

'Your gift is appreciated, thank you. We have prepared the same for you,' she said. At Ruby's nod Archie handed Vladimir a beautifully carved box filled with white powder.

'Thank you. Shall we resume this conversation in two days' time? You will be guests on my yacht, *Grace*, which is moored nearby. We will get to know each other. It will be my pleasure to entertain you.'

Ruby knew that Russian business people rarely made a decision on the spot, preferring to think things through before committing. Therefore, she smiled her agreement as she got up to pour champagne into cut crystal glasses.

'To the future,' she said, raising her glass at Vladimir.

He echoed her gesture. 'To the future,' he said. Perhaps it was a trick of the light, but his eyes seemed to shine as he locked his gaze with hers.

The yacht was a huge gleaming white vessel moored in the fashionable harbour town. It was the largest of the boats, with a sleek long body and the Russian flag flying on top. Ruby had been in constant contact with Vladimir and his people over the past two days, but still she wasn't sure the deal had been done.

Ruby was the first to step aboard. There was a pool on the main deck with sun loungers and drinks tables, and a bar entirely decorated with mirrors that bounced light around the space.

'Enchanted. Please join me in my infinity pool. I don't usually invite guests into my private domain, but, for you,' and here Vladimir stared straight at Ruby, 'I make an exception.'

Chilled champagne awaited them. Vladimir was the first to disrobe and slip into the cool blue water. Ruby glanced at Archie, unsure whether to join him, but etiquette meant they could not leave their host alone in the pool.

Ruby slipped off her coral pink kaftan. Underneath she wore a simple emerald green bikini that complemented her pale skin.

She stepped into the water, accepting a glass of bubbly as she sank down, the cold clear water making her gasp.

'To us,' Vladimir said, holding his glass in a toast.

'To business,' said Archie firmly in response, making Ruby smile.

'We don't usually work with people outside of our networks, so this partnership is a new idea for us. I hope it's somethin' we can all agree on. It's a win-win for us all. What d'ya say, Vladimir?' Ruby's eyes glinted as she spoke. The thrill of making a deal was intoxicating. The fizz from the bubbles, the warm sunshine against the blue sky, the refreshing water and Vladimir's powerful charisma was a heady combination. It was easy to flirt with him, knowing it was just business and her husband was right there. None of it was real – except the money they'd make. It was a deal worth making.

'To our partnership,' said Vladimir.

'That's settled then.' Ruby raised her glass. 'To the future,' she said, knowing that today's meeting had been a mere formality. She'd pulled off the partnership she'd discussed with Lloyd earlier. He'd said that securing Vladimir as a partner could make them millions, and shore up their supply chain. No one would be able to squeeze them.

'To the future. Our deal is done. Now let's drink and eat,' Vladimir replied.

They clinked glasses.

Later, after the afternoon spent eating the finest caviar and blinis, and sipping champagne, they returned to the villa.

'You did it, Ruby.' Archie smiled, kissing her. 'Though I'm officially a jealous man.'

Ruby leaned in to kiss her husband. 'There's only ever been one man for me,' she said as her lips curled in a smile.

'You'll 'ave a yacht of your own for this, darlin'. One twice the size of Vladimir's,' Lloyd said behind them, making them break off their embrace.

Ruby laughed out loud. It wasn't the yachts, the money, even the properties and clothes, which elated her, it was the sheer excitement of the deal that kept her coming back for more.

CHAPTER 44

'To The Locksmith Wine Bar!' giggled Ruby.

'The Locksmith!' cheered back the people all standing around her and Bobby as they toasted the opening of their upmarket wine bar in Chigwell.

Bobby turned to his sister. 'Rube, are ya sure you want me to run this place? It's so . . . so . . .'

'Posh!' laughed Ruby in response. 'Look, Bobby.' She hushed her voice, and nudged him back to a quieter corner of the bar, which they had taken great delight in naming after their humble beginnings. 'This place is yours now. You're a natural. You love people and I've sent one of our associates from Spain to help with the business and accounts side. You're movin' up in the world, brother. I would've run it myself, but I just can't now . . . after everythin'. I can't bear to be here, but I couldn't miss this night . . . your night,' she added.

'Rube, I appreciate everythin' you've done for me and for Belle, but we both know this isn't just a legit bar.' Bobby kept his voice low. So, he'd guessed. She wasn't surprised. They'd grown up surrounded by crime at all levels.

Ruby shrugged. 'It's what we do. It's who we are, Bobby. You must know that by now? Look, I know you're worried about Belle. She's straight, she doesn't understand our world.'

'It wasn't always our world,' Bobby snapped.

'No it wasn't,' Ruby replied calmly. She could see her brother was rattled, but she also sensed that the prospect of owning a bar excited him. 'Belle doesn't 'ave to know anythin' about that side of it – and neither do you. All that is bein' taken care of. All you 'ave to do is enjoy it. It's yours to do whatever you want with.'

Bobby looked conflicted. It was obvious to Ruby that he hated keeping anything from his wife, yet it enabled him to create something of his own, something that wasn't lock-breaking or burglary.

'I'll do it, but you must never tell Belle,' Bobby said hesitantly, unable to meet Ruby's eyes.

'Of course not,' she said softly. *So many secrets*, she added in her mind as the siblings parted ways, him to check in with the bartender, her to circulate amongst their guests.

They'd named the bar for the set of skills that had given them their first break, though it was a long while since they'd needed to break any safes. Money was pouring into the family from their drug trade, but more and more they were finding that what they needed was to launder their money. Hence the need for the bar.

The Locksmith

As Bobby suspected, The Locksmith was a front. Even though Ruby couldn't bear to spend much time in Chigwell she'd decided to keep to the contacts they knew – including the dodgy accountant given to her by Charlie. They would clean their money via London, and the bar would now be an integral part of the process, siphoning money and creating legit funds as a result.

Reluctantly, Ruby had flown back for the opening to support Bobby, but being here for more than a few hours, days at most, was all she could manage. No, it was better if Bobby managed the bar. It gave him a 'respectable' job and kept him in the family business, where she could look after him. She'd kept the mansion, one of her last links with Charlie and Maureen, but it was shut up until Ruby and Archie could decide what to do with it.

She watched as Bobby moved through the room, shaking someone's hand, thumping another on the back amiably. He was in his element.

His path soon brought him back to Ruby, with Belle in tow.

'Bobby's the man of the hour,' Belle announced as she took a sip of her wine.

'To the king of The Locksmith,' Ruby cheered.

Bobby looked both pleased and slightly embarrassed, as Belle nudged him forward. 'Go on, you must go and chat to our guests. I'll be fine here with Ruby.'

Ruby watched as Bobby moved off, rubbing shoulders with local celebrities and upmarket crooks. The place was heaving.

Neither woman spoke as they watched Bobby. There seemed to be a frostiness that had sprung up between them. Ruby guessed this was because of what she'd done. She couldn't blame Belle for judging her. In Belle's eyes she was a murderess now after all, not just a dodgy dealer. As for Ruby, it wasn't the killing that bothered her. She didn't feel one iota of guilt over removing Saban, but George . . . Killing George was something that never left her, that reappeared in her nightmares each and every night.

It was Belle who broke the ice.

'You have to tell her.' It wasn't a statement, it was a command.

Ruby blinked.

'I can't do that, Belle, and by "her" I presume you mean *my* daughter.' Ruby emphasised her claim as Cathy's parent. It didn't go unnoticed.

'It's *your* daughter who rings me every day asking about George. "Where is he? What happened to him? Is Mum lying to me?"' Belle's voice was cold.

Ruby's heart froze. She almost dropped her glass. Suddenly, the room seemed to spin. She clutched onto a bar stool for support. 'Cathy is askin' after George? She's askin' you?'

'Yes, every night she calls. Every. Single. Night.'

'She never told me . . .' Ruby started to say, but then she remembered that the one time Cathy had asked after George they'd closed ranks on her, refusing to talk about him.

'What? That she was calling me? Oh yes, every evening. She's distraught, Ruby, absolutely distraught over what might have happened to him. He did a terrible thing, he hurt her, but he was also her uncle, more of a brother really. You can't expect him to just disappear and not have her ask questions. I can't keep lying to her.'

Ruby's internal world threatened to collapse. Being told that her beloved daughter was reaching out to another woman, even if it was her aunt, felt like a physical blow, but this wasn't the time to crumble. She willed herself to stay calm, though her heart was hammering under her designer dress.

Before she could respond, a well-known chat show host walked past, silencing both women momentarily. Ruby plastered a dazzling smile on her face and exchanged pleasantries, her laughter higher than usual. After a few minutes, the celebrity moved off, and Ruby turned back to Belle. This time she didn't hold back.

'So, you've had an attack of conscience. That's natural. I hate lyin' to Cathy too, but what you don't realise is the truth would kill her, and she'd 'ave to deal with his death on top of bein' raped. So, no, Belle, you won't be tellin' her and neither will I. If . . . *when* . . . she asks you again, you say the same thing: he's gone for good. You got that?'

Ruby stared into her sister-in-law's eyes, hard and fierce. Belle stared back but it was she who dropped her gaze first.

'This is my secret, Belle, mine! I'll take it to my grave, and I expect you to do the same, for Cathy's sake.'

Belle took a sip of her wine, and when she replied, her voice was dull, bleak. 'Or what?'

Ruby looked away, her anger building. She recognised that there was nothing she could do to stop Belle divulging her darkest secret. She just had to hope that, for Cathy's sake, she'd see sense.

Belle, white-faced with fury, hissed, 'What will you do, eh, Ruby? Cut me up and feed me to the pigs just like you did with Freddie Harris? Just like you did with your own brother? No one gets in your way, do they, Ruby? You're a murderer, you're a cold killer with no remorse, none at all!'

Ruby was shocked by the spite in Belle's tone. She looked at the woman again, seeing her as if for the first time. She'd always wondered how someone as nice as Belle had managed to work in a prison alongside men who'd committed terrible crimes. It had been a Category C prison for the least dangerous men but even so, none of them were angels, yet she'd taught a bunch of hardened crooks how to paint with watercolours! She'd had to be made of stronger stuff than she appeared, but Ruby had never seen this before.

In a strange way, Ruby had a new respect for this woman who, until now, she'd dismissed as 'straight' and 'nice'. Well, the niceness had gone, for now.

'All right, Belle. So, the gloves are off. I did what I had to do, and if I had to do it again I would.' Ruby stared back defiantly. Her voice was low but loud enough for Belle to hear every word.

'Is that a threat?' Belle countered, but now she looked on the verge of tears. The woman's anger was melting away, and it made Ruby pause. She saw Belle's guilt and how hard it was for her to be lying to Cathy, who she clearly adored. She saw how the veneer of strength had rubbed away, leaving a woman who cared for her daughter deeply. Cathy might be more like her old self these days but she was still affected, still quieter, more reserved than she'd ever been. Ruby couldn't risk destroying the small steps forward she'd taken.

Yet, Ruby suddenly felt sorry for Belle, seeing the impossible position she was in. 'I'm so sorry, Belle, but it must be this way, for Cathy. I can't control what you do. I can't stop you from tellin' her but I'm askin' you not to. Cathy has started to live again. Oh, it's only small things, like an occasional trip to the shops, or eating dinner with us as a family, but she is starting to cope with what happened. I can see she'll never be that same, innocent girl ever again though, and if she knew I'd killed George . . .' Ruby looked away, 'she'd never forgive any of us. So, I'm askin' you not to destroy my child's life any more than it has been already.'

And with that, Ruby walked away. She left Belle, she walked through the crowd, depositing her glass on a passing waiter's silver tray, and walked straight up to Archie.

367

'I want to go,' she said, and something in her tone told him she meant it.

'Come on,' he said without hesitation, and with his hand on her back, he steered her through the crowds.

Outside he hailed a cab.

'It's time to go back to Spain,' Ruby said as she leaned her head against her husband's shoulder.

He was wise enough not to question her just then. Instead, he nodded.

'Then we go.'

Ruby knew she had to trust Belle to do the right thing for Cathy, or trust that Belle was scared enough of her not to betray her. It was a risk but then again, wasn't everything?

CHAPTER 45

'Come on, darlin', let's go and 'ave a nice day together. We'll get our hair done and go for lunch at that restaurant you like.'

Back in Spain, Ruby was trying to cajole her daughter into going out with her for a girls' day. There was a fiesta in the local town to celebrate the end of summer and the start of autumn, and it was always a joy to see the spectacle, mingle with the crowds, watch the processions, then head off for some pampering.

Cathy was reluctant at first, but after Archie handed her a wad of notes, she brightened. 'Well, there is a dress I've seen. It's gorgeous, Mum, and I'd like to try it on . . .'

Ruby was determined to spend as much time with Cathy as possible after Belle's revelation. If her daughter was going to ask anyone for help, or seek comfort or reassurance, Ruby wanted to be the one who gave it to her. Belle's words had shaken her up.

'Let's go in the sports car with the top down. We'll be really flash today. Anyway, most of the staff will be off at

369

the festival so there's no point hangin' around 'ere. We'll 'ave a lovely day together.' Ruby smiled at her daughter. The sun had left her with a smattering of freckles and a light tan that set off the colour of her eyes, exactly the same shade as Ruby's.

Cathy was wearing a yellow sundress and flip-flops. She wore an ankle bracelet as her only jewellery, and looked relaxed and happy. The sight made Ruby's heart swell.

'You'll be goin' back to school in a few days so let's make the most of our time together,' she added, turning the car ignition and gliding off, the car emitting a deep throaty growl as they went.

It felt good to be out of the villa.

'You OK, darlin'?' Ruby asked as they drove down the road that wound along the hillside. Around them were pine trees firmly rooted in the rich red soil, their branches still in the heat.

'Yeah, I'm OK, Mum,' Cathy smiled, and the words were like warm honey to Ruby. It was the first real smile she'd seen on her daughter's face since the attack and Ruby cherished it. Ruby started to relax too. *She's healing. She's going to be OK, not the same, but OK,* she thought.

They drove to the town, spent the day buying clothes, new shoes and make-up before ending the day at the salon.

It was almost six o'clock in the evening by the time they returned. Ruby's tyres crunched on the gravel as they turned into the villa entrance.

'Where are the guards?'

Ruby looked round as Cathy spoke.

'Oh, I think your dad gave them the afternoon off but I thought he'd left a couple 'ere, just in case.'

Ruby frowned as she spotted a vehicle parked haphazardly outside the villa entrance. It was not the kind of car usually associated with their contacts. It was battered-looking and downmarket with scuffed tyres and dirty windows.

'Who's this? Do you know the car?' Ruby asked, thinking perhaps it was one of Cathy's friends borrowing one for the evening, but Cathy shrugged.

'No idea. Probably somethin' to do with Dad.'

Ruby wasn't reassured by her daughter's nonchalance. 'Why don't you stay 'ere and catch the last few rays of sunshine, darlin' . . .' she started to say, but Cathy had already swung out of the car and was heading for the entrance.

'I'm tired, Mum. I'm goin' inside.'

'Wait!' Ruby said as she got out of the car, and without shutting the door she hurried to the villa entrance. Suddenly, she felt a sense of foreboding. She started to reach inside her bag for her keys and then realised the door was already open.

Cathy, seemingly oblivious to her mum's instincts, stepped inside.

The cool air greeted them. Cathy walked ahead. Ruby heard her heels tap on the white tiled floor, the sound – clack, clack, clack – echoing through the quiet corridor.

Where was everyone? Surely Archie hadn't given them all the evening off? How trusting, how foolish of her husband . . . so very unlike him . . .

Ruby walked towards the large airy lounge. Then she heard Cathy scream.

There was the sound of a tussle, and a man's voice she didn't recognise. A bolt of panic went through her. She pushed open the lounge door. The first thing she saw was her daughter acting strangely, sitting bolt upright in one of the plush sofas, her eyes wide, her mouth open.

'Cathy?'

Then, she saw Archie tied to a chair, his face bleeding, his mouth a single menacing line in his face. He looked up at her but there was no time to ask questions.

'Where's the money?' shouted a man wearing a black balaclava. He marched up to Ruby and pointed his gun directly in her face.

CHAPTER 46

Time stood still.

Ruby turned to face the intruder, staring down the barrel of his gun.

'Tell us and you live,' the gunman said menacingly. His accent was Middle Eastern, his eyes coal black behind the mask.

A jolt of pure fear and adrenaline surged through Ruby's body.

'Give them nuthin'. Open the safe and we're all dead!' yelled Archie from the other side of the room.

Her eyes flicked over to where he was straining against the ties that bound him to a chair. Another balaclava-clad robber held a gun to his head.

The seconds ticked past. Ruby tried to swallow but her throat was dry.

How had the robbers got past the security guards she knew had been there earlier in the day? Surely Archie would never have let them go to the festival, not after what happened with the Albanians? Someone else must've betrayed them – of that she was now sure – but there was no time to speculate. Her life, and that of her daughter and husband, were on the line. One mistake and they were all dead.

As if to make his point, the second gunman slammed his fist into Archie's face. Her husband's nose exploded; blood sprayed across the white marble floor.

'Dad!' Cathy shrieked.

Ruby wanted to scream, to run to her beloved husband, but she was rooted to the spot with fear.

Stay calm, stay calm Ruby, she thought to herself. She mustn't show her panic. If there was anything she'd learnt from the life she'd led up until now, it was that.

'Give. Us. The. Money.' The man stepped closer. The gun was almost touching her face. Her ears strained for any other noise, the sound of other possible assailants, but the villa was silent. She guessed these two were working alone. They'd probably bribed the guards to let them in, a simple trick but effective.

Ruby realised they were all alone. No staff would rescue them. She had to face this herself. The thought, strangely, gave her strength. She was best when her back was against the wall. Throughout her life she'd taken chances, taken risks most others wouldn't. This was the ultimate test. She had to pass it.

She made a decision.

'All right,' she said. Somehow she kept her voice steady, though her heart pounded and she could feel sweat trickling down her back. 'I'll give you the money.'

'NO! Ruby they'll KILL us, d'ya hear me?' Archie dissolved into coughing. He spat blood onto the floor.

Hold still, Ruby, keep it together, she repeated in her mind like a mantra. She couldn't look at her husband in his blood-soaked clothes, tied up and brutalised, or she would break. An angry fly banged against the glass window and the sun shone on the azure sea far below the cliff. She gazed at the view, steeling herself.

'I'll do what you tell me but you don't touch him – or my daughter,' Ruby commanded, drawing herself up tall and holding her assailant's gaze.

The gunman turned to his associate and nodded. The other robber raised his arm as if to strike again.

'You. Don't. Touch. Him,' Ruby said. Her voice was low but there was no denying her authority.

The robbers exchanged a glance and the first one gestured for the other to hold back. It was a small victory but it gave Ruby hope she could get through this – if she held her nerve.

By now, she'd realised that these men could just shoot them all and escape with the paintings. There were several masterpieces on the walls, and it would've been a worthwhile haul. It was their focus on money that made Ruby think these gunmen were nobodies, just two chancers who got lucky. If they were professional crooks they'd know the value of the pieces, which far exceeded the contents of the safes in the villa. The fact they didn't seem to be interested in the pictures gave Ruby hope, but the fact they must have had the funds to bribe the guards left her worried there might be someone behind these crooks.

Their hesitation had also given her time to appraise them. Both wore scruffy clothes and scuffed trainers. They seemed agitated now, rattled. Perhaps they'd expected a woman to scream or faint.

As calmly as she could, she said, 'Gentlemen, I'll get you the money but put yer guns down. You're makin' me nervous and I might forget the combination.' Even as she said the words, she prayed that Archie would stay quiet. She wanted them focused on her.

She smiled, knowing the effect this would have on them. She sensed confusion amid the urgency. Their gazes were darting between each other, and like an animal hunting its prey, she sensed they were unsure now. This was her moment to take the lead. She'd faced down bigger villains than these two gun-wielding amateurs. She felt a surge of adrenaline again.

Both men pointed their guns at the floor.

'Thank you.' Every second that passed gave her the advantage. She turned her back to the men, praying they wouldn't seize their chance and grab her from behind. Nothing happened and so she walked, slowly, across the floor, her heels clicking on the cold, hard surface as she went.

She walked to the back of the room where a large abstract painting hung on the wall. The gunmen were now between her and her family. Sound was amplified.

She heard Cathy moaning, the two men breathing heavily inside their balaclavas and Archie quietly straining against his bindings. Ruby willed herself to keep going, to keep calm.

The painting rolled back to reveal a large safe, one of several in the villa, but she guessed they didn't know about the others. It didn't matter anyway. A plan had formed inside Ruby's mind. She had mere seconds left, seconds which would decide all of their fates. She knew that if she got this wrong, they were dead meat. One bad move, and it was all over. The fact heightened her senses, sharpened her mind.

She glanced back at the men and saw them exchange a look of glee. In that one gesture she saw something animal-like, something uncontrollable, and in her gut, she felt they'd do exactly what Archie said, they'd kill them all as soon as that cash was out of the safe. She had seconds to think. She mustn't let that happen.

She raised her hand to the dial.

CLICK. CLICK. CLICK.

'I always knew this was a dangerous business, and you two gentlemen 'ave proved me right,' Ruby said as the safe opened and she reached inside.

'NO! Don't give those bastards nuthin'!' Archie shouted.

Pulling out the gun she knew was hidden in there, she turned and pulled the trigger, shooting the first man in the face.

The sound of another gunshot ricocheted around the villa. She looked over to the second gunman. Her husband was slumped down in the chair, blood pooling under his body. She turned her gun on the robber and shot him once, twice, three times. She kept shooting, walking towards him, until the bullets ran out. She tossed the gun away and ran over to her husband.

Cathy was screaming.

She threw herself to her knees, Archie's thick red blood soaking into her dress.

'Archie! Archie! My love, are ya there?' She held his head to her. It was heavy, his body lifeless, and she realised he was dead.

'Call the ambulance, Cathy! Do it now!' Ruby yelled, cradling her husband, his head now flopped onto her chest, smearing blood across her. Her beloved husband, the man of her life, lay dead in her arms, slain by the men who lay in their own pools of blood on the floor.

CHAPTER 47

The police arrived in a flurry of sirens and flashing lights. Ruby barely noticed them. She held on to Archie's body for as long as she could, smothering him in kisses, before they took him away, peeling her off him gently.

Zipped inside a body bag was the only man she'd ever loved heart and soul, who was now gone from her for ever.

As she watched them take Archie away, she held Cathy close, the pair drawing strength from each other as their grief painted tears across their faces. Time passed, the officers must have asked questions, but it was all a blur to Ruby.

Their home was now an active crime scene. They were ushered into the kitchen where paramedics checked them both over. She had the presence of mind to discreetly ensure some of the police officers she was familiar with stayed around the villa. She didn't know who to trust, but took a chance that the crooked cops they employed wouldn't want to lose their main source of income. She could barely function, but she knew she had to protect Cathy.

What might have been hours later, their home was released to them – sometimes it was good to have a police chief in your pocket. After Cathy had taken to her bed, Ruby picked up the telephone.

'Lloyd, I 'ave somethin' to tell ya. I don't know how to say this . . .' Ruby's voice broke. Her heart felt wrenched into two pieces, for ever broken.

'What is it, Ruby?' Lloyd said. Both he and Alfie were in England finalising a shipment from Vladimir to their London contacts. They'd been due to fly back to Spain later that day. They didn't yet know they'd be flying home to attend Archie's funeral.

'It's Archie . . . He's dead . . .'

Ruby's words hung in the air. There was silence at the other end.

'Archie's dead?' he said slowly, as if trying to understand. 'My son is dead . . . How did it 'appen, Ruby?' He sounded weary suddenly, like an old man.

In the background, Ruby could hear Alfie shouting. She hadn't realised he was there beside Lloyd, hearing every word. 'No! No, not Archie, not Archie . . .' over and over again. His grief mirrored her own, as overwhelming as a tidal wave.

She barely felt the tears running down her face now.

'Two men forced their way in when Cathy and I were out shoppin'. It's OK, Cathy's OK. I shot them both, but they took my Archie's life before I could stop them. I failed him, Lloyd, I failed my Archie and he's dead because of me.'

'No, Ruby, you were the best wife he could've hoped for. You weren't to blame. Where are you now? Tell me exactly what happened.'

'We're fine, we're safe. It was a robbery. They were after money in one of the safes . . . but . . .'

'It's OK, Ruby. You're OK.'

'I don't know how it 'appened, but they must've paid off the guards. They had money. We came home from a day out and they'd broken in . . . What are the chances it was a straight robbery, Lloyd?'

'Slim, Ruby. Stay safe. Don't leave home. We're—'

'Ruby, Ruby, darlin', I won't stop until I find who was behind this,' Alfie's voice was wretched, choking on his pain. 'I promise ya, I'll rip their heads from their bodies.'

Lloyd took back the phone. 'We don't know they was set up. Not yet. Ruby says they was robbers. Listen, darlin', we're on our way. Don't do nuthin' until we get there.'

Ruby put the receiver down. Exhaling, she dialled her brother's number.

'Bobby?'

'Rube, how are ya?'

'My Archie is dead . . .'

There was a pause at the other end.

'Oh, God, Rube. Are ya safe? Is Cathy safe?'

'I don't know, Bobby,' Ruby said honestly.

Lloyd had seemed to think there might be more to it all than a robbery, but she had no proof.

'We're on our way. Go nowhere. See nobody, sis. Wait for us and we'll work it out. I love ya,' Bobby finished.

His quiet shock, in sharp contrast to Alfie's violent reaction, was somehow more painful to hear. He and Belle promised to be on the next flight over. All Ruby had to do now was wait.

She didn't sleep that night, nor did Cathy. Together, mother and daughter lay on the bed, awake and crying, talking about the man they adored and who now lay in a mortuary on a cold slab.

The local head of police, a man on Archie's payroll, came over the next morning.

'My condolences on your loss, Mrs Willson. It's clear you acted in self-defence. I will make every arrangement necessary for you.'

'Thank you, we appreciate your kindness,' Ruby murmured, holding Cathy close to her.

Ruby went into her bedroom, and sitting at her mirror, she saw a woman, still beautiful, still alluring, yet marred by grief. Her eyes had black shadows and her mouth was a thin line. She hooked a pearl necklace around her neck. It had been a present from Archie, and at the time she'd joked that they were for widows. Well, she'd been right. Standing in front of her, reflected back, was a widow, a woman who'd lost the love of her life, a woman now seeking answers.

Lloyd thinks there was someone behind it. He doesn't believe it was two chancers, it was too well-timed, maybe well-funded, she thought to herself. She had to admit, there were many unanswered questions. Where did they get the money to pay off the guards? She'd called a couple of their guards. They said Archie had given them the evening off. But why would Archie do that after the Albanian set-up? He'd never have left them exposed like that, surely?

She couldn't discuss it with Cathy. Her daughter was distraught, clinging to her mum, crying all day and all night.

Would she ever get over this? Would either of them?

Ruby watched as Belle stepped out of the rental car, squinting at the sunshine. Cathy broke away from Ruby who was standing by the villa doorway and ran to her aunt. Ruby had asked Cathy if she wanted to go somewhere else even for just a few weeks while the horror was still fresh, but Cathy, strangely, had insisted they stay.

'I want to be where Dad was. I want to stay in our home,' she'd said, and Ruby, who was unable to deny her anything, had reluctantly agreed.

'There, there Cathy, it's all going to be OK. I'm so sorry. Come here, darling girl,' Belle said embracing her.

'Come on inside, I don't like hangin' about out 'ere, we don't know if we're safe.' Ruby shivered despite the late-summer sunshine.

Inside, Cathy, Bobby and Belle headed to the lounge to sit together, while Lloyd, who'd arrived with Alfie an hour earlier, appeared in the doorway.

'Come inside, Ruby, we need to talk,' he said. He looked like he wasn't sleeping either, though he was composed if pale. Ruby saw his strength, the strength of a man who ran a drug cartel, a man who, faced with his own son's death, could look at the next move forward.

'Alfie and I 'ave been talkin' it through. The robbery don't make sense. We think there's more to it than that.'

Ruby smiled a thin, sad smile, though her eyes glittered. 'I agree, though we can't prove anythin'. I tell you, if someone was behind this, if someone plotted to kill my Archie, and us, then they'd better run because I'll be after them.'

She looked away as though her thoughts overwhelmed her. She could hear Cathy crying and the soothing low voices of Bobby and Belle. She felt grateful her daughter was finding some comfort, as there was none for her.

Alfie, who was standing with them in the office that Ruby had once shared with her husband, wiped tears away from his face, which was grey with shock and sleeplessness. He drew heavily on a cigarette, and exhaled, running his hands through his hair. His eyes were almost demented. If this was a stitch-up. If Alfie – or Lloyd – found those responsible, she didn't hold much for their chances. They'd be tortured and slaughtered like meat in an abattoir, and neither of them would blink at it. She felt their need for vengeance – it matched her own.

'If, and I do say *if*, there is more to this, then we'll hunt them down and destroy whoever is behind this. Don't worry, Lloyd, Archie's death hasn't made me soft.' Ruby's eyes were hard as she looked back at her father-in-law.

'Let's get the funeral done and out of the way, but behind the scenes, we'll start makin' discreet enquiries among our criminal networks, only trusted allies, but we'll make a start,' Lloyd said. 'Ruby, you need to act the part of grieving widow, victim of a robbery gone wrong. Can you do that?'

'Oh, I can do that,' said Ruby bleakly.

Alfie stepped forward and wrapped Ruby in his arms, trying to offer her some level of comfort.

She stayed in his embrace for just a moment, before she disentangled herself and walked out of the room. She just needed to be alone for a moment.

She tried not to picture Archie's handsome face, the way he smiled at her, that heady mixture of love and lust, which she'd returned in full. Yet each night, when she shut her eyes, there he was, her golden husband, the man of her life. She feared those visions, but she yearned for them too, wanting to remember every inch of him, dreading the day he started to fade away from her mind because that would be losing him all over again.

Once the formalities were over, Archie's body was released for burial, the official explanation being that his killers were dead by Ruby's hands in self-defence. The funeral preparations were then underway. An English-speaking funeral director was appointed by Ruby and the event was planned for two days' time. Lloyd and Alfie rang round their contacts and soon, crooks were flying in from all over the globe in support of the Willson family.

Ruby handled everything on auto-pilot. On the morning of the funeral, she dressed slowly in a black Christian Dior dress and heels. She had chosen a black pillbox hat with a veil that draped down, covering her face. She would also wear dark glasses to hide her eyes from the crowds that would, no doubt, treat this rich widow with fascination and horror.

'Madam, you have a visitor,' Ruby's new maid said, knocking gently on her bedroom door. Ruby rose, straightened her dress and walked down the sweeping staircase. Vladimir was standing at the bottom, a huge bouquet of white lilies in his arms.

'Thank you for comin', Mr Ivanov,' she said. She'd sent him a discreet note asking him to visit her prior to the limousines arriving.

'Call me Vladimir, please,' he said, planting a kiss on her hand.

'Vladimir,' she murmured, leading him away from the entrance so they couldn't be overheard. 'There is somethin' I want you to do for me.'

'Anything, dear lady, anything for such sorrow,' he replied, his eyes boring into hers.

'We are askin' our contacts, discreetly, mind you . . .' Ruby took a deep breath. 'My husband's death and the robbery may 'ave been arranged. We want to know, not think. And if there's a who, we want to know their identity. By now we've built up a business relationship, Vladimir, and as our partnership grows stronger, I wondered if you were in a position to help us?' Her words were barely audible but Vladimir understood.

'You want me to make . . . discreet . . . enquiries?' he said.

'I do,' she answered. 'Lloyd and Alfie are already talkin' to our associates, but as you 'ave so many Spanish connections, I thought it would be stupid not to ask you. Can I rely on your discretion?'

'Of course you can, dear lady. Ask anything of me. I will do everything in my power to assist you – and your family – in these terrible times.'

He looked into her green eyes, holding her steady gaze.

'Thank you,' she said, sealing their unwritten contract.

They walked together to the waiting limousines. Ruby stepped into the first one. Cathy and Belle were already inside. Bobby would follow with Alfie and Lloyd.

The car drew away, making its way slowly down the winding road to the cemetery.

The ceremony was packed, but Ruby was unaware of the others, only Cathy's clammy hand in hers. She felt cold despite the late summer heat as the priest intoned the ritual over her husband's graveside. She watched Archie's casket as it was lowered into the ground, and stood at the graveside to throw in the first clod of earth. She felt as if her body had frozen from the inside, and nothing would ever touch her again.

The wake was a lavish affair. Fears over needing a pauper's funeral were no longer a part of her reality. The villa was filled with flowers, the white lilies Ruby adored. Her staff were catering for hundreds and a large marquee had been erected in the grounds. Ruby watched as Lloyd, as head of the family, hosted the event. She was grateful to be by his side, letting him lead the day. She nodded, accepting condolences from people she'd never met before, as shady men mixed with glamorous models and celebrities, wishing they would all disappear and she could be left with her thoughts. Cathy made her escape early on in the company of Belle, but Ruby wasn't afforded the same luxury.

The hours dragged on, and Ruby finally made her excuses and left the party, slipping into her room and telling her maid to admit no one. Once inside, she peeled off the hat, which had left her feeling claustrophobic, and finally the grief came, washing over her with her tears. She cried for a long time, and when she finally finished, she looked over at herself in her large mirror, a copy of one at the Palace of Versailles. She walked over to it, seeing herself as if for the first time. Her make-up had run and so she wiped her face clean with a scented towelette. She looked again. This time a woman with expensively-cut hair wearing a designer black dress looked back at her. She saw her creamy skin, contrasting with the flash of her emerald eyes. She saw the necklace of diamonds and emeralds glittering at her throat, her wedding ring on her hand, so solid, so tough.

Despite her grief, she saw a woman with her head high, with pride in herself and her family. She saw a murderess, a negotiator, a hardened woman who would stop at nothing to avenge the death of her man. She would bury her feelings. She would carry on, more in control, more powerful than ever. She would become even tougher. She saw herself now, not as a soft, homely mother, but as a businesswoman, a woman of her own creation. It had taken a long time – and many tragedies – to get to this position but here she was at last. Nothing would stop her ever again, and nothing would harm her daughter. Nothing and no one. She would rise from this latest, overwhelming grief, like a phoenix from the ashes of her life.

She didn't know if Archie had died in a set-up, if the robbers were the chancers she'd guessed – or whether there was someone, or some organisation, behind it all. But it didn't feel like it was over.

Her intuition said it wasn't, and she knew she would hunt to the ends of the earth for answers.

Either way, she vowed to use this deep grief, to become so powerful that no one could touch them or hurt them ever again. What happened with the gunmen should never have happened. People should have been too afraid to ever take the chance of crossing them. She had to become untouchable. No one would ever dare take a bribe to let in a chancer. No one would consider doing them over, or trying to harm her family. She had to become stronger, swifter, sharper. Her only safety – and that of her family – from now on was to be on top, to become the most powerful woman in the drug business. Nothing else mattered.

Finally, she reapplied her make-up and stepped back into the events of the day a changed woman. She motioned to Lloyd, Alfie and Vladimir to meet in the office that was now hers alone. She saw Belle comforting Cathy through the large window, the pair sitting together by the pool, and she saw that she couldn't give her daughter the comfort she craved. She knew that she couldn't give Cathy a simpler life, because Ruby wasn't a simple woman. The knowledge was like a blade in her heart. She fought it down, discarding the feeling, knowing that it would be better this way.

'Gentlemen, I've asked Mr Ivanov to help us. I want us to discover the truth. If someone ordered Archie's death, they will pay for what they did. I want their blood. Alfie, Lloyd, work with Vladimir. I want them dead.'

The men looked at her, and she knew what they saw at that moment: a woman without remorse, a cold killer.

Lloyd nodded. In that gesture, he acknowledged a new head of the family. He realised Ruby had stepped up, beyond her husband's shoes and into her power. He saw a woman hell-bent on vengeance.

He nodded to Vladimir.

'Of course, Ruby. Alfie and I will do what you say.'

Alfie nodded then looked away.

Ruby smiled sadly. 'Come now, let's celebrate our continued friendship.'

Vladimir reached for a bottle of the finest vintage champagne from the open drinks cabinet, its shiny surface filling the room with dappled light.

'For a grieving widow, and for our continued friendship. Please accept my condolences. I will do everything in my power to assist you all,' Vladimir said softly.

She accepted a glass filled with bubbly.

'To new beginnings.'

'New beginnings,' the three men echoed.

ACKNOWLEDGEMENTS

The Locksmith is a book that's existed in my head for years, and thanks to my literary agent, Kerr MacRae, it slowly became a reality on the page. Thank you, Kerr, for all your support, insight and belief in my story!

It took a whole team to make this book a reality and I want to say thank you to everyone. Thank you to Jon Elek, Cathryn Kemp, Tara Loder and Rosa Schierenberg for helping me bring Ruby to life. You are all absolute diamonds. This book was written in lockdown, but you'd never know it from the amount of time we managed to spend together; online and on the phone, of course.

Thanks also go to James Horobin and his incredible team of amazing sales, marketing and PR experts. The enthusiasm and energy from this team has been second to none. Also, huge thanks to Alex Allden, Dominic Forbes and Larry Rostant for the cover. I'm not sure I told you, but: 'I love it!'

And a special thanks goes to my dear friend Martina Cole. Martina, who would have imagined that some day I would be the one writing a book? You have supported this book from the start, but more than that, you have been a brilliant friend. Thank you for everything!

ABOUT THE AUTHOR

Credit: Richard Payne

'The first time I held a gun, I forgot to breathe'

Linda Calvey has served 18 years behind bars, making her Britain's longest-serving female prisoner. She moved to 14 different prisons, doing time with Rose West and Myra Hindley. But prison didn't break her.

Since her release, Linda has become a full-time author. Her 2019 memoir *The Black Widow* fascinated readers.

Villains aren't born.
They're made.

But what does a villain like Ruby do
when they're betrayed?

Find out in Linda Calvey's
next book.

WELBECK

PUBLISHING GROUP

Love books? Join the club.

From heart-racing thrillers to award-winning historical fiction, through to must-read music tomes, beautiful picture books for children and delightful gift ideas, Welbeck is proud to publish titles that suit every taste.

Sign-up to our newsletter for exclusive offers, extracts, author interviews and information on our unmissable list:

bit.ly/welbeckpublishing

WELBECK

ANDRE
DEUTSCH

MORTIMER

MORTIMER

WELBECK